Hellhound

Siege Engine

Suzanne Brodine

Eleanor—
Thanks for taking
a chance and reading my
book! It's no maple
syrup commercial — but
we all have to start
somewhere.

Suzanne Brodine

*There is a way that seems right to a man, but
its end is the way to death.
Proverbs 14:12*

CONTENTS

Thank you, Cole, for your unending support and encouragement.

CHAPTER 1: HUBRIS

Tuber. Noun. Slang. Offensive.: An individual who received non-human DNA during embryonic gene therapy. Banned by the Sol Confederation in 2097.
Ex. This bar has really gone downhill, they even let tubers in.

Hour 1006
September 26, 2102

Ignition minus forty-six years.

A scraping, grating sound was dulled somewhat by the thick, one-way glass that was between Representative Sudarshan and the enclosure for Test Subject Twenty-One-G. The Representative had to force herself not to grimace; instead she folded her arms over her chest in a practiced manner that gave her an air of authority. Dr. Jenssen pulled a stylus from his coat pocket and tapped on a control pad in his hand. Data flashed to life on the glass, outlining the subject, displaying vital statistics, and highlighting significant results. Sudarshan ignored most of the glowing text to assess the subject directly. She could only see the top of his head, as he was crouched in a corner. One hand, lightly dusted with short brown hair, reached out to the wall and dragged down the polymetallic sheeting. Curls of material flaked up and away from his nails, deepening two parallel scratches on the wall and assaulting her ears.

"You can see here," Jenssen pointed to a chart and drew a curve to attract her attention, "Twenty-One-G has exceeded conservative projections for all skill areas and resistances. Sensory perception and strength are both far above estimates, and intelligence appears to be within acceptable parameters. Considering the initial difficulty of combining this particular alien DNA into the human genome the team is pleased with the progress toward the physical requirements. Unfortunately, out of the twenty-five subjects that were viable at extraction, he is the only one to remain intact and operational, so our efforts to study and assess him have slowed somewhat as we need to reduce risk of damage for the last living product of the Twenty-One series. Due to this reduction in the test pool, many of the results are open to interpretation, as we have no means of establishing a control or baseline for comparison." Jenssen flicked away the data, and pulled up another set of charts.

He would have continued, but the grating sound started again. Sudarshan watched Twenty-One-G drag his middle two fingers down the grooves in the wall again. "Why is he doing that?"

Jenssen glanced up from his tablet. "Oh, marking territory. We've seen that in eighty-two percent of all viable series to date. The behaviorists believe that it is essential, but my chief geneticist assures me it can be coded out, if it becomes a problem." He gestured with his stylus, "This graph-"

"And his attitude," Sudarshan interrupted again. "Is his demeanor always like this?" She had read the files, of course. That was her responsibility as the new Chair of the Oversight Committee for Defense Research and Covert Operations. The Representative was aware that Project Reform had made tremendous strides in genetic modifications and splicing. The prospect of a new kind of soldier, one that was stronger, braver, and faster than humans but also intelligent was tantalizingly close. However, the challenges were still significant. Congress had spent trillions, would spend trillions more, if requests for the next five year funding allocation were approved, but Project Reform had yet to produce a single individual that could operate in the field.

"Ah, yes," Jenssen cleared his throat and smiled. Fine wrinkles appeared at the corner of his eyes, but his mouth was stiff. "Although Twenty-One-G is obedient and excels in combat simulations, he is withdrawn and has...difficulty...interacting with others."

"Difficulty?" Sudarshan stepped closer to the glass and squatted down. From a lower angle she could see the subject's face. His skin was the same nondescript brown of his hair, or perhaps a shade lighter. His cheekbones were wide and high, his jaw pronounced and broad. The ears were further up on his head than a human's, and edged with long, pale hairs that moved gently in the artificial currents of the hvac system. His eyes were closed, but she knew from the file they were green - and shone red in low lighting. "Is that what you call the maiming of two technicians and the death of another? And I understand he killed five of the six other Twenty-One series models in his group."

"Well," Jenssen coughed and shuffled his feet. "After the challenges with motivation and passivity in the Twenty-series, we made some adjustments to the genome - which was extremely successful. The results were exactly what we were hoping for."

"Dead scientists?" she murmured. Her eyes traced over the broad shoulders and heavy musculature of the subject. His simple gray scrubs were stretched tight around long limbs. Thick hair was tied into a ponytail at his nape, and darker brown hair grew on his face and neck. "That is not a promising goal, Doctor." She could hear umbrage rising in Jenssen's voice.

"The staff...incidents...were the result of security procedures that were not properly followed. Dr. Gillian was aware that no personnel are allowed direct contact with the subjects unless they are anesthetized. Despite that, she entered the enclosure to begin an unapproved behavioral study. When Twenty-One-G attacked, the technicians intervened."

"I read Gillian's report. She stated that increased socialization would curb the violent tendencies and establish trust and loyalty." The Representative studied the subject's feet. They were larger and broader than an average human. She recalled from the file it was a result of increased height and body mass; the design supposedly aided in speed and agility. His toes were pressed against the floor, his heels raised and under his body.

"Yes," Jenssen's tone was saturated with derision, "And the former Oversight Chair took those concerns seriously. We did institute controlled interactions between subjects - which resulted in aggression and violent outbursts between them. Of the fourteen that were still viable at the time, G killed five that were in the same control group. The sixth was left alive with only non-lethal puncture wounds on the neck." The display on the glass flickered, and new data, including images of subjects that had refused food and one that killed himself by puncturing his abdomen with his own claws. Behind her, Jenssen was sounding more confident. "The other control group was declared non-viable within a few months. Gillian's research is pedantic, at best. If we threw out the behaviorists and psychoanalysts and focused our resources on the hard science, I promise you we could produce the outcomes the Committee is looking for in another two or three series."

"Such ego," Sudarshan murmured under her breath. She pressed her palms against her knees to stand, and in the split second that her attention turned from the subject, he exploded into motion. Later, review of the security footage would show that he had braced himself to move and his eyes had been focused on a faulty seal at the bottom of the glass. It would be hypothesized that he could see or sense the residual heat from the bodies of those in the observation room as it seeped out under the window. Whatever reason he had, however he accomplished it, the result was a terrifying impact when his body slammed into the mirrored side. Four inches of reinforced plastiglass shuddered and cracked in a spider web pattern. Sudarshan fell backward onto her hands with a strangled gasp. Jenssen screamed.

Alarms sounded and high inside the enclosure, vents opened releasing a sedative gas. Sudarshan flinched, her heart stuttering, as Twenty-One-G hit the glass again, the second time with his fist. Small chunks of material splintered and fell out of a tiny hole that centered on the impact. The Representative stared into the subject's eyes. They were pale green, flecked with brown. Despite the fury etched on his face, Sudarshan saw something else there too. The sedative took effect before he could connect a third time, and both the observation room and enclosure were swarmed with security personnel. Sudarshan refused assistance and stood up on her own, watching as they strapped the subject down and loaded him into a confinement chamber the size of a large coffin. When she finally turned around, she was unimpressed to find Jenssen, pants soaking wet, breathing from a portable oxygen canister and ranting about protocols and autopsy schedules.

Sudarshan ignored him and pulled aside one of the guards. "Take me to a secure line, and get me the next most senior staff person. Now."

One subject, under constant surveillance, had tricked dozens of scientists, security personnel, and Sudarshan herself. He had nearly overwhelmed the best containment money could buy. That destructive power was impressive.

Two days later, Representative Sudarshan was on a transport back to the Sol System. Dr. Jenssen's contract had been terminated, and he was strongly encouraged to review the binding non-disclosure and non-compete portions of his agreement. Dr. Gillian, fresh from transplant surgery, had been reinstated and promoted as the head of research. She had insisted on foregoing her scheduled skin grafts and reconstructive procedures to begin work immediately. Project Reform was under new leadership, and a new strategic plan. The Representative accepted a drink from her assistant and settled in to listen to reports on the latest debates on the Congressional floor regarding oceanic reclamation. She could afford to focus on domestic matters, assured that she would soon have exactly what humanity needed to search out their enemies and erase them. Her last act, before she closed the files on her tablet, was to authorize a new code name for the black operation.

Project Barghest would make her career.

CHAPTER 2: LUCK SOMETIMES VISITS A FOOL

Klimovsk Service Pistol, a.k.a. *Klim.* Proper noun. standard issue semi-automatic pistol issued to Sol Coalition forces which is capable to holding up to five types of ammunition. The Klim integrates into the personal tech of each soldier, allowing for ammunition selection, assisted targeting, and safety measures for crowd control.
Ex. Just because your Klim has non-lethal rounds doesn't mean you should use them.

Hour 0432
March 3, 2148

Ignition minus fifty-one days.

"That was a hell of a hickey I saw on your neck in the showers last week." Dan Rodriguez didn't smile, but his dark skin crinkled around the eyes. Under the shadow of the dirty hat that disguised his standard issue Sol Coalition haircut, he held a vapor pen to his mouth. It wasn't switched on, but he made a show of using it periodically.

Sergeant Maker kept her eyes on the entrance to the poorly lit commons area they had been staking out for almost twenty-four hours. The niquab that covered her hair and lower face was hot in the recycled air of the station, but it made her pale skin less noticeable in a crowd where humans were typically stained and scarred from deep mine gases. Without looking at the newly minted private, she responded, "I saw you there as well. My condolences on your shortcomings."

Unfazed, Rodriguez continued, "Just say the word and I could give you better."

"Fraternization between junior and senior personnel is prohibited, Fuzz." It was true that Maker hadn't been an officer very long. Also true that there were more experienced, older soldiers on the mission, but she was second-in-command, and most of her team didn't like her to begin with, so there was no point in giving them any infractions to hold against her. Rodriguez had slept with an impressive number of the women on their ship, and some of the men, so shutting down his advances wasn't a hardship. On this mission, the soldiers on the same level of the mining station were on the same channel, but that wasn't enough to keep the playboy in line.

"But what is fraternization, really? Surely a little rub and su-"

Faint static in their sub-dermal receivers cut off whatever the private had been about to suggest. "Not to interrupt you, ma'am," Bretavic drawled, "but we have movement at Position Two." Maker leaned across the small table to pour more of the low-grade alcohol into Rodriguez's cup. He slouched in his seat, affording her a better view over his shoulder and easing his hand closer to the service weapon concealed in a pocket of his baggy pants. When she took her seat again, she turned so she faced a service corridor. The station was in the middle of a mining shift, so there were only a few stalls open and even fewer patrons milling around or seated at the common-use tables in the center of the space.

"Copy that," Maker replied quietly. Rodriguez stared at her face, his mouth tight while he waited for her to assess the situation behind him and for command to make the call. "Two Nicks, could be our targets." Native to the Cancri System, Nicks were easy to identify. They were bipedal, but had reverse joints and four limbs of equal length. Officially, their species was known by their home system and planet. Unofficially, any human who had served outside Sol used the derogatory term for the lightning fast thieves. Maker focused the scanning capabilities embedded in her contacts; in less than two seconds, she had information on the radiation signature of their technology. It matched the mission file. "Identity verified. Confirmation?"

"Identity confirmed," came Bretavic's low response from the second position. Bretavic had been on more operations than the rest of the team combined. While he didn't seem to respect Maker it obviously had more to do with his thoughts on officers than her personally. His call could be trusted. That should have been all she needed to request the Go order, but Maker hesitated.

"Position One, status." The Lieutenant in charge was stationed out of her line of sight with his own partner, down a service corridor. His voice snapped with command, bordering on irritation.

"Status," he said again, this time demanding an answer. It wasn't intuition, or some gut feeling; no sixth sense stopped her from making the call so the Lieutenant could send her fire team into action. She didn't think it was fear. She couldn't have said why, but she took three long, deep breaths before she opened her mouth.

"Hold." Their transmitters barely vibrated with Bretavic's whisper. A third figure, shorter and more fluid than the Nicks, eased around the edge of the corridor and hovered at the entrance. "Sarge?"

The question was breathed more than spoken, but Maker was already scanning. *Culler*, she thought with a new iron ball of anxiety settling in her belly. She double-checked the readout overlaid on her vision before she spoke. None of the mission briefs said anything about Cullers, but if there was one on the station, so close to the border, her superiors would want to know why. There was only one way to find out.

Her heart was beating too quickly.

"Command, Position One reporting unknowns. Relaying data." She casually tucked her hands in her sleeves, surreptitiously pressing the code on her bracer that would send the image to the lieutenant.

For a few tense moments it was quiet, then the Lieutenant's voice was in her head again. "Field call. Additional targets. Alive, if possible."

Maker's gut was churning. Bretavic's fire team at the second position would provide backup. There were another two covert soldiers on the level below them, and two in the docking bay. That left the pilot and medic on the ship. They had set out with four people from the squadron, including the lieutenant and his partner, ready to take down two Nicks. Standard operating procedures required a minimum of four heavily armed soldiers for every one Culler. That meant that Rodriguez and Maker would have to deal with the two Nicks on their own. She swallowed and perspiration beaded at her temple.

"Additional objective," she confirmed. "Painting targets." With a subtle press of her fingertips against the palm of her glove she transmitted visuals to the rest of the team. Through the tech of her contacts, she watched each of the Nicks and the concealed newcomer light up with a yellow glow.

"Party crasher is ours, Team Two." The Lieutenant' voice was flat. "Team One, you have original targets. Secure and detain. Collateral authorized."

Maker could feel sweat was sliding down her back and spit collecting in her mouth, but her voice didn't waver, "Copy." She and Rodriguez weren't prepared to handle two Nicks on their own but there wasn't any alternative. Bretavic's and the Lieutenant's teams would have the significantly more dangerous target; without any heavy munitions they would need backup as soon as it was available. That meant Maker and the fresh-out-of-training-camp private needed to work quickly. The Nicks moved closer to the tables, close enough that Maker could see, unaided, the sand papery texture of their skin. The third opponent hung by the entrance for several long minutes before easing into a narrow alley behind a row of stalls.

"Go," the lieutenant ordered.

There was no response from the other maneuver team, but Maker knew they were already in action. She stood and stretched, slowly, before picking up the alcohol carafe and moving around the tables toward a bar. It was the distraction that they had planned to begin with, but her palms were clammy with sweat under the added pressure to succeed. Both Nicks watched her; her contacts tracked the movement of their eyes as she crossed in front of them. She purposefully tripped over a metal chair as she passed, and Rodriguez used the noise to conceal his approach behind them; as soon as he was in position, Maker tossed the alcohol straight into one Nick's face.

The action was recorded by her contacts. Rodriguez slapped cuffs on the upper limbs of one Nick, but the rookie didn't move quite fast enough to complete the circuit on the ankles. His opponent whipped around, prehensile tail emerging from its tunic to slap the gun out of the private's hand. Rodriguez rolled to avoid a follow-up kick, but was hit with the tail on its reverse swing. He slid across the floor, knocking over a table and chairs with a shout of pain. The Nick leaped after him, the open end of a pair of electronic cuffs dangling from one leg.

Maker had no time to spare a thought for her partner. The alcohol served in the mining station was poor quality, but high proof. Her Nick bellowed with rage and its tongue slithered out of its mouth to swipe at the liquid burning its eyes. It seized the table between them with a lower limb and flung it out of the way - leaving Maker to stumble backwards into a chair, pulling her weapon and firing as she moved. The first shot from her Klim was wild, narrowly missing Rodriguez. The second short burst hit the Nick in the hip. Blue blood spattered the floor and tables behind the creature and it stumbled, letting out another deep cry. Its tail lashed around dangerously. *Move, move,* her mind chanted. She used the chair as a springboard to fling herself onto the roof of the bar. Her foot caught in the chair back, wrenching her ankle and knocking the seat into the Nick's legs. She had to crouch awkwardly to fit between the thin metal sheets and the duct work for the common space, but the height put her out of arm's reach. Maker toggled through her ammunition menu for a compressed wire detention net. The first shot tangled up the Nick's left arm; she cursed. The second hit the center of mass and brought one hundred eighty kilos of tail-slashing anger to the floor. Maker activated the trigger to magnetize the net. She had forgotten to check the setting. It was higher than was recommended for a Nick. The alien would likely have cuts from the pressure, but at least she could be certain it would not move while she assisted Rodriguez.

He desperately needed help.

The Private had managed to pull a secondary weapon, but not his net gun. The whites of his eyes were large with fear and Maker's sensors were sending off alerts in the periphery of her vision that his adrenaline had spiked beyond acceptable margins. Other alerts were softly flashing for the four soldiers in the alley and she could hear shouting. One soldier's indicator light went out. *This is so, so stupid,* her brain was pointing out to her, but she ignored it. Rodriguez fired three bursts in rapid succession and Maker took some slag in her shoulder as she pushed off the roof, reaching for a handhold on an HVAC pipe. She fired a net at the ground near the Nick's feet. At the same time her hand connected with the hot metal cylinder. She could feel her grip slipping, and only prayed she could hold on long enough. Her heavy boots swung out toward the Nick's face, but she had not caught it unawares. The creature hissed and ducked, turning and flicking its tail to wrap around her ankles and yank her from the ceiling.

She lost her grip on the pipe with a sharp curse and a friction burn that was painful even through her glove. Maker into the floor, and her already injured shoulder clipped a chair on the way. She was stunned for a precious few seconds, while her display was screaming at her that her team was in danger and a target was closing in. Maker fumbled with her Klim and switched ammunition in time to fire point blank into the bare foot of the Nick as it was poised to stomp on her chest. It screamed and flinched from her, scrambling for purchase but unable to crawl away from the magnetic lock of a net Rodriguez fired. The Private was pushing to his feet, one arm was bent unnaturally but her tech notified her that he had already used his field meds to dull the pain. She was panting as she stood and, with a command on her bracer, she dimmed the stats for Rodriguez. With the closest proximity individual muted, her tech turned towards the next member of her squad.

The Lieutenant was dead.

Maker's breath caught in her throat. She scrambled with the controls in her bracer to pull up a locator map. His body was only a few feet from the corridor where he had been positioned. The Culler had taken him out before he could even fire his weapon. As she verified the readout that specified brain death, her stomach clenched and the hairs on the back of her neck stood up higher. That thing, the enemy, was still on the station with them.

Maker was in command.

Another indicator on her display went dark. Another soldier was dead. Her back was throbbing, but she ignored the med kit on her belt. She didn't have time for it, and her tech was streaming reports of Bretavic's team that made her swallow curses. "Secure and notify transport of incoming," she ordered Rodriguez. She didn't wait for his nod or acknowledge the pale strain in his expression before she forced herself into a jog. There was no one to dodge or yell at to get inside as she approached the far end of the commons area. All of the walkways had been deserted within moments of the first shot. Some shops had been hastily closed. Others held the telltale anticipation and occasional terrified movement that betrayed their occupants.

It was quiet and dark when she approached the alley, and Maker's breath was hot inside the veil over her face. She almost tripped over a body a few feet from the entrance and she quickly put her back to the wall to scan her surroundings. The corpse at her feet wasn't alone. Parts of another lay half in- half out of a shop; a dark, shiny wet smear the width of a man's shoulders trailed up the side of a building and onto the roof. She double checked her display. The second position team was alive, their stats below desired levels but steady. With a press of her fingertips into her palm she activated her locator. The two soldiers were outlined in blue, one hidden from normal sight by a twisted pile of sheet metal and debris. The other lay halfway down the alley, faintly visible in the indirect glow that bounced off of the ceiling.

"Eyes," she whispered into her comm. Her legs were shaking. Her belly cramped and she had the inconvenient urge to urinate. The word was inaudible, but the vibration in her throat was picked up by her implant and transmitted.

"Eyes plus thirty," she heard the quiet voice, knew it was Bretavic under the debris. His stats were not good, but he sounded more angry than in pain. "Your right, roofline."

Maker kept her eyes moving over the buildings, searching for movement while she quick stepped to his location, and knelt next to an opening in the debris. "Status." A long piece of hair had worked out of the veil and stuck to the sweat on her temple.

"I can cut free with my torch - maximum sixty seconds. Gonna be noisy." She couldn't see his face, but she could hear the wince in Bretavic's voice, "Right leg is toast. We both used our meds, my partner took another hit to the head."

Maker was supremely aware of the slight weight of her med kit against her hip. Each soldier had only been issued one for the mission. Nicks were tough, but four on one was a good bet with the element of surprise. The third enemy had put them on the losing end of all but the longest odds. It didn't matter. A Culler needed to be dealt with as soon as it was identified, and Maker wouldn't have minded some answers for why the mission was blown all to hell. She swallowed and brushed the sweat from her eyebrows. *Why the Lieutenant is dead. Why Private* - she silenced her thoughts with a shake of her head and focused. Without her med kit, she could only take one, maybe two hits before she went down. An officer's first priority had to be the mission, then the team. Her gut churned. She didn't know any of the men well, but she didn't think she could sacrifice them to ensure success, Cullers tracked quick movements easily, so escape would be difficult. Unless they had a distraction. Or a decoy.

So, so stupid, she repeated to herself.

"Wait for my signal, then get cutting. Grab the bodies, if you can." She stayed close to the left wall of the alley, running her fingers a few millimeters over the uneven surfaces of poorly repaired shops, and jogged forward. She scanned the area, visually and with her tech while she unclasped her kit, folding it open with one hand and toggling the dosage on the transdermal syringe. She crouched in preparation, and then her transmitter crackled.

"Cullers! Down, three down!"

The all team channel was wide open, something that could only be done by the commanding officer unless casualties were taken. Weapons fire was close enough to be heard through her transceiver over the screams of the soldier six decks below. Kerry, heavy weapons support for the nondescript little hauler they had come in on, had gone through basic training with her. His familiar tone was even despite his volume and situation.

"Transport down! Cullers! Two in the bay, one in the weeds! Request immediate assistance! Respond!" Maker almost dropped the kit, her brain trying to claw its way out of her head with fear, *Trap! Trap! Trap!* They had all recognized the Culler that followed the two Nicks into the commons, but none of them had anticipated more. She cursed herself; it was her fault, her fault that they hadn't immediately notified the transport. It had been her call after the Lieutenant went down to maintain transmission silence with the ship that was waiting for them in the docking bay. Her fault that two soldiers were dead on their level and three more bleeding down below.

"Go!" This time she yelled the command while she jumped away from the wall. She slammed the blunt end of the syringe into the soldier's neck hard enough to damage the skin and dosed him with everything she had. Maker's boots pushed against the floor, adrenaline and terror surging through her veins. The sound of a gasp for air and the sudden rise of the soldier behind her barely registered. "Retreat! Cargo is expendable, if necessary! Go, Go, Go!"

She knew that they obeyed her orders. They were well trained, and her display tracked their movements until she pushed team location to the bottom of her tech priority. An explosion shook the entire deck, making her careen to one side in her sprint. There was only the flash of yellow across her vision as she reacquired a painted target. The Culler was on her. Thirty kilos of damp cloth and wiry muscle dropped from directly above, striking her wounded shoulder and back. The impact sent her flying forward and she didn't manage to tuck before she hit the floor. Maker flopped over and raised up one forearm in defense. She scuttled backward on one hand and her heels as the Culler bounded forward. The hooked talons of its arms easily pierced the ceramic weave of her body armor. Her visual display winked in and out as the circuitry in her glove and sleeve was ripped away, leaving a long, shallow gouge in her arm that welled blood. Its head pressed close to her and she gagged on the smell of rotting plant matter. She tasted bile in her mouth.

"Human," it said, making the sounds of the word despite not having a mouth. The talons withdrew and rose again.

Maker fired.

Her weapon was at an odd angle, given that she could barely feel her hand, but four incendiary rounds punched into the vulnerable skin between shell plates in rapid succession. An unholy sound of pain and fury, like dry ice grinding together, pierced her ears. The fifth and sixth rounds tore chunks of white flesh away and found purchase in the ceiling. Incendiary rounds were stupid, and overkill. Her weapons instructor would have had her running laps, full gear, for firing at that range in an enclosed space. *Lucky for me, he's not here*, she thought wildly, *or lucky for him.*

Then her ammo exploded. A splatter gore hit her and she curled up to protect her head before the structural beams above began to fall. Two heavy weights, one after the other, dropped on her back and neck. She wasn't sure how long she lay flat on her stomach, but when she became aware of the wet veil sticking to her lips and tasting of rot she threw up. She tore the material from her face and rocked to the side, away from her vomit. The motion jostled debris off her back, freeing her. The floor was slick with the ichor of the Culler and her own blood, and she fell twice, banging her knee hard, before she could brace herself upright. Her vision slid sideways, or maybe it was the floor that was moving, but she crashed into the wall and fell again before the world righted itself.

"Report," she rasped, pressing a palm to her forehead to push away the ringing in her ears and the black halo that threatened to seal her vision and drop her back into unconsciousness. Without the connection to the tech in her armor the communication implant was barely functional, little more than an open channel, but she tried to contact her team anyhow. "Report," she demanded again, this time louder. She forced her legs to work, and although she felt the pain in her knee and back it was a distant second to the fire in her arm. She switched her weapon to her off hand, which was in better condition as it only had a single puncture wound at her collarbone.

"Two levels below you, Sarge." Rodriguez's voice sounded far away, and she could hear the tremor in it. "I made you a short-cut." She saw what he meant as soon as she cleared the alley. A smoking hole, approximately two meters in diameter, had been blasted in the floor of the commons area. Bretavic was leaning heavily on his partner, standing at the edge. He lowered the body of the lieutenant down carefully. Then, between the two of them, they managed to shove a snarling, netted Nick through the hole before seating themselves on the lip.

Bretavic looked over at her, but Maker didn't hold his gaze. The corridor the Nicks had first entered through was full of shadows that had not been there moments before. All of the artificial lighting had been turned off, leaving the space one large darkness. Maker's throat felt tight, she was sharply aware of the warmth of blood as it ran down her arm and pearled on her fingertips before plopping against the metal floor plates.

"One in the weeds, confirm please," she whispered. Bretavic slowly turned his head to follow her line of sight.

Kerry's voice, thick with breathing sounds, came through, "Correction. One cold in the bay, two in the weeds. Both bloodied."

Two Cullers, holy hell, she thought. An inappropriate urge to giggle pushed against her lungs from the inside. If her tech was still operational, it would have been flashing medical warnings and situational readings. She shifted her weight and bit off a scream when the exposed meat of her arm brushed against her hip. *Tech would have shorted itself out anyway, trying to record this FUBAR mission.* One Culler had wrecked two soldiers and nearly ripped off her arm. In her current condition, with the second team wounded and vulnerable in the center of the room, two of the aliens would leave nothing behind but bloodstains and service tags.

"Status," she said. Even she could hear the high-pitch in her voice.

"Position Four - 'A' KIA, 'B' Med. Position Six - 'A' Steady, 'B' Med, Position Seven... 'A' Med, 'B' KIA."

Two more dead, in addition to the Lieutenant and his partner, including the pilot. The medic injured and out for the fight, same for Kerry's partner. The only other soldier they had with real flying and maneuvering experience was Bretavic, and he was several floors and two Cullers away from the ship. And injured. And exposed. And staring down the barrel of another attack.

It was supposed to be a simple snatch and grab - two Nicks that intelligence reported had flight records and communication codes for some runs through Culler space. Nicks were strong and fast, but not well armed. It was why she was assigned second-in-command; her first time out as an enlisted officer was supposed to be an easy assignment. *Brass will have a hell of a time evaluating this.* The giggle warped into a full out laugh and she had to swallow it hard. She was now responsible for seven other lives, plus at least one Nick that she was supposed to bring back still breathing.

And the bodies of the fallen.

And a Culler that should be taken in for questioning.

Only eight days as a sergeant had to be some kind of record.

The darkness in the corridor shifted. Maker blew out a long breath and brought up her Klim - elbow slightly bent, both eyes open. She toggled through the magazine selection menu with her thumb. Incendiary and pellet rounds were empty. She had a full load of armor piercing. From the corner of her eye she watched Bretavic free his weapon; the faint blue glow of his munitions selector mirrored her own.

"Team Two en route." Maker stated calmly. A distant part of her mind was proud of that, despite that sour ball of fear trying to rip through her gut. Bretavic turned his face to hers, and his mouth was turned down in a frown that threatened argument. He knew what she was planning, and he didn't like it. If she had been faster, or a better shot, or had any experience outside of boot camp and eighteen months on border patrol, she might have come up with a better idea. But she wasn't. She didn't. She was responsible for the team, and they need to get back alive - or at least in as few pieces as possible. For that they needed a pilot. "Sending you wings, transport." Bretavic hesitated, then nodded subtly. "Fuzz has the cargo. You are on mission. Repeat. On Mission. Fire it up and you are go to launch at will. I am in the weeds. I say again. I am in the weeds." Bretavic wrapped his free hand around his partner's vest and his bicep bulged under his armor as he lowered the man into the hole and let go. His eyes stayed on the shadows, but he lifted one hand above his head, and she could clearly make out his middle finger as he gestured toward the corridor. "I read you Team Two." She responded. "Out." Bretavic pushed off the edge and disappeared below.

There was almost an equilateral triangle between Maker, the corridor, and the hole, but the leg that would have been her likely escape route was heavily littered with broken tables, chairs, and unidentified bits of tissue that might have once been a Nick. She tripped over a table as quietly as she could, not that the small movement was easy to hear past the whine and grate of tons of stressed metal and machinery that made up the mining station and the alarms set off by Rodriguez when he blew a hole in the floor. She went down on one knee and braced her weapon against the edge of the table. Surprisingly, her injured arm obeyed her command and managed to rip the detonation pack from her belt. She raised the pack to her mouth, and tasted copper and salt on her lips as she ripped it open with her teeth. Two coils of shaped plastic explosives, each spiraled like a snail on a peel away sticker, fell out along with a simple detonator. She removed the backing from one and pressed it against the tabletop - dead center. The other she tucked into her pocket.

It was the first rule of munitions training not to put things that go boom anywhere near your genitals, but Maker wasn't expecting to live long enough to worry about the condition of her reproductive system. In the deep recesses of her mind, she felt a little distant regret for that. Then darkness shifted again, and she could barely make out the shine of emergency lighting on wet, gray skin. She took a deep breath, ignoring the stabbing pain in her back and clicked out the first Culler phrase she had learned in Basic Training.

I've got garbage that is faster! You're too weak to eat!

The effect was both better and worse than her xenospecies linguistics instructor could have ever known. The scream that rent the air was painfully high pitched and accompanied by a blur of movement from the corridor. One Culler streaked to the right, towards the hole, while the other barreled straight for her. There wasn't time for multiple shots. With a gentle recoil that belied the force of the projectile, an armor piercing round fired. Maker didn't watch to see if it hit the target near the hole, but surged to her feet with everything she had, throwing herself back toward the alley and pressing the detonator.

Time slowed down. A white haze pressed around her, vibrating slowly in synchrony with the hum in her ears. Her feet were strangely hot, but there was a breeze on her face. She could feel her heart beating, pushing blood through her veins, into her head, forcing her to think. *This was a bad idea.* Maker blinked, and then time caught up with her. She slammed against the back wall of the alley, shoulder first, breaking through the thin metal of a poorly secured door and crashing into an empty shop. Her armor reacted accordingly, the layer of kinetic gel hardening to absorb the energy and then releasing into a fluid state again. It wasn't enough to keep her from feeling it - and did no good at all where her suit had been damaged. Agony lanced up her arm and radiated from her back like a fission reaction. She thought she cried out, but she couldn't hear any sounds. She brought a hand up to her head, trying to find the split that must be in her skull because her brain felt like it was going to explode. Sticky, hot liquid coated her fingers and made the grip on her weapon wet. She stared at it for a moment, dumbly, wondering why her ears were bleeding.

The last Culler found her like that, slumped against a dirty wall and looking at her own blood. It was on her before she even knew it was there. Bony legs, slippery with the mucus secreted by Culler skin, pressed into her thighs. One talon stabbed into the wall by her face, flicking curls of metal against her cheek and forcing her to look up. The other talon found the hole in her less damaged shoulder and dug in, twisting and turning until she thought she would pass out from the pain. Its two spindly fingers, attached at the base of its talon, prodded at her wound.

It was bleeding. Thick, goopy liquid coated its carapace, pumping from a hole in the chest. She briefly considered that the wound was almost exactly center of mass - just like during training. Then the creature twisted that talon again and she screamed.

"Human," it said. It made several clicking sounds, and then, "Human was waiting for the traders." Maker's pants were wet, not from urine, she was fairly sure, although that wouldn't have surprised her, but from the combination of cold sweat and blood that was dripping off her body. The Culler leaned in close. Its eyes, larger and blacker than seemed possible, dilated, revealing a silvery center that seemed to bore into her. "Why."

Maker felt like a ton of bricks had been pressed onto her chest. Her brain was being squeezed, and it hurt. *Holy hell, everything hurts,* was all she could think. There was more clicking, and the talon withdrew from her shoulder. Both razor sharp appendages reached toward her face, pricking lightly against her flesh - just enough to break the skin. "Human." The word sounded tinny, like it was coming from far away through an old fashioned megaphone. "Tell." As if in slow motion, the skin of its jaw and neck split. It wasn't a mouth - Cullers didn't have mouths according to xenobiologists. It was a beak and stomach. Like an octopus, Cullers ground their food and ingested it directly. Maker had never seen one outside of a textbook. It was less attractive in person. Her head was ringing and her tech was flashing and blinking with red warnings. The beak moved sideways, grating against the hard plate of bone underneath. It sounded anticipatory.

Maker squeezed the trigger.

The bullet burned against the top of her thigh where it grazed her, ripping right through her armor until it connected with the pelvis of the Culler. Its beak gnashed shut and she was grateful for the blood in her ears so she couldn't very well make out the shrill sound of its scream. It fell backward, flopping, almost comically, like a fish out of water, and flailing with its talons - less comically. One bit into Maker's calf and she let out a guttural shout. Her bloody, numb right hand wrestled for her net gun, and when she finally got it to fire, it only captured the Culler's top half. She had no way to turn on the magnetic locks, so it was just a wire mesh that the thing couldn't seem to cut through, even with its deadly talons. Maker stared at it for a few precious moments, mostly stunned that she was alive.

She holstered her gun, and an overwhelming sense of exhaustion came over her. The niquab still covered her hair and neck, but it was too difficult to remove. Maker decided that was fine, because while she had been too hot before, she now felt a shiver dancing along her skin. She might have curled up right there, tried to rest in the shell of the building, if the owners of the shops had not started to reappear. She saw one on the far side of the commons, barely noticeable with the near-dead flicker of her contacts. Another leaned out of a building, speaking into a communicator and pointing to the trail of Culler-bits that had been smeared across the floor. The mission was supposed to have been easy, quiet, and not leave any impression with the locals that the Sol Coalition had any interest in the little mining station. Somewhere in her most-definitely concussed state, she realized that plan would be blown to hell once station security arrived to find her, the shot-up Culler, and all of her Coalition issue equipment.

"This is Command, respond." She struggled to her feet and only had to pause for fifteen or twenty seconds to steady herself and prevent whatever might remain in her stomach from becoming reacquainted with her mouth. "Command calling, over." Her throat felt hot and raw, but she kept repeating the call out, softly, as she picked up one twisted corner of the net. The wires bit into her glove every time the Culler moved, and Maker finally turned and shot the thing in the foot with her Klim. It still struggled, but not so violently. She bypassed the hole in the floor, knowing she would not be able to jump down two levels, even if she used the Culler as a landing pad, and headed for the corridor.

Locals were noticing her, and they were not friendly. Several armed residents of the station followed her progress closely. "Command here, call back," she continued to try to raise the transport as she limped down the hall. There was a small stand-off at the lift doors, and Maker wasn't sure what finally made the armed miners move: the sight of her gun, or of the snarling, shrieking Culler behind her. She kicked the creature in the head with her boot once she had it in the lift. The movement sent a spear of fiery agony up her thigh and into her back. At the push of a button they descended to the docking level without any further noise from the prisoner. Unfortunately, it seemed to come around as she approached the bay and the growing stench of rotting plants. What little was left of a Culler after a vapor round from a heavy rifle dripped from the walls and ceiling. It made her prisoner thrash wildly. She shot at it again, but missed. "This is Command, please respond."

"Transport here, Command." Static and crackles accompanied Bretavic's deep voice, but the transmission was understandable. Maker's heart seized hard and then started beating in double time in relief. The pilot continued, "Locals are starting to rumble, time to go."

Maker entered the bay to find the ship prepped and ready; the thrum of the engines reverberated dully against her throbbing ears. A loose group of ten to fifteen miners blocked the door to the operations center; there would be no leaving the station without accessing control for the docking doors. Rodriguez was braced against the hydraulics for the ship's ramp. Next to him, holding a heavy rifle and surrounded by spent cartridges, was Kerry. Rodriguez looked pale, but determined, as he kept his eyes on the crowd. Kerry was as complacent as ever, his weapon on the miners. He glanced at her quickly, and spoke to the private with his usual calm tone.
"Sarge could use help."

Without responding or looking away from potential hostiles, Rodriguez holstered his Klim and held out his arms for the rifle.

Kerry drew his service weapon and sidestepped toward her. Maker would have met him halfway if she didn't have to stop twice to kick at the snarling Culler. Adrenaline was wearing off, and pain and exhaustion were rapidly taking precedence. She issued orders in what she hoped was an authoritative voice, but she doubted it came out that way, "Warm up the forward cannon." Kerry took the net from her and hauled the Culler up off the floor with ease, never losing his targets. He moved quicker than she did, easily picking his way through the blue Nick blood that streaked the ramp even with his thrashing package.

"I'd appreciate it if you'd open the door," she called out to the miners. Her voice sounded strangely far away and outside her own head. A few men shifted, looking at one another, and one raised a gun.

"Target painted," Rodriguez said softly. She was close enough she could have heard it without the transceiver, if her ears weren't still bleeding sluggishly. Her tech flickered, for a moment showing the aggressive miner outlined in yellow.

"Hold targets," Maker stated flatly. She couldn't feel the gun in her hand, couldn't feel much of anything past the pain. So much pain in her arm. Shoulders. Back. Thigh. Calf. Head. So much pain that it blended together into a red haze that surrounded her vision. The mission was mostly screwed. They were supposed to bring both Nicks in alive; one was dead and she wouldn't be surprised if the other followed soon, if the amount of blood he left behind was any indication. They had involved locals, and although their armor was unmarked and mostly covered by civilian clothing, the miners would have had to be brain dead to not suspect the Sol Confederation. One fourth of her team was unconscious, another quarter dead, the rest severely injured. *We're already FUBAR,* she thought, *there is really no reason to be polite.* She focused on the crowd.

"You can open the door," she told them, "or I can." She stepped onto the riser for the transport and spoke lowly so that only the transmitter would pick it up, "All aboard, raise the hatch." As the hydraulics began to work, she called out to the miners, keeping her gun ready, "You have two minutes."

As soon as the ramp was sealed, Bretavic leaned out of the cockpit to nod at her, but she couldn't manage a response as she stared at the floor of the cargo hold. All of their dead had been recovered, and someone had attempted to cover them with a cargo tarp. It wasn't large enough. *Too many bodies*, she thought woodenly. Only their faces were concealed; their legs stuck out, stiff and spattered with fluid. Maker couldn't stop staring at the boots. The Lieutenant's were polished to a high shine. Despite orders to remain covert, he must not have been able to help himself. Habits ingrained during training were hard to break. She looked down at her own feet. Her rough brown boots had been already dusty and scuffed before they became covered in blood. *I should take better care of them.*

Rodriguez found her standing in the hold next to the stretched out corpses of her team. He escorted her out of the cargo area and helped her to lie down on an empty bunk where he could administer meds and emergency bandages. Maker was vaguely aware of Bretavic noting the dock doors opening and ordering the team to strap in, but she could focus on little past the sweet relief of pain killers as Rodriguez injected her. Kerry found them there once they were in open space.

"Passengers secure?" Her tongue felt thick in her mouth, and Kerry's dark hair and skin looked fuzzy. The flat nose and wide cheekbones that signaled his genetic modifications blurred a little, so that all she could clearly make out was the dark slashes of his mouth and eyebrows.

"One Nick, one Culler. Both pissed as hell, but they'll live," he responded and took a seat on the floor in the narrow walkway between the bunks, his back against the bracing near her feet.

She glanced at the bed opposite her and could make out a soldier's form. "The others?"

"They'll make it," Rodriguez replied. "Although you might not. Shit, Maker," worry seeped into his voice, "why the hell didn't you follow Bretavic down? You're lucky those Cullers didn't eviscerate you." She pulled her eyes away from Kerry's head to look at the private. He was frowning, the expression making his handsome face broodingly attractive. He was only a year younger than her, but in that moment of drug-induced simplicity he looked sickeningly youthful. *Eighteen,* she recalled from the mission brief files, *probably not even done filling out yet.* He could have died, like the others. *Hell, I almost shot him myself...a couple of times.* Rodriguez cut away the clothing and what was left of her armor over her chest and shoulders. She had never seen anyone die before. Suddenly she felt sick again, and had to close her eyes and breathe shallowly to hold back the urge to vomit. The private didn't seem to notice as he continued to work, or he attributed it to pain. "There's nothing I can do for your shoulder joint, anyhow. Hopefully the medics at base can save it. But you're going to be in surgery for a day or two, at best."

Maker swallowed several times, and was aware of the weight of Kerry's head, leaning back against her uninjured leg. She should have been more concerned with her shoulder, but what had been fiery agony was subsiding into a dull throb that seemed far away. Everything seemed far away. She realized it was the meds, making her comfortable and loosening her tongue, but it didn't stop her from mumbling, "Just make sure they take the det cord out of my pocket, first."

CHAPTER 3: SKINNER BOX

Eugenics. Noun. A social philosophy and the actions to carry it out which aim to design the human race through selective breeding. It had a resurgence of popularity in the United States and United Kingdom in the early 20th century and was later a key component of Nazi regime policies. Embryonic gene therapy was criticized through the early twenty-first century as a tool of eugenics. Most detractors were silenced in 2047 with the approval of a select list of health-related and minor aesthetic changes covered by insurance and ensuring equal access.
Ex. If you desire tall children, marry a tall spouse; it is simple eugenics.

Hour 1630
March 28, 2109

Ignition minus thirty-nine years.

Bee lifted his head slowly above the vegetation where he had been hiding. He could smell the animal ahead of him, and his mouth watered, but he swallowed it down and waited. The white coats called the game Group Dynamics Planning Exercise One, but Bee and the others called it what it was: surround-wait-pack-pounce. There were lots of things that had two names. There was the name the white coats spoke, and the name Bee and his pack spoke. He was Bee, or sometimes Twenty-two-B when they were talking about him instead of to him, but his real name was long-crouch. His favorite game was sniff-listen-follow-find, but the white coats called it Sensory Perception Assessment and Expansion Exercise Three. The white coats had funny, long names for most things - even themselves. Sometimes the white coats spoke too short. Today the first meal was called Protein Supplement MRE Six, but the pack knew it was hot-meat-ran-fast-ate-green-good-death and oily-smooth-salty-swimmers. The white coats were smart, and they knew where the food was and how to open the doors, but they weren't very good at naming things.

Second meal had been smaller than normal, so Bee and the others had known there would be a food game. Ghe had complained and pouted, but Bee and the others were excited. Food games were fun, and the food was tastier and more...more... Bee struggled with a description. Game food was bright and big in his mouth and sometimes crunched or squirted when he bit down. It was wet and hot sometimes, and it made his nose feel full and tingling with scent. It was just *more*.

It had been nearly time for third meal, and his stomach felt empty, when the white coats came. Soft-rough-mother was with them, and that made the whole pack even more excited. The white coats called her Doctor Gillian or Wendy or sometimes Boss, but when she watched a game, at least one of the pack was always picked to do something special afterward. It was hard to always tell how to get picked. Sometimes she wanted the fastest, sometimes the most patient, sometimes she picked the one that made all the rest of the pack listen.

Bee thought he had it figured out, though. The white coat that was sweet-flower-bitter-herbs always sat by the window after second meal to watch them. She used a stick and wrote on her bright square and if Bee came to the window, she would watch him. He knew she was writing about him, because sometimes she drew pictures too. He recognized himself from the mirrors in the enclosure. She made his fur dark and his mane streaky. And she wrote his name next to those drawings: Twenty-two-B. That was him. He had watched sweet-flower-bitter-herbs long enough that he knew some other words too. Like Positive. Pat. Training. Good. Obedient. Alpha.

That was what soft-rough-mother wanted, he was sure. The white-coats said that word 'alpha' a lot, and although none of the rest of the pack seemed to recognize it, Bee knew what it really meant. First-kill-hot-blood-protector-front-walk-listen. Sometimes Ae was that. Once or twice it had been Jay, but usually they worked together, mostly, and if there was a problem with their plan, each of them tried to win on their own. But soft-rough-mother wanted one of them to be in charge. She wanted one of the pack to make the others listen, even if something went wrong with a plan. Soft-rough-mother was going to give special treats and attention to the one who could make the others listen. The way the white-coats listed to soft-rough-mother.

Bee wanted special treats. He wanted attention from soft-rough-mother. He wanted her to put her hand on his head and use her good-boy-good-girl voice and tell him he did well. He wanted to be allowed to sit on the ground next to sweet-flowers-bitter-herbs and watch her draw him, to lean against her warm leg. Bee wanted to be the alpha.

He tried to explain it to the others after second meal, but only Ae had understood at all. The words were hard - hard to make sounds that meant what he was thinking. When third meal was late, he had finally given up trying to convince them.

Follow, he had growled. *Listen. My plan. My kill. Pack bite hot meat hot meat hot meat. Obey. Hot meat hot meat hot meat.*

Then soft-rough-mother had come in and the game began. "Group Dynamics Planning Exercise Number One, attempt number thirty-four, series Twenty-two primary group." She held up her clicker and pinched it three times, *click-a-click-a-click-a,* and that meant listen. "Covert. Team. Hunt. Ready." She held her hand flat in the air, and brought it down as she said,

"Go."

Bee and the rest of the pack were good at that part. Before her hand could reach her side they had scattered into the plants that were thick around the walls of the enclosure. Bee was as quiet as he could be, climbing up a rock and laying on his belly in the deep shadow of a tree. He watched the clearing below and the game box that was lowered to the center. He could smell his pack, waiting, watching. He could smell the white coats. There were more than usual, and not just soft-rough-mother in the enclosure with them, but also the trace of sweet-flowers-bitter-herbs that filtered through the vent under the glass and others too. One in the enclosure and many in the corridor and behind the glass.

Bee flicked his ears, and his hairs told him that the air was changing direction. The scent of the game animal blew toward him, and then the game box opened. He tensed, alert, and his surprise was only overcome by the spike of ready-smell that Jay and Ee were giving off. Bee tensed his throat and moaned as low as he could. They had all been practicing making the sound. The white coats couldn't hear it, but they could feel it or see it move in Bee's chest if they were close enough.

The ready-smell died off, and Bee knew they were waiting for another signal. That was good. They listened. Listening meant alpha. He turned his full attention back to the game food. It wasn't hairy, but had ridges on its back that looked hard to chew. It moved, slowly, and that surprised Bee. Game food had never moved before. It also excited him. He wanted to chase. To pounce. Bee dug his claws into the rock to help himself stay put and moaned again. If he wanted to chase, the others would too. They couldn't, not yet. He had to wait first to learn the rules.

The game animal crawled off of the metal box that held the prize. It moved cautiously, curled up and taking tiny steps that made its ridges stick out. Bee waited, the hot smell of blood and the sound of it pumping through the game food making his mouth water even more. It seemed like forever, longer than forever, longer than the pack had ever waited for game animals. Then the animal relaxed. It picked up a broken leaf from the ground and rolled over onto its back to hold the green thing while it ate. The game animal had a soft, soft belly.

Bee dug in his blunt toe claws and leaped, without making a sound. He landed a little further from where he had wanted to be, but he still got one hand buried into the game animal's belly. It made a shrieking sound and thrashed, but the rest of the pack was there. Jay stepped on its tail, even though it had little spike that made his foot bleed. Ae dug her claws under its chin, and Dee rammed his face under one flailing leg to bite at the joint. Bee roared. It sounded loud to him, and all the pack but Ae and Jay backed away and circled the game animal. Bee looked to Ae, just to make certain she knew he was first-kill-hot-blood-protector-front-walk-listen and then he snapped his mouth around the underarm where he could hear and smell the blood pumping hard. It sprayed on his face, and the game animal stopped moving.

There was a click, and the prize box opened. The pack smelled excited, ready. A few even let out whimpers and whines. But they waited. They were listening. Bee stepped away from the game animal and walked carefully to the box. Spit was starting to leak out of the side of his mouth, but he ignored the feeling in his stomach that said he should take all the food. He reached in one hand and pulled out the largest piece of food. He took one bite, one big bite of hot-meat-ran-fast-ate-green-good-death and then he used his claws to cut it into two halves. He gave one to Aa, and one to Jay.

Aa waited, although her lips were shiny with spit too. Jay bit into his, then stopped when Bee growled. Jay sat down and waited too. Bee was still hungry. His stomach felt even emptier, but he was sure that he knew what soft-rough-mother wanted.

He couldn't help but sneak a glance at her. Her face was flat, but she smelled happy. Bee felt a rush of happiness too. He would be alpha. He would be good-boy-good-girl head-pat-pat. Bee stepped away from the prize box and called to the others.

My plan. My kill. Good pack. Eat. Eat. Eat.

And they did. The pack yipped excitedly and bunched around the prize box. Since Bee hadn't taken a full share, there was a little more for everyone. Bee knew that was important. He promised the pack if they listened, they would get more. That made trust. The white coats liked trust. The pack liked trust too. Bee made sure everyone ate equally, although he had to snap at Aech to keep him from sneaking a second piece. Then he walked over to soft-rough-mother. He sat down at her feet and waited. When she didn't immediately praise him, he began to worry that her happy smell wasn't for him. Then she slipped her clicker into her pocket. She bent a little at the waist, she was tall for a white coat, and smoothed her palm down his head to rest her fingers against the back of his ear.

"Good boy, Twenty-two-B. Good job."

Bee closed his eyes and leaned into her warmth.

***

"It isn't conclusive, not at this age."

Dr. Wendy Gillian acknowledged her fellow researcher with a nod, but continued to watch through the one-way mirror. After the resounding success of the Group Dynamics exercise, she had let Twenty-two-B choose his own reward. That too, was a test of sorts. She knew he had to be hungry, but when presented with a choice between a double-portion of protein, fatty acid, and simple sugars or a single portion of protein and physical contact with her assistant, he had chosen Lupe.

It made sense. All of the primary group had an extra twist

to their genetic structure, a marker that made them want to please. But B had always shown an extra willingness, desire even, to seek praise. Gillian was surprised, however, that he had been the one to finally leap into a dominate role. There were others that occasionally showed capacity for it; J in particular was more aggressive than the rest of the pack. Aggression, as exhibited by many species on Earth and on Keres 6b-3, was not always an indicator of leadership skills.

Dr. Bantan was going on about personality fix milestones and cognition development. Gillian ignored most of it. She had heard it all before, even published some of it herself. It was an old argument. She interrupted him instead, "Have you noticed he watches her stylus?" Gillian toggled the camera to zoom in on B's eyes. He was following Lupe's progress with her drawing and accompanying notes carefully. The male was sitting on the ground at her feet, leaning into the side of her thigh to peer over her arm. His food had been finished long ago, but Gillian was content to let the special treat last at least until Lupe was finished with her current assignment.

"Hm." Bantan moved to stand next to her, and then pulled up the feed on his tablet. He replayed it several times, drawing a few lines over the image to highlight B's gaze. "Well, I'll be damned," he said quietly.

"What?" Gillian pulled her eyes away from the subject and research on the other side of the mirror and glanced down.

"I think he's reading." Bantan shook his head. Gillian was just as disbelieving. The Twenty-two series had been genetically dialed back, as the specialists termed it. They were less human and more animal than many previous series. The return to something closer to the original subject species was an attempt to better understand where the sequencing and accompanying training had gone wrong. From a strictly genetic standpoint, they were animals with some human DNA. Not the other way around. Reading, and other high-level intelligence tasks, had been hypothesized to be years down the road in their development - if not completely impossible.

"Send Lupe a text," she decided suddenly. Bantan typed while Gillian dictated. They could both see the moment the message went through. B stiffened and his eyes snapped to the tablet in Lupe's lap. She tapped on the screen to pull it up, and they watched B's eyes scan over the text.

Count to five, then read aloud: Twenty-two-B is a good boy.

Lupe frowned, but they could see B nearly vibrating with excitement *before* Lupe spoke. All of the subjects had been conditioned to the phrase 'good boy/girl' and the praise of a head pat. Gillian's heart picked up pace, but she tried to keep her excitement in check. She dictated another message, and B leaned so far over the tablet when the chime sounded that Lupe couldn't see the screen.

Pat Twenty-two-B.

The subject turned and faced Lupe so fast he almost knocked the stylus out of her hand. It took her a moment to realize that he was waiting, head lowered and hovering under her free hand.

"Son of a bitch," Bantan whispered.

Gillian stared at him with wide eyes. This was it, she was sure. Nearly two decades of her life, full use of her left arm, and half of her face had been given to the project. The tall, furry six year-old on the other side of the glass was the breakthrough she had been hoping for - had thought was years and another two or three attempts at sequencing away. Her theories could be proven. Here. Now. Nurture conquers nature. Gillian had to breathe deeply to keep the sheer exhilaration, the joy, from exploding. "Design the test - I want to start tomorrow. For all of them, this group and secondary. Keep the team small - Eyes Only. We need to get this figured out before Congress decides to send the twenty-twos to war."

CHAPTER 4: UNASKED DEBT

Peppermint. Noun. Slang. Offensive.: An individual who did not receive standard embryonic genetic therapy to remove non-desirable aesthetic or minor health concerns. Such an individual may have had medically threatening genetic material removed, such as markers for Tay Sachs or Cystic Fibrosis. Often shortened to 'mint', or 'minty'.
Ex. He's handsome, for a peppermint.

Hour 0900
March 14, 2148

Ignition minus forty days.

Maker clenched her jaw and tried to ignore the hot ache in her shoulder joint. The surgeon in charge of the bone reconstruction had protested her discharge, claiming the artificial ligaments needed more time to fully attach to the new clavicle. Unfortunately, an official inquiry into her actions on the last mission superseded medical authority. The doctor had practically snarled as he had tossed a sling at her, growling about barbarian recovery procedures. She had left the sling in her bag in the corridor before she was escorted into the hearing. Standing before a panel of officers, at least one of whom she knew had a personal dislike of her, was not a time to look pathetic. Lieutenant Commander Soon had made it clear during her time stationed aboard the *Pershing* that he felt it was his responsibility to make her life a living hell. Maker didn't know why, but she wasn't about to expose any weaknesses. *Any more weaknesses,* she snorted to herself.

Most of the bruising on her face had faded, but there was no doubt that she had been injured. The brace that kept her two new vertebrate properly aligned made her uniform coat bunch and strain. Unlike the sling, she couldn't just remove it. Vertebrae were much more sensitive to misalignment than ball and socket joints. Just thinking about it made her shoulder throb.

"This inquiry is called to order," the Commander chairing the meeting stated. She dropped the gavel with enough force to echo in the mostly empty room. Lieutenant Commander Soon sat straight, nearly leaning forward in his chair in anticipation. To the Commander's left sat an older officer who took no pains to hide his bored expression from the intimidating woman speaking. "Sargent Clara Maker, Service Number SC2144-E56-00861, you have been notified of Questions of Concern regarding the performance of your duties and the accuracy of your field report during the mission noted as," she paused and consulted the tablet in front of her, "2148-RS-237." Maker was vaguely surprised that there had been two hundred and thirty-seven Recon and Secure missions authorized so early in the year. *At least I only have to fill out the forms for one*, she thought sourly. "Do you understand the Questions as they have been posed?"

Maker didn't shift her gaze from the Commander, although she could feel the attention of the other two panel members on her. The Questions of Concern had been listed in the summons she received while she was in the infirmary. Although a lot of statute and protocol was mixed into the language, the message was basic: they thought she fucked up. It wasn't an unsurprising conclusion. Her sergeant's stripes weren't even broken in, and a simple bag-and-drag had resulted in the death of nearly half of her team, including the commanding officer. The killing of two Cullers and capture of another only added a layer of strange to the fucked-up. The blatant flaunting of the order to remain covert was a frosting of insubordination. A bitter sprinkling of incompetence from the damage inflicted on the mining station was the final touch on her shit sandwich.

Incompetence on insubordination on strange on fucked-up, she summarized internally. *Yeah, I understand the questions.*

"Ma'am, yes, ma'am," she said aloud.

"Very good," the Commander said, scrolling through her files. She flicked the one she wanted onto the wall display. "Let's begin with a review of the field footage." The lighting dimmed.

Maker tried not to fidget or relax her posture as they forwarded through hours of pre-incident footage from the multiple angles offered by each soldier's personal recording device. The playback was paused only a few times to highlight the lieutenant as he gave orders to switch shifts or stay focused. Her back ached and her shoulder burned; her arm felt like a lead weight pulling down on the socket. She was unsuccessful at controlling her blush when they slowed the images down in time to catch her exchange with Rodriguez. The older panelist chuckled. The Commander remained impassive. Lt. Commander Soon sent her a glare. After that, the film became uncomfortable to watch. She flinched when her own video feed was enlarged to show her clumsy attempt to back away from the Nick she had thrown alcohol on. The muscles in her back twitched in remembered and real pain as she watched her fall from the pipe to hit the floor. The tech displays were overlaid on the recording of her vision, and Maker stood still while she watched her team's lights go dark all over again.

Kerry's transmission seemed louder and more frantic as it played in the meeting room than it had on the mining station:

"Transport down! Cullers! Two in the bay, one in the weeds! Request immediate assistance! Respond!"

"Retreat! Cargo is expendable, if necessary! Go, Go, Go!"

Her video shook as she had run down the alley, and then the Culler was on her. Maker broke out in a sweat, just watching the attack. Then the video feed went dead. Sound had continued to record, and the room sat in silence, listening to her heavy breathing, her grunts and screams of pain, the grating words of the Culler. Video flicked in and out a few times. Once it showed the blood-soaked face veil as she ripped it off and vomited on the ground. Her arms had been shiny-wet with blood welling out of her body armor and making her gloves slick. The second time lasted longer, and captured Bretavic on the edge of the hole in the floor, his gesture to the corridor, and the first charge of the Cullers. Her shot had gone wide, ripping through the wall of a shop.

Then there was the noise and confusion of the fight, the explosion. Maker watched while a cold sweat made her skin clammy. The increasing desperation in her recorded voice as she tried to raise someone on the comms made her nauseated:

"This is Command, respond."
"Command calling, over."
"Command here, call back."
"This is Command, please respond."

Then there were her threats to the miners, and her discussion with Kerry and Rodriguez on the transport. The feed ended, and the lights slowly brightened.

"Sergeant Maker, is the evidence shown here, incomplete as it is, accurate?"

"Ma'am," Maker had to pause to gather enough spit in her mouth to speak. A trickle of sweat slid under the collar of her uniform. Her stomach was twisting again, with fear or guilt she wasn't sure. "Yes, ma'am."

"Do you expect us to believe that you took out three Cullers on your own, Sergeant?" Soon leaned forward in his chair, his fore-arms braced on the table. "What really happened while your video was out?"

"Sir, I could never have terminated those targets on my own, sir." Maker swallowed again. In another time and place she would have savored the smug look on Soon's face, knowing she had the power to wipe it away. Reliving the disaster of her first command obliterated the petty impulse. "The first target, Spe-cies Cancri 8 -"

"Nicks, I believe you called them." The older officer who had laughed at her exchange with Rodriguez smiled.

Maker nodded stiffly, and continued, "That was dumb luck. As you could see, my aim was off and I nearly broke a leg trying to get to higher ground. The second one was as much Rodriguez's success as mine. Likely more."

The Commander glanced down at her tablet. "That would be Private First Class, Rodriguez?"

"Yes, ma'am," Maker agreed. "The Culler in the alley-"

"The one who killed your commanding officer," Soon inter-rupted. Maker nodded jerkily. "But you had no trouble with it." His contempt was obvious.

"No, sir," she disagreed. "Bretavic's team had already wounded it, and it still dislocated my shoulder, punctured my leg, and destroyed my tech."

"Thing probably died more from the ceiling crashing down than the girl's shot," murmured the old man in amusement.

Maker didn't wait for Soon to interject again, she was desperate to get the inquiry over with. Her body hurt, and she didn't want to think about what had happened on the station for a moment longer than she had to. She spoke quickly, "The other kill and the capture were similar. They were already injured, and I took wounds, from the enemy and my own actions, and destroyed a significant amount of personal and corporate property, in order to survive. The mission objectives, as stated by my commanding officer prior to his death, were achieved. The subsequent loss of life and breaches in protocol are solely my responsibility. I am prepared for whatever decision this body hands down."

The room was quiet for a moment, then the Commander spoke reproachfully, "This is an inquiry, not a court martial, Sergeant. No sentences will be handed down today."

"I have heard enough," the oldest member stated, rolling his shoulders. "This evidence and testimony, combined with what we reviewed earlier, confirm for me that Sergeant Maker acted to the best of her ability within the confines of her orders and the situation." The official statement was spoken with a practiced tongue, and the officer casually slapped his palm onto his tablet to sign his decision.

"I object," Soon said flatly. His eyes sparkled with malice. "I am not satisfied, nor do I feel that Sergeant Maker has conducted herself in a manner befitting a member of the Sol Coalition forces, much less an officer. I recommend that this case be forwarded onto the Justice unit for an expedited court martial." He, too, pressed his palm down, but with a barely suppressed smile. The bottom fell out of Maker's stomach. She had wanted it to be over, but she hadn't honestly expected that result. Her eyes turned to the Commander.

"The circumstances presented here are unusual in the extreme, as are the actions taken by Sergeant Maker," she said slowly. Soon's white teeth flashed in a savage smile. His satisfaction was premature, "The veracity of her statement is not in dispute, and has been confirmed by other accounts. However, given the preparation and intelligence provided for the mission, and the challenges posed, as well as Maker's own inexperience, I believe that she displayed quick-thinking, courage, and grace under pressure. These are the basis for a fine soldier, and a fine officer."

"Provided she doesn't blow herself up first," muttered the third member.

"Indeed." Maker might have imagined it, but she swore she saw a crinkling at the corners of the Commander's eyes. "This body has a majority. All Questions of Concern have been addressed, and no further action is indicated." The Commander sealed her palm print to her tablet and then banged the gavel again. "The meeting is concluded. Sergeant Maker, you are dismissed." Soon stormed out of the room; the Commander followed more sedately. Maker simply stood, blinking, for a few moments wondering what exactly had happened. She slowly pulled her injured arm to her chest, cradling her fist against the opposite shoulder.

A voice at her side startled her, "That was quite a thriller you treated us to," said the older officer. Maker was surprised to note the bars on his cuffs. His badge read, Sullivan.

"Captain, sir," she said weakly.

He chuckled, "In my day we would have pinned a medal on you for killing those Culler bastards. Still, try not to end up here again, eh?" She turned to follow him out, and they parted at the doorway. He threw a wink and a comment over his shoulder, "And tell your mother, next time you see her, not to worry about the favor. I don't like serving on these things, but reading this mission report was the highlight of my week."

Her mouth fell open, she was sure, and she stared at his back as he walked away.

Maker wasn't sure how long she stood there, trying to process that she wasn't going to be disciplined - and *why*. It was Bretavic that finally caught her attention as he limped around the corner, a cane gripped uselessly in his hand like a club and a brace on his leg. "Hey," he called out, drawing the attention of several administrative staff in the hallway. He ignored them.

"Shouldn't you be in the infirmary?"

"I could say the same for you," she answered automatically. Then she shook her head to clear it. "Inquiry," she said shortly. Her shock at Captain Sullivan's comment was wearing off, to be replaced with anger.

"I take it everything went okay?" At her nod, he continued, "I tried to tell them, but that Soon was a real jackass." She began a slow walk back toward the lift, her ire continuing to build. *Favors, it always come down to favors*, she thought. She needed a painkiller, and a soft bunk, and some method of reaching through subspace and misguided, unwanted maternal protection to slap someone. Her shoulder throbbed as Bretavic explained. "Rodriguez asked me to wait around for you after he got done with them, but I had to report for a physical."

"Everybody okay?" Concern for her team pushed aside the irritation for a moment.

He named the soldiers, two of whom were still in the infirmary listed as critical. "Kerry and Rodriguez are clean. They had duty this shift. So..." His voice trailed off, and Maker shot him a glance. The big man looked uncomfortable. He was substantially cleaner and healthier than the last time she had seen him. She hadn't known him well before the mission so she couldn't determine if uncomfortable was usual for him. His jaw was showing a five o'clock shadow, strange since it was barely 1200 hours, and his uniform had a few creases. Enough to take a penalty from a strict officer, but not so many that she couldn't reasonably ignore it. She might have stripes on her sleeve, but Bretavic had seniority over her. Between that and flying her out of the FUBAR mission on the station, she wasn't inclined to mention anything about regulation dress.

He shifted a few times and an awkward silence grew between them. "What?" she finally asked. She pushed the button for the lift and stepped in when it almost immediately opened. They were alone in the car, and Bretavic let out a pent-up sigh as the doors closed.

"I have a card game on Thursdays." He said it with an air of challenge, as if Maker cared that he engaged in gambling. It was prohibited, but not enforced, and it wasn't like she was going to get into trouble. "Stop by, if you want."

Oh. Maker blinked. Despite coming completely out of the blue, she recognized an offer of friendship when she saw it. *Maybe I will get into trouble.* She reflected on the meeting she had just been subjected to. *Screw it.* "Yeah, thanks. Where at?"

"Maintenance Bay Six. Security code 1234." He grinned, showing off straight, even white teeth that almost made him handsome. He was at least a decade older than her, but still a private. Maker could guess what had held back promotions. *As if it was just one thing.* "It's ironic."

"I get it," she responded dryly. A tone sounded and the doors opened.

She heard him call after her quietly as she walked away, "And find a fucking sling, Sarge."

Her surgeon was fairly upset to find out she had let the weight of her arm hang from his "perfectly good capsular ligament", resulting in dislocation. He had a nurse hold her while he reinserted it - sans anesthesia. When she woke up, she found that she had been restricted to bed rest in the infirmary for a further two days. It wouldn't have particularly hurt her feelings, if she hadn't been itching to make a call. Rodriguez visited once, although he spent most of his hour flirting with a medical resident. Kerry came as well, and, in the true vein of the friendship they had forged during basic training, he mostly sat quietly and listened while she talked. Although he surprised her by sending a few new novels to her net account as well. It gave her something to do besides practice the lecture she was waiting to give.

Within twenty minutes of being released, she was back in her own quarters. She shared with another non-commissioned officer, but her bunk mate was luckily on duty. Maker flipped on her display and opened her net account. She had to look up the number, but the call was picked up right away.

"*Perry*-niner, here, state your business." The voice was clipped and professional. Maker expected nothing less from a member of that crew.

"Sergeant Clara Maker, Service Number SC2144-E56-00861," she responded. She didn't bother sitting up straight, although she knew the communications officer on the other end could see her. As was protocol for an active-duty ship, the camera on that end remained dark until permission was granted by a senior officer. "Requesting to speak with Captain Yamamoto, immediately."

"Sergeant," the officer's voice dropped about ten degrees. "That is not in your pay grade. Submit a formal request."

"Is Commander…" she wracked her brain for the man's name. It had been years since they met. "Alarcon available?" There was a long pause, and Maker vacillated between anger and hope. Anger for the Captain. Hope that the Commander remembered her.

"Go." The single command came from a new voice, just as concise as she recalled.

"Commander Alarcon, this is Sergeant Clara Maker. I need to speak with Captain Yamamoto as soon as possible, sir."

"Sergeant," he hesitated, and then the display activated. A middle-aged man, his skin dark and silky looking, stood with the communications officer behind him. "The Captain is off duty. Can this wait?" His face was calm, but not unkind. His raked over the yellowed bruises on her face and the sling.

"No," she said, just as evenly, "it cannot." The display went dark again and a protest by the communications officer was abruptly silenced. There was a minute of nothing while the indicator lights at the bottom of the screen blinked to show the communication was being held in the system. Then they flashed green.

"Yamamoto, here." Her voice was a little rough, she had obviously just woken up.

"Lin," Maker said flatly. The camera on the *Perry* immediately switched on. Yamamoto looked the same as when Maker had last seen her, almost two years prior. Her skin was a flawless almond. Her hair, despite the mess of sheets and dented pillow on the bed where she sat, lay in a smooth black curtain just past her jawline. The blue pajama set was not standard issue sleepwear, but they displayed to advantage a body that had been well-taken care of for the last four and a half decades.

"Clara," she didn't raise her volume, but her eyes widened in surprise. "Is something wrong? I thought you would be in the infirmary for another few days, at least."

Maker tried to keep her anger behind a cold voice, "Why would you think that? In fact," she could feel her blood pounding in her ears and had to grip the edge of her desk to keep from pointing an accusing finger at the screen, "How did you know anything about my injury?"

"That," Yamamoto frowned and waved a hand as if it wasn't worth mentioning. "I would never know anything about you if I waited for you or your father to inform me. The Chief Medical Officer on the *Pershing* is a family friend. He notified me as soon as you were admitted." Maker ground her teeth together with fury, but her mother continued as though she couldn't clearly understand the expression on her daughter's face. "Your surgical report showed several coral grafts and some artificial bone. Are you rejecting them?"

"Why ask?" Maker spit out, furious. "Why not just ring my doctor and ask him?"

"Clara, that would put him in an awkward position, don't you think?" Her gentle chiding sent Maker's blood boiling. "Now, if you would simply add me to your information release form, we wouldn't need to go through this. I barely had enough time to call up your grandfather's old classmate to help smooth out the inquiry."

"Captain Sullivan-" she began, but was cut off.

"Yes. I hoped you were sufficiently respectful during the inquiry. You will never get a decent posting once you are commissioned if you don't-"

"I will say this once." Maker leaned in close to the screen, focusing on her mother's face. She kept her voice low, knowing that the walls in her quarters were not thick enough to keep her neighbors from overhearing if she shouted. "I have no intention of being commissioned. I will not re-sign once my obligatory two years' service is up. I do not want your help. I do not want to use the Yamamoto name or connections. I. Do. Not. Want to speak with you. Stay out of my life, Lin."

She ended the transmission and logged out of her account, locking the station. As soon as she had her breathing under control, she grabbed her dopp kit, towel, and a change of clothes and went to wash.

It was a short walk to the showers in her section, and they were nearly deserted. When she finished, Maker wiped the steam from the mirror. Her wet hair looked nearly black, the unruly waves slicked down against the back of her neck. The white of her skin looked deathly against the purple smudges under her eyes. Freckles, cultivated during a childhood spent under the Earth's atmosphere, had faded to nearly nothing; but they took on a green cast under the harsh lighting. Her new scars were minimal, courtesy of laser stitching and low-impact techniques. Only slightly shiny patches on her pale skin denoted where a talon had pierced her calf and the bullet trail across the top of her thigh. A silvery line, barely wider than thread, traced down her arm to end in a faint starburst where her damaged tech had burned her. With the mirror, she could see the still healing pink tissue on each shoulder; her left was surrounded by fresh bruises from the recent dislocation.

It didn't seem like enough. Four soldiers were dead and she had to search for a visible sign of her injuries.

It was too much. She hadn't wanted to be a soldier, would never have joined if it weren't compulsory. Nineteen years old. Four months left to serve and she wanted nothing so badly as to just go home.

She could feel hot tears pricking at the backs of her eyes, which made her angry. She shouldn't be crying. She wasn't hurt anymore; she didn't have the ashes of a loved one on their way home in a jar. She didn't have any good reason to cry. Maker yanked on standard issue loose gray shorts and tank - the contrast to Yamamoto's attire was satisfying. On the way back to her quarters she kept up a pace that was uncomfortable for her still healing body and fell into her bunk before any moisture leaked out onto her face.

CHAPTER 5: RECOMBINATION

Societal Collapse. Noun. The end or diminishing of a society, culture, or civilization most commonly resulting from economic, environmental, or cultural change. Forces contributing to such a collapse include sub-replacement fertility, prolonged armed conflicts (internal or external), and natural disasters.

Ex. The fall of the Roman Empire was predicated with internal political struggles, a series of expensive military expansions and overextended borders, and low birth rate among the ruling class.

Hour 0830
January 1, 2115

Ignition minus thirty-three years.

"Five series, Dr. Gillian. Five." Representative Sudarshan punctuated the number by pressing her palms flat against the table on either side of her tablet. Her manicured nails clicked against the steel. "I have provided everything you have insisted is necessary for the success of Project Barghest. The Oversight Committee for Defense Research has spent more on funding your facility than on cleanup of the Michigan-Pennsylvania and Showa crash sites combined. And yet, I have here your most recent quarterly report." Gillian opened her mouth to respond, and Sudarshan glared to let her know she wasn't finished.

"And yet," she repeated, "as I was on my way to a session hearing, sipping my coffee and listening to my daily calendar, I read this: '...twenty-six series is not viable for field deployment...'." Sudarshan flicked one finger across the surface of her tablet, "...inability to assume effective leadership..." She looked up, brushing a non-existent stray hair back into her chignon. "I understood you had corrected that defect in the twenty-twos. So why is it, then, *Doctor*, that despite trillions of credits, years of research, and the brilliant minds recruited to this staff, that you still have not produced results?"

Gillian remained silent for a long moment, her jaw clenched in obvious anger. The white scar tissue that covered nearly half of her face remained smooth, while her undamaged skin was showing the inevitable signs of aging. It only reminded Sudarshan of how much time had been lost. If her election went well, in less than a year she would be moving into a Senate office and handing the leadership of the committee and Project Barghest over to a junior Representative. She needed progress, concrete proof of success. Her entire career had been dedicated to finding a solution to the loss of life against Culler forces - and all of her bets were placed on Barghest and Gillian.

"If I may, Representative?" Gillian motioned toward the door. Surprised, Sudarshan nodded. She stood only a beat behind the doctor, picking up the tablet, and followed the white-coated woman through a security door - not the one by which she had entered the office - and began walking down a corridor. "Series twenty-six does display some undeniable indicators that they will not perform in the field as the project requires. However," she cut her eyes to Sudarshan and the representative bit back a tart comment. "However, that does not mean they are incapable of ever being utilized as soldiers." The two women entered an observation area, not unlike the one Sudarshan remembered vividly from her first visit to the facility. On the opposite side of the glass was not a small sterile room, but rather a large space not unlike a public school gymnasium.

Two rows of pre-teens, mostly boys, faced each other. A bearded man in generic exercise clothes walked between them, calling out commands for a set of exercises. Each child performed perfectly in sync with the others. Each increasingly complicated task was done without hesitation. The leader reached the end of the row, nearest the glass and turned. Sudarshan could not help but make a small noise of surprise when a short-haired brown tail flicked into view - attached to the man's backside.

"That is Twenty-two-B, and this series follows his commands easily - far better than any of our staff. I believe it to be instinctual."

Sudarshan studied the man more closely, but could not quite believe he was the same individual she remembered from the many reports on him and his series. "The aging flaw," she said uncertainly, remembering the primary reason for the discontinuation of the Twenty-two series.

"Correct. From the outset, one of our objectives has always been to reduce maturation time of the subjects - dropping the total cost of ownership and the investment period in each individual. With the Twenty-twos we managed to achieve maturation at the chronological age of eleven years, but the cellular degeneration in most subjects could not be prevented from continuing at that rate. Bee is one of the few that responded positively to treatments to slow his progression, but still his aging makes him unsuitable for the field."

"Yes. And while it may be considered efficient of you to have found a use for outdated models, I did not come here for a history lesson, Doctor. If these subjects can take orders, something which you vehemently stated was not possible, then in what way are they unsuited to their purpose?" One of the young men in line muttered something out of the corner of his mouth, startling a laugh out of the boy next to him. Their instructor, tail whipping angrily, was in their faces in an instant. Although no sound was being piped into the observation room, it was still clear that the youths were put into their place as they dropped to the ground and began push-ups with twin grimaces of shame.

"The Twenty-two series had cellular degeneration issues. The Twenty-threes were too empathetic. The Twenty-fours were incapable of the spacial learning required for modern weapons training. The Twenty-fives had hormonal imbalances that made them emotionally unstable. We have corrected all of those problems with the Twenty-six series, and-"

"But," Sudarshan interrupted, "You have brought back an old one. I would think you, of all people Gillian, would know the inherent danger of a hybrid killing machine that refuses to recognize authority." She had intended the comment to give the doctor a reminder in humility - and warn her to stop wasting time. It resulted in an unexpected smile. The rough skin of Gillian's cheek pulled down on the corner of her mouth, making the toothy grin nearly grotesque.

"Indeed - but that is not what we have here. What we have are killing machines - exactly as you requested. Intelligent. Strong. Agile. Capable of ending life but with an understanding of the value of the same. Physically, mentally, and emotionally mature at approximately fourteen years from extraction. They only need one change in your deployment parameters to make them effective."

"Are you suggesting," Sudarshan narrowed her eyes and gestured with a disgusted motion toward the fanged, tail-sporting male on the other side of the glass, "that I recommend to the SC brass that they send a dog into battle to command their elite forces?"

"Bee is not a dog," Gillian bit off. Silence fell for another moment while both women tried to rein in their tempers. "And I would not recommend he enter the field, even if he does live long enough for these subjects to be deployed. She turned tightly on a low-heeled shoe and opened another security door. "I am recommending," she said in a calmer tone, "that the twenty-sixes receive additional training and classification as general support forces while the twenty-seven series matures.

Once ready, the twenty-sevens will be capable of commanding their predecessors as well as receiving additional training for special forces missions and highly independent decision-making." They passed through two security doors, the second guarded by another individual with a tail.

The female, wearing a modified version of fatigues, greeted the doctor with a dipped head and a smile that bared pointed teeth. She sniffed overtly at Sudarshan.

"She is with me, Ae," Gillian stated calmly. The guard was dedicated to her duty. She took their security cards and carefully compared the photo on Sudarshan's to her face and the information terminal on the wall before scanning them in and stepping aside. Sudarshan did her best to keep her expression from not reflecting the morbid curiosity that swirled in her mind as a brown tail flicked at the button to open the door. She followed Gillian inside and the door shut behind them, leaving them alone in a five by five room.

"Decontamination will take a moment, breathe normally," Gillian instructed. Sudarshan had toured research and medical facilities before, so she was prepared for the cool hiss of gas and the glow of UV lighting against her closed lids. After ninety seconds, a chime sounded and another door opened. The room she stepped into was another observation space, but this one was manned with several technicians at computer stations and lab tables. The quiet activity would have been commonplace in almost any biotech facility, if not for the wall of glass that dominated the room. On the other side were four bays of artificial wombs, clustered in groups of twenty-five per bay. The mass of technology that was supporting the lives of one hundred genetically designed beings was phenomenal.

The costs of it all was equally staggering. Sudarshan had never seen the gestation lab, but she was aware that no hospital on Earth, or anywhere in the Sol Coalition, could boast the level of care in the Barghest facility. *With good reason.* Artificial wombs had been declared restricted technology, usable only to save viable pregnancies if the parents did not have any other children. Even if they had not been so carefully controlled, the expense of a single device, even for the few months to mature a regular human infant, was far beyond the means of all but a tiny percentage of the population. Before her were enough machines to grow an army from nothing but artificially constructed DNA, nutrient packs, and energy.

"These are the twenty-sevens. They are the culmination of my work, Representative, and that of hundreds of other scientists." The quiet pride in Gillian's voice was obvious.

"When will they be ready?"

"Extraction is typically around forty-six weeks, since we corrected the aging issue."

"When will they be ready for deployment," Sudarshan clarified. She could not take her eyes off of the small bodies, visible as shadows in the pearly liquid of the wombs. So much potential. So much expectation.

"Like the Twenty-sixes, they will be mature at fourteen years." Dislike hardened her next words, "But I strongly recommend that they spend at least an additional year in field training exercises."

"Noted," Sudarshan turned to face the doctor. Tearing her eyes away from the tiny soldiers growing at her direction. Tearing her mind away from the possibilities of the future. "Our losses pushing the Cullers out of Near Sol space are unsustainable. We need those soldiers, doctor." She handed back the tablet loaded with reports and data on the project and turned to leave. "And for gods' sake," she tossed over her shoulder as she pressed her palm against the security lock, "stop naming them after the alphabet. It makes the field reports damn confusing."

CHAPTER 6: SMOKE FILLED ROOM

Judicial Equity. Proper Noun. Refers to a series of bills passed from 2088-2092 allowing criminals accused of avoiding mandatory military service or violent crimes, and later some non-violent crimes, to serve a reduced sentence through labor. Although the Confederation and some member nations still operate prisons and work sites, most individuals found guilty of felonies or repeat misdemeanors are ordered to one of the many contracted labor sites run off world by corporations.

Ex. He chose service of ten years in the terbium mines on Europa rather than twenty years incarceration for involuntary manslaughter.

Hour 1325
April 13, 2119

Ignition minus twenty-nine years.

"This morning I was on the Senate floor, a wet Paris spring outside the windows, listening to debates on the war and reading a live transcript of a strategic planning session on Kuiper Station, and now here I am having lunch in Omaha with you. Many of my colleagues lament the loss of the good old days, but, Avani, I vastly prefer the advances of modernization."

Sudarshan nodded politely, but she did not drop her guard, despite the casual surroundings. The noodle shop was far too small to be expected to offer indoor dining, but an April snowstorm had covered the sidewalk tables in a layer of wet, cold snow. The owner had squeezed a tiny table and two chairs in a corner between the counter and the front window to accommodate the Prime Minister, leader of the Sol Coalition Senate, for a luncheon meeting. Most of the business seemed to be in deliveries made out the back entrance. Their meal was undisturbed except for the polite service of cups of delicate tea and steaming bowls of fragrant broth.

"I find it especially striking when I come home. To think, my grandfather used to bring me here when he came back from Washington. That was just after the Repulsion of the Culler invasion, and he was overseeing the reverse engineering of the alien ships that landed on American soil. Oh," the older woman reminisced with a smile, "the base here in Omaha was so small then - barely equipped to deal with the soldiers and scientists that all flooded in, doing everything they could for the war effort - to ensure the survival of humanity." The Senator smiled and took a bite of her noodles, "Mm, delicious as always. You can't get Vietnamese anywhere that is better than this. Not since the Red War."

Sudarshan, despite her tension over being summoned by the Prime Minister more than seven thousand miles from the Sol Coalition Congressional Hall, relaxed somewhat as she also began to eat. The highest member of the Senate, the Prime Minister, was an unassuming American woman. Her hair was thick and white; unlike most people her age she had forgone pigment treatments. It contrasted nicely with deeply tanned skin and bright blue eyes. The woman was quite fit, which was appropriate given her campaign persona of a hard worker and no-nonsense legislator. Sudarshan had only met her a few times before, and never in a one-on-one meeting, but she found the relaxed, friendly manner of the senior Senator to be at odds with the whispered rumors that she was a tenacious political shark.

The Prime Minister set down her spoon and took a sip of tea

before continuing, "He would not recognize the city now, my grandfather. Tripled in size and home of the Sol Coalition's largest research facility on Earth. I imagine he would be quite proud of some of our accomplishments."

"Due, in no small part, to your efforts, Prime Minister," Sudarshan ventured tentatively.

"Oh, no, I cannot take responsibility for that. North America pooled its resources to establish this base, the location is entirely a logistical issue. Besides that, to claim, even privately, that my achievements as a public servant are mine alone would be rather egotistical, don't you think?" The Prime Minister smiled as coolly and charmingly as on any of her campaign ads. Sudarshan hesitated, sure that the jaws of the conversation were preparing to snap closed.

"We are all only working towards the greater good," she responded slowly. The senior politician's smile remained, but her gaze hardened into something that sent a shiver down Sudarshan's spine.

"Sam," the Prime Minister called out. A cook popped out of the kitchen, a damp towel in hand. "Give me a few moments, please, would you?" He nodded and immediately disappeared into the back. The sounds of water being shut off and muffled conversations abruptly stopped as a door slammed shut. Sudarshan was suddenly very aware that the only person who would witness the remainder of the lunch was the Prime Minister's personal security guard.

"The greater good," she said the words slowly, as though testing their flavor like a Vietnamese noodle. The shiver froze around Sudarshan's spine, and she felt a tightness in her chest. "It is interesting that you would use such a phrase, Avani. Exactly what greater good were you working toward this morning when you voted against the Emancipation and Suffrage bill?"

"The party has always held conservative views toward the GMH population," Sudarshan quickly responded. "I was only-"

"And who, exactly, told you that a publicly promoted conservative view translated into a vote against the E&S? Or did you deduce that little nugget on your own?"

Sudarshan bristled. She had been prepared to be chastised for something, but she wasn't about to put up with personal insults, not even from the Prime Minister. "I know what the party supports, ma'am, perhaps even better than you, given your tone. The future of Genetically Modified Humans is not one of Emancipation and Suffrage, at least not yet, and if you do not understand the gravity of this matter, of what it means to us all, to the *war*, then-"

"You twit." The Prime Minister's expression did not change. She still smiled and held her cup of tea with an easy gesture, but her voice dripped with anger. "You want to play at shaping the future, at determining the fate of a species? I should take you over my knee for that kind of ignorance. You want to use your former position in Congress, your knowledge of Project Barghest to justify your actions. If you think that one operation is enough to support such a conclusion, that the party wishes to see GMH individuals held as property indefinitely, you are far more stupid than even my most pessimistic assessments."

"I have the support of-" Sudarshan began hotly, but she was cut off.

"You have the support I allow you to have," the older woman said sharply.

"If we want to win the battle in Near Sol space, we need-"

Again she was overridden, "Battle, you think this is about *a* battle?" The Prime Minister set down her cup with a definitive clink. "I am shaping the future of our species, and you want to throw away our best defense, your career, the power of our party in the Senate, the security of our solar system - for one battle? Do not be so shortsighted," she spat. One bluntly manicured nail pressed into the cheap table as she made her point. Blue eyes glittered like ice. "You have seen a fraction of the intelligence, the scouting reports, the research assumptions. Cullers," with a hard breath she dismissed the species that had come close to heralding the extinction of homo sapiens, "what are they but cannon fodder - a prelude to something more? Humanity is on a galactic stage now, one battle, one war, is nothing in contrast. Our plans must be designed to carry us forward, to ensure survival, physically, culturally - morally - beyond species that have not yet even crawled out of the oceans on planets that spin thousands of light years away. I am smoothing the way for humanity to endure, to thrive, to expand and seize our future - to *command* our future, and you whine about *one battle*?"

The Prime Minister sat back in her chair, lips pursed. Sudarshan did not move. Every rumor, every whisper she had heard ran screaming through her brain.

The General of the Army calls her before he scratches his ass.

She put the last President in office.

The People's Empire of China retained entire countries after the Red War on her recommendation.

She had killed a Culler with the severed limb of another soldier during her mandatory military service.

They were all a shadow in comparison to the woman before her. There was no denying that the Prime Minister was the power behind her party - and her party was the power behind the Sol Coalition Congress. It ate at Sudarshan to humble herself, to admit to wrongs she still didn't believe she had committed, but the Prime Minister was capable of decimating her career without even getting out of her chair. Possibly worse.

"Ma'am," she began, but one creased palm made her swallow her words.

"I. Am not. Finished." She closed her eyes for a moment and then opened them slowly. "Gillian has requested a new chairperson for the Oversight Committee. Tomorrow, the Chair will tender his resignation from Congress and you will recommend Representative Soledad Venegas as a replacement. Once the session closes next week, you will go visit your family home in Renukoot. When session resumes, you will change your views on the GMH issue. You will admit that you have reconsidered and you were wrong. When the Emancipation and Suffrage bill is reintroduced, you will support it. Eloquently and emphatically."

"The voting equilibrium will be disturbed. There will be members of the party that will be unhappy," Sudarshan warned. She chafed at having her vote determined for her, chafed at the prospect of admitting publicly that she had made a mistake - when she truly felt she was acting in the best interests of humanity. "Members of the opposition will try to take advantage of any discord in the upcoming elections."

The Prime Minister frowned, "At least you recognize that much. Perhaps you are not a complete loss." Blue eyes relaxed, and she sat back, considering Sudarshan with a calculating gleam that made the younger politician's skin crawl. "Reparations will be made, do not concern yourself. In the meantime, you are going to become a moderate candidate, Avani. I am going to save your career, but do not ever think to assume such grand plans without consulting me first."

"I can take care of my own career," she said tightly.

The Prime Minister arched one pale eyebrow. "It was never yours to take care of." Quietly, she listed the names and amounts of every contributor to the first campaign that had gotten Sudarshan into a state office position. "Did you really think your supporters saw your social media outpouring and handed over their credits?" Sudarshan could feel the blood draining from her face as the realization sank in that her life had been so carefully manipulated without her knowledge. "You succeeded because there was something in you that could be useful to me. There still is, if you can follow orders. You want the war with the Cullers to end? It will happen, but there are those of us who know better how, and when, and in what way it might benefit *the greater good.*"

"Ma'am," the woman's security detail held out a phone, the screen indicating it was on hold, "An urgent call from the Minster of Defense, ma'am."

"We're done," she dismissed Sudarshan and took the phone with the same hand. With a knot of humility, anger, and fear in her stomach, Sudarshan rose and stepped toward the door. Behind her, the Prime Minister answered in her practiced, cool voice.

"Helen Maker, here."

CHAPTER 7: ACES HIGH

Impacoral. Noun. Proprietary plasma compound designed to absorb kinetic energy. The compound remains in a liquid state until sufficient kinetic force collides with it. Upon collision, the compound hardens, absorbing the energy, and then re-liquefies. It is commonly found in vehicle safety restraints, personal and structural armor systems, and medical immobilization devices.

Ex. The private felt the generic Impacoral in his combat suit harden under the extreme pressure of a sudden ISG exit.

Hour 0900
March 18, 2148

Ignition minus thirty-six days.

Two shifts of mind-numbing light duty and an equal number of mandatory counseling sessions - required after a live weapons fire exchange, and Maker had herself under control again. She wasn't better. She didn't feel less guilty - although the psychologist had worked hard to try to get her to admit to the emotion. But she had pushed it down far enough that she could function. Although if she was never assigned deep frequency communication array maintenance and updates again it would be too soon.

Kerry was waiting for her when she got off her shift on Thursday. It wasn't too surprising, he often went with her to the mess or a rec hall if their schedules lined up. It was illegal to discriminate towards Genetically Modified Humans, had been for years, and the SC enforced the letter of the law. But it did not stop anyone from thinking less of people like Kerry. *Can't outlaw ass-holes*, Maker thought as they walked together. She pushed back a string of black hair that had escaped her regulation style; the movement made her shoulder spasm. It had been a long day working in the communications department.

"Workout?" Kerry asked quietly. "Today is Thursday, you are cleared for cardio, right?"

"Yeah, I- Thursday?" Maker paused, recalling her ride in the lift with Bretavic. "Actually, I was invited to a card game, but-"

"Bretavic," Kerry nodded, "he asked me too."

"Really? I - I mean, that's great but -"

"Surprised he asked a tuber like me?" Maker rolled her eyes at Kerry's easy use of the derogatory term, but her friend's quick smile forgave her assumption. "I was too." They walked in silence for an entire section. "So," he said casually, "do you want to go?"

"I'll lose," she said seriously. "I am terrible at cards, you know this."

"You have money?" Kerry's thick, dark eyebrows lifted in question.

"Some." She hesitated, "I could spare a few hundred credits, I guess."

He snorted, "That'll ensure they invite you back, if you lose that amount."

"If I'm going, so are you," she hit him lightly in the ribs with her elbow. "Today everyone has to get out there make a new friend. Even if it hurts."

Kerry stopped them at the lift and hit the controls. "It almost always does. Except without the friend. And getting out there most often consists of a bar fight."

"Yeah," Maker smothered a laugh, "but I maintain the last one was not my fault."

"Of course it wasn't." Kerry fell back into his customary silence after that, and they made their way to Maintenance Bay 6. Maker punched in the door code, and Kerry frowned.

"It's ironic," she informed him with a smile.

"I do not think you know what irony means," he replied seriously.

It took them a few minutes to find the cluster of soldiers in a far corner, behind a stack of crated repair parts. Two tables had been set up and the men and women were using storage containers for chairs. Several field canteens were being passed around to fill a variety of cups. As Maker and Kerry approached, talk slowed. Most of the faces were carefully blank, but a few looked hostile. Maker was about to suggest that they turn around when Bretavic stood and offered them each a cup. Maker's smelled like the unholy offspring of lighter fluid and cheap vodka.

"You'll play at my table," he announced loudly. There was some place shuffling and resettling, but the release of tension was palatable. Hands were dealt and Maker relaxed for the first time since the mission. An hour later - seventy-two credits in the hole - Maker folded early, sitting back to drink contraband moonshine that was probably melting her stomach lining and listen to the conversation around her.

"Sounds like a lot of talk to me," a soldier stated flatly. She took a swig of her cup that left Maker wincing, but the woman didn't even flinch. "Election campaigns will start in a couple of months - the liberals that want to run for office always throw out the idea of pulling back the military to get the voters stirred up."

"Right," Uesugi, the man next to her, snorted, "and then nobody ever says anything concrete about plans, and next thing you know mandatory service levels are increased or recruitment quotas go up. Anyone that believes Congress wants to downsize the fleet should have their genes examined. Idiots," he added and increased his bet.

"I'll see it," the woman responded. She tossed in chips and continued, "A politician saying they want to bring home soldiers is like an officer saying tubers are valued team players," her voice dripped with condescension. "A whole load of shit that looks nice on a poster." She glanced up at Maker, then her eyes slid to Kerry. "No offense." She shrugged.

"None taken," Kerry said evenly. "I'll see and raise you five."

"Little bit taken," Maker said dryly. She was the only officer at the table. The woman laughed.

"I'll see your five and call." Bretavic swore loudly as he lost the hand to Kerry. He poured himself another drink while the younger man cleaned up the markers on the table. "Suck it up, Maker. You're going to be an officer, you have to get used to being hated."

"Not hated," Useugi corrected, "just don't expect friends."

"And here I thought maybe later we would braid each other's hair and trade diaries," Maker deadpanned. She spoke in a monotone, "Now my feelings are hurt. Ouch." They all laughed and drank and played another hand, which Maker quickly folded out of so she lost only the ante.

"Point is," the female soldier said as though the conversation had never stopped, "it doesn't matter if the Cullers stay outside Far Sol Space for another five years. As long as there are reports of the slimy little fuckers anywhere in this arm of the galaxy, no one is going to want to reduce Earth's defenses." She took the hand with a crow of triumph and counted her markers.

"Lucky for us," Bretavic said sourly.

"You're damn right," Useugi agreed, either ignoring or not noticing the large soldier's sarcasm. "That's job security. As long as there are Cullers - they'll need somebody to blow them straight to hell. I get paid to make greasy smears out of space lobsters. That's easy money."

"You should really needlepoint that on something," Maker said. Blank looks met her archaic reference.

Kerry explained, "It's like a recruitment poster."

"Ha!" The woman laughed and punched Useugi in the arm, "that would get re-enlistment numbers up." She spread her finger out and outlined an imaginary advertisement in the air over the table, "Come, sign up with the Sol Coalition. Make greasy smears out of space lobsters."

"Don't forget the easy money," Bretavic pointed out, frowning as a new hand was dealt. "I think that sums up this whole war nicely."

"Easy money," Useugi and woman repeated in sync, then laughed. Their chuckles were only lightly scented with alcohol, but Maker couldn't help the shiver that danced along her spine. She might have agreed with the sentiment a few weeks ago, but after the mining station, she didn't see a lot of humor in the idea. Thankfully, conversation soon turned to a recent training test that had been completed by one of the many platoons aboard the *Pershing*. Maker picked up her cards. She had a pair of twos and an ace. *With my luck,* she thought, *I'll end with just the twos.* She threw in her marker with a sigh of resignation. Her contemplation of what to keep in her hand was interrupted by an argument between Useugi and Bretavic.

"-the hell! No way you scored that high!"

"Jealous, Bretavic?" Useugi smirked, "Try getting onto the mats every once in a while, instead of using fights with new recruits to polish your martial skills."

"I call bullshit," the woman said, tossing her cards and folding. "If you scored that high, you'd have already been flagged for special ops. You're a liar *and* ugly - it's not a good combination."

"You weren't saying that last night, Tremaine," the veteran soldier grinned. She flipped him off.

"The score isn't the only requirement for special forces," Kerry said quietly. All eyes turned to him in surprise, he hadn't spoken much since the game had begun. The heavy muscles in his shoulders shifted under his uniform as he shrugged. "Genes." Maker saw the flash of pity in Bretavic's eyes, while the other two soldiers remained silent.

Kerry gradually stiffened, as he realized he had drawn attention to himself. They couldn't know for certain, although Maker did, but they could easily guess how well a Genetically Modified Human would do in training tests. Kerry had been specifically bred to be a soldier, which was fairly obvious from his build and reflexes. Maker had been with him at every step of their training and could attest to his near perfect scores in anything related to strength, agility, or motor skills. Her table companions had been right when they made the comparison to politicians' promises. No tuber, no matter what was said about equality, was treated fairly in the Sol Coalition. It was a load of shit.

"That explains it," Bretavic broke the silence, pointedly looking over the veteran. "Too much Neanderthal DNA, right?"

The table was silent for a long minute, and Maker held her breath, wondering if Bretavic had stepped over a line. Finally, the woman barked out a laugh and slapped Useugi on the shoulder. "He caught you out, idiot! I always suspected - what with the back hair!"

The veteran slouched in his chair and grinned, "It's a sign of virility - back hair."

"Keep telling yourself that," Bretavic mumbled, disgusted.

Maker let out a silent exhale, grateful that the attention was off of Kerry. Her friend had a difficult enough time as his appearance was so obviously caused by now-illegal gene treatments; he didn't need his first social gathering on the *Pershing* to single him out from other soldiers. The nickname, tubers, already spoke volumes about how most people felt about the technology that created him - and thousands more like him. Only those who were truly desperate to set their offspring on a different path chose Genetic Modification.

When the procedure was banned in Sol-controlled systems, black market operations sprang up on independent mining stations and colonies. Those couples that paid for a GMH pregnancy in the years following gave everything they had - and oftentimes the assurance of years of future income - to scientists that promised the world but rarely had the credentials or equipment to deliver on those guarantees. Even with a successful treatment, having genetics that were labeled superior or desirable did not ensure an easier life.

Although GMHs were given full access to citizenship rights almost ten years before either she or Kerry were born, his assignments reflected how his superior officers felt about tubers. Especially ones with matte blue skin and the physical skills to show up most 'good' soldiers.

Eighty-five percent of Sol-born humans received embryonic gene therapy to maximize their DNA. Symmetrical facial features, skin tones ranging from honey and caramel to a deeper mocha, and three generations of selecting for height resulted in Kerry's stocky bulk being an anomaly in almost any crowd. And that was before his bluish skin was taken into account.

Although Maker wasn't as obviously different as Kerry, her

father's choice to restrict her gene therapy to only medical needs and leaving her appearance up to nature had resulted in the same prejudice under a different slur. Scorchingly pale skin and short stature had ostracized her nearly as much as her friend's non-human gene additives. Maker often felt she didn't deserve the sort of dedicated loyalty Kerry gave her, but she did her best to offer him the same.

She picked up her cards without really looking at them and determined that the hand would be her last. She was almost out of money, and Kerry seemed comfortable enough to stay without her - if that was what he wanted. She had a new duty rotation the next day, and wasn't looking forward to slogging through training on too few hours of sleep.

"The bet is to you, Maker," Bretavic leaned around Kerry's bulk to catch her eye. "Just fold already so I can collect my winnings." He grinned.

"What the hell." She smiled back and tossed in a marker. "This is my last hand anyway. Call."

"Past your bedtime, little girl?" Useugi grinned. "Probably for the best, as you won't beat my straight." He laid out his cards and sat back, crossing his arms smugly as the woman next to him groaned. Both she and Kerry had folded early.

"Fuck all," Bretavic swore, tossing down his hand. "Two pair, you lucky bastard." The veteran was actually reaching toward the pile of winnings in the center when Maker put down her cards. She blinked in surprise, not having paid much attention to her final game. Bretavic barked out a laugh, "A Full House, Aces over twos! Get your hands off the credits, Uesegi!"

"You been setting me up for the long con this whole game, Maker?" The veteran, Uesegi, frowned, but he didn't sound upset.

Maker shrugged, smiling. No one could be angry about what was clearly a lucky hand. She had lost more than she won over the course of the night, so no one could say she came out ahead. "Yeah, that's it. You caught me. A few more weeks of losing my paycheck and I would have had you just where I wanted you."

"Now you've done it, Sergeant," the woman laughed as Maker picked up the markers, "You'll have to come back and lose next time just to prove Bretavic didn't bring in a ringer."

"That won't be a problem," Kerry deadpanned.

Maker elbowed him while everyone else grinned and chuckled. More drinks were poured as she tucked her winnings into her uniform jacket. She didn't admit it, even to herself, didn't even let her thoughts go there, but as she walked back to her shared quarters, she felt a little less guilty. A little more at peace.

CHAPTER 8: SOCIAL HIERARCHY

Lightfoot. Noun. A person born in space, rather than on a planet or planetary satellite. So called because most spaceships and stations are set with gravity slightly lower than Earth standard. *Ex. John is a real lightfoot, he knows all the trade routes like the back of his hand.*

Hour 0700
January 8, 2122

Ignition minus twenty-six years.

Malak handed his second MRE bar over to Ondrea and let his mind wander while he watched her eat. It was test day. Figuratively speaking, it was always test day for research subjects like him. He and the rest of his pack had been watched by cameras, scientists, guards, and untold number of medical devices since before their birth. *Decanting,* he dryly reminded himself. That was what some of the less respectful technicians called it. Dr. Gillian referred to it as 'birth', even though it wasn't really, when she spoke to the subjects. When she wrote in her notes it was 'extraction'. Bee, in the growling language that came easiest to him, called it 'waking'. As strange as most of the natural humans found Bee's ideas, Malak had to admit that his Basics instructor - the only test subject to hold that status – had come up with the best name.

Since his Wakingday, he had gone through twenty-five test days.

That I can remember, he clarified to himself. Malak always tried to be precise, even in his own mind. *Precision leads to success.* This day was number twenty-six, and it had the most pressure riding on it. Or perhaps he was simply old enough to understand how important the tests were to the future of his pack. A test meant changes, depending on how individuals and the group did. Sometimes it was different MREs - more protein or less protein, more fats or less iron. Sometimes it was colder quarters, or hotter classrooms, or longer training sessions. Once they had received an art instructor, who stayed for over a year, then was inexplicably removed.

Ondrea finished the meal bar and grinned her thanks before walking back to the table she shared with Smierc and Parshav. The three laughed and jostled each other while they finished their water. Malak would have been welcome to join them, he knew. Welcome to join any of the other four tables where his pack was finishing their breakfast, but he didn't. There was too much on his mind. *Test Day.*

They weren't supposed to know the parameters or objectives prior to tests, not unless Dr. Gillian or one of the other senior scientists explicitly told them. But there were a few individuals in Malak's group that were very, very good at keeping their ears and eyes open. On this day, Malak's pack, Series Twenty-seven-two, were going to be introduced to the rest of the Twenty-sevens. Groups one, three, and four were going to join them for a day-long training exercise. Ostensibly, it was based around co-operative learning. Which was true, Malak knew. He also knew that it had a much more important purpose. Malak had shared his suspicions with Bee, who agreed that it was likely.

Dr. Gillian wanted to find the Alpha.

Not an alpha, lower case a, Malak thought. *The Alpha.* Malak was the leader in his group. His pack had followed his orders since before he could remember - although there had been a brief week where the twins tried to take control. The whole pack went without test rewards for three days before the two females stepped down and submitted to Malak. It had all been fairly painless, although mildly humiliating for the twins. It wasn't always that way, though. Bee had told him how the twenty-sixes selected their alphas. Three of the four groups had bloody fights. No one died, but it had been a near thing in one case. Malak wasn't sure how the other alphas would react to taking commands from him - but it wouldn't matter.

The outcome would be the same. Malak was going to be the Alpha, because he didn't know those other twenty-sevens. He couldn't guarantee that they would watch out for his pack like he did. It would be more responsibility, three times more. Instead of twenty-five he would be in charge of one hundred. One hundred research subjects who frightened their scientists as often as they pleased them. *One hundred soldiers,* Malak reminded himself.

That was the point, really. They had been grown - decanted - to be soldiers for the natural humans. He understood. In the six years since his Wakingday, he had learned a great deal about natural humans and the war they were fighting. The Cullers were his enemy, and his purpose in life was to protect the natural humans from them. To kill Cullers. Malak knew he could do that. He was stronger than anyone else in his group. He was quicker than everyone except Smierc. He was just as smart as Parshav, although not as good at coding. Four more years and he would go on live training exercises. Four years after that, he would go up against the Cullers in real missions. That was what he was made for, and Malak knew he would be good at it. There was another purpose, though, one which was more than just a lesson learned or something bred into him. He needed to protect his pack. To do that, he had to be the Alpha.

Smierc slipped onto the bench opposite him, her water cup in hand but empty. She held it up to her mouth - a proven method for making certain the cameras couldn't track the movements of her lips. "Parshav just gave the signal. Lupe is on the way with Gillian."

"Hn." Malak turned his cup between his palms. His stomach felt unsettled, like he hadn't eaten, or maybe like what he had eaten hadn't been quite dead.

Smierc ran her fingers through her shoulder-length red hair and pulled an elastic from around her wrist. "You good?" She asked while she made a quick ponytail.

"Hn," he nodded, despite the itchy feeling growing in his legs and hands. Smierc snorted, rolling her eyes, clearly not believing him. Malak breathed deeply and tried to find a calm spot in his mind. That is what he needed - to be in control of himself. Then he could control others. He could smell the familiar scent of his beta, a mellow sort of orange in his nose that mixed with the standard issue soap they all used. The mess hall smelled like disinfectant and the dry, nutty-oat flavor of the MRE bars. Parshav smelled like rotten leaves and sweat - which was probably because he had been last in the night before so had early morning duty cleaning one of the training arenas. It was all familiar.

Smierc picked up her cup again. "You'll be fine," she assured him. "We all will. And if those others don't submit-" Smierc set down her cup and bared her teeth at Malak. The expression started his adrenaline flowing. "We'll make 'em."

"Hn." He offered her a nod and a small smile. Smierc was second, behind him, for a reason. She was absolutely loyal, positive, and swift to protect the pack. He hoped the other groups would have some like her.

The doors to the mess hall slid open with a whisper of air pressure. "Good morning, everyone," called Dr. Gillian. Half of her face was wrinkled with age. The other half was scarred smooth from an old accident and subsequent surgeries. She had once told the pack it was her good side. "I hope you have all finished breakfast."

Lupe grinned and waggled her eyebrows. The younger scientist was always joking with the pack. "It's the most important meal of the day," she sing-songed to several smiles and chuckles.

Test day, Malak thought again and rose to lead his group out.

***

"That's the last of them," Lupe announced, selecting a video feed from her tablet and throwing it onto the wall with four others. "Twenty-seven-two is in position. One, Three, and Four are ready to go whenever you want to start, Dr. Gillian."

Gillian stood a little straighter, ignoring the chair that some well-meaning and unintentionally condescending research assistant had placed behind her. She had banked a great deal on the results of today's exercises. Almost seven years ago, she had assured Representative Avani Sudarshan that the Twenty-seven series would be the answer to Department of Defense's problems. She had lied through her teeth and promised that they would have no trouble commanding the Twenty-sixes and going into battle at age fourteen. *Fourteen, for god's sake,* she chastised herself, not for the first or last time. It was a brutal schedule, a brutal childhood. *But they aren't really children, are they?* Not technically. Although the Sol Constitution had been amended in 2120 to give citizenship rights to Genetically Modified Humans, it was debatable whether the subjects of the Barghest project would meet the rather vague interpretation of 'human'. Either way, they had been created far outside of the Sol system and the legal reach of Congress.

Equal rights aside, the Twenty-sevens hardly looked like average children. At six, they appeared eleven or twelve. By the time they would be ready to march off to war, they would be physically and mentally in their early twenties even though chronologically they should only be in middle school. Gillian glanced at the video wall and picked out the alphas for each group. Skoll led Twenty-seven-one, his gangly arms and legs causing him to tower over those around him. He was strong, and bigger than the others.

Malak stood quietly with Smierc at his side. She barked orders at the others in Twenty-seven-two, while he nodded and spoke in a low voice. Malak was serious, highly intelligent, but also extremely protective and even tempered. He was smaller than Skoll or even Smierc, but he hadn't hit the age six growth spurt yet.

Giltine stood at the front of an organized formation of Twenty-seven-three. Her brown hair was braided tightly and her body purposefully relaxed. She was the only female alpha, and her group followed her commands like a well-oiled machine. Gillian was aware that Giltine was the first choice of the military adviser that had been assigned to the Barghest Project. She was the perfect example of a soldier, following orders to the letter and keeping her subordinates toeing the line.

In group four, Almaut knelt in the center of a tight knot of bodies. His pale hair and skin stood out sharply among the more common reds and browns of the subjects. He was clever, sometimes to the dismay of those in charge of training his group, and imaginative in his solutions to test situations. Any of the four would be excellent Alphas for the series.

If they are capable of it, she thought worriedly. Gillian didn't allow her concern to show on her face. But the capacity of her research subjects - *these children* - was the crux of the matter. The twenty-six series had been saved from destruction because Dr. Wendy Gillian had promised the Oversight Committee that the next series would be able to control them. If none of the four alphas on the screen could lead their entire series, there was little hope the Twenty-sixes would listen. If that couldn't be accomplished, then they would be of no use to the military. Trillions of credits spent on a project that did not produce results made for some very angry Congressional Representatives. It made for a whole lot of unemployed scientists.

It makes for several hundred dead test subjects.

Gillian forced those thoughts aside and glanced at the center screen. A flag was placed in the middle of an open field. The subjects need to get the flag, but it would take all four groups, working together, to get past the obstacles in their way. They would need one leader.

"Give me the mic," she said calmly, holding out her hand to Lupe. Her former research assistant handed over the slender mic and reached forward to press the transmit command. "Good morning, twenty-sevens," Gillian spoke and heads on the screens stopped and listened to the receivers they each wore just behind their ears. "Today, you must capture the flag…"

***

"That was a good catch," Almaut said admiringly. "I didn't see the looping patrol, without your advice we would have walked right into it."

Malak nodded in acceptance and tried not to shift his weight. Fidgeting was a sign of weakness, and in his case it would reveal actual weakness. He had twisted his knee during the exercise, and the joint was already starting to swell. He flexed his jaw and ignored the pain.

"Not so impressive," the female alpha, from group three, narrowed her eyes at him. Malak had immediately pegged her as his biggest competition for Alpha. "My scout saw it, we could have gotten through easily."

"Yes, yes," Almaut chuckled, "and then what would you have done if the Ones weren't ready to back you up? An odd number in your group makes it difficult to do a tandem crossing, right? You'd still be on the other side of the ravine."

"I'm sure Giltine would have figured it out," said Skoll. The taller male was attempting to fold his shirt back together, with no luck. The garment had been completely shredded when he pushed one of his own pack members out of the path of a drone. Malak had been impressed. Skoll was willing to take serious injury to protect another. He was a good leader. And a bit of a peacemaker. "No need to dwell on it. We won, with no serious injuries, and everybody gets rewards tonight, so good day, right?"

"Good day?" Giltine bit off. "You won't be saying that when they don't pick you. I for one won't follow-" Malak rubbed the back of his head, and from across the gathering space Smierc, ever watchful, gave a signal. Parshav suddenly tumbled into the female alpha's back, cutting her off.

"What? Oh, so sorry!" He stood and tried to help her out, brushing at her clothes and loudly apologizing. Giltine backed away from him, baring her teeth in irritation, and ran into Malak. He quickly leaned forward, letting the disarray of her braid hide his mouth.

"There are two cameras watching us right now. They'll know whatever you say, so cover your mouth when you talk." The others heard him, and both Almaut and Skoll stared wide-eyed as Giltine spun around and faced him. She looked mad enough to chew through plastiglass, but instead of speaking, she pulled the elastic out of her hair and bent to shake out what was left of her braid.

"How did you know?" she muttered, her face towards the ground.

Malak considered how to answer as the other three alphas watched him. He could say that he had mapped every camera in the research station, and had his pack report to him if anything was added or moved. He could say that although he didn't believe that Dr. Gillian wanted to hurt them in any way, he didn't trust her to look out for the pack's best interests either. He could say that he wasn't an animal, or an experiment, but a person - the natural human government had said so. Malak had seen the documents that confirmed what he already knew. A person deserved to have at least some of his thoughts remain private. He could say that he was a soldier, and a soldier looked for and took every advantage he could get, even in peacetime. It turned out he didn't have to say anything, because Smierc choose that moment to come retrieve Parshav. She slapped the back of her pack-mate's head and pulled him down into a headlock, concealing their faces.

"Because he's the Alpha," Smierc stated plainly. Malak could hear it in her voice, in the rumbling command behind it. Alpha with a capital A. The Alpha. Three pairs of eyes turned toward him. One considering, one accepting, and one assessing.

"Hn."

"Prove it." That came not from Giltine, but from Almaut, and the female was quick to agree.

Malak had thought about that eventuality, he had discussed pack a few times with Bee. He didn't want to force submission. He didn't want to become Alpha by tasting blood - but he would if he had to. There were other ways that he would try first, though. Malak let his arms fall to his side and took in a deep breath before opening his mouth. The roar felt good. It filled his chest with sound and rustled the leaves above him. It was a declaration, a warning, one that his ancestors - the alien animals, not the humans - had used to intimidate enemies and claim territory. When he was done, he looked out over the small field where all of the twenty-sevens had gathered. To a one, they were looking at him. Some jaws hung open. Some heads tilted to the side in displays of submission. Some had fallen to one or both knees.

My pack. My territory. Obey.

Bee was the Basics instructor for all of the Twenty-sevens, he had taught them his simple language and they all understood Malak's claim. He stood, waiting, hands loose and prepared for a fight, his eyes on the other alphas. Almaut tipped his head slightly, bearing his neck with a slight smile. Skoll nodded deeply, stepping back and splaying his arms out to his sides. Giltine flared her nostrils, scenting him, he was sure. Whatever she smelled, it made up her mind.

"I guess that's okay," she said slowly. She reached up to scratch at her nose, covering her mouth. "The pack comes first, or I'll take your place."

Malak nodded, "Agreed."

CHAPTER 9: FRYING PAN

*Interstellar Gravity Drive, a.k.a. **ISG**.* Noun. Propulsion device reverse engineered from Culler ships which crashed on Earth during the Repulsion. Speed varies based on ship design and quality of dark matter fuel, but exceeds the speed of light utilizing. ISG is prohibited within star systems and near large gravity wells, such as black holes, without authorization.

Ex. The new ISG got the ship from Sol to Polaris in four weeks.

Hour 0900
April 11, 2148

Ignition minus twelve days.

Maker did not shine at poker; she was even worse at the game than she had admitted to Kerry. It wasn't until their fourth night in Bretavic's storage room that she won again. "That's it, I'm out," she declared, pulling the pile of chips towards her. *Quit while I'm ahead,* she thought to herself.

"Come on, Sarge," Useugi laughed, "you're on a hot streak."

"That win just used up all the luck I'll get this decade," Maker smiled, but the fine hairs on the back of her neck stood up. She told herself that the maintenance bay was climate controlled for storage, not leisure purposes. "This *almost* makes up for half of what I've already lost." She pulled open an inner pocket in her jacket and began dumping in chips. "I'll collect tomorrow after my shift, but I'm headed to bed before someone asks for a loan."

"Hey Maker," called a soldier from the other table, "Give us a kiss first, I could use a little luck."

"Not even with Kerry's lips, Niamey." Both tables laughed. A female enlisted, *Gonzales* stamped on her uniform coat, leaned over and locked lips with the man. There were chuckles, whistles, and some lewd suggestions. Then the emergency signal sounded.

"Code Red. Code Red." The pre-recorded voice was calm in the empty room. "Report to your stations." The poker players blinked at each other for a moment before training kicked in and they swiftly stood, leaving their bootlegged alcohol and cards behind. "Code Red. Code-"

Maker tuned out the alert, focusing instead on getting to her assigned post. She clipped shoulders with another crew member on the way out of the lift. If Kerry hadn't been behind her she would have fallen. He stepped in front of her, acting like he might make her a path all the way to the Level 3 Communications Lab, but Maker pushed him away. "Go," she felt like she shouted, but the corridor was busy and loud with bodies, called out orders, and alarms. "They'll need you in munitions. I'll be fine!" He squeezed her shoulder hard, and then he was gone. It took her another five minutes to make it to her destination, but by the time she got there her tech was broadcasting new orders. Maker stood on her tiptoes to see over the crowd that was swiftly changing directions as they all received the same information. The same Uesugi she had been playing cards with flashed her a grin as he jogged past her from his post in Level 3 Security toward the infantry deployment bays, his wrist control bracer flashing until he punched in the acceptance code. The bracer on her arm flashed with the Master Sergeant's identification code, and then a reassignment: *Maker, Clara - deployment.*

Maker tapped her wrist on autopilot, not quite believing what was happening. She was a second year recruit and her training outside of basic rotations through ship's systems had all been in small team reconnaissance and communications. It had been sheer bad luck that had landed her on the mining station field mission which resulted in fatalities.

Duty assignments during an engagement with an enemy, a Code Red, were ranked based on priority. The *Pershing* carried three battalions of specialized infantry - a thousand soldiers each - in addition to ship's crew and the fifteen hundred or so fresh recruits, like Kerry and herself, whom were rotated through various positions to determine their strengths and supplement career soldiers. If she was being ordered to deploy, then the forces they were up against must have been enormous. She made her way back to a lift, and then jogged to the large bay where her gear was stored. The locker room was full, soldiers on every bench and cubicle getting ready to take fire. She caught the door of a toilet stall as it swung open, slipping inside before someone else could claim it.

Her skin was clammy, her chest tight. Maker stood facing the rear wall and breathing deeply, trying to get her thoughts under control. Her shoulder ached with the memory of a long, finely serrated claw drilling through the bone. The skin on the side of her thigh where her own weapon had dug a groove tingled unpleasantly. Metal between her stall and the next, too thin to keep out sound, dented under sudden pressure as someone hit it. Retching and the smell of vomit overwhelmed Maker, and she too bent over the toilet.

A heavy fist banged on the door, "If you're scared, fuzz, go puke in your helmet. I need to take a dump before I suit up!" The only response from the next stall was another wet cough. The banging started again. With a shaking hand, Maker wiped her mouth. She relieved herself quickly before opening the door to find an angry soldier, his kit half on and half off. "About time," he snarled as she slipped by. "Fucking fresh recruits."

His outburst drew attention, and Maker was very aware of the eyes on her back as she washed her hands and face. She bit the inside of her cheek and kept her spine straight as she found her locker. Her stomach was still trying to escape - through her mouth or any other orifice - but she refused to let it show on her face. Ship boots, pants, and her jacket were shoved into the narrow storage space assigned to her. A few poker ships clattered to the floor. She hastily picked them up and retrieved her body armor and boots. New combat contacts, still in the packaging, slipped onto her eyes easily and automatically synced with her bracer and the tech in her armor. She tugged the form-fitting charcoal suit over her underwear and shirt and fastened it up to the collar before sitting to put on her boots. A hand reached into her locker and pulled out her helmet; she looked up to see Useugi dressed and offering it to her.

"Come on, Sarge," he said with a small smile. "Stick with me."

"I'm fine," she insisted quietly. Her cheeks were burning, sure that everyone around her could hear him offering her assistance.

"Yep, sure are," he purposefully misinterpreted and whistled as he looked her over. "I got to keep an eye on all that fineness, or I won't have a chance to win back my credits."

Maker blew out a hard breath that tasted like vomit. She stood, grabbing her helmet and reaching into her locker for gum. "Fat chance, old man," she smiled shakily and shoved a minty tab in her mouth. "I'm on a hot streak. All aces from here on out."

He clapped her shoulder with a laugh and shoved her locker closed. She was grateful, in the moment, that Useugi decided to walk with her to the ground transport and was issued a pack and a rifle right behind her. Grateful that he strapped in on the seat next to her and pointed out that the rude soldier whom had needed in the toilet so badly had soaked the front of his armor. It was probably water, but Maker did not feel at all bad about suggesting it was something less sanitary. She was grateful that Useugi's laugh was the last thing she heard before she pulled on her helmet and snapped closed the ring that sealed it to her armor suit. The quiet voice over her comm, announcing the countdown to interstellar space exit, didn't seem as ominous with Useugi beside her.

"...one. Disengaging ISG Drive." The usual soft notice over the communications system was not accompanied by a shudder and the hum of sub-light engines warming up. The ship around her shuddered, as it always did, but then it began to shake. It rocked, hard, as if something had hit the hull. Traveling through star systems or coming out of ISG in the middle of a star system was, at best, a calculated risk and prohibited by the Sol Coalition except in times of extreme need. The rude soldier was thrown from his seat - his harness had not been fully fastened. The press of her own harness into her armor didn't have enough force to activate the kinetic safety features, and Maker felt the sharp jab of her in-suit breathing tubes against her collarbones. "Secure personnel and all level 3-"

Pershing's automated safety procedures were cut off by a live transmission, "This is Captain Yardley." Maker didn't recognize his voice, but she could picture the dark hair silvering at the temples and the tall, thin figure that she had once seen heading to the officers' mess. "We are under heavy fire. Any infantry units already in position - deploy. All others, prepare to be boarded."

She didn't have time to think about the implications of that statement. New information was pouring into her tech. Coordinates, maps, unit deployments and enemy troop movements. A series of comm codes that barely finished downloading before the ground transport rumbled to life. The ship-to-surface vessel was not equipped with windows, so she couldn't see the doors on the floor of the bay slide open or the descent into open space. Twice before she had been launched planet-side in a similar fashion, and Maker had no desire to watch the ground drawing closer, faster than sound, as gravity performed the task of bringing them to the battle.

"Listen up, fodder!" The Lieutenant commanding the company yelled through the comms. "When those doors open, I want your weapons hot. We have intense Culler activity on the ground and in the sky. *Pershing* doesn't have time to help us out - they have a *Ferox* Class ship in need. Our job is to stop Culler deployment from the surface to give the Captain some breathing room. So keep your eyes open and stay with your maneuver team until you reach the regroup point." Coordinates flashed on Maker's display along with an overlay image of the planet surface. Their touchdown location was dotted in red, with a line leading to the regroup point. "Keep your gear tight and your-"

A blast rocked the transport and tremendous pressure pulled Maker's arms and legs to her right. "Fuck!" The comm cut out abruptly as the lieutenant must have switched channels to find out what was going on. In her periphery vision blackness grabbed her attention.

The rest of the transport was gone.

The metal edges of the ship were exposed, liquid-smooth where a high-heat blast had cut through the hull. A third of the company, still strapped in on the other end of the transport, was falling away from them, spinning end over end. There was no sound in space, but there was plenty of light to see the carnage clearly. Between the two shells of the transport there was a field of debris, quickly thinning out as gravity took hold. It was mostly parts of bodies that had been caught on the edge of the blast. Maker tried to stay focused on the black space outside the damaged ship - on the surreal spray of blood that froze within seconds of contact with a vacuum, but she could not help herself. Her eyes turned of their own volition. Where Useugi had sat down, two legs and the left side of his torso remained. The rest had been vaporized by the heat of Culler weapons fire. Red droplets floated up from a few open edges of flesh that hadn't been cauterized.

The transport rotated gently, and the view of the *Pershing* above them was stunning. She was firing into the side of a Culler cruiser. The rail gun moved regularly, hammering away at the alien hull shields with projectiles while the fighter squads deployed. It looked was a ballet: sleek, flat SC ships, manned by two soldiers each, darted through a wall of spiny Culler vessels. Like sea creatures, the small gray craft floated around their cruiser, waiting to sting anything that came too close while the larger ship recharged its laser cannon to fire again.

Rotation took the *Pershing* to the side of her helmet, and Useugi's blood broke into tiny red crystals as it hit her faceplate. Maker heaved, but she had nothing left to lose. *Zero gravity helmet vomit,* she thought, in a strangely detached way, *would be a real bitch to clean out.* The *Pershing* disappeared, and another ship came into view. A *Ferox* class, it was listing slightly, but still firing away. It was smaller than the *Pershing* by design - a third of the crew and three times as much firepower. It had taken significant damage, but didn't appear to have any hull breaches. *Yet,* Maker thought. It was realistically only a matter of time. Three more Culler cruisers were parked around the *Ferox*, and while she already had her squadrons of fighters at work, only one enemy cruiser had taken enough damage to cease firing. Maker's transport continued spinning.

"Listen up!" The Lieutenant's voice crackled over the comms, hard and serious without a hint of fear. "We are in for a hard landing. Struts are out, maneuvering is out, and shielding is gone. Seats twenty-five through thirty-four-" Maker glanced to her right again, Uesugi had been in seat thirty-four. "-unstrap, move up, and secure yourselves before we hit atmo. We are using controlled fuel releases to make certain we hit face first, but if you are too close to that breach, consider yourself bar-b-que. You have forty seconds"

Her hands were shaking as she unclipped her harness. The other soldiers were moving carefully, quickly, walking hand-over-hand along the seats toward the front of the transport. Seat twenty-nine had trouble with their straps. Maker activated her proximity comm.

"Hold still," she said ordered. If anything, the soldier's struggles with their harness increased. Maker gripped the service knife that was strapped to her thigh and unclipped it from the holster. With as sharp of a movement as she could make without gravity, she rapped the hilt on the other person's helmet. "Hold still, meathead!" The struggling stopped, and Maker looked away from the opaque faceplate to the twisted straps. Carefully, she slipped her gloved fingers between chest armor and harness, then inserted her knife.

"Thirty seconds!"

Heavy breathing increased over the proximity comm. "Holy hell, private," she said, trying to get the soldier's attention off of their deadline. The first strap snapped and she moved on to the second. "My sheets don't get this tangled up during sex, how the fuck did you manage it?"

"You're-" a panicky-familiar voice gasped for air, "you're doing it wrong then. I'd be happy to help."

"Rodriguez?" She asked, surprised. The second strap broke and she nearly lost her grip as he began to float toward her.

"Twenty seconds!"

He reached out and grabbed onto her wrist with one hand, hauling her forward with him as he turned. His voice was gradually becoming stronger, "Yeah, just can't get enough of me, I see. It must be kismet, us on the same transport."

"Not likely," she snorted, and suddenly realized that her nerves had calmed down as he did.

"Thanks," he said quietly, pulling her in close and bracing his feet against a wall support. "I don't like to be trapped."

"Move your asses! Ten seconds!" Maker glanced up at the Lieutenant, strapped into his seat at the front of the transport. All of the other soldiers from near the breach had moved forward and secured themselves by lacing arms and legs through the harnesses of those that were still in their seats.

"Hold on," Rodriguez said, and then pushed off. They bumped into the last two available spots and he quickly released her to slip his toes into the clips on the floor and press his back against the chest of another soldier. They locked arms together. Maker turned and did the same, just as the transport began to rock with increased pressure.

"Here we go!" Flame, first orange and then white hot, shot up and around the edges of the transport. Ceramic plates, designed to deflect the heat, broke off the hull and slapped against the open edge before disappearing in their wake. Maker's teeth rattled, and she clenched her jaw closed to keep from biting her tongue. Whispered prayers, curses, and heavy breathing filled her proximity comm. Someone nearby threw up in their helmet. *Should have gone before we left home*, she thought. That was the last coherent thing in her mind for a long eighty-three seconds. There was heat, and pressure, and enough g-force that she might have blacked out for a moment. Then they hit. The sound was concussive, pounding against her helmet; it probably would have blown her eardrums if they were exposed. The transport surged up again, and Maker's stomach went with it, before falling back down. The second time, liquid poured over the open edge of the transport, flooding the space.

"Unstrap and move! Check your tech, shore is to your starboard." There was a flurry of activity, and Maker managed to get her boots unhooked before the soldier behind her roughly shoved her forward.

"Get the fuck off, before we both drown," the woman snarled through the comm. With liquid crashing into the transport and soldiers scrambling over the seats to reach the surface, it took a moment for Maker to realize her shoulder was dislocated.

"Let's go," Rodriguez said from behind her. There was no other choice, she needed both arms to swim. Both arms to fight. Both arms to flail with appropriately manic fear. Maker gritted her teeth and threw her body against the hard surface of the floor. The joint clicked back into place and she screamed into her helmet. Rodriguez cursed, but followed her when she used her good arm to yank on his pack and pull him toward the opening. The transport, which had landed on the nose, was tipping back to the surface of a large lake. Maker's tech brought up a map, showing her where they had landed and the thankfully short distance she would have to swim to shore. She hoped there wasn't anything living in the water.

That thought made her pause, perched at the lip of the sinking transport and watching soldiers dive into the lake and make their way towards shore. The brownish liquid steamed a little when wet armor suits and helmets made contact with the air. Maker frowned, pulling up the scant information downloaded into her tech about the planet. *It's too cold for water to-*

A scream ripped through the comm and one soldier flailed and fell under the water. Suddenly, it clicked in Maker's mind and she stuck her hand into the water to allow her tech to analyze it. "Bromine!" She yelled over the comm. "It's mostly bromine, not water! If your suit is ruptured, it can paralyze you!"

"Help him!" the Lieutenant's command was loud and clear. Soldiers snapped to attention and two grabbed the flailing man under his arms and began dragging him to shore. Maker glanced worriedly at Rodriguez before they both dove in. After one hundred slow, agonizing meters her feet could touch the bottom and she stood to assess the rest of the company. Out of one hundred, only twenty-eight had made it to shore, of those, two were suffering effects from bromine getting into their armor. She glanced back at the lake. The transport had completely disappeared, leaving only a few bubbles of air and ripples on the surface. "Maker," the Lieutenant snapped out through her transmitter.

"Yes, sir." Her tech provided his location further from the shoreline. She jogged to his side, Rodriguez following her.

"You're the senior comm officer now, so get me a clear line. And you," he pointed at Rodriguez. There was a brief pause while he seemed to be searching through his files. "You're not listed in my transport, Private Rodriguez."

Maker stepped between the two men as she removed her pack. "His first drop, sir." She tried to think quickly of an acceptable excuse. "There was a mixup, and another rookie got on his transport. It left before we did."

"Huh, well, it won't matter until the debriefing, so until then - what the hell is your specialty, private?"

"Mechanics, sir," Rodriguez answered.

"Fine, stick with comms and make yourself useful. When I need you, get your ass where I want it before I even ask. Got it?"

"Yes, sir." The lieutenant was moving away before Rodriguez could finish his salute. "What now," he asked, dropping to the ground beside Maker.

"Now we find out if my equipment survived with less damage than I did, then we bring comms online." She unsealed her pack and found the emergency communications unit intact inside its protective casing. Maker pulled it out and hooked it into the holster on her belt before syncing it with her tech.

"How's your shoulder?" Maker glanced up at the question, and frowned when she found Rodriguez's hands empty. He was greener than her, and had still seen more close action in the last six weeks than most recruits lived through in their mandatory two years.

"Weapon out, Fuzz. We're in hostile territory." In truth, her shoulder was throbbing, but with most of her company dead, it seemed inconsequential. The comms came online, and Maker noted that there was some interference in the atmosphere that was shortening radio range. Luckily, she found another unit's signal close enough to be received. "Company India, Company India, Company India. This is Company Juliette -Niner. Over." There was a pause, and then a request for security clearance. Maker tapped her code into the system and waited for acceptance. The Lieutenant was barking out orders and pulling together a movement formation, injured soldiers in the center. Gradually, the black of armor suits were being switched over to a camouflage setting to match the dark greens, purples, and browns of the planet.

"Juliette this is India-Niner, come in."

"This is Juliette, we have taken heavy casualties on a bad dismount. Desire assistance on the move. Over."

"This is India. Roger. Stand-by." The Lieutenant had the group ready to go and gestured to her to hurry up. Maker nodded, but remained crouched down in case they came under fire. The company began to move, and Maker readied her pack while she waited for a response. "This is India. Rendezvous at coordinates, over." Her map automatically maximized to overlay on her vision, the location where her group could meet up with another company slowly flashing.

"This is Juliette. Roger, India. Wil-co. You make the coffee, I'll bring the biscuits. Over."

"This is India. I can taste them already. Out."

Maker disconnected and ignored Rodriguez while she jogged

over to her commanding officer. The Lieutenant was pleased with the news, but he quickly sent her to the rear to monitor communications so he could focus on the terrain. Maker spent the next hour quietly explaining radio code to Rodriguez while she scanned the horizon for Cullers and listened to the airwaves for transmissions. It was a long march. They spent an hour in double-time, until the terrain became rough, and then another three making their way through sharp rocks the color of a week-old bruise and thick, dark grasses that shot ten or fifteen meters into the air before arching back towards the ground. Pink, feathery seed heads the size of a toddler weighted down the vegetation until they touched the ground in some places. The distant sun was small and red in the sky. Lights and vapor trails occasionally streaked the atmosphere as the battle between the Culler ships and the Sol Coalition continued.

As they closed on the rendezvous point, Maker left Rodriguez to catch up with the Lieutenant. "Sir," she spoke crisply, doing her best not to irritate a commanding officer who was having a worse day than she was. "Shall I radio India Company to let them know we are inbound?"

He nodded sharply, his eyes scanning the ridge line that had appeared on their right an hour previous and continued to rise until it was several stories above them. "Next time, Sergeant, do what you know needs to be done instead of pissing in my ear. I don't have time to babysit your every move."

"Sir, yes, sir," she responded, stepping out of line and pressing her back against the ridge wall to allow the column of soldiers to pass. *Yeah right*, she thought sarcastically, staring at the lieutenant's back, *you want me to take initiative right up until I don't read your mind - or I do, and it ends up getting someone injured. Jackass.* That wasn't entirely fair, she knew. Maker had been in command – however briefly and tragically. It was difficult and frightening and the worst experience of her life. She wasn't envious of the Lieutenant given their current situation or any other.

"What's up?" Rodriguez asked as he reached her. Maker fell into step beside him and tapped in the codes to activate her comm signal. There hadn't been any traffic since her conversation with India Company, but she assumed that all of the units that had been sent to the surface were, like hers, having to hoof it from less than ideal drop points to their intended coordinates.

"FYI - I think the Lieutenant is immune to your charm, so you've been warned."

"No one is immune to this," he pointed at his opaque faceplate. Maker could only assume he was waggling his eyebrows or doing something equally stupid.

She rolled her eyes, knowing her couldn't see it. "I need to make a call." Her display notified her it was ready to transmit. "Company India, Company India, Company India. This is Company Juliette - Niner, over." She waited, but no response came back to her. Maker frowned and double-checked her comm system. It was set to the correct frequency, and it showed that India had an open comm - so they should have received her message. "Company India, Company India, Company India. This is Company Juliette - Niner. Come in." As she repeated the call, the two soldiers in front of her glanced backward. Maker slowed her steps so that the proximity comm wouldn't transmit her voice to them.

She radioed India again, but when they did not respond, her stomach began to twist. "Fuzz," she said softly, "run up to the Lieutenant and let him know I am having trouble reaching India. I am trying other channels, but we may be walking into something." Before the Private could take off, she grabbed his elbow. "Rodriguez, keep it quiet, okay?" He nodded. Maker switched channels, hoping that the comm officer for India was an idiot and had accidentally tapped one channel higher or lower than he had been assigned. There was no answer.

She knew Rodriguez must have reached the head of the column, but she was too short to see over the soldiers. Maker switched to the emergency channel, "Break-Break. Company India, Company India, Company India. This is Company Juliette. Over." Regulations determined that she should repeat the call three times before moving on to the next level of urgency. Maker's stomach was in knots and the hairs on the back of her neck were so stiff they hurt. She changed to a wide-band. Any comm officer would be able to hear her, if his equipment was turned on. "Charlie, Charlie. This is Company Juliette. Any receiving, please respond." She waited a full minute, mouth dry, before speaking again, "Charlie, Charlie, This is Company Juliette. Any-"

"Maker." Her Lieutenant's voice came over a dedicated comm, interrupting her transmission. Maker winced. She should have set up a direct line instead of sending Rodriguez. It was a stupid oversight. She glanced up to see that the line of soldiers had stopped, each turning in a standard formation to take turns resting and watching for movement. "Status."

"India is non-responsive, Sir. I-"

"Company Juliette. This is Company Oscar." The man directed Maker to move to another channel.

"Lieutenant, sir," she quickly spoke into the direct comm, "I have a contact, shall I - I'll patch you in." Rodriguez was nearly back to her position by the time she had the Lieutenant and Oscar on the line together. "Company Oscar, you have Juliette-actual, go ahead."

What followed was a nightmare for Maker, whose duty it was to stand, silently, monitoring the channels and listening to the conversation without reacting. Oscar had also lost soldiers on their descent, due to a minor hull breach that changed their trajectory and destroyed one of their landing airbags. Eighty-six of the one hundred assigned to their transport were in fighting condition. Oscar had contacted the nearest company, India, to rendezvous before heading to the target - much as Maker had done for Juliette - but his commanding officer had ordered regular radio checks every half-hour. Maker grimaced. *My mistake. Again.* It wasn't standard procedure, but if she had thought to do the same, they would have known there was trouble long before they were within firing range of India's position. She didn't have long to berate herself, as Oscar continued,

"Last transmission cut out. Comm is active but unresponsive. Scouts detected weapons fire in India's approximate position. Over."

"Oscar, this is Juliette-actual. Stand-by." The Lieutenant switched over to a private channel. "Maker, get your ass up here." She moved, Rodriguez right behind her, as the entire company was given orders. "Another company may be in distress. We are moving now, weapons hot. Try not to shoot any friendlies." Comms switched again, including Maker, Rodriguez, and the one soldier equipped with a heavy gun that had survived. "Gunner, set point on comms. Rodriguez, you're reassigned to gun support. I want you so intimate with that weapon it'd make your mother blush." Their 'sir's' were cut off as he took Oscar off of hold. "Oscar, this is Juliette-actual. We are moving to verify situation. Wait - twenty for Juliette-niner. Over."

"Juliette, this is Oscar-niner. Wil-co. Out."

Maker didn't need the order, she readied comms for herself to Oscar and the Lieutenant, as well as the newly designated gunnery team. They reformed into an open vee, moving slowly through the grasses that grew closer and closer together as they approached India's position. India had made good time from their drop site, helped considerably by the terrain. They had landed in a shallow river valley. The water itself was only a slow-moving stream a few meters wide, but the shore was another twenty meters on either side. Steep banks rose up three or four meters in places, and then the dense grasses took over. Maker found herself crouched between two huge dark clumps, pink seed heads brushing against her shoulders, as she looked down on the valley. There were bodies everywhere. India must have landed near another company, because there was too much blood, too many scattered limbs, for only one hundred people.

She had never been so happy that she couldn't smell anything through the air filtration system in her helmet. Steam was still rising in the air where high-heat energy weapons had seared flesh. A splintered bone, charred and dry, protruded toward the sky like a barren flag pole. One soldier, his helmet cracked and broken, had died with his fingers thrust into the soil of the embankment. His legs were missing.

It had been a massacre.

"Jesus," someone whispered over the proximity comm. Maker had to keep her eyes off of the bodies, or risk vomiting again. Instead she focused on the weaponry. Several heavy guns were in a state of partial set-up. Tripods had been erected, and one gun was mounted in place, but none had their control panels lit up. No shots had been fired from those weapons. Standard-issue rifles littered the gray-green mud near the stream. She counted sixty-two guns. Assuming that each of the two companies had been short a few soldiers, that still only accounted for less than half of them managing to get out their primary weapons. That indicated a quick attack.

"Maker," the Lieutenant's voice startled her out of her assessment, "find me the comm box." Every communications unit, once activated, also became a passive field recorder. Although the tech for each individual soldier recorded their movements, it was difficult to access that information in enemy territory. A comm box could be manually plugged into to any other and the information downloaded. It provided easy sharing of knowledge between units and a quick way to make certain that no important tactical data was left behind. She minimized all of the tasks she was managing and pulled up an electronic scan of the area. Several comm boxes responded to her ping, but only one was active. She painted it in her vision and copied the location to the Lieutenant.

Moments later, a two-man maneuver team slid down the embankment and began slowly moving toward the box. They were half-way across the beach when Maker lost signal strength - for just a moment. She took a deep breath, frowning. *What could have-* Heat and light lanced across the valley, and the man who had been facing them was cut in two. Maker's eyes widened and chatter exploded on her proximity comm.

"What the fuck!"

"Christ!"

"Where is that coming from?"

"Get down!"

Someone let out a choked sob.

"Can it!" The Lieutenant roared over the comm. The soldiers fell deathly silent, but Maker could see on her display the active line between the commanding officer and the one soldier still alive in the mud. She had been bending down to shift aside a body, and she fell when the laser cannon fired. She lay, motionless, her left arm pinned under the smoking corpse of the other half of her maneuver team. "Maker," the officer finally cut through to her channel. "Tell Oscar what is up, and that we will need fire support from the opposite bank if we are going to retrieve wounded and get that comm box. And see if they can get eyes on the ridge behind us."

Maker began her communication with Oscar while the Lieutenant issued orders to the rest of the company. Rodriguez helped the gunner set up his equipment, although there was little to aim at aside from the thick canopy of grasses that sheltered their position from the ridge line. Maker was extremely conscious of her suit, and the cooling and heating circulation system. If the exterior temperature of their helmets and armor hadn't been the same as the ambient air around them, it would have been a simple thing for the Cullers to target their thermal signatures and fire away.

Fish in a barrel, she thought. "Roger," she said aloud to Oscar. "Awaiting your arrival. We'll keep the light on for you. Over."

"This is Oscar. I expect a mint on my pillow. Over."

She snorted. Both she and the other comm officer could see the writing on the wall. They were engaged in what would either be one of the shortest deployments in SC history, or a long standoff with Cullers who were far better designed than humans to wait through a night that would get down to -40 degrees Celsius. "This is Juliette. Turndown service is extra. Out." Maker cut the line and rechecked her equipment and transmission status, making sure she was still receiving the wide-band ping from the *Pershing*, signifying that the ship was still operating. The soldiers around her were settling in, forming up watch positions further back into the grass and rest locations nearer to the embankment. There was no discernible movement from the valley, as the downed soldier was overshadowed by the bodies around her. Those corpses had saved her life.

Maker couldn't imagine how horrifying it would be to have to lay out in the open, surrounded by dead - one a close comrade. She checked her tech and opened a line with the woman, Gonzales. "This is Comm," she said quietly, so as not to startle her. "How are you doing, Private?"

There was a long pause, "A little too much sun for my taste."

Maker let out a startled laugh, "Grunts ask for leave and they ask for leave - finally get a chance to lie out and relax, and all they do is complain."

"Didn't mean to sound ungrateful, ma'am," Gonzales responded. Her voice sounded tight, but not like she was panicking.

"I'll let it slide, this time," Maker said. The smile felt stiff on her face. There was no getting around the fact that they were in a pinch point, and Gonzales was exposed. "You know," she flicked through her comm lines again, checking for activity, "the way you are all belly-flat out there reminds me of a dog I had once."

"What?"

Maker ignored Gonzales' confusion. If she was listening, then she wasn't thinking about her situation. It was the least Maker could do. "Yeah, a dog. Laziest damn animal..." Eight hours later, Maker's throat was raw. She had told Gonzales about her lazy dog, the second graders that had toured her dad's farm and accidentally flattened an entire cornfield, the first horse that had been allowed into private ownership in decades - for educational purposes - and how Maker had 'misplaced' it for three days, and why mincemeat pie didn't have any meat. Gonzales told her about the apartment on Titan where she lived with her younger brother and her aunt and uncle and cousins, the ice floe races that were held every year on the surface, how her parents had met at basic training, and the woman she had loved and lost more than a year ago.

Maker hadn't bothered with a direct line, so other soldiers had chimed in on the proximity comm. Rodriguez had told a very strange story about his older sister and brother getting him drunk on 19th century wine at the tender age of eight. The gunner talked about his dad's roasted okra, with just a hint of sweet pepper, and the cool feeling of a shady pond on a humid summer day. Another soldier talked about his younger brother, recently transferred to Opik Station in the Oort Cloud and head-over-heels in lust with his superior officer. Sunrise was still a long way off when Maker's raspy retelling of an old family joke was interrupted.

"-pickle slicer. She was fired too." The laughter of the soldier closest to her faded when a priority communication came in.

"Company Juliette, this is Oscar-niner. Over."

"This is Juliette-niner. Go ahead."

"This is Oscar. We have eyes on your shooters. Seven laser cannons in a defensive alignment. Over." He sent a coded file, and when Maker opened it her map maximized and an image file overlaid it. The ridge behind her was slightly concave, the top leaned out over the grass forest between it and the valley. It explained why her company had not been fired on as they moved toward the river. As soon as they had cleared the shadow of the tall vegetation, the two soldiers on the maneuver team had been visible to the Culler position. *Weird*, Maker thought. There really wasn't another word for it. Cullers used planets as resupply and repair stations, not permanent bases. Maker had never heard of them setting up perimeter defenses. She scrolled out on her map. Behind the ridge was a massive crater. The images were flecked with several small, dark dots. Maker zoomed in, but could only make out what appeared to be openings in the ground. Whether they were deep pits or shallow tunnels, she could not be certain. Of greater interest were the shiny, hunched forms along the edge of the ridge. Scouts had caught at least forty Cullers in a single image. Maker's shoulder twitched.

"This is Juliette. Roger. We have an access point, at least two hours to reach shooters. Stand-by for Juliette-actual." She radioed the information to the Lieutenant. "Oscar will be pinned down, sir, unable to cross the valley to get to the checkpoint until those shooters are taken out."

"I am aware, Sergeant," he snapped back. He was quiet for a moment, but when he answered, he surprised her. "I'll take a strike team to the ridge with the heavy gun. That should keep the Cullers off of Oscar long enough for them to cross the valley, pick up Gonzales, and meet up with you here. You'll take command of the remainder of Juliette and head with Oscar to the rendezvous."

"Me, sir?" Maker winced at the squeak in her own voice.

"You are an officer, aren't you?" His irritated words reverberated inside her helmet.

"Yes, sir, I mean-" Her apology was interrupted by Rodriguez tapping on her shoulder and whispering through the proximity comm.

"I finished the inventory. Two more emergency comm units, 40 MRE bars, a spare water recycler, parts for the heavy gun, sixteen ordinance packages, eighteen det cord rolls, and two basebots."

The Lieutenant was still dressing her down on one channel, and Rodriguez was complaining about the uselessness of a basebot when they didn't actually have a base to maintain. Maker ignored them both, her brain itching with the image of the emergency exit Rodriguez had blown through the floor on the mining station. "Fuzz," she broke into his litany, "how many meters of rock can one ordinance package go through?" He blinked and then answered, going on about detonation mechanisms and rock composition. She interrupted again, "Great, I'm going to patch you in to the Lieutenant. Sir," she said as soon as the lines were connected, "I have Private Rodriguez here, and he may be able to take care of your shooters without climbing the ridge."

"I'm listening."

Maker rushed into an explanation, "The ridge isn't too thick, maybe 250 meters at the base, according to our maps. We can get right up under the shooters, using the grass here as cover, and place ordinance on the wall. Blow the wall - the Cullers will all come down. Any that survive should be a lot easier to pick off."

At the other end of the loose grouping of soldiers, down the embankment to the south, the Lieutenant stood. His head nearly touched the curving roof of grass that protected them from enemy fire. "Rodriguez, you have munitions experience?"

"Some, sir." He swallowed audibly, "It is more of a...hobby, sir." He rushed on before that comment could be questioned. "I can do it though. We have enough cord to link the explosives and set off a controlled detonation. I should only need about two-thirds of our supply."

"Maker, go with Rodriguez. I'll monitor comms here. You have forty minutes to get to this point," he sent her map coordinates, directly below the shooters, "and get those charges in place. If this doesn't work, I'll take a team up the ridge." Maker's mouth fell open a bit, and she was grateful for the opacity of her helmet so no one could see the mixture of fear and surprise that was churning in her gut and no doubt plastered on her face. "What are you waiting for, Sergeant? A guided tour? Move it!"

"Sir, yes, sir!" It took less than ten minutes to transfer comm control, notifying Oscar that Juliette-actual would have the line, and gather up the supplies they would need. Despite Rodriguez's reminder that she had carried det cord a lot closer to her than the bag suspended between them, Maker was not comfortable. She kept her rifle out in front of her, scanning the narrow spaces between clumps of grass as they moved. At a slow jog, it took another twenty minutes to reach the path they had been walking the day before and follow it under the ridge to the detonation point.

The back of her neck was prickling and her eyes felt hot and dry. Her stomach was knotted and her fingers were shaking as she followed the younger soldier's instructions to set up the explosives. Although the Cullers had been on the ridge when she walked under it the first time, it was different to know that they were directly above her. They ran a line of cord back into the grass, about a hundred meters from the rock.

"Sir," Maker called the Lieutenant over a shared link with Rodriguez, "we are in place here, sir. Ready to detonate on your order."

"Hold," he responded. Sweat was dripping down her back, making her shirt and underwear stick to her skin. Her suit regulated temperature, so she knew it was nerves. *Scared sweaty*, she thought without any humor. "On my mark. Three. Two."

Maker glanced over at Rodriguez. His helmet was pressed into the dirt, his body laid out like hers along the ground. The hand that held the detonator was steady, but she could see his stats on her display. His heartrate was almost as fast as hers.

"One."

Light burst in little pinpricks through the vegetation, the controlled blast forcing most of the energy into the rock. In the next second a boom washed over the grass forest, a strong wind following behind and nearly flattening the pink seed heads to the ground. Far in the distance, Maker swore she could hear the shriek of a Culler. Dust clouded the air and a rumble, low and deep and reaching up through her feet to flip her heart upside down, shook the ground.

"Move!" Rodriguez shouted. She was up a beat behind him and just ahead of the horizontal rain of sharp rocks that erupted from the collapsing ridge. They were both panting, lungs and muscles screaming for more oxygen, as they dodged clumps of grass and flying debris. "Got any-" Rodriguez gasped, "more ideas?" Maker didn't answer, too busy watching her feet and trying not to run into the other soldier's back. She did, in fact, have one other idea. Unfortunately, it was not as helpful to their situation.

If forty Cullers set up a defensive perimeter, how many more were hiding behind it? A rock smacked into the back of her helmet, and that thought was her last before she blacked out.

CHAPTER 10: KIN SELECTION

Ministry of Defense. Proper noun. Military branch of human government, created in 2084 with the ratification of the Sol Confederation. The Minister of Defense is appointed by the President and affirmed by Congress. Undeniably the most powerful member of the Presidential Cabinet, the Minister of Defense directly oversees the Sol Coalition forces including the Army, the Fleet, and the Sol Intelligence Service.

Ex. Requests for new body armor were denied again due to budget constraints; the Ministry of Defense must have needed new office chairs.

Hour 0700
November 10, 2126

Ignition minus twenty-two years.

"Test day?" Malak's head was turned down, executing a difficult form that would position him for a strong back kick. The older training room was empty except for the student and teacher. Despite the ragged exercise mats and outdated equipment, Malak and Bee preferred to spend their individual sessions there. The cameras had not been upgraded in years and were simple to adjust out of focus.

"Yes," Bee answered him, poking Malak's hips with his practice staff to put them into a better alignment. "No," he continued contrarily, using his own bare foot to urge Malak into a wider stance.

Malak breathed in through his nose and out through his mouth, slowly pivoting on the ball of one foot. As he turned, he shifted his weight until his right leg was free of any pressure. Bee could speak. He was intelligent, Malak knew that from experience and the test scores that Parshav and Almaut had hacked from the research station's computer system. However, Bee had been designed to be much closer to their animal base code than the Twenty-six or Twenty-seven series. It was evident in his long tail, fangs, and abundant hair. Beyond that, his vocal cords and thought patterns weren't intended for complex speech. He spoke the same language as everyone on the station, and understood perfectly well, but his vocabulary was limited. It was necessary, though, to express ideas outside of immediate needs or dangers.

"A test for the Twenty-sevens?" Malak pulled his right knee in close to his chest and bent at the hips, angling his body to look over his shoulder. The muscles in his stomach burned under the excruciatingly slow tempo Bee demanded for their practice.

"Some," Bee acknowledged. "Alpha." *A test for me only*, Malak translated.

"Did you take this test?" Sweat dripped down his face, stinging his eyes, but his leg moved with precision. Foot flat. Heel leading. Pausing before over-extending the knee.

Bee put pressure on the top side of Malak's foot, first lowering it a few inches to demonstrate the correct position, then to force Malak to support more weight on tense muscles. "Yes. Passed," Bee smiled, the wide grin a learned expression that displayed his sharp teeth. "You pass too." They went through three more forms in silence, while Malak's thoughts raced. It had been four years since the day when the other groups in his series submitted to him. In that time he had learned to work well with Skoll, Giltine, and Almaut. Giltine still challenged him the most, but they all followed him without question during training exercises. He had even established a weekly meeting, among the four of them, to review what each group had done, how individuals were testing, discuss ideas. It had been easier to arrange than he had hoped, but the research staff had been ecstatic that he took initiative and organized a hierarchy. Not that they told him as much. They couldn't, not and maintain professionalism and experiment structure. Parshav had found that information in the computer system too. That and comments questioning how well Malak's tactic of soliciting input would work for test A-13b.

Today's test was A-13b, Malak was fairly certain. Parshav had been working as quickly as he could without getting caught, but so far had not found out anything about the conditions or purpose of the test. Malak had the other alphas looking into it as well, but other than figuring out it was important, and that visitors had arrived on the station to watch, little information had been found.

Bee finally called an end to the training session, and they both took a seat against the wall. Malak rubbed his face dry with a towel and finished off his water before he spoke again. "What happens if I don't pass?" It was a difficult question to ask; it put Bee in an untenable position. Technically, Bee was a research subject - one of only three from the twenty-two series to still be 'extant non-viable'. He was alive, had survived whatever experiments were run on his genome and then after his waking-day, but he wasn't approved for their intended purpose. Bee was a failure, as far as the military was concerned, because he couldn't fight against the Cullers.

Malak considered his instructor while Bee struggled with an answer. The twenty-twos had been extracted from the artificial wombs over two decades ago, but there had been a problem with their aging processes. Bee was still fit, his chest and leg muscles were well-developed under the fine layer of brown hair on his body. His eyes were still sharp and his bones strong. He had streaks of silver though, at his temples and on the end of his tail. Around his eyes were lines that matched those of human technicians more than twice his age.

Malak was ten, but he was already close to his full height. Some of his packmates were done growing taller. The medical physicians expected he would still put on more weight in muscle; he had just started a new protein diet and strength program to accelerate the process. He would never have hair like Bee - none of the Twenty-sevens would, but he had noticed thicker, darker growth on his jaw. The females, like Smierc and Giltine, had already filled out and been started on a new training program as well. Some of the males, like Parshav, had been issued razors. As fast as Malak was growing though, it was nothing compared to what Bee had undergone. The Twenty-two series was mature by the time they were Malak's age, and then they kept getting older. Most had died, the rest had been labeled 'non-viable'. However, Dr. Gillian had made those that survived valuable in other ways. Guard duty, training younger subjects. *Enrolled them in a new experiment,* Malak thought bitterly. That was the crux of Bee's struggle. He was a test subject, but also a teacher. He was part of the authority that oversaw Malak, but he was also less human than the Twenty-sevens. Malak experienced a twinge of regret for making Bee wrestle with his duty. He reminded himself that the future of the pack could be dependent on the day's test - and how prepared Malak was to perform.

Bee's tail flicked with agitation. "Pass, good. Good for little alpha. Good for pack." Malak nodded, trying hard not to look impatient. "No pass." Bee paused, and blew out a hard breath, his face grimacing. "For little alpha pack, no good, no bad." He stopped again, screwing his eyes closed and leaning his head against the wall. *An order to keep quiet,* Malak thought. It was difficult for Bee to ignore direct orders from the researchers whom he had been conditioned to obey. A direct order could only be overridden by a higher authority, in Bee's mind, regardless of what he personally felt.

Malak growled, unintentionally, slapping his sweaty towel against the floor. He usually controlled his emotions carefully, but seeing Bee struggle between doing what he thought was right and what he had been programmed, genetically and behaviorally, to do was frustrating. Infuriating. Humiliating.

Sorry. Bee's soft whine caught Malak's attention and his eyes snapped to the older male's face. Although Bee had, with greater frequency in recent months, asked for Malak's compliance rather than demanded it, the submission in his posture was new and surprising. Bee's head tipped to the side, his shoulders hunched and his tail tucked down. *Sorry, Alpha.* Malak blinked. Bee had never before used that sound. It had a different meaning than alpha, or little alpha, as he often called his favorite student.

"It's-" Malak cleared his throat, not sure what to say. It had felt natural when the other twenty-sevens submitted to him, but having Bee, his teacher, his senior, do the same felt heavier, harder. There was a responsibility that came with it. Something more than looking out for his pack. More than leading the other one hundred subjects in his series. It had never occurred to Malak that he might have to operate in a larger framework. To gain the respect and obedience of anyone outside of his group. It was daunting and exciting and a little bit frightening. *Okay.* Malak found the rumbling, soothing sound that Bee would understand best, then he paused, trying to find the right emotion to calm Bee without giving up his newfound authority. He hummed, *Good pack.*

Bee immediately relaxed, his body un-tensing in a way that Malak had never seen before - as though years of pressure were suddenly lifted from him. "No pass - before pack." Bee paused again, searching for the right words. The Twenty-sevens, in Bee's mind, were the *now* pack. The Twenty-sixes were the *be-*

fore pack. "Alpha pass, before pack good, now pack good. No pass, now pack no good, no bad. No pass, before pack bad." It took a moment for Malak to make sense of Bee's words. *A test only for me, that doesn't affect the Twenty-sevens. One that if I fail, will only affect the Twenty-sixes.* Malak's brain was running over itself to generate possibilities, few of them good, and ways to succeed. Bee's shoulder nudged his, and Malak met the green eyes of his instructor - so like his own. "Before pack - bad followers. Alpha make them follow, or before pack done."

Done. It was a serious word on the research station. Done only had two meanings: either the subjects were ready for independent field work, or they were 'non-viable, non-extant'. Research subjects that had no value were a drain on resources. Malak closed his eyes briefly, swallowing down the anxiety and fury that were battling inside him. His stomach felt like it was being twisted in knots. His lungs were too tight. His head was pounding.

If he failed the test, the Twenty-sixes would die.

***

Dr. Wendy Gillian watched through the video feed as Lupe ushered the VIP guests into the observation room. Representative Soledad Venegas was with them, which was expected as he was the Chair of the Oversight Committee. There was a scientist from the Science and Research division, and two staffers. The Sol Coalition military liaison was there as well, and she had brought another officer with her that Gillian didn't recognize. Gillian's hand shook as she reached for her cane, and she frowned. Nerves were not unsurprising, but she didn't want them to ruin the presentation. She had enough to deal with keeping her aging body under control.

Eighty-two years old, and the stresses that had been put on her were beginning to show. Thirty years on a space station that wasn't quite earth gravity combined with injuries sustained early in her career resulted in weak joints. Of course, she could have undergone procedures to correct the osteoporosis hollowing her bones. But it would have required a long period away from work that Gillian didn't feel she could afford. Not with all that still needed to be accomplished. Her career, *her life's work*, would be tested in front of the visitors from Congress and the Coalition - bureaucrats and politicians that had no idea how much trial, error, loss, and brilliance had gone into the final product. The Twenty-sevens were a miracle of science, the perfect combination of genetic research and applied psychology. The lessons learned from them had already been refined and applied to three more series that were in various stages of production and training.

Gillian and her team had created a designer species to exacting specifications. Project Barghest would do for war what robotics had done for industry. Faster, cleaner results with fewer human losses. It would revolutionize society in the same way. Where low-skill laborers were a thing for history books, so too would become human soldiers. Gillian's subjects would free humanity from the need to fight and die for their security. Free them to explore their minds and the universe around them.

She took in a deep breath and stood, using her cane to take pressure off of her knee. Perhaps once the Twenty-seven series had proved themselves, then she could take a break. Gillian smiled to herself as she hit the door control and walked to the observation room. *Unlikely,* she thought, *always another deadline. Another project.*

All eyes looked up when she entered, and Gillian acknowledged them coolly. "Ladies, Gentlemen, welcome to Erasmus Station. I am Dr. Wendy Gillian, Head of Research for Project Barghest. It has been noted that my presentation technique is rather dry," she smiled, and as expected they all smiled back. *Ingrained behavior,* Gillian thought, *exists in every species.* Her knee was aching. "I won't bore you with the technical details of this project.

You have all received the briefing, but please indulge me, and allow Dr. Lupe Martinez to provide an introduction."

Lupe stood and walked to the front of the room while Gillian took her seat at one end of a curved table. She watched the faces of the visitors as her former assistant began to speak, "As you are aware, Project Barghest was first approved as Project Reform in 2091 with the intent to create a supplemental or substitute force for the Sol Coalition's engagements against aggressive species. Although research and initial genetic trials exceeded expectations, and significantly furthered our understanding of theories of cross-system evolution, subjects were deemed nonviable for the proposed purpose."

"That is a rather couched term, Dr. Martinez," Venegas said with an arched eyebrow, "given the loss of life and property during the previous administration here. Let's be blunt. They were a waste of money."

"You are correct, of course, Representative." Lupe nodded her head and swiped data from her tablet onto the wall. "As you can see here, as a percentage of funding spent, positive milestones towards the goal were limited. Although," another chart came to the forefront, "ancillary developments and applied research have resulted in significant benefits, both monetary and tangible, for the Ministry of Science and Research."

"We are not here to discuss your bank statement, Dr. Martinez," the military liaison scowled and leaned forward in her chair. "We are here to see soldiers."

"You bring me to my next point," Lupe smiled charmingly, but Gillian could see the tension in her shoulders. Her assistant and the liaison had never gotten along, and it was only the audience that kept Lupe from telling the female officer exactly what she could do with her opinion. Lupe's fingers danced on her tablet and the data slid off to one side of the wall, minimizing into a narrow column. The majority of the space became transparent as the plastiglass was activated. The viewing window looked down on a six-acre training arena that had been designed to reflect the natural landscape on many of the breathable planets encountered in the Orion-Cygnus Arm of the Milky Way. Fine dirt, the color of almonds, was sparsely dotted with clumps of dark sedges. Three rocky outcroppings mimicked hills or canyon openings, and those were covered with lichen and moss in oranges and greens. The lighting in the ceiling some hundred feet overhead had been set to mimic mid-day under a dwarf-red star.

"In 2102 it was determined that genetic advances alone would not be adequate to ensure success. Under the leadership of Dr. Gillian, the project was renamed and Erasmus Station began a heavy emphasis on psychology and nurture, not just nature. The results have been tremendous. Over the last twenty years we have refined our techniques to produce the last two series of subjects. The individuals entering now are the leaders of the Twenty-six series." A panel opened on the left and three figures stepped forward. They were too far away to make out easily, but Gillian did not need the zooming camera view that Lupe provided. Kapziel was the alpha for the entire series, but his domination had come at a high price. The Twenty-sixes were no more aggressively designed than the Twenty-sevens, but hierarchy had been established through brute force just after adolescence. Kapziel had maimed the leaders for groups two and three, leaving himself with his original beta and the former leader from group one. Lessons had been learned from that situation, primarily that groups should be introduced slowly to each other at a younger age, before maturity.

"Kapziel, here," Lupe centered his face on the screen, "leads the Twenty-sixes. They have met or surpassed all of the benchmarks for-"

Lupe's recitation and the various charts and graphs she displayed on the screen was interrupted by the new officer. His security badge read, *Thomas*. "What do you mean by leader?" His sandy-blonde hair was cut to regulation standards, his uniform crisp and perfectly tailored.

"Exactly that. Kapziel is the commanding officer for his series."

Before she could get back to her presentation, Thomas spoke again, "Commander? Your packet," he gestured toward the tablet in front of him, "refers to them as subjects, not soldiers."

"My language choice is first and foremost intended to help you understand the dynamics involved, and secondly to label these individuals, sir," Lupe smiled, showing most of her teeth. Gillian reflected, not for the first time, that the woman had spent too much time with Bee. She looked nearly feral. "They have been engineered and conditioned to act as a cohesive military unit. It is, in part, why their base code contains the portions of alien DNA that were selected. Project Barghest subjects have a deep - gene deep - loyalty to their groups. These groups will form the actionable units that will be put into the field. It is a reflection of the priority needs expressed by the Committee when the parameters were first designed. They thrive in strong hierarchies and, unlike most humans, find a measure of self-actualization in successfully carrying out orders and contributing to the survival of their group."

"Isn't that counterproductive?" He argued, "if they are so focused on survival, how can they successfully risk their lives in the place of human soldiers?"

"Group dynamics and altruistic behavior," Lupe answered simply. "Sacrifice by one makes a group stronger. In early humans, this might mean one man taking the lead in a mammoth hunt - risking being gored - in order to bring rewards to his group. Humans still have this instinct, but it has been dulled over time. The military reinforces it though training exercises." She waited a beat for further questions. "We have advanced both the instinct and the training. Project Barghest subjects are dedicated, their purpose is to defeat the enemies set before their groups."

"And who determines the enemy, Dr. Martinez?"

"We do," she responded. Three flags appeared on the training ground, each marking a black box. Kapziel and his followers immediately crouched, waiting and assessing the situation.

"Forgive the interruption," Venegas interjected, "but your reports indicate that the Twenty-six series are hesitant, even aggressively opposed, to taking orders from human staff. Do you mean to tell me that you have corrected this flaw?"

"The flaw, as you phrase it, is a genetic one, so it could not be corrected after extraction. However," Lupe tapped her screen and another panel in the arena, at the far end of the space, opened. "We have worked around it."

Gillian watched the close-up camera as Malak walked into the training area. In comparison to Kapziel, he looked painfully young. The Twenty-sixes had already reached physical maturity. They were in the tallest point five percent of the human population, and their bulk was obvious. Musculature made thick by design and careful training made for impressive soldiers. Even on the zoomed in view, the differences from a human were minor, but unmistakable. Heavier jaws and brows, slightly pointed ears. Thick stubble and chest hair on the males. Gillian knew too, although she never mentioned it specifically in her reports, that both genders had incisors that were too sharp to be passed off as human.

Malak was almost as tall as Kapziel, three centimeters shorter, but he had only recently entered puberty. His face was more peach fuzz than stubble, his figure more lanky than bulky. For all of his youth, chronological and physical, mentally he was far more mature than any of the Twenty-sixes. Gillian suspected he exceeded most humans of any age as well. His green eyes were cold, his mouth flat and jaw set. He scanned his surroundings and the distant Twenty-sixes as though taking in the play on an uninteresting board game. He wore the same day uniform as all of the subjects: a long-sleeved undershirt and light armor jacket, durable cargo pants, and boots. The Twenty-sevens wore black. The Twenty-sixes wore blue.

Skoll stood on Malak's left, his height and thick chest overshadowing his leader. Almaut was similar in Malak to build, but his pale hair and skin stood out sharply against the brown backdrop and coloring of his companions. Giltine walked just in front of Malak. At first, the researchers had worried that the female did not fully accept her position below Malak in the hierarchy. It had become apparent during training, however, that she had become a forward scout and quick strike weapon for the group. It often seemed to be Malak's intention, too, to mislead others regarding his position.

"The Twenty-sixes have repeatedly proven that they will follow orders only from an individual they feel is worthy of their loyalty - which does not seem to include any humans. The twenty-sevens were designed differently, and so don't have that issue. We intend to create a new unit, composed of both series, with a single leader that will act as the control factor - accepting commands from a military handler or commanding officer and enforcing them with the rest of the subjects."

"The conclusion?" Venegas asked.

"We will see it today," Gillian interjected. "Lupe, ready the communication implants, please." Gillian turned toward the rest of the table while Lupe typed commands. "Each of the leaders will be given an objective and instructed to work with the other group to capture their flag. The Twenty-sixes will target the blue flag, the Twenty-sevens the black flag."

"What's the red flag for?" A staffer at the back of the room blurted, then blushed.

"Outliers," Lupe responded absently.

"One group will have to be dominate to succeed. Both series will then be ready for the final stage of training and deployment - as the military sees fit."

"If this one," Venegas paused and scrolled through his notes, "27-2-Malak, can't bring the others to heel?"

"Then we will have wasted our afternoon, but the data collected from the twenty-six series will still benefit us as we move forward, and the twenty-sevens will still be viable and extant." *I hope*, Gillian added silently. There was always the possibility that Kapziel would kill Malak and the entire project would be canceled. She nodded to Lupe, and the communication feeds for each of the seven subjects appeared at the bottom of the viewing window. An eighth feed popped up in the corner for Bee, labeled 'instructor'.

"Go," Bee's gravelly voice was loud in the observation room. Kapziel immediately sprang into action, ignoring the twenty-sevens and racing toward the blue flag. Malak, conversely, scaled the nearest rock formation with Giltine behind him while Almaut and Skoll took up defensive positions at its base.

"Your golden boy isn't off to a great start, Gillian," Venegas noted dryly.

***

"Thoughts?" Giltine asked him quietly. Despite the distance, she seemed concerned that the other team might hear her. She knew about the Twenty-six series, Malak had compiled a large amount of information on them from various sources and required his pack to memorize it, but he knew she wasn't going to risk their senses being stronger than her own.

"Assess first," Almaut responded through the new subdermal transceivers they had been implanted with. The faint vibration of the technology irritated everyone's skin, but Malak ignored it.

"Act second," Skoll added in his much deeper voice. Giltine scanned the area around the black flag. It was subtle, but they had all played similar games and knew what to look for. Faint depressions, no more than dust that was laying differently than the surrounding area.

"Pressure plates," Giltine confirmed what Malak had already noted. "Grid. Rough Delta pattern. Reverse on Two B, Fifteen K, and-" the rest of her words were cut off as an explosion sounded from the opposite side of the arena.

Malak depended on Giltine to keep her eyes on the flag while he turned his attention to the Twenty-sixes. They had apparently discovered the same defense system around their flag, and determined to simply set it off rather than move around it. Clumps of vegetation, thrown with enough force, could set off the pressure plates and allow them to move unimpeded. The system that monitored the defenses could not reset quick enough to stop the other team from making progress. It was a risky tactic, but it provided the greatest potential for speed. Malak's stomach was knotted so tightly it cramped. He ignored the anxiety and focused instead on forming a plan.

"Skoll," he ordered. His beta bent at the knees, breathing deeply and evenly while he scented the air.

"New obstacle," Skoll reported. "Four - correction, five Cullers." Malak felt his jaw harden. They had faced the enemy before, but never with those odds. It was a clear indication of how serious the test was. "Interior holding cell, blood scent." At least one was injured, giving off the bitter smell of their internal fluids, but that only tended to make Cullers more violent. The twenty-sixes were approximately one-quarter of the way through their minefield, but one of them was moving awkwardly, as though injured.

127

"Changing targets," Giltine reported. Malak watched as the flags changed color, rotating in a clockwise pattern. There was a sharp snarl of frustration from the Twenty-sixes, and then they raced across the arena to the new blue flag. The injured member of their group lagged behind and waited while the others began setting off pressure plates near the new target - this time at twice the speed. There was a screaming, grating sound, and then the first of the Cullers emerged from within one of the rock formations. Malak's mind was working through contingencies at a furious pace. Each of his team was armed only with a service knife; he watched as the injured Twenty-six pulled one as well. A second Culler was released, and the two aliens paused for a moment before leaping down from the rocks to make room for a third.

"Almaut," Malak said shortly.

"Wait," he was whispering under his breath, watching the timing of the pressure plates and the flags, "wait…"

"Almaut," Malak demanded.

"Thirty-two seconds, plus or minus three seconds per engaged plate," Almaut answered quickly. The entire exercise was designed to require both groups to select a single target and work together. Even then, they still stood a good chance of taking losses. The Cullers were splitting off; the first three turned and began their bounding step toward the Twenty-sixes. The next one did not hesitate but came at Malak's group.

"Giltine, Skoll - play tag. Almaut, with me." Malak didn't have to waste any time looking to make sure his orders were followed. Giltine was on the ground before he could even move, following Skoll across the dirt. She made a sound, high in the back of her throat, which immediately grabbed the attention of the Cullers.

Chase.

The sound and meaning of her call sent a tingle down Malak's spine, but he ignored that as well and jumped down to run in the opposite direction. "Can you disarm and rearm one of those?" He asked Almaut. The paler boy in his peripheral vision nodded. "Good. Conscript the injured Twenty-six and get it done." The first three Cullers had already reached the pressure defense system. Two had taken leaps over the traps and were nearly upon the tall leader. The last one had triggered a release and been thrown backward. It was oozing fluid, but still deadly. As they drew closer, Malak could clearly make out the expression of fear on the reddish skin of the male standing outside the defense zone. His knife was drawn and ready, but his left leg was twisted strangely and his pants were wicking blood.

Malak sheathed his own knife and directed his path to intercept the downed Culler. He didn't stop to engage, but set one hard boot against the chitinous rear leg of the alien. With his other, he stepped up and slammed the reinforced toe into the shoulder joint. It cried out, the scream painful to his ears, and swiped at him with its free arm. Malak had planned for the counterattack, and never slowed down. The serrated edge of the claw caught the back of his jacket, slicing through the lightly armored material and drawing a shallow line of pain on his back. The leaping kick carried him over the creature and past the first line of pressure plates, which had already reset. Malak trusted his team to carry out their orders and focused on his own task.

Dodging the plates wasn't difficult, given that he knew the pattern. It was made more challenging by attempting it at a dead sprint. He could feel the sweat dripping down his back, stinging where it met the open flesh of his wound. He counted out the grid while he ran and tracked the movements of the enemy in front of him. One Culler was more mottled than the other and it reached the Twenty-sixes first. The alpha Twenty-six, taller and more muscular than his female beta, turned and crouched into a fighting position, waiting for attack. Malak would have cursed, if he hadn't needed the oxygen to keep up his pace. The Cullers were clicking back and forth at each other. Although Malak did not have an ear for it, he could guess that they were planning a rush. Sheer size, speed, and available cutting edges would give them the advantage. The older alpha didn't seem to recognize that, or he wasn't willing to allow for the possibility of failure.

Obey. Malak growled as soon as he was close enough. *Wait. Listen. Ambush.* The twenty-six alpha began to snarl, diverting his attention from the mottled Culler, who reached out one long appendage and swiped at the male. He took the blow on the leg, which quickly spurted blood. *Obey,* Malak snarled. *Obey or die.* Then he turned his head toward the enemies and whistled. The high-pitch caught their attention, just in time for Malak to draw his knife and slide to the ground. His momentum carried him under the alien at the rear, and the reinforced blade sank between the hardened plates of the thigh and body. He could feel resistance as he hit the fibrous tendons, then they gave way and the Culler shrieked. It stabbed down into the dirt after him, barely missing his head. Malak rolled, just short of a pressure plate and took off back the way he had come. He could scent the bitter odor of the Culler behind him, its broken gait slowing it significantly. There was another scream, and a bark of victory. The air around him was sprayed with the scent adrenaline and the fluid of his enemy. *Two down,* he counted to himself. He jumped over the last line of defense systems to find the injured Twenty-six tearing off the head of his Culler opponent. Almaut, covered in ichor from the waist down, had a dusty pressure plate in his hands, using his knife like a screwdriver.

"Forty-seconds," he yelled without being questioned.

Malak compared that to his internal countdown for the flag change. *Three, two, one.* A yell of frustration behind him signaled that his count had been correct. The flags changed again and he could hear the Twenty-sixes making their way out of the pressure field. The timing would be close. Giltine and Skoll were rounding the far end of the arena, only two of the enemy behind them. A third body was piled in a heap at the base of a rock formation, fluid coated the surface with shiny steam. "Home run," he rasped, lungs heaving, but his transmitter picked it up. Skoll grabbed Giltine by the arm, sling-shooting her over a low ravine before following with a powerful leap. The ten-foot wide fissure was nothing to the Cullers, who crossed it with only a screech of irritation.

"Thirty," Almaut called. From the corner of his eye, Malak watched the injured twenty-six stand and bare his throat. Malak braced his feet. There was only the faint crunch of a boot on vegetation to warn him, but he was ready. Just as he had practiced a million times with Bee, he ducked and pivoted, sweeping out with his leg. The other alpha knew the move, and changed tactics quickly. He snarled, reached down and grabbed Malak's collar as he jumped over him. The two tumbled together, barely remaining standing, and Malak was at a disadvantage for weight, reach, and experience. A knife buried itself in his shoulder, and Malak had to grit his teeth against the pain.

My kill, the other alpha snarled, his dark skin twisted with fury and determination.

Malak didn't respond, but threw himself forward, further onto the blade. A brief moment of surprise flashed across his opponent's face, and then Malak's legs were free and he kicked up and over the other alpha's back, taking the knife with him. He turned, and they slowly circled each other. Malak pulled the weapon out of his shoulder, clenching his jaw to keep from grimacing. He held one knife in each hand. His right dripped with Culler ichor. His left with his own blood. He bared his teeth and roared.

"Twenty," Almaut yelled. "Ready to deploy!"

"Skoll, Giltine," Malak growled into his transmitter. "At your mark." He kept his eyes on the other alpha, but his ears were tuned to the sounds of his team. Almaut grunted as he set up the pressure plate. Giltine made her high-pitched sound again, egging on the Cullers. Skoll counted.

"Five. Four. Three. Two. Now!" A cloud of dust rose around Almaut and then there was an explosion. The screams of one Culler cut off abruptly, while the other continued to whine and thrash in the dirt.

"Report," Malak ordered.

"Good to go," said Skoll and Giltine at nearly the same time.

"Peachy," gasped Almaut with a cough. Malak couldn't spare him a glance, his eyes still locked on a potential threat.

Obey, Malak growled again. His voice was lower than he was used to, but his head was also getting a little light from blood loss.

"Get the flag," the other alpha countered. It was a challenge, a demand that Malak prove himself before he would be accepted as dominate.

"Giltine," Malak immediately called out. She was at his side in an instant, Skoll a moment behind her. "You," he pointed at the other Twenty-six, the female beta, "run." He yelled over his shoulder as he sprinted toward the flag that had started out black, then had become blue. Its current red color was sharp and bright against the artificial background. "Count?"

"Twelve," came Almaut's reply.

"Step where I step," he ordered the beta and began a breakneck race through the pressure plates. There were only two rows left, and the beta was right behind him, when Almaut screamed out a warning. The flag changed colors turning black, and the pressure plates all reset. "Hand," he yelled. Her eyes were wide, her mouth dry and gasping, but she stuck out her arm. Malak dug in his heel and rotated, launching her across the last twenty feet.

She ducked and rolled, but was still covered in scratches and dirt when she finally stood. Her hand touched the box at the base of the flag, and a tone sounded in the arena, signaling the training sequence was over. He waited, bleeding and breathing heavily through his nose, while she brought him the box. Her green eyes were downcast as she handed it over, tilting her head slightly.

She walked behind him back to the others, where Giltine and Skoll were watching over the other alpha and Almaut was still rubbing his chest where he had impacted with the pressure plate. The other member of the Twenty-six series stood to the side, glancing between the two alphas. The twisting feeling in Malak's stomach was gone. Perhaps he had overcome his anxiety, or perhaps the blood loss and sudden drain of adrenaline was making him delirious. Either way, he was ready to accept submission and get back to the barracks. He had no desire to waste time on posturing for the sake of the Twenty-six's ego.

"Obey," he said clearly. The twenty-seven puffed up his chest and opened his mouth. Malak's expression didn't change. He was too tired to react. "Obey," he repeated. The Twenty-six paused again, sniffing, then lowered his head.

"Great," said Skoll clapping his hands together with a smile. The friendly action was made slightly less appealing by the gash over his eyebrow and the wet, sticky sound his ichor-covered palms made. "Anyone hungry?"

***

Kapziel and his two betas had gone with him to the infirmary, and then later to the mess hall. They had sat down, interspersed with Giltine, Skoll, and a severely bruised Almaut, and eaten with no incidence. Malak had even found a moment to submit a request to Dr. Gillian that Kapziel be granted permission to join his weekly meetings, as well as combining some of their training sessions. He didn't expect any problems with the re-

Suzanne Brodine

search staff, but it was always better to be prepared for the unexpected. Which was why he had assigned Parshav to monitor anything strange on the Station. Several hours after the test, Malak listened carefully to the audio feed that Parshav had been listening in on while Smierc kept the barracks guards busy with a minor distraction.

"-impressive. Imagine what they could do with body armor and weapons from this century," a woman's voice said with admiration.

"It doesn't even give you a moment's pause, does it?" A man, cooler and far less impressed, spoke.

"Why should it? This is what we have been looking for - a new weapon. And finally I get to report something other than resource losses and budgets thrown down the toilet."

"There is a difference between a rifle and a high-yield drone. You-"

The voice faded out and Parshav fiddled with several settings on his tablet.

"Where is this coming from?" Malak asked quickly.

"Section C, distal access corridor," Parshav responded while he tried to find his quarry. "I've been tracking them using a piggyback on the security cameras, but I could only get audio - so far. I think they are headed to- ah, there."

"-take it?" The woman's voice sounded clearer than before, and after a second Parshav held up his tablet, displaying the live video footage.

"Would you?" The man wore the insignia of a colonel on his shoulder. He was tall, for a human, and his hair was yellow. Malak recognized the woman from previous observations she had made,. It was jarring to see her an expression of disgust and superiority on her face.

"A personal request from the General?" She snorted, "If someone

134

with that kind of power asks you to walk their dog, you do it."

"Batma didn't call me personally, and you would be wise not to bring it up again. Those kinds of requests have a way of being forgotten on a black book project." He stressed the word, *requests*, and the woman blanched. "And these are no dogs." The man pressed his hand against a security pad, and there was a tone notifying them that the lift was on its way. "I'd sooner handcuff myself to a feral Rottweiler than share a ship with the tubers they have cooked up here. At least I could trust the Rottweiler wouldn't shoot me."

"I would have never thought you, of all people, would be afraid of a few kids."

"Were you watching some other demonstration? Those aren't kids, they are killing machines. And if we are very, very lucky, they'll be somewhere deep, deep in Culler territory when they figure out what we have done to them."

What's that? Make them soldiers?"

The two officers stepped into the lift. As the doors were closing, Malak heard the man's response, "*Make them slaves.*"

.CHAPTER 11: FIRE

James, (i.e. *a james*) noun: Derogatory term for a late twenty-first century real-time language translation program. So called after the Sol Coalition implemented use of the first models during negotiations with another species. Misuse of a common alien phrase resulted in the imprisonment and later execution of the political liaison in charge of discussions, Randolph James. Resistance among troops to use the infamous device resulted in a preference for human interpreters.

Ex. "Should we ask them to put away their weapons?" "Our unit has a james, not a translator." "Oh, might as well start shooting then."

Hour 0330
April 23, Year 2148

Ignition minus twelve hours, eighteen minutes.

"You can't just go and play your two right out of the gate!" Gonzales' irritated voice was loud enough to be heard even over the staccato bursts of heavy weapons fire and the occasional whine of laser cannons.

"Why not?" asked Rodriguez. "It's my two, and they can't take the point. Seems like a good play."

"It's a stupid play," Gonzales argued. The two other soldiers playing cards with them snickered and sat back against the rough rock walls of the trench. Maker tried to press her head deeper into her pack to drown out the sound. For a moment she wished that bringing down the crater wall had given her more than a blackout concussion. *Something more permanent might be nice.* It wasn't possible to get more than ten feet away from another person in the tight quarters of the ditches, but she had done her best. Duty shifts were long, frustrating, terrifying, and boring. What little off duty time she had she wanted to spend unconscious on the muddy, uncomfortable ground instead of awake, dreaming about regular rations and listening to Rodriguez piss off every human being that spoke with him for more than ten minutes. "-makes your partner want to kill you," Gonzales continued. "That's why it's stupid!"

"But we *are* winning," Rodriguez pointed out calmly, "so it's not stupid. It's an amazing play. Tell her, Sarge," Rodriguez called out. More than almost anything in that moment, Maker did not want to be dragged into conversation.

"You're an idiot, Fuzz," she said with a sigh, finally giving up on sleep. "Play the way Gonzales wants you to, or find another partner." She rolled onto her back and stared up at the sky. The atmosphere on the planet was breathable, but a little thicker than Earth's. Maker tried unsuccessfully to pick out Sol in the darkness. The little yellow star was too dim to see unaided at such a distance. She wondered how Kerry was faring. Her friend had been deployed to a different company, and his comm placed him at the far side of the trenches. She pulled up her tech and checked on him again - an abuse of her position as comm officer, but she was beyond caring. Kerry's signal pulsed comfortingly, as did to the ping on her display from the *Pershing*. The ship was still in orbit and active, but it had been nearly two weeks with no reinforcements and no comms. Everyone was on edge.

"Mmm," Rodriguez murmured suggestively to Gonzales, "how do you want me to play, *partner*?"

"With your tiny brain," she hissed, "instead of your tiny-"

A company-wide communication cut off Gonzales' reply. "Code Red. Incoming. Weapons hot." It was indicative of how long she had been there, how long they had all been there, that Maker didn't react to the order with more than a grunt and a quick, muddy glove across her hair to keep it out of her face before she pulled on her helmet. Less than two weeks ago, the same warning had been issued on the *Pershing*. Code Red: Enemy Engagement. Then, she had thrown up in a toilet before she could even get her armor on. After everything that had happened on the hellhole of a planet where the Cullers had hunkered down, it had become situation normal.

"SNAFU," Gonzales said aptly through the proximity comm. Maker snorted along with several other soldiers, and then they were lined up on the edge of the trench, weapons out. The shrapnel grenades came first. They were thrown from a fair distance, so only half of the lobbed devices made it close to the trench.

"Down," shouted Maker. The soldiers nearest to her all ducked below ground level as a grenade rolled across the ground. It stopped short, but the resulting explosion sent bits of metal flying out in 360 degrees of pain. A few rained down on helmets, but the trench protected them from direct impact. Gas grenades were next, but they were ineffective as long as a soldier's suit remained intact. Thankfully, no one near her had any issues - this time. It was agonizing to listen to the screams of a soldier suffocating in his own helmet. Then there was always the shine of floodlights on moist gray skin as the Cullers approached. After the first few days, the aliens had stopped charging in a straight line, and now loped, jumped, and crawled unevenly across the slippery mud between the trench and the enemy outpost. The planet had no moons, but the emergency floodlights that had been erected illuminated the hull of a Culler ship that sat in front of the crater.

Munitions had disabled it before Oscar and Juliette companies had ever arrived, and every three days a squad was sent in to repeat the process. So far, the ship hadn't been able to take off or turn its powerful weaponry against the humans. The small victory came at a steep price. None of the squads had returned.

"Heads up," Maker called out, focusing her sights on a target. Other Cullers were painted in her vision as the rest of the soldiers locked in their guns. A laser cannon cut a wide swath through the trench to her right; the screams of soldiers were loud over the proximity comm. "Ready!" The first of the Cullers came into range, and Maker's tech notified her of their approach. "Fire at will!" Rifles were mostly quiet, compared to the noise of heavy guns and Culler weaponry, but the sound of projectiles hitting targets was grating. Shrieks, screams, and the wailing ice-dragging-against-ice sound of Culler language were like a ragged fingernail trailing up Maker's spine.

Waste!
Die!
Insects!
Humans!

She had heard it all many times since their landing, and would hear it again, and again, for eternity it seemed, until reinforcements arrived. The waves of Cullers were unending; no matter how many they cut down, more emerged from behind the stationary ship. Maker aimed carefully and fired again, tracking her incendiary round as it passed through the upper chest cavity - where she knew from personal experience the beak and gut were located - and then into the Culler behind her target. The first creature fell, screaming and writhing, to the ground. A beat later the second followed with less noise and more splatter as the round exploded. The enemy closed within fifteen meters, and Maker quickly slung her rifle over her shoulder and pulled her Klim.

"Close range," she yelled, but didn't have time for anything else. The Cullers were faster than their awkward, bony limbs looked like they should be. She was aware of that, aware of how quickly they could cross a space so that they were breathing rotten air into her face and piercing her skin with serrated, bony claws. Not everyone was so fortunate.

Maker fired. Once. Twice. Three times and the Culler in front of her dropped to one foreleg, ichor dripping out of its lower abdomen. She pulled her service knife and climbed over the edge of the trench, ready to cut anything that came too close. Their exoskeletons and redundant organ systems enabled them to continue moving - and posing a threat - long after a human would have died. A bullet to the brain was the best way to ensure that a Culler stayed down. One foreclaw rose up, and she hacked reflexively with her blade. The move had been a feint, and the alien surged to its feet. Maker stumbled backward, tripping over undetonated ordnance and falling to her back. The clumsy action saved her life as another laser blast ripped through the Culler and one of his comrades, before gouging deep into the opposite trench wall. *They are killing their own,* she noted, far more calmly than she should have. A small, introspective part of her wondered if she was in shock. Wondered if she had been in shock for weeks, and what would happen when the numbness wore off.

"Get it off!" Someone screamed. Maker rolled onto her belly to see a Culler had avoided the laser by leaping into the trench. It had one soldier pinned to the dirt and was ripping away at the armor over his chest. Rodriguez stood off to the side, firing repeatedly. Most of his shots slid off the tough back carapace or lodged in non-vital areas. Gonzales drew her service knife and slashed at the Culler's face. It reared back, shrieking, giving Rodriguez a chance to pull the injured soldier out of the way. Maker toggled to non-lethal ammunition and just as the Culler tensed to attack Gonzales, she fired.

Metal wires, thin but strong, swirled out from the projectile in midair. They wrapped around the Culler's outstretched arms, locking them together and dragging it down to meet gravity. It screeched, thrashing and turning, but unable to defeat the magnetic lock on the wire. The thin sheen of mucus that always seemed to cover their skin mixed with the thick ropes of gray and pink blood that pumped out of damaged areas to soak into the cloth wrapped around its abdomen and upper legs. The material had more in common with rags than clothing.

Maker crawled to the edge of the trench, conscious of the notice over the comms that the barrage was over and of the blinking indicator lights for the health of nearby soldiers. She fell more than climbed down the embankment, coming to a muddy stop just out of reach of the Culler's legs. Gonzales was still standing ready, her gun in one hand and a knife in the other. Rodriguez had started first aid on the man with the chest wound. Three other soldiers stood behind her, shifting their weight. The air felt heavy with expectation.

"Humans! Die!" The Culler clicked. The grating wail of its voice continued, *"Trash in the universe! Enemy to them!"*

Gonzales swore and raised her gun.

"Don't," Maker warned. She got to her feet, and circled around, as best she could in the narrow trench, to approach the Culler from near its head. Priority with a captured live Culler was information. That was a standard command which, more often than not, was ignored in the field. Few soldiers were willing to risk further injury or enemy escape when shooting it would be simpler. They could always claim later that it looked like the Culler was about to break free.

"Ma'am-" Gonzales started, but Maker ignored her. There was something that had been bothering her about the Culler installation on that planet. It was unnatural, their entire operation, behaviors, the sheer numbers of them on a planet nowhere near any human colonies, stations, or trading routes was beyond strange. It was unlikely. It was suspicious. *It is downright fucking irritating, is what it is,* Maker thought sourly. She holstered her gun and drew her service knife. Her voice was raw from lack of sleep and shouting commands, but she managed to form the language that every soldier was forced to watch a short video on during Basic. So few human could understand it, and fewer still could speak in the alien clicks, that training wasn't even offered to new recruits.

"*Human,*" Maker repeated. The Culler's black eyes dilated, its frantic movements stilling. "*Human finds you. Human kills you. You stay. You like to die by human talon.*"

She didn't have a wide vocabulary, and she was sure her grammar was terrible, but the alien understood her. That much was obvious when it suddenly fought against the restraints, legs digging into the mud and sending muck and blood flying.

"*You came to us,*" it said. The furious pace of its clicking was difficult for Maker to understand. "*We were not ready yet, but the human trash will die, as you always die. Their enemy will be crushed beneath our numbers.*"

Maker felt almost hypnotized by the pools of darkness; pinpricks of silver dotted the very center of its eyes, drawing her in. Cold sweat ran down Maker's back, and her scalp shivered inside her helmet. The skin over her forehead and temples felt tight and dry, like at any moment it would split and expose the bone underneath.

The alien's carapace parted on the chest, forming a vee that had its widest part near the head. Gray flesh, wrinkled and oddly tender looking compared to the hard outer shell of the Culler's body, shone wetly in the ambient glow of the floodlights. It folded back to reveal the hard beak inside.

"*You will die,*" it promised, grinding the hard, sharp parts of its mouth together. "*You will die, and we will ravage these stars.*"

If there had been anything in her stomach, Maker would have thrown up. If she had not been stretched taut with fear, she would have collapsed to the ground. If she had never before felt the strange, terrifying sensation of her brain trying to crawl out of her eye sockets to escape the dragging, scratching awareness at the top of her spine, she would have screamed. The familiarity of it, from her experience on the mining station, did not make it less horrifying. Less disgustingly invasive. Less unbelievably frightening. Maker pressed her knife to the place where the skin split, just below the beak.

"*Weak*," she said, her cheeks and tongue forming the hard clicks while her vocal cords tightened to make the high screeches. Her nerves were crying out for relief, for her to look away, to run away from the cold cutting along her central nervous system. Maker put her weight behind the blade and the Culler jack-knifed, making a sound that was not a word - but meant pain.

"*Weak*," she repeated, "*and dead.*" She leaned hard and felt the sudden release of pressure as her knife cut through the sinewy sheath around the nerve bundle that lay behind the beak. It functioned like a brain stem, and the silver light in the Culler's eyes winked out as the point of her blade pierced through to the carapace on the other side. The pressure on her head let up so quickly she almost fainted. Instead, Maker overcompensated, windmilling backward and crashing the opposite trench wall. She slid to the ground, dropping her knife and clawing at her helmet.

Thoughts raced through her suddenly unfocused mind. *Can't breathe, can't breathe, can't look, oh hell, killed it. Cut it, stabbed it. Murdered. My head! Can't breathe!* She was hyperventilating, her brain was on fire as though she had no oxygen, despite her display telling her everything was normal. Her vision darkened, tunneling into a bright white light surrounded by darkness. It reminded her of the Culler's eyes. Hands pressed against her shoulders and neck, and for a moment Maker struggled, slapping at the arms gently holding her down.

"Sarge," a voice said quietly, and then, with more authority,

"Clara."

Rodriguez.

Maker's hands fell away, and he was able to find the catch that released her helmet. She gasped for air, and as soon as it was removed the Private was pushing her head down so that she faced her knees. "Breathe," he said softly. She realized he had removed his helmet as well and was practically whispering so that the other soldiers would not hear him. "Calm down, it's okay. Just-" he stopped himself, seemingly at a loss for words. Maker found her gulps softening into deep breaths while she wondered what he had wanted to say. "Just think of the celebration when we get off this rock." She could hear the arrogant swagger returning to his voice as his volume increased. "Me, the brave, incomparable hero, beautiful women and men fawning over me. And my commanding officer - no more will you have to lie alone and unsatisfied. Admiring enlisted and officers alike will line up to taste your-"

She shoved him roughly. "Finish that sentence," she rasped, eyes narrow, "and you won't have anything to celebrate *with*, private." Rodriguez grinned, and Maker found it easier to breathe while she was looking at his stupidly handsome face, dirty and bruised like the rest of them, instead of at the gore and remains that she had so recently been speaking with. Gonzales let out a relieved, snorting laugh. The other soldiers relaxed as well, organizing among themselves to toss the Culler body over the back of the trench - where other alien corpses had been left to rot.

"Didn't know you were a lobster-er, speak Culler," Gonzales said quietly.

Maker shrugged uncomfortably. "Watched the same tutorial during boot camp as you. Hell," she tried to smile away the awkward discomfort emanating from all the soldiers in the trench, "I could have been insulting its mother for all I know."

"Maker, Rodriguez," the snapped command that came over her tech was easily identified as their Lieutenant. "HQ, ten minutes."

They shared looks of sympathy with the other soldiers as they got to their feet and began the winding trek to the bunker that had served as headquarters for the last week. Basebots - Rodriguez had found a use for them after they had done the majority of the trench digging - had built the structure with blocks 3-D printed from crushed rock and sand. It was ugly and dark and dirty, but it was solid and the walls thick enough to withstand a laser cannon.

At least once.

Maker's stomach rumbled as they approached. She glanced at Rodriguez, only to receive a wink. They were all hungry, after days of half-rations, but he was the only soldier she knew who seemed to get randier when he was slowly starving to death.

The Lieutenant was waiting for them at the makeshift conference table in the center of the single, large room of the bunker. "Maker, we're down a comm officer after that attack. You're up."

"I just got off duty," she said without thinking, then winced. "Er, yes, sir." The Lieutenant frowned at her, but motioned at the narrow table covered in equipment in various stages of repair. Maker scowled as she approached; she had last been sitting in the same spot only two hours previous. She synched the more powerful base comm station with her tech and began monitoring communications and troop positions, as well as sending the regular ping to the ships orbiting the planet. *Pershing* responded, as always, with the automated signal that it was manned and active - but did not reply. The *Ferox* class bounced back her sign without a reply ping. The ship could be running silent, or it could be dead in space. Maker had weeks of practice, but she still had to force herself not to think about why the *Per-*

shing had not contacted them.

Why the *Ferox* was unresponsive.

Why no other ships had arrived.

The Major leading the ground forces arrived with a string of curses and a spatter of blood. A medic followed behind her, trying to check the field bandage covering a wound on the officer's forearm. A snarl, threatening to send the would-be nurse to the front line, had the man scampering out of the bunker. "This the one?" Ben-Zvi asked, looking Rodriguez over as she cut apart an emergency blanket to create a makeshift sling. The woman had aged ten years in the last four days - since the Colonel that had been deployed with them had been killed during a barrage. Maker was empathetic, but immensely grateful she was not in the major's shoes.

"Yes, ma'am," the lieutenant responded.

"I understand you have some skill with controlled detonations." Major Ben-Zvi raised her eyebrows when Rodriguez didn't immediately respond. "That wasn't rhetorical, private."

"Ah, yes, ma'am. Some, but I haven't yet gone through my munitions rotation."

Maker kept one ear on the comms, and the other on Rodriguez. He was smiling with a sort of boyish charm, but his voice was too faint to maintain the fiction that he was unaffected by his situation. A private being called before the commanding officer of a battalion was never good news. Although she was sure he was worried he was going to be disciplined, Maker was more concerned that he might be about to receive a reward for his service in blowing up the ridge.

What would they even need a demolitions expert for? There isn't anything around to explode except - oh, no. Maker's eyes widened.

"Good. As you are aware, we have a bit of a problem with a Culler ship on our doorstep, blocking line of sight into the crater. We can't get a good look at the size of the enemy, and if they get that cruiser working, we might as well-"

"No," Maker blurted out. All eyes turned to her. Rodriguez looked afraid and confused and trying to hide both emotions. The Lieutenant looked pissed. The Major had leaned back into her hips, as if she couldn't quite believe she had been interrupted. Maker couldn't believe it either. It was insubordination to deny an order, but if Rodriguez did what she was sure the Major was planning, he would die. Just like the squads before him. If he closed position on the Culler ship, he would not come back.

"Did you say something, Sergeant?" Her voice was cold enough to freeze blood in the vein, and Maker was struggling with the desire to shake her head and drop straight through the ground to hell, which conflicted with the undeniable impulse to save Rodriguez's life.

"Ma'am," she started hesitantly. Her mind was whirling, trying to find any excuse to keep the private that had so recently talked her out of a panic attack from marching to his death. "Ma'am," she began again, then paused. They did need to see what was behind the Culler ship. Without any knowledge of how many enemies they were facing, the SC forces had to assume that the Cullers could keep chipping away at their numbers until there were no humans left to stand against them. Then it would only be a matter of time before they repaired their ship and met the *Pershing* and *Ferox* class vessels - which had already taken heavy damage and had no support forthcoming. Forty-five hundred soldiers would be dead on a planet so unimportant it only had a number, no name, and two Sol ships would be charred space junk. Thousands dead, and still no one would know what the Cullers had been doing, or why they were acting so strangely. "Ma'am," she said, more confidently, as a stupid, crazy, suicidal idea began to form.

"If you say 'ma'am' one more time," the Major interrupted with flared nostrils, "you will spend the rest of your time on this backwater swamp on cremation duty."

"Ma-" Maker swallowed the reflexive title. "If you just want to know what's behind that ship, there's a better way."

"Are you suggesting you know better than me how to carry out our objectives, Sergeant Maker?" Retribution, fueled by days without sleep or enough food, days of blood and dirt and death, lit an unholy light in Major Ben-Zvi's eyes. Maker wasn't too proud to admit to herself that she was ready to retract everything she had said under that angry glare.

"Hear her out, Pilar," the lieutenant said gruffly. He collapsed back onto a hard bench that had been carved out of the floor. "The kid isn't a complete idiot, despite indications otherwise." Rodriguez was shaking his head, silently gesturing for her to shut her running mouth, but the Major was waiting impatiently.

"The crater sits on a tunnel system," she began quickly, before she could talk herself out of saying anything. She minimized the comms into the background of her display, and used her bracer controls to flick through the image files stored in her tech. When she found what she was looking for, she sent it to the tablet lying on the briefing table. "Here," she painted the dark spots at the bottom of the crater rim interior with red, "you can see the entrances."

"Those could just be caves," the lieutenant pointed out.

"Could be, sir," Maker agreed. "But here is some footage taken by Delta company." She sent another file out. "They passed by the ridge we detonated about an hour after us, cleaned up a few Culler strays. You can just make out, in the rubble, the edges of a collapsed tunnel system. I think that these run throughout the crater's rim and underneath of it. If-"

"You think? When you interrupt me, you better be damn sure, Maker." The Major sounded angry, but her expression was losing its feral edge.

"The openings are symmetrical," Maker quickly pointed out. She used one finger to highlight the round shape of the tunnels. "That isn't natural. The Cullers obviously have some reason to defend this ground - more so than anything else we have ever seen." A shared look, full of meaning, passed between the two senior officers. "It stands to reason that whatever the Cullers are using this planet for, they made some adjustments to make their activities easier. These tunnels could be why intelligence didn't detect any large numbers, tech, or heavy equipment on this planet. We weren't prepared, because they went to great lengths to prevent us from suspecting anything."

"Let's say, for a moment, that I might - maybe - buy into your theory, Sergeant. How does that help me get rid of that ship?"

"It doesn't," Maker shook her head, and then realized how her response sounded. "I mean," she said quickly, "we can use that information to get around the ship. If we figure out what the Cullers are protecting, get a look at their setup from the other side, we can come up with a plan that doesn't-"

Kill anyone, she had been about to say, but that wasn't true. There was no way, no plan, which would get them off of the planet without more loss of life.

Suck, might have been a more accurate way to finish her thought, but just as likely to end with her on cremation duty.

"Modified explosives," Rodriguez murmured, saving Maker from trying to complete her sentence.

"You have something to add, Private?"

Rodriguez, all traces of his hesitancy and confusion wiped away by sudden understanding, nodded. "Modified explosives," he said more clearly. He reached one hand over his shoulder and into his pack, pulling out an undetonated Culler frag grenade. Maker had a brief moment of vindication - only the Fuzz would casually carry around dud ordnance. "My observations only account for a small portion of the trench, of course, but I've seen one in every three of these things fail to trigger. The casing is heavily modified - I thought maybe they were trying to add something more deadly to the shrapnel mix, but I think these might actually be mining explosives that were modified to be weapons. The chemical makeup is right for it."

"Mining," the Lieutenant repeated it slowly, as if he had never heard the word before. "Cullers. Mining. For what?" His bafflement was a stark contrast to the sudden, hard resolve of the Major.

"You can get in there?" She asked Rodriguez. "Without drawing too much attention?"

"Yes, ma'am, I think so." He straightened his shoulders and stood tall. His reflexive swallow was the only indication of nervousness.

"We'll need to go with a smaller team," the Lieutenant said to the Major, pulling a tablet to the center of the table.

She responded, "Who's the most experienced with covert?"

Maker felt a little dizzy. The two officers were moving on her idea as though it was completely normal for a second-year Sergeant to plan an intelligence gathering mission. She did not fail to notice that Rodriguez was only in a slightly less dangerous position than he had been before she interfered.

"An hour ago it was a tie with these two," the Lieutenant was gesturing to the tablet, "but an entire section of the trench caved in during the last attack. If they are still alive, they won't be in great condition once they are dug out."

"Going into their base, it would be better if we had a translator."

Maker was still trying to decide if she should say anything else, perhaps mention that there had to be someone else, anyone else, with more experience than Rodriguez when the idiot opened his mouth, "Sergeant Maker speaks Culler." Three pairs of eyes turned her way, and Maker was uncomfortably aware that the fairly rare ability to learn the alien language was not viewed by most soldiers in a warm light. Of the derogatory names she had been called because of her dubious linguistics skill, 'lobster mouth' was perhaps the least offensive.

"Do you, Maker?" Her Lieutenant was looking at her with a fascinated sort of disgust.

She straightened her shoulders and lifted her chin, *in for a penny*, she thought, "I understand more than I can speak, sir, but I know the basics."

"Basics are the best we have," the Major stated. "You'll go in with Rodriguez, here," she pointed to the map still displayed on the tablet. "Lieutenant, get her the short list from the scrapped op. Maker," a hard gaze pinned the younger woman down, reminding her of how much was riding on her success. *As if I needed another reminder,* she thought. "Pick four others and help Rodriguez find whatever equipment he needs. I want you out of here in one hour."

Maker snapped a salute a beat behind Rodriguez and stumbled out the door behind him. An incoming transmission from the Lieutenant containing a list of names tried and failed to grab her attention. She was a communications officer, a glorified radio technician and telephone operator rolled into one, not a special forces soldier. Two close encounters with Cullers - a phantom shiver traced up her back at the memory - was enough for a lifetime. She had no desire to sneak into their base. No burning patriotism was pushing her to carry out orders. No love of the adrenaline rush urged her to run towards danger. And yet, that is what she found herself doing. *Again.* Not for her culture or species. Not for the glory. For the soldiers that risked their lives beside her. Rodriguez was going on about needing some parts, and she could still hear the Major talking inside the bunker.

"-and get me another comm officer, even if you have to draft someone."

The list of potential soldiers finally caught her eye. Two names stood out sharply - Gonzales and Kerry. Gonzales had the experience to make the roster; Kerry had no doubt ended up on it the same way he got most of the dangerous and unappealing assignments - by way of being genetically different. If she had to go into enemy territory, there was no one she would rather have watching her back than Kerry. She didn't want to ask, because she knew he would say yes. Frustration at their situation, and being forced to fight and die without any choice nearly overwhelmed her.

"-requisition anything we need," Rodriguez was saying as he moved away from her. She stepped up to follow, trying to compartmentalize and shove away everything but the series of tasks before her. *Step 1, pick a team.* "You know what that means, right?" The teenager, more handsome than he had a right to be and far too aware of it, waggled his eyebrows.

"You can finally get that economy container of lubricant you've been dreaming off?" She replied offhandedly. *Step 2, load up on ammo*

"Ha – no. Although," Rodriguez grinned manically, "I am very interested as to why that came to mind."

"Because you're a perv, Fuzz," Maker answered. *Step 3, map a course that will take us undetected to the crater wall.*

"No - well, yes. But more importantly," he leaned forward, the lascivious anticipation on his face setting off warning bells for her. "We can hit up the ration distribution. All the MRE's we can eat!"

"That's greedy," she replied automatically, thinking that the rations were determined to maximize nutrients for everyone. "And kind of gross." There weren't many things that she could think of that would be less appealing than nutrient bars to gorge herself on. *Radishes, maybe.* Her stomach rumbled, painfully hollow. "We'll stop there first."

CHAPTER 12: INCLUSIVE FITNESS

Calque (KAL-kuhk) slang, verb: calculated the risk and determined it to be acceptable.
Ex. Failure to properly calque ISG exit coordinates may result in fatal hull stress and gravity kickback.

Hour 2200
December 25, Year 2130

Ignition minus eighteen years.

"Drop is in thirty minutes. Get the teams ready."

Malak nodded at Colonel Thomas' order, but it wasn't necessary. He had already checked in with his team leaders. Giltine, Kapziel, and Almaut were all prepared, and Malak trusted that the soldiers serving under each of them would be too. He adjusted his shoulders under the new body armor issued for the mission; it fit tighter than he was used to, but the dark material did not impede his range of motion.

It was a soldier's uniform.

It was what they were now - or would be once the mission was complete - no longer research subjects but soldiers. It was a status that meant more than the purpose for which he had been created. It meant a measure of rights. Malak would never say so - and he had ordered the others to keep their thoughts on the issue to themselves - but he knew what kind of legal position they were all in. Almaut had unfettered access to the net. Under the Emancipation and Suffrage amendment to the Constitution, they were all people. Citizens of the Sol Coalition.

The Constitution required every citizen to serve two years in the military, and then they were granted secondary status. They could vote and own property. Another ten years of service granted primary citizenship. Those citizens could own corporations and run for public office. They were eligible for appointment to various government positions and received pensions. Malak didn't have his sights set quite that high. He wanted to be in a position to exist, outside of a black-budget research station. He wanted that choice available to all of those he was responsible for. He had already been through one test mission with Skoll and Kapziel's two betas. He knew how laughably easy war would be for all of them. The military leaders and scientists, with the exception of Thomas, were impressed by small things.

Thomas was a difficult human to impress.

Killing Cullers was no problem; it was what they had been designed to do. Thomas, however, expected more. He wanted Malak to gain intelligence about enemy movements. He wanted prisoners for interrogation and technology for reverse engineering. He wanted black boxes from Culler ships and codes for their communications. He wanted more than battlefield success, he demanded from them an end to a nearly century long war. And he insisted that it take place so quietly that the humans would never know where the Cullers disappeared to. The colonel's attitude made it clear that he did not like Malak; he had expressed more than once his support of the ban on GMH research in the Sol System. Malak vividly recalled his comments, years earlier, comparing the research subjects to Rottweilers. However, Thomas had gained respect for the Alpha. The Colonel had an inkling of what the Project Barghest soldiers were capable of and it made Thomas both cautious and demanding. Malak understood that.

He locked in the last set of commands to his armor tech and picked up his helmet. Thomas stopped him with a raised hand before he could exit the compartment. "Before the Repulsion, every army and regiment on Earth had its own motto. They used to put it on grave markers when soldiers died in combat."

"Hn," Malak answered coolly. The colonel had a habit of trying to teach lessons about Earth history and early human military tactics. Usually they ended in a critique of some action Malak had taken. The Alpha had found that a blank expression and curt response curbed most humans' desire to engage him in conversation. Unfortunately, the Colonel was not so easily deterred. Thomas shook his head, finally looking up from his seat. Thomas waited, fingers irritatingly tapping - his favorite tactic when he felt Malak was being too reticent.

"I do not intend to die," Malak finally elaborated, simply wanting to end the conversation and go to his teams to prepare, "and if I did, there would be no grave, and no marker. As you are aware."

"Yeah, fine," Thomas waved the response away, making Malak clench his jaw. "But what would it say?"

Malak was quiet for a long moment. The question struck him as surprisingly important. He rolled his shoulders, subtly testing his armor. He was born to fight for the humans. Despite how he had been created and the circumstances of his training, they had never physically abused him. He had no choice but to serve, but it was his *instinct* to protect. Malak's future was not his, and yet Thomas had spent an interminably long time explaining how the pay system would work once they were confirmed as soldiers of the Sol Coalition, how hierarchy and combat assignments were structured in human battalions. It was a strange dichotomy - breeding them to serve and remain hidden, but expecting them to desire, and be content with, the meager rewards of a soldier.

A soldier's rewards without a citizen's rights.

In spite of that, the humans deserved protection from the Cullers. He, and his teams, deserved to be allowed to do what they could do best. A tone sounded over the ship's communication system, announcing that they were twenty minutes out from the drop, and everyone needed to be in position.

"Just think about it," Thomas said gruffly. "See you in forty-eight hours. Try not to destroy any equipment." He picked up his tablet and began scrolling through the mission file, muttering, "I hate requisition forms."

Malak hit the door activation but paused before stepping through. "Natus at mortem," he replied in a low voice. Thomas didn't acknowledge him, but Malak turned the phrase over as he entered the bay and took his position opposite Giltine and Kapziel, and next to Almaut.

Born for death.

It seemed appropriate. A banner, as well as a curse.

***

"Count thirty-four," came the low whisper over the transmission system. Malak pulled up the map of the underground tunnel system on his display. The pale blue trails overlaid his vision, showing potential paths to the chamber that Giltine and her team were investigating. Thirty-four was a lot of Cullers, but not overwhelming, not with concussive grenades and the high ground. Giltine had positioned her people in the tunnels opening into a series of ledges at the top of a large cavern. Intelligence had indicated a heat mass, approximately 20 meters below those ledges. Giltine had confirmed that thermal bloom to be the enemy.

Malak knew his mission was to order an attack and destroy the supply post of alien repair parts and fuel cells. It would have been a simple thing, with the combination of technology and superior senses, for his teams to surround the Culler stronghold, initiate combat with high-temp, low-percussive detonations and then cut down any survivors that tried to escape the tunnels as they collapsed. It was expected he would give the order.

He did not. "Hn," he stated flatly.

Parshav spoke over the command channel that only fed to the team leaders, and Malak noted his position with Smierc and Almaut deeper in the tunnels, seventy meters below, "Hold for note." There was a brief pause, then, "This isn't a natural tunnel." Malak stared at the veined stone in front of him. Trails of heat made by a native microbial life form glowed in his night-vision. Parshav wouldn't have bothered using the restricted channel if his observation wasn't important.

"Assess," Malak instructed.

"Laser cuts and some heat-vaporization," Parshav finally determined. "High energy requirements."

"The brief said this was 'a hiding place of opportunity'," Kapziel quoted. His curiosity came through clearly.

"Suggesting intelligence got this one wrong?" Almaut sounded distracted. "Shameful."

There was a long pause while Malak considered the ramifications. It was a training mission, one designed to ensure that they could follow orders, kill the enemy, and withdraw quietly. It hadn't been openly stated, but it was reasonable to assume that the targets had been chosen for their control factor: well-researched, containable, and with limited possibility of anyone - Culler or human - stumbling upon them. So, he had to wonder why - on an insignificant, relatively uninteresting rock - why had the enemy expended significant resources to improve existing tunnels. The twelve soldiers in Malak's group waited in complete silence behind him for an order. He toggled through his stat display to check on the dozen he had left on the surface as a perimeter guard. Culler excavations were an unknown factor that could destroy his mission success - and the lives of a hundred soldiers. Malak determined that he would, at his earliest opportunity, put in a request that some of his people be trained to review intelligence and plan missions. He would be better prepared for missions and it would significantly reduce the number of humans he desired to put on permanent disability leave. Malak controlled his breathing, and his temper, while he waited for more information.

"Hold," Giltine spoke again. "Count revision." Parshav was feeding information into the shared network regarding additional excavations that had not shown up on the satellite scans. The Cullers had dug thousands of meters beyond the tunnel system they had in their maps. Whatever was down there - it was important to the enemy. "Count eighty-two."

That changes things, Malak thought to himself. Giltine's group was now outnumbered more than three to one. They weren't impossible odds, particularly if he directed Kapziel to relocate and assist her. The teams would likely sustain casualties, deaths perhaps, during an engagement on that scale. Malak did not want to lose anyone. Not on their first mission. Not ever, if he could do anything about it. He also wanted to know the purpose of the new tunnels. A significant portion of his education had been on Cullers: anatomy, behavior, culture, technology, language. They were not a colony-building species. At least, humans had never observed that kind of behavior. Although a point of origin for Earth's enemy had not been established, it was assumed that supplies were transported from there, as Cullers did not have fuel mining or harvesting stations, agricultural resources, or any permanent bases. The closest thing to strongholds for them were supply caches like the planet selected for the training mission. Cullers utilized such places for ship repairs, regrouping, and resource transfers between military units.

The natural tunnel system had been periodically monitored by the Sol Coalition for almost two years. Information collected by surveilling the waypoint had been developed into strike attacks on larger, more important battle groups. Traffic to and from the planet had dropped in the last six months, which was why it had been selected for termination. No movement meant no intelligence, which was the only reason to leave Cullers alive. They had lost their value, and so Malak and his teams were instructed to use them for target practice.

Two years, Malak thought with disgust, *and the SC never noticed a large-scale excavation.* It was only his second time commanding a field operation, but so far he was not impressed with the tactical directives of the Sol Coalition. It was too late to do anything about that, and it would only stir up resentment and division among his people if he spoke what was on his mind, so Malak remained silent. The original plan had been to send Giltine to the cavern with the known heat-source to eliminate any Cullers there. Kapziel and Almaut had each lead exploratory teams into the tunnel systems in different directions to ensure that no Cullers were left alive or useful technology abandoned. Malak had split his own team into a surface guard and a strike group to secure the exit and assist any of the other three if they encountered trouble.

If he changed the mission parameters, it would increase risk for everyone.

"Team Two," he spoke quietly to Kapziel, "split forces to support Team One and secure the exit." The soldiers behind Malak shifted, their breathing changing for a moment as they listened to him deploy other units to take their position. All maintained silence. "Team Three," he trusted Almaut to relay his instructions to Smierc and Parshav, "prepare a grid search protocol.

Three squads." He switched channels to speak with his own group. His display was lighting up with information about their physical stats, and Malak turned the notifications down, pre-ferring to rely on his own senses to keep tabs on the soldiers. "Relief watch is on its way. Check weapons and tech. Explore and Assess." The command was well received by individuals who were bred and raised to fight and had found themselves spending their first mission without any chance of action. In the quiet of the tunnel, Malak picked up increased heart and breathing rates. He glanced back at his team and saw red eyes flashing in the darkness. His nose almost itched from the adrenaline seeping into the air. Thomas would have told the soldiers to 'settle the fuck down'. Malak let it go. His own body chemistry was beginning to tick up; so as long as the others remained still and silent, he didn't feel a reprimand was in order.

Kapziel's beta and eleven other green dots appeared at the edge of his proximity map, so Malak ordered his team to move with him. It took nearly thirty minutes for him, walking slowly and stopping frequently to check his surroundings, to reach Al-maut's position. The pale-skinned soldier was waiting for him, helmet off.

"There are two main channels here," he said quietly. He gestured to an opening at the far end of the wide corridor where his team was grouped. The subdermal transmitters echoed his voice, despite their proximity. The devices were not programmed to take non-human hearing into consideration. It was another thing Malak would need to address. "Sonar indicates this one," Almaut tapped the command pad on his sleeve and the right tunnel was painted yellow on Malak's display, "splits again in another two hundred meters, about sixty meters down. Past that, we can't get a read with all of the zinc and lead in the rock."

Malak turned off his display and removed his helmet for a mo-ment so that he could take a look at the walls without any digi-tal overlays on his vision. Midway down the tunnel, the ceiling took on a swirled appearance, as though a corkscrew had been pressed against it and turned. After another five meters, the walls alternated the same pattern- sometimes on both, in other places on just one. Where the tunnel diverged in a 'Y' junction, every surface was grooved rather than smoothly uneven like the natural tunnels behind him. Malak compared the dimensions to what he had been crouching in for the last two hours. Where the soldiers had entered the system, rock had been cleared away by some ancient river hundreds of thousands of years ago and remained approximately four meters in diameter, sometimes much larger. Where the grooves began, the walls had narrowed. Malak ran his gloved fingers across the stone. The resulting shafts that had been cut were a symmetrical three and a half meters.

"Three-point-eight meters," Almaut clarified, without having to hear a question. "Down to the millimeter. Parshav measured four times." Malak crouched down, keeping his weight balanced on the balls of his feet, to stare down the steeply sloping floor of the artificial passage. Almaut continued to speak quietly, regarding the composition of the rock, the microscopic filings left in the floor grooves. The traces of slag melted during laser cutting. The potential for increasing levels of lead and other elements that would block communication signals as well as the sonar and other mapping tech. A slow breeze moved through the air, bringing with it scents from deeper in the ground. *Mica and iron. The tang of zinc and the musty, damp smell of old wetness. Rot with a sickening sweetness - Cullers.*

"What," Malak asked slowly, as Almaut began to wind down, "is three point eight meters in diameter?" The pale soldier blinked in surprise, and then his brow furrowed. The Alpha let him think about it as long as he wanted, sure that he would come up with a response. Malak had already run through a few possibilities. Cullers were driven by a single motivation: to eradicate humans. They could be surprisingly inventive in their tactics, but never had they undertaken terraforming or base building. They lived on ships, leaving only to fight the Sol Coalition forces or to trade supplies and equipment with each other. They were not stupid or wasteful. Cullers would not spend valuable resources on such an extensive project without a justification - a rationale that would result in a loss of human lives. There was only one reason to make a tunnel: to go through it. So the question remained, what, or who, did the Cullers need to transport under the surface of an out-of-the way, nearly abandoned planet that had no readily available natural resources?

"A TUNA is three point seven meters," Almaut said slowly. Malak kept his face carefully blank, but his brain was sifting through possible reasons for an obsolete aquatic vehicle to be on a planet with no liquid water. The Cullers had used TUNA's in Earth's oceans during the the initial invasion of Earth, and a few had been found abandoned on other liquid ocean planets in nearby space. Almaut gestured with his helmet, the matte black face shield turning to regard each surface. "It is the right shape, wider on the sides." Malak followed Almaut's gaze to the ceiling, "Ridgeline...the propulsion system would be hot enough to create zinc sphalerite slag..." His voice faded away, and he alternately nodded and frowned to himself.

Whatever the Cullers were doing on that planet, it needed to be investigated. Malak stood and replaced his helmet, Almaut a beat behind him. He flipped over to the command channel. "Team Three and I are going deeper, communication range is limited. Remain at your positions. In six hours, execute the mission objective and evac to the extraction site."

"Confirmed," Kapziel responded without hesitation, although his voice sounded irritated. Malak assumed the older, brasher soldier would have preferred exploring rather than continuing to wait.

"Secondary extraction?" Giltine asked.

Suzanne Brodine

"None," Malak responded. To his credit, Almaut did not flinch at the news that if he and his team could not make it back out by the deadline, they would be left behind. Malak doubted human soldiers would have reacted the same.

Giltine was silent for a long moment, and Malak knew her instinct to obey was fighting with her desire to tell him how stupid she thought his plan was. "Confirmed," she finally responded.

"Count begins now," he started a timer on his display that would be represented for the rest of the command staff as well. "Malak out." He turned to Almaut, "Split your teams. You take the left, Smierc and I will take the right and divide up at the fork. Comm silence unless you hit trouble, or find the end."

"Yes, sir," Almaut said. His helmet concealed his face, but Malak was sure he was grinning. Everyone wanted to test themselves, to do and see something new, and Almaut was no exception.

Malak led twenty-four others, including Smierc, down the steep grade of the right-hand channel. Where it split, he and Smierc divided as well, exploring with their weapons leading the way. His tech continued to map the area around him, long after he lost the signals from the rest of his people. Something he had not felt before trickled down his spine in that moment. *Fear,* he recognized belatedly. Malak - all of the subjects from the research station at Erasmus – had been put through isolation tests, but never had he been so effectively separated from his pack. He could not see, hear, or smell any but the twelve soldiers behind him. The knowledge that they were, actually, out of reach - not just in the next lab, room, or training facility - stopped him cold for a moment.

Like a ripple on a pond, he could feel his temporary unease moving through the others. Malak shook himself. He was the Alpha; they were his responsibility, and if he could not control himself, he could not expect them to do the same.

"Nose up," he ordered quietly, and then began to move again. There were several audible inhales, which had the effect Malak had desired. The familiar scents of the comrades with them made each soldier feel more secure. They walked for close to three hours. A six hour deadline meant that they could only go so far before they would not be able to return in time to make the extraction. What ground they covered in four hours at a cautious walk, they could retrace in two hours at a jog, or 45 minutes if they ran flat out, but that would leave them open to attack. Malak wanted desperately to find something. The end of the tunnels, a secret Culler munitions stockpile, even an ambush. Anything would be better than the constant, pressing decision of whether to turn back or keep going. With each step, his boots felt heavier. The armor across his shoulders was tight, his back and neck strained with tension. The three-hour mark came and went. His timer display changed from green to red. Still, the tunnel continued down.

They had just passed the four hour mark, and Malak was about to call for a ten minute rest, when he noticed a sharp drop ahead. He held up one fist, signaling the group to halt, then crept forward silently. A hole in the floor, the same size as the tunnel itself, plunged into a darkness unrelieved by the faint glow of the microscopic trails in the rest of the rock. After about fifty meters, it lightened considerably.

Where there was a light source, there was something worth looking at.

Malak gestured two soldiers forward, and between the three of them they quickly drove pitons in a triangle around the lip of the hole. Malak used hand signals to let them know he would go first, and half of the group would follow after a count of twenty-five. The other half would remain to guard the rear.

The cable attached to his gear belt whispered as he lowered

himself without touching the rock around him. As he drew closer to the end, he could see that the shaft opened into a larger cavern, but nothing was visible directly below him. Cautiously, he utilized his tech to map the room with sonar and heat. There were enormous concentrations of thermal mass, but nothing moving in the space below him. He relayed the information to the rest of his team and then released, dropping the last five meters to the stone below. Malak rolled to cushion the blow and came to a stop in a crouch. His back was to the wall, which curved around in a rough oval shape randomly dotted with small piles of rubble and the occasional chunk of stone. Several other shafts dropped from the ceiling, and a large opening had been cut in the center of the floor. Evenly spaced around that hole were three large machines glowing bright white in his night vision. Malak blinked and forced his eyes to switch perception. The space was dark, except for the machines which gave off a subtle red luminosity. His tech alerted him that they were also producing low-levels of radiation that would be harmful if he remained there too long. Malak tried to come up with a comparison, but they resembled antique jet engines more than anything he had ever seen. The propulsion end was secured to the rock; slag melted the metal casing directly into the stone. The intake end faced toward the ceiling. Each one was directed toward a larger central shaft above them - for venting or fuel, he wasn't certain.

Another soldier dropped down beside him, and Malak gestured for him to secure the area. The Alpha moved closer, making certain he was recording everything he saw. He approached the closest machine and focused on the exposed circuitry near what looked like a terminal panel. Upon closer inspection, the center of the room was a meter deep depression shallowly filled with water from an unseen source. Piping led from the water to each machine, possibly for cooling. Responsibility for his soldiers, his pack, was warring with his duty to his makers - the Sol Coalition. A grinding, scraping sound echoed into the room, and Malak glanced back at his men. All six had taken up position along the wall, near a large hunk of stone that appeared to be a remnant from the excavation. Moisture was seeping through the rock, making the wall shine in the low light. Malak felt exposed as the sound grew louder. He dropped to the floor and backed against the machine between two thick support struts. The heat against his back, even through his temperature regulating armor, was intense.

The grinding sound stopped suddenly, and the clicking, screeching language of the Cullers took its place. Although no one on his team had managed to be able to replicate the sounds, they all had translation software installed on their tech and it was enough to get an idea of the discussion.

Test. Deaths. More fuel. Stage two. Transport.

What else they might have said was lost as one of them screamed and then shots rang out. Malak's display bloomed to life - the signals for Almaut and his team flashed in his vision, showing their positions grouping together on the far side of the cavern. Malak ran around the machine in a crouch. Four Cullers had been towing a TUNA, the hull dented and in disrepair. They had abandoned it and attacked Almaut's team as they descended from another ceiling tunnel.

"Support fire," Malak ordered his team. The Cullers were quickly caught between the two squads, and when it was over, there were only minor injuries reported on his display.

"What the hell are those?" Almaut asked, quickly tying off an arm wound and gesturing at the machines.

"Get whatever information you want, then set detonations," Malak ordered. "We need to-"

Another screech, this one louder and longer and peppered with gunfire, reached his ears. Seconds later, Smierc's location showed up on his map. "Coming in hot," she breathed heavily into her comm. "At least sixteen behind me, and more joining. Seems I stumbled into a party."

"You, you," Malak gestured to two of his soldiers, "Positions, either side of the tunnel, prepare for a siege." His heart was beating in double-time, but rather than anxious, Malak felt exhilarated. His mind was clear and focused, his body ready to act. He ordered the six that had remained above to run back to the tunnel complex entrance and meet up with Kapziel's team. "Report to him. We're right behind you."

"Yes, sir," they echoed, and then were gone.

"Almaut," Malak barked. The soldier was directing three of his men to set up explosives while another two rapidly scanned the machines for data. White hair was exposed as Almaut removed his helmet and jogged over to his alpha. "Find me an exit, fast."

"Find it fast - or make the exit fast?"

Malak growled, his carefully cultivated expression of calm slipping. Almaut didn't lose his attitude, but he obeyed. "Both - got it," Almaut grinned and spun away. The excitement of finally seeing action, even if, or perhaps because, it threatened their lives, was affecting nearly everyone. Even Malak was aware of the pump of blood in his veins and the way smells seemed sharper than usual. The Alpha organized the rest of the soldiers to watch the other ground-level entrance and prepare to assist Smierc. She entered, as Malak expected, with a shower of explosions. Four soldiers proceeded her, running flat out and their stats signaling that they were wounded. Smierc was in the middle of a carefully ordered retreat. She and seven other soldiers pivoted gracefully, making up a moving wheel of firing weapons and occasional melee attacks. Those that rotated toward the front would toss carefully aimed grenades behind the group - into a swarming mass of Cullers.

Malak had never seen so many in one place. Even in video footage of ground attacks, where thousands of Cullers would engage the Sol Coalition infantry, they did not look so numerous. Long, knobby limbs moved with surprising speed along the ground. They were so close together, some were pushed up against the walls, their claws digging into the stone so that they could run perpendicular to gravity's pull. The sound was deafening; even past the bursts of percussive explosions, there was a constant screech and grinding gnash of their language. One alien surged forward and caught its hooked claw in the armor of a soldier. She was yanked backward, toward the mass of the enemy. Malak aimed with precision. As the second claw moved up to pierce the soldier's torso, he fired. An incendiary round exited the back of the creature's head and then ignited. The force threw the injured soldier and several splatters of ichor and tissue over Smierc's head and into the chamber. Malak's team were ready. As soon as they had clear shots, they began to take down Cullers. Each death slowed their advance - enough that Almaut's team could prepare their detonation.

"Clear!"

Soldiers dove for cover and the ground shook as the tunnel collapsed over the Cullers. A few managed to propel themselves past the debris - straight into the waiting line of soldiers. They were dealt with quickly, freeing Malak to order emergency first aid and perimeter security before checking in with Almaut. The Alpha did not have to ask for a progress report.

"Smierc is going to love this - you, not so much." Almaut gestured toward the center of the room. "I still don't know the purpose of the things, but at least part of it is an exhaust system. With enough pressure, it will make a decent cannon to get us out of here."

"Those," Malak said calmly, even while the soldiers close enough to overhear laughed or snorted with disbelief, "are radioactive. And we are not cannon balls."

"Okay," Almaut continued. He turned to the closest machine and with a spring leaped up onto the primary structure. He seized an access panel with both hands and ripped it away with a grunt. "Bad analogy. I'm going to force air out through this thing with enough pressure to blow a hole straight to the surface. I estimate I only need to get through about a hundred meters - give or take twenty-five - of solid rock. Then we can climb out, detonations are on a timer. This Culler base will be destroyed, we'll be free and clear. Everyone can have a nice meal supplement bar before Thomas picks us up."

"I believe you may have left out some pertinent details," Malak said dryly. The plan was not impossible. It was not ideal, but it wasn't impossible. He calculated the amount of time it would take him to free climb several hundred meters. Not all of the soldiers were as strong as him, and some had been injured. Responsibility and duty, instinct and reason were tangling inside of Malak. Their weight was an albatross trying to pull him down. With decent handholds, he could probably free climb to the surface in fifty minutes. But there was no possibility that the injured could keep up at that speed, and the Cullers would be able to dig into the chamber and disarm any explosives before Malak and his teams could get clear of the blast. Malak tried to determine how they could get thirty-six soldiers into the one available TUNA.

Malak's eyes roved over the chamber, assessing each individual, counting the remains of the enemy, before finally coming to rest on the damaged TUNA. "How much water is behind that wall?" Both men glanced at the wet stone, dripping moisture onto the floor, then at the dented alien transport.

Almaut's eyes widened, "You want to-"

"Check it out, but do the math quickly." Malak reached for his gun again as shifting rocks alerted him that the Cullers were trying to dig through the cave-in. Tactical Unit Nautical Assault vehicles were named by North American scientists after the Repulsion in 2056. They could carry 25 Cullers from splashdown sites to port cities and up onto beaches and docks. Even the smallest of Malak's people had at least twice the mass of a Culler, but their bodies were better designed for compact spaces - fewer hard shells and splayed joints.

One Culler arm punched through the loose rubble and was quickly removed by a standard-issue service knife before another controlled detonation sealed the chamber off again. Blasts of hot air – the temperature high enough to melt rock, rushed out of the venting ports on each devices and hit the ceiling. Where they combined, a hole began to grow. Malak monitored Smierc's progress in securing a secondary tunnel while he waited for Almaut to report.

"This is, quite possibly, the most amazing thing I have ever done," Almaut announced through the comm system. Malak glanced up to see him standing in the center of the room, supervising a small group that was relocating the TUNA to the cooling pond. "When they replay this footage, I hope Thomas notices how completely brilliant this is. I deserve a promotion. Or a raise. Maybe a handshake and thanks - from the President."

"You don't have a rank," Smierc noted over the comm from her position on the front line of the tunnel. "You don't get a paycheck, and the President probably doesn't know you exist."

Almaut signaled to a soldier near the dripping wall, and he secured two rolls of det cord to either side of a much more significant charge. "Oh, then the raise takes priority. Definitely." Metal rubbed against metal, loud in the room, and the rear hatch on the TUNA opened.

"Contacts approaching," Smierc noted calmly. Her team began to fire down the tunnel.

"All aboard," Almaut called out. "Keep your helmets on, your hands to yourself, and use your emergency oxygen if your ears start to pop. Or bleed." Malak stood by at the entrance, making certain everyone squeezed in and covering Smierc's controlled retreat. "If this doesn't work, we will be sitting ducks." Almaut scratched at his pale chin with his helmet and then shot at an unfortunate Culler that had broken away from the front line.

Malak ignored the comment. "Give me the detonation code." He punched it into his tech, and held the activation ready. *Instinct and duty.* The rotten sweet scent of alien ichor and the familiar musk of his pack flooded his nose. Almaut followed the last soldier onto the TUNA, squeezing in and grabbing the hatch lever. Without another word, Malak spun in a tight circle, slamming the sole of his boot into the exterior of the hatch and quickly shutting the TUNA.

"Wha-" came over the comm.

Smierc's voice crackled through his transmitter at the same time, "Don't, Malak." The two words were tight with anxiety.

Cullers surged out of the unprotected tunnel, snarling and shrieking. Malak holstered his weapon, secured his helmet, and detonated the charges.

***

The silence was loud in the debriefing room. Dr. Gillian sat off to the side, along with the Chief of Medical, but the hearing was run by the military. Representative Venegas was flanked by Colonel Thomas and a General that had traveled from four star systems away solely for the meeting. The playback from Almaut's tech was frozen on the image of Malak's face, set and unyielding, terrifyingly composed without his helmet, his foot outstretched to shut his team into the damaged Culler vehicle they had commandeered. Gillian, even thirty-six hours after the group had returned from the mission, was in shock. The subjects had been programmed for loyalty, quick-thinking under pressure, and dedication to the Sol Coalition and defeat of the Cullers. Decades she had worked toward creating an undefeatable weapon that would save human lives. A soldier that was stronger, faster, and less inclined to allow fear to control decisions. Those *children* - the twenty-sevens were only fourteen years old, regardless of how mature their bodies were - had found a nest of enemies four times larger than reports had indicated. They had taken it upon themselves to gather intelligence, decimate a secret facility, and completely eliminate all Cullers on the planet, without any loss of allied life.

Except one.

Gillian was in shock. Representative Venegas looked furious. The General appeared overwhelmed. Thomas was smiling. It was a little thing, just a tiny quirk at the corner of his mouth, but it made Gillian's stomach twist.

Venegas continued berating the research subjects, "You put the lives of half of the deployed forces at risk in a non-working, seventy-year old alien vessel and allowed your superior officer-"

Almaut raised his hand, but didn't wait to be acknowledged. "Actually, it turns out we don't have ranks." Venegas' mouth snapped shut, his brown skin turning a purple shade. "I know," Almaut said easily, as though confiding in an old friend, "I was just as surprised. Did you know we don't get pai-" Kapziel yanked the other male backwards, making his mouth shut with an audible click.

"Excuse me, sir," Giltine smoothly stepped forward. "We followed the Field Manual for Special Operations to the letter, including our exit strategy."

"And where, young lady," the General asked, both silvery brows raised, "does the Manual recommend building your own water gesyer and riding it back to base?"

"Don't ever march home the same way," Thomas said quietly.

Gillian didn't recognize the rule, but she had only read through the manual once, prior to designing training exercises for the twenty-two series.

"Section Four: Retreating," Giltine answered without hesitation, ignoring the colonel's comment.

"Do not retreat," Kapziel began.

"But if your position is overwhelmed," Giltine continued, standing at attention and looking the General in the eye, "utilize surprise and any advantage offered by the surroundings to distract the enemy while moving to higher ground."

Almaut lost his easy humor and spoke seriously for the first time in Gillian's memory, "Use any means necessary to ensure the enemy's losses are greater than your own."

"Your recall is as impressive as I was lead to believe. However," the General said, his dark face equally serious, "that section ends with one extremely important command that you seem to have forgotten."

"Leave no soldier behind." Malak stood as he spoke, his wheelchair rolling away as he pushed out of it. Even with the plaster on his leg up to the hip and half of his neck discolored and strangely shiny from the skin graft that had not had time to fully take, he looked impressive. At more than two meters, he was taller than anyone else in the room. He had never gained the bulk that Kapziel had, but his shoulders were broad, his thighs and arms corded with muscle. His light brown beard was usually kept shaved, but he had demanded release from the infirmary to attend the debriefing, and his thick stubble and unkempt hair reflected his hasty departure.

Gillian's stomach twisted again. Malak was the pinnacle of her research, the lynchpin to the success of Project Barghest. He was trillions of credits, decades of work, and the trust and hope of two generations of government leaders. They had almost lost him.

Not to the enemy, she reminded herself, fear still gnawing at the edges of her shock, *but to his own moral code.* He had sacrificed himself to kill the Cullers and ensure that all of his team made it out alive. If they had taken the conventional route and climbed out of the tunnels, he could have come out with few injuries. Most of his series would have survived. Malak's actions flew in the face of conventional training. His behavior was not genetic. It was not programmed by psychological training. It was entirely of his own choice.

The realization terrified Gillian.

"Malak," Venegas started, having finally regained a semblance of composure, "you determined to seal your team into a damaged vessel, which you could not be certain would remain intact, and blow them to the surface with a scrambled-together plan, and then face a swarm-"

"A swarm would imply insects," Almaut interrupted again. "Cullers are categorized as-" Malak made a low noise in the back of his throat and the blonde male abruptly ceased speaking. All three betas stood at attention.

"I trust the judgment of my team," Malak responded. His deep voice had gained a gravelly note since his neck injury. "If I did not, they would not fight alongside me. Almaut stated the pressure would be sufficient and that the TUNA would hold. It was apparent that it would be under significant strain given our numbers, and chances of success were greater if someone remained outside to properly time the detonation of the initial blast to create an exit and seal the secondary tunnel. Then the subsequent blast to release the water."

"And if there had not been enough volume to reach the surface?" The General looked fascinated.

"Almaut placed additional charges and an emergency fuel cell on the lower compartment of the TUNA. In such an instance, Smierc would have ignited it to provide enough thrust to crest the shaft entrance."

"And if you had been incapacitated or killed by Cullers before you could activate the second detonation?" The Representative asked with reluctant interest.

Malak turned his gaze on Venegas to answer his question. Gillian stared at the cold, green eyes of the Alpha as if she had never seen him before. *Perhaps I haven't,* she thought with an anxious realization, *not truly.* The lack of inflection in his voice made it clear how little he thought of the suggestion.

"The possibility was below the parameters set by the Manual for assessing risk."

"Awfully high opinion of yourself," Venegas ground out.

"Sir," Malak rolled his shoulders slightly, as though throwing off a weight on them, "there were only thirteen intact Cullers that survived the tunnel collapse. Given that the majority of my engagement with them was under water, where their anatomy is poorly suited for movement, it was unlikely I would be unsuccessful."

The General let out a barking laugh, "So you flooded the room, shot a dozen Cullers, and swam 500 meters to the surface."

Almaut muttered out of the corner of his mouth as the Representative spoke, "Shot twelve, decapitated one after he ran out of ammo."

"Not successfully," Venegas argued, ignoring Almaut's low commentary, "You were dead when your team found you washed up on the dirt."

"I would interject, Representative," the Chief of Medical spoke up, "Malak's vital signs were only recorded as flat for fifty-seven seconds, and his brain activity did not cease during that time.

Even if his team had not gotten to him, the AED in his armor would have auto-energized and restarted his heart in another three seconds."

"That is not a risk that should be taken with an asset of his value!" Venegas exploded. Gillian barely contained her wince. Although the subjects were all cognizant of their purpose and the circumstances of their creation, she had worked hard to ensure that they were not spoken to as if they were property - regardless of how the Oversight Committee considered their status. It belied the psychological programming she had designed.

"Colonel Thomas," the General turned to the man who had overseen the final stages of training for the subjects. "Do you feel these individuals, the twenty-six and twenty-seven series of Project Barghest, are capable of field duty to the full extent expected?"

"Yes, sir," Thomas nodded his head, "they will exceed it. I am certain."

"Excellent. Then on your recommendation, the Sol Coalition Forces will take over from here. Project Barghest is now under the auspices of the military, not the Oversight Committee. No need to interrupt your schedule, or your Congressional budget, anymore, Representative Venegas." The Representative did not reply, but his chair scraped loudly on the floor as he pushed it back and stalked out of the room. "Now," the General glanced down at his tablet, clearly pleased with the results of the test mission, "by the authority granted to me by the Defense Minister, I hereby create the Thirteenth Legion, under the command of Colonel George Thomas, as an Operations and Support Special Access Program. Malak," the General paused, looking up and frowning at the injured male, "do you have a last name, son?"

"No, sir," Malak answered coolly, although he must have been confused by both the sudden familiarity from a human officer as well as the insinuation that he should have a family name.

"Hm, well, we'll consider Malak your surname - makes the paperwork easier. As I was saying, Malak, I am commissioning you into the Sol Coalition Terra Forces at the rank of Lieutenant 2nd Class with Field Command of the Legion. You will report to Colonel Thomas. Thomas, you have the full authority to commission additional officers below the rank of Lieutenant 2nd Class, as you see fit, from within Legion ranks, and submit requisitions for additional personnel if necessary. A discretionary budget will be transferred to you by the end of the week, and I expect a preliminary operations report and deployment recommendation by the time I get back to Sheng Station." He pressed his palm against his tablet to sign the order. The General's smile was bright against his dark skin when he looked up. "Dr. Gillian, I expect that you will prepare a final report for me as well. Until further funding is determined, Erasmus Research Station is on hold. If there is nothing else, I'll leave you to it."

Gillian was reeling. Her project was a success - the military was apparently ecstatic with the results. However, she was not. There was something wrong with Malak - with the entire research group. They had not turned out the way she had intended. They weren't supposed to behave the way that they had.

"Sir," Thomas stood as the General pushed away from the table. "I would like to inform you that the Legion has adopted a motto."

"Motto?" He chuckled, "Black ops means it won't be published anywhere, but go ahead, let's hear it."

Gillian stared, wide-eyed, as Thomas glanced to Malak and then back to the General. "Natus at mortem," he stated. The twist in Gillian's stomach became a wrenching cramp, the pain making her want to double over. Bile rose in the back of her throat. A fear she had never felt - not even when the Twenty-one series became feral and attacked her - froze her joints.

Born for Death.

What have we done?

CHAPTER 13: A LIE HAS NO LEGS

Black. Adjective. As used by the government, specifically military, to describe operations, budgets, and files that have the highest top secret classification. Only those individuals directly involved (writing the budget, carrying out the operation, etc.) and a single superior officer are aware of the situation. Those involved may be disavowed at any time.

Blackout. Adjective. A level above black for classified information. Individuals who gain any knowledge about the situation may be terminated by those authorized to have knowledge. Those involved do not exist.

Hour 1700
January 2, 2131

Ignition minus seventeen years.

"You have reached your destination," the transportation AI stated in a soothing British accent. Soledad Venegas stepped out of the car and took a deep breath. It never ceased to amaze him how fresh the air in the deep farming country of the United States was. He knew it could not be attributed entirely to the environmental efforts of Congress; the area had simply never been close enough to any heavily populated areas to experience the smog and acid rain that had plagued his home city of Rio. He stretched and grabbed his bag, waving to the security personnel that were nonchalantly guarding the farmstead.

A voice called out from the shadows of the open barn door, "Be with you in a moment, Soledad." The Representative shivered under his wool coat. Thankfully, no wind blew, but early January ensured that there was a hard crust of snow on the ground and his breath was visible. A gray speckled horse was lead out of the barn by an older woman. Her long, white braid was topped with a worn brown cowboy hat. Thick, serviceable denim pants, a heavy coat and well-used boots gave her the look of a seasoned worker. She pulled off a leather glove as she drew close enough to shake his hand. "Glad you could make it."

"I'm only sorry I missed the holidays, Helen." He smiled and quickly put his own hand back in his pocket. "Was the weather cooperative?"

"A white Christmas, as you can see," she nodded at the large snow piles in the yard. "Santa had plenty of space to land the sleigh. Come on, I'll walk you to the house." Helen turned, clucking at the horse, and began a leisurely stroll. Venegas slid the strap of his bag over his shoulder and followed.

"The little lady of the house was excited for her presents?"

"You would think my granddaughter was turning ten, instead of two. Waiting by the fireplace until she fell asleep there. And of course my son spoils her something terrible. Still, I reminded her you were coming, so I don't think you'll get away without a gift of your own."

"Oh, I remember when my children were young," he chuckled. "I brought something I think she'll like."

"How did it go?" The question was asked in the same tone, as though the conversation was still focused on weather and holiday plans.

"As expected. General Batma appointed Colonel Thomas to oversee the Legion." He patted his chest pocket. "I'll have to destroy it later, but I made you a copy of the mission film - it was quite remarkable."

"Legion," Helen snorted. "Batma could have had a career in marketing. I told him it was unnecessary to give them their own designation - it will draw attention before we are ready for it."

"Ah, then you will really be pleased that Thomas has apparently already named them. Keres Legion, he calls them. Although why, I have no idea."

"Well, aren't they just full of creativity," she murmured. Soledad couldn't tell if she was irritated or pleased. "The Keres were old gods that carried spirits to the underworld."

He whistled, making the horse's ears flicker. "That explains their motto, *Born for death*."

"Those two are like peas in a pod. I wonder if Batma was aware that Thomas has such a flair for the dramatic." Soledad shrugged and they walked in silence until they were nearly to the main house. Two stories of old-fashioned white painted clapboard and large, four pane windows was decorated with lights and garland. "Gillian and Batma know you'll shut down the program?" Helen looked at him for confirmation.

"Oh, I was very convincing. Even left in a huff." He stopped and turned to her before they came into earshot of the guard on the front porch. "The twenty-eight series are performing well in preliminary trials, and the twenty-nines have passed the benchmarks for their maturation rate. The thirties will be ready for extraction soon, on the schedule you dictated. I signed off on the budget to complete their training before the mission report came in. No one will be surprised when there is no funding for another series."

"Good." She placed one gloved hand on his sleeve to keep him from moving. "Soledad," she said seriously. Although she had more lines between her brows and around her mouth than when he had first met her, Helen Maker was still a handsome woman - blue-eyed and pink lipped. And even stronger and more determined than she had been at the start of her career. "I know you could have moved on to the Senate years ago, or retired, but I needed you on the Oversight Committee. Thank you."

He covered her gloved hand with his bare palm. The cold stung his skin. "What are old friends for?"

"Favors?" A smile quirked her mouth. "There is another issue we need to discuss, before you leave on Monday." Venegas repressed a sigh. Helen was a *very* old friend, but she was tenacious and dedicated to goals he could only understand a fraction of. A door banged open and a squeal interrupted further conversation.

Venegas held out his arms with a grin as a bundle of pink snow pants and black hair nearly tumbled off the porch in excitement. Blue eyes just like her grandmother's sparkled with happiness. He quickly stepped forward and swept her into a hug, "Happy Birthday, Clara!"

CHAPTER 14: KNOCK, KNOCK

Basebot. Noun. A mobile 3-D printer used by the Sol Coalition to build initial fortifications and temporary housing. Local source material such as sand or dirt can be extruded into nearly any shape including building blocks, interlocking pavers for temporary roads, even simple equipment such as helmets.
Ex. The basebots don't build attractive barracks – but it sure as hell beats a tent.

Hour 1130
April 23, 2148

Ignition minus four hours and fifteen minutes.

Maker watched with a combination of surprise and respect as Rodriguez reprogram the basebot. It was an older version, blocky and painted an unattractive shade of green that was supposed to distinguish it from competitors' models, but it had earned a reputation for poor-quality 3-D printing that quickly ended the contract from the Sol Coalition for purchase of the units. A meter tall cube which housed the printer sat on top of tank treads. Two specialized arms were designed with broad scoops to gather material.

The team of six, including herself, had been followed through the grass forest by a clunky robot. After a tedious walk far around the battlefield to reach a relatively unprotected side of the crater, Rodriguez had requested a halt under the canopy of grass to prepare the basebot. He had pried open the back panel. Then he had spent the next forty-five minutes murmuring sweet nothings to its innards. By the time he was finished, the robot would be modified to dig into the solid rock wall of the crater. It would be less noticeable, by far, than explosives, but Maker hadn't really believed it might work. In fact, when she had suggested that det cord might reduce their chances of remaining covert, she hadn't expected Rodriguez - or anyone else - to come up with an alternative. But he had. One that was both crazy and simple.

Simply crazy, Maker thought.

"Come on, baby," Rodriguez crooned, not for the first time. "You know you want to." Maker glanced to the side uncomfortably. Kerry was purposefully staring straight ahead, watching the narrow strip of exposed ground between them and the crater, and ignoring Rodriguez. Gonzales looked a little turned on.

Or not, Maker tried to reassure herself, *that could just be gas. Hopefully.*

"Gotcha!" The private's whispered exclamation drew the attention of the other two soldiers that had been assigned to guard their flanks.

"Are we good?" Maker asked.

"Just one more little - there." He returned a calibration tool to his pack and typed in a final command before closing the access panel on the robot. "She's good to go. Just get her up to the wall, and we'll be inside before you can offer me your gratitude."

"You don't get gratitude, Fuzz," Maker said, in an attempt to garner some degree of professionalism from him. "You get a paycheck. Which you cannot spend if we get mowed down by Cullers while we are waiting for your little friend to do its job. So, how fast will it be?"

Rodriguez did not appear chastised in the slightest. "You're welcome, Sarge." His eyes became a little unfocused. Maker was familiar with the gaze. The display provided by their stand-ard issue contacts was essential to interfacing with each other, their weapons, and their environment, but a large amount of such information was difficult to process while still really see-ing beyond the lens. Like a store window that had too many sales ads drawn on the glass, it could be nearly impossible to see the fresh produce behind all the words. "Looks like maybe ten-fifteen minutes at full power, but I think we should go slower. She'll be quieter at lower speeds. I recommend fifty percent."

Maker did some quick calculations. "You can have eighty per-cent, no less. Gonzales," the other female soldier was already at attention, helmet in hand and ready for orders. "Keep your partner on our rear, I don't want any surprises. Peters, set up for long-range support. I don't want anything coming over the top at us." The sniper, easily the most experienced of her team, nodded calmly and began to set up his rifle. The location wasn't ideal, with the crater ridge another twenty meters above them, but it had been selected for the small hill where they had stopped to work on the basebot. The rise would give them a running start to reach the crater wall, and was the only ad-vantage she could offer Peters. "Kerry, you're on point until we reach the target, then you take left. I have right."

Maker looked around at the faces of her team. Peters was just finishing his second tour. More than twenty years of experi-ence in the Coalition had given him a hard expression, an iron backbone, and a wicked scar that deformed his nose and pulled the corner of his mouth down in a perpetual frown. Gonza-les looked determined. Whatever trauma she had experienced from being trapped under her dead partner for eight hours had been shoved down so that she could do her job. *The SC shrinks are going to have a field day with her when we get back,* Maker thought with sympathy. The woman's new partner was even greener than Rodriguez and the pallor of his face gave the im-pression that he might puke at any moment. Maker wouldn't have held it against him, as long as he did it before they were under fire.

When she caught Kerry's eye, he nodded. "Okay," Maker said. She took a deep breath. "We get in, we look around, if we find something we can take advantage of, I'll consider it. Priority one is to get whatever information we can on a weak spot back to the Major. Secondary is to cripple the enemy, if possible. Got it?" There were no questions - not that she had much of anything else to add - so Maker put on her helmet. The others did the same and she opened a comm to the team. "Everyone comes out of this." She stared at their black, opaque face plates. It was supposed to be encouraging, but she could hear her own voice. She sounded too serious. Too low. Too real. She tried again, "Everyone goes home." Maker was still certain that her words were more ominous than comforting, but there were nods of agreement around her, so she gave up trying.

"Hotel-Quebec, Hotel-Quebec, Hotel-Quebec," she punched in her authorization code as she spoke, leaving her line open for the rest of her team to hear, "This is Zulu-actual, over."

"This is Hotel-Quebec-niner, over."

"This is Zulu, we are in position. Over."

There was a slight delay, then, "This is HQ-actual." Maker recognized the authority in Major Ben Zvi's voice. "Proceed as you will. Over."

Her palms felt clammy in her gloves. "This is Zulu. Tango minus twenty-five. Over."

"This is HQ-actual. Good Luck. Out."

Maker's heart shuddered under the weight of responsibility. There was a great deal left unspoken in that statement.

If you fail, another, even less experienced, team will be sent to sabotage the Culler ship. They will not come back.

If you fail, there is no one to pull you out.

If you fail, we will all die.

The countdown timer on her visual display turned red, indicating there were only ten seconds left. "Everyone goes home," she repeated through the team channel. She didn't have time to think about if she sounded encouraging or not. Commanding or not. Afraid or not. The timer hit zero. "Go, go, go!"

Maker and her team rushed down the hill, the base bot following behind them. In the distance, the loud echo of heavy weapon fire reverberated along the crater wall, signaling that the rest of the Coalition forces had begun an assault to help conceal Maker's approach. She was conscious of Peters on the hill, waiting for a Culler target to appear. Of Kerry, running just ahead of her, his weapon scanning with his eyes for danger. The sound of combined breaths over the comm was a quiet background for the percussive beat of her boots against the ground.

It was over in seconds, the mad sprint to the crater wall, but it was a full five minutes before Maker's heart stopped racing. She dropped to one knee, rifle braced against her shoulder, watching for any approach. She did not turn to look at the others, hoping they were following orders. If they weren't there was nothing she could do about it while still protecting their flank. Her proximity comm alerted her to Rodriguez's progress. The wet, vibrating sound of the basebot cutting into rock seemed loud in her ears. She checked the decibel level. Acceptable. Not ideal, but acceptable.

After ten minutes, she spoke into the team channel, "Check in."

"Left, clear," Kerry said calmly.

"Rear One, clear," said the rookie. His voice was still shaking. Whether from the run or nerves, Maker couldn't tell.

"Rear Two, clear," said Gonzales.

"Rear," repeated Rodriguez with a chuckle, "I'll bet your-"

"Mechanics," Maker snapped. She had to work to keep from letting her smile into her voice. She was sure Gonzales was barely holding back from smacking Rodriguez.

"Mechanics, on target," Rodriguez replied. "The volume is louder than-"

"Leave it," Maker interrupted. She would have preferred that they work quieter as well, but speed was equally important. The longer they were exposed against the wall of the crater, the more likely it was they would be discovered. *And shot. Or stabbed. Or slowly eviscerated and then quartered. Ground between beak and bone like hamburger.* Another ten minutes had almost passed, and Maker was getting ready for a check-in, when Peters' voice came through.

"Movement, on the ridge. Three unfriendlies. Twenty meters, your left. Closing fast."

Maker could feel the immediate tension in the team as easily as she could feel a twitch building in her neck. There were few things that unsettled a soldier quite like knowing the enemy was at behind them. "Hold positions. Mechanics, cut power." The low whine of the basebot died off and the sound of cutting rock faded.

"Ten meters," Peters said. "Slowing." Maker held her breath and carefully put her finger on the trigger. "Full stop," Peters announced quietly. "Shooting solution for only two." Maker knew there was no way that Peters would be able to hit all three. She trusted him if he said he could get two before they climbed down the crater wall, but even that would be a miracle of precision aiming and speed. If they were lucky, only one Culler would land on their position and kill two or three soldiers before they could take it down. If they were unlucky, it would go for backup.

"Hold," Maker ordered. There was still a chance that they hadn't been spotted. She had chosen the location carefully, and the base bot was digging just under an odd rock outcropping. Unless the Cullers leaned far out over the side the ridge - purposefully looking - they might not notice there were five humans right underneath of them. She toggled her ammunition for a gravity net. It could take a half dozen shots to bring down a Culler, and she doubted she would have time for more than two. The better play was to immobilize, rather than terminate.

"Recount," Peters announced. Maker wanted to swear as the sniper kept adding worse news to bad. "Five unfriend-lies. They're..." his voice died out, then he swore creatively. "They're moving a laser cannon. To your right, five meters and increasing. Ten...Twenty."

The rookie let out a sigh of relief, but Maker felt sick. Although it had just become significantly easier for them to breach the crater, there was only one reason that the defensive weapon from the ridge above them would be moved. The Cullers were going to step up the assault on the base trenches. "Mechanics, resume. One hundred percent." The Coalition forces had been barely maintaining position and managing losses. If the Cullers abandoned their defense plans and turned all of their firepower on the Coalition, it would be a bloodbath. *They'll be lucky to survive the day*, thought Maker. The rasp of blades on rock and the whir of the water mister picked up pace and volume. There was no further talk on the comms, and Rodriguez quietly an-nounced he was finished only eight minutes later.

The robot backed out of the cut. Kerry stepped into the tunnel first. He had to turn almost sideways to fit his broad shoulders through the narrow space, but after four meters he announced that it opened up into a wider passage. *Lucky day*, Maker thought with relief. The tunnels had been a good guess, not a sure thing, and the fear that they had spent so much time and resources on a potential boondoggle had been weighing heavily on her. The others followed Kerry in, leaving Maker to bring up the rear. She punched in the shutdown code on the basebot, then opened a direct channel to Peters.

"Four hours," she said, to be certain he remembered the agreed upon wait time. "Keep this exit clear, if you can. But if you haven't heard from us by then, blow the bot and get the hell out of here."

"I thought 'everyone goes home'," Peters said, an impressively small amount of sarcasm in his voice.

"That includes you, veteran," she answered. "I'll take care of these yayhoos, you just keep yourself alive, and don't let anyone airbomb my tunnels before time is up."

"Yes, ma'am." He had turned on the camouflage feature in his armor suit, and she could barely make out the flicker of movement as he saluted. Pink, feathery seeds and thick dark grasses swayed in a slight breeze around him.

"Damn straight," she responded. She was gratified, as she entered the tunnel, to hear his snort of laughter before the rock of the crater prevented communications.

CHAPTER 15: STRATEGIC MILESTONES

Vindloo Factor. Noun. Standardized test evaluating the subject's ability to cope with stressful situations and decisions which may harm others or the subject. Lower scores indicate aptitude for compartmentalization and suitability for front line or high-tension assignments. Higher scores indicate a tendency towards emotionally charged responses to pressure and development of post-traumatic stress disorder.

Ex. Incidence of high Vindloo Factors have been steadily decreasing over time, making for a more robust fighting force.

Hour 0700
October 21, 2138

Ignition minus ten years.

"Gregory Maker," the Prime Minister said with exasperation into her phone, "are you honestly telling me you are going to deny your child the right to see her mother?"

Avani Sudarshan did her best to appear as though she could not clearly hear the conversation. She sipped her coffee and kept her gaze resolutely on the colorful leaves slowly falling in the garden. During her tour of Versailles when she first took office as a Representative, the guide had pointed out significant renovations and historically sensitive additions. The Palace could accommodate offices and meeting rooms for over eight hundred elected officials as well as the Congressional halls for the lower and upper houses. Additional structures had been added nearby, along with an extensive excavation under the palace itself, to provide space for staff and government appointees. Everything had been done according to French regulations - giving the entire campus the uninterrupted look of a 17th century planned community. No vehicles were allowed on the grounds, and so politicians and gardeners alike were often seen walking into the surrounding city to get transportation to Paris, where the President's offices were located. Her attempt to focus on the details of gardening and architecture was interrupted by the Prime Minister's voice.

"You won the court case, Greg....Yes, however- please don't interrupt...Do you think she will entice a ten-year old away? I doubt it...There is nothing more important to that woman than her career. Clara is a smart girl, she will see that...Thank you...Yes, and please let me know how it goes. I love you too." The phone was handed over to a guard. Behind dark glasses and a stoic expression he was doing a much better job than Sudarshan of looking disinterested. "Children," Helen Maker said with a charming smile, "they call for asking advice - but really are hoping you'll say what they want to hear."

Sudarshan smiled back reflexively and nodded. The older woman took a seat. She poured herself a cup of coffee, adding milk and sugar from the provided tray. They sipped in silence for a few minutes, while Sudarshan tried to determine why she had been summoned. It had been nearly twenty years since the last time she had met privately with the Prime Minister. A reprieve Sudarshan had been grateful for. After being exiled to India for that summer so long ago, she had returned in the fall of 2119 to her seat in the House of Representatives and given her support for the Emancipation and Suffrage bill. It had taken years once the Constitution was amended to give GMH individuals rights for her to regain her popularity. Sudarshan should have been proud of what she had accomplished since then. Huge strides in environmental efforts in Earth's oceans. Reform for the punitive work colonies. A relaxation on corporate restrictions. Her election to the Senate in 2128 should have been a crowning achievement.

However, in the back of her mind, she could always hear a whispered reminder: *your career was never yours to take care of.* Knowing how delicate a hand had guided her election to the House only made her question every victory, every failure. Which were hers, and hers alone? Did it matter? She had done good things, great things, improved lives. She had done some things that she was not proud of either, but not since the E&S bill had she ever been asked to vote contrary to her beliefs. *I am my own person,* she reminded herself. *No one owns me. I can leave at any time. I will leave,* she resolved, *publicly, if the Prime Minister thinks she can push me to act again.* With those thoughts strengthening her spine, Sudarshan set down her cup and opened her mouth.

The Prime Minister beat her to it, "I have decided to step down."

Sudarshan blinked and snapped her teeth shut. Vivid blue eyes waited placidly for her response, but she had none. Helen Maker had cut her teeth on international politics. She had held the seat of Prime Minister for a record three terms. The idea that the wolf in sheep's clothing in front of her would willingly give up that kind of power was unbelievable.

"That...must have been a difficult decision for you," Sudarshan floundered.

"Indeed. However, it is time for something new, a bit more out of the public eye." The junior Senator felt like she was listening to an extremely unfunny mad lib - none of the words made sense. Helen Maker was the least public politician in the Senate. She rarely took interviews, stating that her voting record spoke for itself, and was notorious for holding marathons of private meetings and closed town hall sessions with her constituency. She had once been quoted as saying that inviting the press to listen to an official answer questions was the surest way to hear a lie. Sudarshan wasn't certain if that was something the woman actually believed or merely election propaganda, but either way the Prime Minister was rarely in the public eye.

"Oh," she responded inelegantly.

"Perhaps something that peaks my interest will open up when the new Administration takes office." The Prime Minister picked a dainty toast point from the tray and spread it with clotted cream. "So many appointments change hands when a President is sworn in."

That comment turned Sudarshan's bewildered silence into a sharp expectation. Nothing the Prime Minister ever said was flippant or one-dimensional. A junior Senator from the subcontinent was not so egotistical to think she had been summoned to a private breakfast meeting just so that she could be the first to hear of Helen Maker's pending retirement and personal observations on administrative offices. It was also exceedingly strange that the woman would speak as though an incumbent, from her own party, would not be reelected. As far as Sudarshan knew, the President's party nomination was already assured. The press called his reelection a shoe-in.

"That is true," Sudarshan said after a long silence. "But a fresh perspective might be beneficial to some agencies."

Steam rose from a delicate porcelain cup, creating a warm mist in the cool autumn air. "It is unfortunate that you missed your train today." The Prime Minister's abrupt change of topic had Sudarshan reeling again. "But since you did, you might as well stay the weekend in Paris. Perhaps you will even run into some old friends this evening. Jon Ainsley and his family have an apartment on the Seine. They often eat at a little place on the river." Maker named a small restaurant that Sudarshan had never heard of, but she committed it to memory. She had, of course, met Ainsley, the chair for her political party, but she would not have said they were *old friends*. "If you should see him, do be certain to say hello for me."

The Prime Minister asked her guard for the phone, and Sudarshan took that as her dismissal. As she walked past manicured lawns and artfully trimmed shrubs, the Senator was reviewing every scrap of information she had heard about Jon Ainsley, Helen Maker, or the Sol Confederation President. There were hundreds of possibilities, all with repercussions that went far beyond a simple election.

***

Two Years Later...

Soledad Venegas knew he shouldn't take another skewer of grilled meat and vegetables. He certainly didn't need it. The former Congressional Representative ran one hand over the love handles that had appeared around his sixty-fifth birthday and had stubbornly remained. He glanced over at the media coverage playing on a wall display. The news anchor was still making small talk. It could be another hour before the election results were announced. He shrugged and took a third shish-ka-bob. It was real beef, after all, not the printed protein that tasted like meat. An expensive and rare treat that Helen Maker only offered her closest friends.

"Uncle Sole?" Clara's freckled face, followed by a frizzy black ponytail and knobby, skinny body, popped around the doorway from the dining room. He wasn't really her uncle, but he and his wife had been spending a significant amount of time at the Maker farm since his retirement from politics. "Daddy wants to know if you need another beer."

"Clara," Helen reprimanded lightly from her place on the sofa with Venegas' wife.

"Sorry, Grams." Clara did not sound at all sorry, and it made Venegas grin. "Uncle Sole," she began again in an overly formal voice. She affected an accent that he thought was supposed to be British. "Would you care for another refreshment, sir?"

"I thank you for the offer, kind miss, but I am fully refreshed." He gave a little bow and was rewarded with a bright smile full of sparkling braces. The orthodontics were unusual to see anymore, but Greg Maker had insisted that his daughter not receive any genetic therapy if it wasn't medically necessary. It was already apparent that the eleven-year old was going to be shorter than average. Venegas wondered what other challenges Clara would face due to her father's bohemian views.

"Thank you, Clara," Helen called out as the child waved and bounced back toward the kitchen.

"Wow, grandma," Venegas teased, "are you the manners police?" He sat in a nearby armchair, but did not have the opportunity to even take a bite before his wife was turning up the volume.

"Shh, they are announcing it," she said.

"Votes from all precincts have not yet come in, but the results are conclusive. Avani Sudarshan has swept the election. In January, Ms. Sudarshan will be sworn in as the next President of the Sol Confederation. Let's go to Henri, reporting from the government district in Paris." Venegas sat down his plate, the beef forgotten.

"Well," his wife exclaimed, muting the reporter again, "who would have seen that coming eighteen months ago?"

"The public can be unpredictable," Helen agreed. Venegas didn't say anything. Helen hadn't spoken of it directly, but no change in their political party - especially one at the highest level - happened without her input. He could guess that she had done far more than comment on a replacement that was so unexpected.

Greg and Clara entered, and Venegas' wife turned to them to discuss the results. Helen's phone rang, and she stepped into the study to answer it. The door, right behind Venegas' chair, was not closed all the way, so he heard clearly when she spoke.

"Congratulations, Avani…I am sure you have a celebration waiting for you…" There was a long silence. Venegas watched Clara, pretending to be sworn into office. She had her right hand on an empty cookie plate, in place of the Sol Constitution. "Thank you for considering me, Avani," Helen finally continued. "I would have to think about it, of course. My decision to retire was not one I made lightly.…If you really feel I would be able to do some good…Yes, I'll let you know next week." She offered congratulations again, that time in Hindi, before stepping back into the living room. Their eyes met briefly. Venegas felt, in that moment, every one of his years. He was nearly three-quarters done with his life, and Helen seemed like she was just getting started.

"Grams, do you think I would make a good President?" Clara was standing on a footstool, failing miserably at looking impressively Presidential in her torn denims. She held a half-eaten skewer of beef and vegetables in one hand, using it like a microphone, and the cookie plate in the other.

"Oh, you can be anything you want, my dear. And I am sure you will be exceptional at it." Helen smiled, and Venegas was struck with a cold reality. His old friend had the same expression for her granddaughter that she did when manipulating military leaders. "Why stop with such a limiting career?"

Greg laughed, and so did Venegas' wife. He couldn't manage more than a tight smile, though, as Clara took the suggestion with all the seriousness of a child. "Right!" She threw her arms open wide, "Empress Clara! Benevolent leader of the Galaxy!" The remains of her shish-ka-bob flew off of the stick and hit the wall with a splatter of marinade and smoky tomato. "Well," she said, looking at the mess and the disapproving expression on her father's face, "that or a jockey."

"Go get a rag, Empress Jockey," Greg ordered. Clara grumbled and slumped away.

Venegas was looking at Helen. The calculation in her gaze, focused entirely on a little girl, was frightening.

CHAPTER 16: NOSEY NEIGHBORS

Dark:(noun) as in, *The Dark*. Space between solar systems where the effects of the gravitational pull of objects (e.g. stars) has no discernible effect on ISG drives, providing the widest margin of error for safe departure and reentry into sublight space travel. Note: also allows interstellar travel that leaves no commonly monitored trail.

Ex. The freighter captain made certain to take a deck of cards as her route would require three months in the Dark.

Hour 0630
March 11, 2148

Ignition minus forty-three days.

Malak wrapped his fingers around the edge of the table in his ready room and squeezed. The metal could withstand his grip, and the crew working on the bridge could not see him, so he considered the small loss of control acceptable. The dark brown skin over his knuckles whitened under the pressure. Almaut was still speaking on the main screen, his pale forehead furrowed with irritation. Smaller windows at the side of Almaut's image showed the other betas. Kapziel was cleaning a weapon while he listened. Giltine had a tablet in front of her, on which she was doubtless taking notes. Skoll leaned far back in a chair, frowning thoughtfully. Their weekly meeting had started poorly and continued to deteriorate.

"- ignoring requisitions is one thing, misplacing intelligence is another. I forced the brief through the new firewall, it will pop up on Admiral Tsang's defense system feed in twelve hours, but what he does with it will be another matter entirely. Thomas said he would speak with Batma about it, but the General is scheduled to be in meetings at Opik Station all week. I can hack a direct comm from Thomas to Batma, but the local station security will know about it within a few minutes."

"Without Batma, Tsang will be listening to his Congressional liaison," Skoll noted, still frowning. "If recent actions are an indication, he is more likely to favor caution rather than risk letting the public get ahold of any news of a surge in deployments."

"Sending a single scout ship to the VK10 System," Giltine made a sound somewhere between a snort and a laugh, "he might as well direct them to fly into a quasar, for all the good it will do."

"The Coalition would be better off leaving the Cullers on VK10 alone and letting us take care of it, if they can't get an entire task group in there." Skoll leaned forward, causing the blue-tinted light of the planet he was on to glint in his eyes. They shifted from red to green. "You're sure you can't send that message to Tsang?"

Almaut growled, uncharacteristically losing his humor. "If I had known that the SIS was going to graduate from annoying misplacement of supplies to blackballing our intelligence, I would have taken care of it. But I can't tell the future."

"You could push it through, if you weren't working so hard to keep the humans from finding out about us," Kapziel stated with feigned nonchalance. Skoll snapped his teeth with impatience at the old argument. Giltine hissed a warning. Almaut ran a hand over his face.

"That is true," Malak finally interrupted their conversation. All eyes snapped to him, and he knew they were surprised by his comment. It had grown increasingly difficult in the last eighteen months to carry out their directives without letting the rank-and-file of the Sol Coalition know they existed. Or worse, handing the SIS – the Sol Intelligence Service - proof of the Thirteenth Legion's actions. The SIS had been a minor irritation for years, but had recently stepped up from paltry attempts at disrupting requisitions to a blockade of information between the Legion and Coalition leadership. The situation was growing intolerable.

Malak knew his people were good. Better than human soldiers. The best at what they did. However, they were still only 500 individuals. Less than a full battalion. Although they were faster, stronger, and trained for nothing but war, they could not be everywhere at once. Almaut had eyes and ears across the local arm of the galaxy - and some a good deal further away than that. His intelligence pointed to a massing of Culler activity on a small planet in the VK10 system. The activity was suspiciously like a few other instances that they had investigated, and destroyed, over the years. Only once had they found any indications that the type of work discovered during their training mission was ongoing, but Malak was constantly wary of it. That had been the first documented Culler defense base - a permanent outpost with installations and apparent research being conducted. He had planned to investigate the possibilities as soon as the mission docket was lighter.

That was the crux of the matter. There were always other missions. Skoll was seven star systems away from their base of operations - in the opposite direction from Malak. He had the bulk of the twenty-eight and twenty-nine series, each a full company of one hundred, serving under him on Legion business. Their position was necessary to combat a cell of Culler ships which were moving toward Sol-controlled space. Giltine had most of their own company, the twenty-sevens, with her on a deep Dark run to get around a human-Nick trade route and destroy a Culler supply base. Kapziel had just completed a mission a thousand light-years from Sol and would be weeks returning. Almaut had his hands full managing his intelligence network and dodging the childish spycraft of the SIS. Malak was the closest to the VK10 system, but he was supervising a training exercise with the youngest company in the Legion. The thirties were not ready for live combat on that scale.

There might not be another opportunity.

"Finally going to bite the hand that feeds you, Lieutenant?" Kapziel's use of Malak's rank, afforded by the Sol Coalition, added a tone of disrespect to the question. Malak had carried the same title for eighteen years, and expected to do so for the rest of his life. All in service to his creators. Malak did not have to say anything; he turned his stare on Kapziel and the beta lowered his eyes after a few seconds. The older male did not intend to challenge his Alpha, Malak knew, but they were all bitter over their position within the military. Kapziel was simply more outspoken about it. Regardless of how much their place out of sight and mind sometimes chafed, they were all dedicated to their duty. Protect humanity. Destroy the enemy. Humans, intentions aside, had created the Legion. Cullers had killed Legionnaires. With the two combined, his choice was easy.

"No," Malak answered finally, "but we will save the Coalition from the interference of the SIS."

"Again?" Skoll asked with a grin that revealed his sharper-than-human teeth.

"Okay," Giltine agreed, "but you'll have to kill gravity drives in that area, or you know Tsang will send someone to take a look-see and then all hell will break loose."

Almaut flicked some information onto the shared screen. "Malak, it looks like you have all of the equipment in your inventory. Parshav shouldn't have any trouble building a few Gravitron Apples for you. The rookies will get some good hands-on experience out of that." Malak considered the proposal. Almaut had come up with a device for disrupting interstellar travel shortly after they were promoted to the field. He and Parshav and refined the idea, a Gravitron Apple, but had only tested it once. Malak would have preferred to take care of the problem himself, but that wasn't an option. The best alternative then, was to make certain that the Cullers already at VK10 couldn't leave, and that no reinforcements could arrive. There was an outside chance that the Sol Coalition might send a ship into the system on sublight engines, but it would take weeks to reach the planet even if they came out of ISG drive on the edge of the Dark. And that was assuming they had any captains in the vicinity. Captains that were extremely dedicated to duty, overly ambitious, and risk takers. It was unlikely the SC would have anyone in place before Malak could finish the training mission, return the thirties to base, and get back to VK10.

"Giltine," he said quietly. The rough quality to his voice had not faded from his injury on that first mission, and the sound reverberated against the plastiglass door of the ready room, causing the bridge crew to raise their heads and glance his way. "We will hit VK10 in five weeks." He said nothing more about the matter, but continued on to the next subject that needed to be discussed. "The new ship design under construction by the SC is inferior. How would you improve upon it?"

While they discussed various flaws in the plans, he accessed information about Coalition deployments. There were no ships in the same sector as VK10, but a *Sidus* class battleship, the *Pershing*, was in an adjacent system. Her current course was taking her away from VK10. Another Coalition ship, the *Perry*, one of the new *Ferox* class destroyers, was on her maiden voyage. It was likely she had been ordered to stay on course and test her engines. She was so fresh from the construction yard at Europa her paint was probably still wet. *A newly-minted captain,* Malak thought. *Too young and worried about getting their crew under control to take a chance on investigating.* That was good. The less interference in his plan, the better.

The next topic gained his full attention. Almaut said, "I pulled a couple of the humans-"

"Falcon Platoon," Skoll interrupted. Of all of them, he was the most careful to never denigrate humanity. Despite their physical superiority, Malak and his betas knew that the humans had several advantages over the Legion. Numbers. Political power. Varied experience and education. Freedom.

"I pulled some soldiers from *Falcon* away from admin and intel," Almaut amended with a roll of his eyes. "I've got them working on our side project, but if I don't make headway soon, I'll have to agree with Thomas that it's time to turn it over to the Ministry of Science and Research." For nearly two decades they had been analyzing the data, and what few pieces of technology had been salvaged from their training mission, to try and determine what the Cullers had been up to on that planet. It had been an exercise in frustration. Just as they were prepared to give up, some new whisper of intelligence or abandoned Culler devices would give them a hint and send them in a new direction. Malak hoped, privately, that VK10 might provide some answers.

"Give Falcon Platoon six months," he decided. "If they don't have any breakthroughs, we're finished with it." Malak had worked hard to get a unit of humans - trained scientists, researchers, and support staff - cleared through military security and assigned to his command. He couldn't allow any misuse of their talents and time. They spent another twenty minutes discussing personnel issues and some minor mission intelligence before Malak ended the meeting.

He stepped out onto the bridge of the small ship Thomas had requisitioned for training exercises. It was an older, retrofitted cargo hauler. From the outside, and over visual comms, it looked thirty years out of date and barely capable of reaching the next star system. Behind the flaking ceramic shield and cargo doors pock-marked from micro-impacts, the *Lead Belly* held a tremendous amount of firepower. Old-fashioned high consoles on the bridge concealed technology that had not yet been released to the rank-and-file Coalition. Narrow, dark corridors split off into dozens of bunk rooms and well-equipped training facilities for the hundred new soldiers on board and the twenty-six senior personnel that were supervising them. The cargo bay was packed with military grade supplies. What had once been passenger rooms had been converted to house enough weapons to start a small war. Or end one.

Smierc turned toward him as he entered. "That freighter is hailing us again. They have altered course slightly to come alongside us."

"Assessment," he stated, coming to stand beside her at the command console.

"No tactical threat." She paused, a smile quirking at the corner of her mouth. "I believe they want to socialize." Malak raised one eyebrow. It wasn't too surprising. Long-range cargo ships could spend months between ports. While the Legion was not immune to the effects of isolation, humans were not as conditioned to tolerate it. It was a common practice, and considered a courtesy, when crossing paths with another hauler to cruise together for a few days and exchange social customs. As a black book unit the Legion could not allow themselves to interact with the general population. The sight of a ship full of genetically modified soldiers would be unsettling to civilians – at best. At worst, it was a violation of his mission parameters and would require the termination of the civilians. It would be a waste of ammunition and result in significant hours filling out forms. And would require action to make certain they never spread a word about it. "I told them I would notify the Captain.

They are waiting on a response."

"Standard rejection," Malak ordered.

Smierc nodded and punched up a comm line. "*Dolcezza*," she said calmly. Her smooth, low voice was as familiar to Malak as his own growl. "This is *Lead Belly*. Unfortunately, my Captain has denied the request to dock. We have a mild outbreak of influenza, and that means no unnecessary air exchange until we get it locked down. Hopefully there will be a next time. Over."

"This is *Dolcezza*," a male voice came over the comm. "Sorry to hear that, *Lead Belly*, but we don't mind a few runny noses if you don't. We're just happy to see a friendly smile. Over."

Smierc let out an irritated breath and glanced at Malak. He shook his head and walked over to the sensor station to check the readout on the other ship himself. If it was anything more than a lonely hauler, the crew of the *Dolcezza* was hiding it exceptionally well.

"This is *Lead Belly*. That does sound nice, *Dolcezza*, but as I said earlier, our visual comms aren't working quite right. We'll have to wait until we make it to port to let our hair down." The soldier manning the sensory station gestured with a half-eaten MRE bar and mouthed 'hair down' with a questioning tilt of her chin. Malak ignored her. He spoke a few Earth languages, but the idioms rarely made sense. Smierc was better than most of them at using the strange phrases correctly. It was why she was assigned comms. She passed for human better than most of them.

"This is *Dolcezza*. I have a few mechanics over here that are pretty good. How about we come over and give you a hand." There was a chuckle that was no doubt intended to be disarming. Malak found it annoying. "Promise we won't kiss anyone with a fever."

Smierc was looking both amused and frustrated, so Malak motioned to her that he would turn on the video feed. *Better to get this over with*, he thought. He hated acting. Smierc pulled a worn civilian jacket from a crate near the console, and took out her ponytail. Her long red hair covered her pointed ears. The soldier at sensors pulled on a hooded vest and handed a checkered cloth to Malak. He carefully draped it over his head and around his neck. The disguises worked well, in low lighting, as long as there weren't any humans standing around for comparison. A female trainee from the thirty series, just learning the weapons post, snapped a headband over her ears with an excited grin. Malak gestured to his own pointed teeth, reminding her not to show off her canines, and pressed the command for visual comms. The forward wall of the bridge pulsed to life, revealing a sharp image of the bridge of the *Dolcezza*. A man in his prime sat in the captain's chair. Several other males, all the same age or slightly younger than their leader, were standing eagerly nearby.

Ah, Malak thought with growing irritation. He was aware that the researchers on Project Barghest had spent several series trying to curb the instinct to procreate. The Legion was designed to be fully focused on their duty. Of course, some of the Legionnaires who spent long periods with individuals not related to them - such as Falcon Platoon - exhibited a desire for intimate activities. Still, it was surprising to him how focused humans were on their need for sex. Even in the poor lighting, Smierc would be considered attractive by the humans. Add her physique and odd eye coloring to that of Ondrea at sensors and the rookie at weapons, and the *Dolcezza* would be nearly impossible to get rid of.

"Thank you for the offer, *Dolcezza*, but it looks like our mechanics are already solving the problem. We won't trouble you. Over."

"No trouble, *Lead Belly*." The captain leaned forward in his chair, and Malak could see the man's eyes traveling over Smierc's open jacket. Smierc had been raised as pack, comparable to a sister in human families. She shared a significant portion of his DNA as well - everyone in his series did. In the abstract, he could understand that she was attractive. But having fought, eaten, slept, and showered with her since he could remember killed any desire that genetics and behavioral programming might have left alive. Even the rookie was pack - family - to him. The delay due to the attractiveness of his *sisters* was aggravating. "Maybe we could learn something from you," the Captain cajoled. "We can have a small boarding party over there in ten minutes."

Smierc did not look over at her Alpha, but she made a low, questioning sound in her throat. It would have been easier to get rid of friendly traders who wanted to help a ship in need. Lonely, instinct driven males would be more difficult. *Instinct.* Although the Legion was more in tune to survival and hunting than procreation, the crews on both ships had the same urges. The same instinct for self-preservation. It could be used to advantage. Malak stepped around the command station, looming behind his beta. Smierc was tall, but he would dwarf even the largest human male he had ever met.

"No one boards my ship," he said calmly. The unavoidable rough burr in his voice made the Captain flinch.

Smierc noticed and continued diplomatically. "Our crew can take care of any necessary repairs, and the standard Sol Confederation Health Procedure demands that we minimize risk of infection. Sorry, again, *Dolcezza.* But I'm sure we'll see you out there." The Captain finally seemed to come to terms with the situation, but still transmitted his course and a direct comm code to Smierc before he cut communications.

"Next time," Ondrea said after a long pause, "can't we just shoot them?" Smierc snorted and then ducked her face to let her long hair hide her laughter.

The rookie hesitatingly asked, "Are they all so....insistent about making friends?"

"That man," Ondrea said between barely suppressed chuckles, "did not want to be Smierc's friend."

Smierc ignored Ondrea, and replied to the younger female, "When we get back, ask one of the Falcons to explain it to you."

"Do not encourage such behavior," Malak said disapprovingly. The rookie whined submissively at his tone. Some of the Legion might have embraced a deeply buried biological imperative, but it would make missions exceedingly difficult to plan if that became standard practice. They had more important issues to deal with, starting with preventing the Sol Coalition from walking into a Culler ambush. "Have Parshav in my ready room, five minutes," he ordered Smierc. "You have the bridge."

As he returned to the utilitarian space that doubled as office and conference room, he heard Ondrea speaking to the rookie. "Alpha isn't pissed at you, kid, so no whimpering. I'll draw you a diagram later."

Smierc choked back her laughter long enough to mutter under her breath, "Maybe Malak should have someone draw *him* a diagram."

Malak let the insult go as if he hadn't heard it. The training mission had been long, and the crew deserved a little lightheartedness. He closed the door behind him and let out a hard breath. Maybe they all needed a break. *We last took leave...* Malak sucked in air, surprised at his own calculations. It had been almost a year since any of the Legion was off duty. Leave for them was restricted to a few days on uninhabited planets, but the value of that time unconcerned with danger or duty was incalculable. Malak resolved to schedule some rotations as soon as the issue with VK10 was settled.

He stared out the window at stars slowly passing at sublight speeds. It wasn't just the lack of vacation. They were born to be soldiers. *Born for Death*, he reminded himself. They didn't technically need any time to recover, psychologically, from war. There were other aspects to their duty, however, that wore them down.

Tedium.

Reports. Frustrated intelligence and missions thwarted. Covert encounters with irritating humans. As he waited for Parshav, Malak came to the realization that he was verging on burnout. It was inevitable, he supposed. Even he could only go so long without a challenge, without new experiences. He picked up a tablet and opened the files for the Gravitron Apple. Blockading a star system was new. Perhaps, if he was lucky, when he returned to deal with the Cullers they might present a piece to the puzzle Almaut and Falcon Company were working on.

CHAPTER 17: WHO'S THERE?

Technological and Biological Interface Device, a.k.a. *TABI.* Noun. Also commonly referred to by the generic term, implants. TABI comprise a wide range of software and hardware components that can be integrated into the human body, surgically or by injection, to regulate, stabilize, or increase performance in physical or cognitive areas as well as provide increased interaction with technology outside the subject body.
Ex. She had two TABI: a standard communications implant and neural sensors for a prosthetic hand.

Hour 1400
April 23, 2148

Ignition minus one hour forty-eight minutes.

Maker crouched across from Kerry and tried to breathe quietly. Although the perfectly shaped tunnels made walking easy, they also carried sound long distances. Because a high zinc and iron content in the rock interfered with the range of their tech, they were forced to rely on more primitive means of searching for the enemy. Their ears.

Kerry was well suited to the task, but it made Maker nervous. In order to best use his genetically superior hearing he had removed his helmet. With her night vision switched on, the warm skin on the back of his neck glowed soft and vulnerable. Cullers were faster than humans. Their hearing was better. They made up for poor color sight with a sort of echo location that gave them eerie accuracy, even in the dark. Sneaking around in their base without using every advantage she had would be stupid. *I've done stupid things before,* Maker reflected as she considered how easily a Culler talon could pierce Kerry's skull. *It wasn't that bad.* A phantom pain in her shoulder belied her thoughts.

Kerry gestured to the y-intersection a few meters ahead of them. He placed his hand over his mouth to keep his words from echoing and spoke quietly. "At least three on the right, moving away quickly. One on the left, maybe, but there is some clanking."

Maker raised an eyebrow. Kerry was usually concise and specific to a fault. "Like a mechanical sound?" Her words were transmitted directly to Kerry's implant. He paused again, tipping his head and listening, then nodded.

A bead of sweat trickled down her temple. The tunnels ran deep, and they had been slowly making their way lower for nearly two hours. She was hot, and could smell her own nervous sweat in her armor suit. They had only run into one Culler, who had seemed just as surprised to see them as they had been to see it. Kerry, in lead position, had shot a non-lethal round at point-blank range. Right into the alien's face. Although the hit had made it viciously angry, it had also disabled its vocal ability. Suppression rounds fired by four weapons and Kerry's knife in the thing's hip had taken it down far easier than Maker had anticipated. Since then, the only signs of life they had come across were distant movement. All of the Cullers were making their way to the front line to face the Coalition. Except one. One Culler and a clanking sound. Maker knew well the expression about cats and curiosity, but in this instance she couldn't ignore the whisper in the back of her mind.

What is so important to keep a Culler from the fight? Why dig these tunnels? Why defend them?

"Left," she ordered. "Slow and steady. I've got point. Kerry, behind me, ears open." She knew he wanted to argue, but she wasn't going to stare at his exposed head for the rest of the mission - imagining what his brain would look like spattered on the wall. It was another twenty minutes of soft steps, pauses, and listening before Kerry tapped her shoulder.

"Twenty meters." His voice was so low her receiver barely picked it up. "Down and curving around to the left."

"Weapons ready." Maker added, "Assess first and try not to shoot me." A nervous giggle, presumably from the rookie, came over the comm and then was stifled.

One step. Two. Five. Each footfall sounded loud in her helmet. The slight crunch of dust and pebbles under boots made her stomach clench. She reached the bend before she could hear through the proximity comm what had alerted Kerry. Faint clicks and soft shrieks, like muttering, was interspersed with an irregular mechanical sound. Clanking was a fair description. Or uneven grinding. She held up one fist, ordering a silent stop, and took a deep breath. As slowly as possible, she eased around the corner.

Orange and white light bloomed in her night vision from something extremely hot. Her display flashed a radiation warning, which she ignored. The stupid part of her brain whispered that things were beyond shot to shit if radiation poisoning was not top priority. Unfortunately, there were more pressing problems. *Like what the hell is that*, Maker wondered in consternation. In the center of a large cavern was a ten meter tall cylinder, approximately three meters across. A tubular casing surrounded the middle section, and from it supporting struts stretched to the ground. The central component graduated out in size below the casing, until it was nearly fifteen meters across where it reached the ground. Through the soles of her boots she could feel a slight vibration that was timed with the grinding sound. Directly above the device, a shaft opened in the ceiling. Maker checked her map and guessed the shaft was one of the dark openings she had first noticed inside the crater. If that was the case, there were at least three more devices like the one she was looking at.

She transmitted her view back to the others, with a command to hold position. The clicking was still audible, but muffled. Piles of debris, rocks and dirt mostly, were scattered near the cavern walls. *Stupid, stupid, stupid,* she cursed internally. Maker sprinted to one and pressed her back against it, keeping the top of her helmet below the meter-high barrier. Abruptly, the clicking stopped. Maker held her breath. *One-mississippi. Two-mississippi. Three- missi-*

Vermin. The Culler voice sent a chill of fear down her spine. *Finished by now if they weren't crawling into the equipment.* Maker let out a silent, shaky exhale. Cullers tended to use the word, vermin, to describe humans. Apparently it could mean any small, irritating creature. Faint, scratching steps alerted her to the Culler's movement. Its lower talons snagged in the dirt and kicked pebbles across the ground. A frisson of electricity spiked up her nerves, and Maker's hair prickled. The Culler paused, and then spoke again, as if into a comm device. *Close, close.* He used some words that she could only assume were a measurement. *Synchronize the others. Reinforcements will be ready for you...* The clicking sounds grew unintelligible. Partly due to unfamiliar vocabulary, and partly to something muffling the Culler's voice. Another bolt of electricity turned Maker's stomach. The Culler paused, almost like it was listening. *Yes. Pull back to the ridge before the seismic activity.*

Abruptly, the tension pressing down on Maker released. She hadn't realized how much pain she was in until it was over. She found herself curled into the sharp rocks, clutching her belly. Her head was pounding, her vision swimming with pixelated lines and sharp blurs of light. When the pressure released, she sagged in relief. A loose stone dislodged from the pile and rolled across the floor. A scratch. A whisper. Then, before she could grip her weapon, the Culler was on her.

Vermin! Trash! It shrieked. Its knobby rear legs, the joints sharp with bone spurs, dug into her hips through her suit. The talons drove toward her helmet, and when it could not break through, the huge claws bent backward to expose the hands. Kobby fingers, like green, warty wood, tapped against her face shield. The beak was already exposed, thick mucus dripping onto her helmet. *You cannot stop* - Its threats cut off abruptly as containment netting wrapped around its torso and pulled it to the ground half beside, half on top of Maker. Kerry was there an instant later, silencing the shrieks and clicks with a projectile straight to the exposed jaw. Maker's head was still reeling, her eyes having trouble focusing on the bright heat of Kerry's face in her night vision. Slimy spit, or snot, or digestive juices smeared across her face shield.

"Are you hit?" He asked quietly.

"Sarge, you okay?" Rodriguez was far louder over the proximity comm.

"Fine," she managed to sound far more in control than she felt. She swiped one forearm across her helmet. "Fan out. Secure the room." Kerry sat her up and then moved away, listening and looking for threats. There was one other exit from the cavern, in addition to the way they had come in and the vent in the ceiling. By the time each team member was reporting, 'clear', she had blinked away the blur and lights in her vision. A dull throb of pain at the base of her skull remained constant as she stood, echoing the bruises she was sure were forming where the alien had landed on her.

"Rodriguez," Maker called out, "what am I looking at?"

The Private had already moved closer to the Culler device, and was carefully studying an open access panel. He did not touch the control systems. *Smarter than he acts*, Maker thought. "Not sure yet, Sarge." He murmured to himself, then lay down on the ground, pressing his face close to the edge where metal met dirt. "A drill, maybe? Do Cullers mine? Hydraulics," he drifted off into muttering, "open pit would be more…"

There was a noise of surprise from Gonzales, and Maker frowned. Mining indicated a permanent presence or at least resource extraction. As far as she knew, Cullers brought all of their fuel and supplies with them from their home system. *It's never been located,* she considered. *How far away must it be for the SC not to have found it yet? And how much energy is wasted hauling everything needed to support an army?* She walked over to the machine and squatted down next to Rodriguez. Humans had pushed out into neighboring arms in the Milky Way. Intelligence networks and trade alliances with other species extended that reach even further. It was reasonable to assume that wherever the Cullers were from, it was a long, long way away from Sol. *Maybe on the other side of the galaxy,* Maker thought. That brought up a host of other questions that she didn't have the time or pay grade to consider at the moment. Such as reasons to attack a pre-interstellar culture like Earth if there were thousands of systems separating the two species. More importantly, it was an easy jump to conclude that it would be more efficient to get some of those supplies locally. Bringing an army across a galaxy would have enormous cost - in time and resources. Finding fuel and materials at the destination was tactically and economically beneficial.

"Status," Maker requested as she stood and walked around the device.

"Clear," Kerry repeated. The vibration was still going, but there was no product anywhere that Maker could see. Mining activities should result in ore, or gas, or *something.*

"Clear," said Gonzales. Maker put one booted foot up on a strut and hauled herself up to look under the casing. Exposed circuitry and what looked like pipes were putting off enough heat to glow white. Her radiation sensor began to chime a warning.

"Uh, clear," the rookie stated, his voice trembling a little. The pounding in her head had synced tempo with her radiation alarm, and Maker was irritated by the sound, the pain, and her inability to come face-to-face with a Culler without feeling like she was going to lose the contents of her stomach. Her spine still felt cold and tingly.

"I think this might be a matter regulator," Rodriguez said. Maker glanced down to see he had removed his helmet. *Maybe not so smart.* He held a small tool in each hand and was adjusting something inside the open panel. *Exotic matter,* she thought, but didn't say. It was an area of research that had been on the cutting edge of human science before the Repulsion and had only recently begun to be explored again. Suddenly, he pulled back his hands, stepping back as far as he could with one stride. "Maker," he said seriously. "Get down. Now." She obeyed quickly. Rodriguez wasn't the type to give orders unless the situation was dire. He opened a direct comm line to her. "This isn't a mining operation."

"I didn't think so," she answered. "So what is it?"

"I have no idea, but we do not want to be here when it is done charging. See this indicator?" He pointed, and Maker switched off her night vision to get a better look. The device emitted a faint red light, and where Rodriguez was pointing, a display showed a meter that was nearly full. "Whatever they are doing here, they aren't pulling something up - they are pumping it down."

Maker swore. Long. Creatively. Using words her father would have been ashamed to hear she knew. She could think of a few reasons to collect exotic matter in large quantities - none of them were good. *Blowing up a planet for one.* She was certain there were others - all probably less good. "Can you reverse it?"

"Uh," Rodriguez shrugged, "maybe? If I had a whole team that knew what the hell they were doing and a few days?" He scratched at his head and scrubbed on hand across his face. "Look, Sarge, I've had basic mechanics training. I'm only making some guesses here."

"Worst case scenario?" She unclipped her helmet, wincing at the rotten-vegetable smell of the dead Culler and the hot, humid metal taste in the air. Maker brushed sweaty hair off her forehead. "Give me your best guess."

"We fiddle around with this, screw up the pressurization, and ka-boom. No more VK10 system."

"Okay," she said slowly, "let's not do that. How about we-"

The rookie screamed as he was tossed across the cavern like an old pillow. Maker's contacts displayed his status, showing that his armor had engaged and he was alive. She had little time to focus on that as two Cullers surged into the room. One dug his talons into the rock wall and ran along the vertical surface, shrieking. The other headed straight for Rodriguez and her. Maker acted without thought. She swung her helmet and hit Rodriguez in the gut, sending him sprawling to the ground, then the Culler was on her. She barely managed to get her helmet between her chest and its body. The talons were free to rake along her sides, catching and tearing at her armor. It was clicking at her, but she couldn't concentrate on the words past the wave of hot pain in her head and the frantic struggle to keep her face and belly away from sharp claws and crushing limbs. It took two hits in rapid succession, the weapons fire unsuppressed and deafening in the rock chamber.

The Culler rolled off her and then braced for another attack. It was just enough time for Rodriguez to aim and fire. An incendiary round went right through the thing's eye, sending a rain of wet tissue and thick blood shooting out behind its head. It kept coming. "In the neck!" Maker screamed kicking out at the knee joints and slamming her helmet against one talon to pin it to the floor. The Culler shrieked. It reared up and lifted one mangled appendage, the claw at the end missing. Thick pink-white gore was clotted with dirt - embedded with shards of bone and chitin.

"I was aiming for the neck!" Rodriguez shouted back. He fired again. Three standard projectiles hit in rapid succession. Two bounced off of the plates across the chest. The third wedged in, sinking under the skin. Abruptly, the Culler staggered back, swiping its good arm at the wound. Maker didn't hesitate, but pulled her service weapon and unloaded an entire round. Her position on the ground angled the shots up underneath the creature and the exoskeleton that protected it. It fell to the dirt in a heap.

"Report," Maker snapped out. Her brain was throbbing, her eyes swimming. She tried to scroll through her display to check on the members of the team, but couldn't focus on the text.

"Clear," Kerry answered, slightly out of breath.

"Minor wounds, I'm good," Gonzales' voice sounded faint.

"My only injury was from you," Rodriguez panted. "I'm clear." The rookie didn't respond. Maker rolled to her feet, walking carefully to keep the spinning ground under her.

"I said report," she said into the comm. The private had been tossed against a pile of rubble, and for a moment, Maker thought that he was just catching his breath. As her vision cleared, she noticed that his hips were twisted almost perpendicular to his shoulders. She maximized his stats on her display. He was alive, barely.

"Rook," she said softly, kneeling on the ground next to him. "Hey, rookie, no laying down on the job."

"I-I-" His voice was soft and wet, from tears and snot or blood, she couldn't tell through his helmet. "I can't feel my legs."

"Well," she said calmly. She was disturbed by how collected she sounded. "That's not surprising. Your back is broken." Maker had her own med kit, and the private's as well. She could dull the pain. She could stop external bleeding if he had any. She could inject him with stabilizing foam to keep the broken bones from crushing his spine. She could not make him able to walk, much less run, through enemy territory. "Don't sound so down about it, Private. No big deal." She replaced her battered helmet and hoped it would conceal the fear – the truth – on her face.

"Wha- what?" He gulped loudly.

"We deal with this sort of thing in the field all the time," she lied. "Right, Gonzales?"

"Oh, yeah," Gonzales responded easily. Maker noted that she had resumed her position watching the entrance. "No sweat." Gonzales continued to speak calmly, telling a story about a previous mission she had been on where a soldier lost an arm and a leg and apparently continued to man his heavy gun.

Maker opened a direct line to Rodriguez and Kerry. "Fuzz, I need something to stabilize the Private. Whatever you can find to make a back brace - rip the struts off that device if you have to. Kerry, scout ahead a bit. We need a fast route out of here. Preferably something with few obstacles and lots of sensitive equipment to blow up." They both answered affirmatively, and she turned her attention to trying to boost her comm signal while she administered first aid. There was nothing on the wide band frequencies, nor could she get through to Peters. Maker checked her countdown clock. There was only an hour left before her sniper was scheduled to leave his position and head back to the main force.

"-treats that prosthesis like a damn miracle," Gonzales was saying. "My friend swears it is better than the real thing. He can jump out of a transport at twenty meters and not even feel the landing." Maker opened up her comms as far as they could go, rerouting power from her armor suit's internal sensors and reaction system to extend the signal as far as she could. Her display was crowded with information on her team's stats, the signal penetration through the crater rock, and map coordinates aligning their position with the surface. A hand on her knee startled her concentration.

"Sarge," the private whispered. "If I'm...going to die here, please...please don't let the Cullers get me." His fear was a palpable thing, gripping her heart with two hands and squeezing.

"Shut it," she said sternly. "That's an order. You're on my team, Private. And there is no whining on my team. Got it?"

"Yes, ma'am." He didn't sound relieved, exactly, but he stopped talking about dying.

"I have movement, one hundred meters," Kerry said quietly over the team channel. "Stand by."

"It'll be rough, Sarge," Rodriguez said, approaching with a coarse cut metal brace and his tool kit. "But I think I can-" He continued talking as he began assembling a frame, but Maker tuned him out as her communications equipment flared to life.

"-Two, you have left. Team Three, you have-" the signal cut out and Maker stood and worked desperately to narrow down on the channel. After what seemed like minutes, but was probably only a few seconds, the gravelly deep voice returned. "-eapons hot. Crater blows in T minus forty minutes. Legionnaires, keep your-"

"Team leader," Maker spoke quickly, hoping whatever soldier was on the other end could hear her, "this is Zulu-actual. There are friendlies in the crater. I repeat, there is an SC unit in the crater, be advised. Over." No response came, but she could see the line was still open. "This is Zulu, I am sending you our coordinates." She flagged the shafts that marked where devices like the one next to her were probably operating. "Do not, I repeat, do not fire upon the targets. There is unknown tech - extremely volatile. Confirm receipt, over." Sweat was running down her back and chest, stinging where it met the lacerations made by Culler talons. "Team leader, do you copy, over."

Kerry spoke softly, "All clear."

"Get this strapped on and you can ride all the way back to base," Rodriguez said conversationally to the injured private.

"This is Zulu, do you copy, ov-" The communication was cut. Maker stood motionless, feeling the vibration in the floor and the distant, muffled booms of heavy guns and laser cannon fire. *We're going to die here.*

"Sarge?" Gonzales was backing up, preparing to guard their rear while they tried to get out.

"Kerry," Maker said. Her chest felt too small for her lungs. *We are going to die.* "Get back here. You're on transport duty. Gonzales, on the rear. Rodriguez, you have flank."

"Which one, Sar-"

"Your fucking choice," she bit off, too scared and angry and *scared* to let him make light of the situation. "I have point." Kerry appeared back in the cavern, moving quickly. His helmet was secured to his belt. "Let's move." It was everything she had not to pick up her quick step to a jog. A jog to a sprint. She had not set a timer, but the countdown was still rolling in her head. Trickling down to the beat of her pulse. Forty minutes until the unknown team detonated explosives, or called in an airstrike, or set a few laser cannons to self-destruct. It didn't matter how. When they brought the crater in on itself, it would bury her team alive.

Forget bodies. When those devices go, we'll be lucky if there is enough left for the Coalition to identify the planet.

Her breath was coming fast and hard, not from the pace, which was far, far slower than she would have liked. From fear. Fear that she was going to die. Fear that her team would die. Fear that the thousands fighting in the trenches - who didn't even know they had been depending on her - would die. Fear that whatever the Cullers had really been doing on that stupid, mud-slicked purgatory would go unreported. It was like an icy pit in her gut that grew heavier and colder with each thought until it threatened to rip a hole straight through her.

Five minutes out they ran into a Culler patrol. Gonzales took a talon to the leg. Rodriguez's stats bottomed out before coming back on - she didn't see what happened, only that his suit looked burnt and he spoke with a slur afterward. She was too busy trying not to choke on the river of blood coming out of her nose and the flashes of light across her vision. Culler activity was becoming frantic; singles and small groups were harder and harder to avoid. Each word in their language was a pin directly into the tender tissue of her brain.

Fourteen minutes out Maker almost walked off the edge of a cliff. She barely caught herself, collapsing back against the rock face. Her toes hung off a narrow ledge above bottomless darkness. The sound of heavy guns grew louder.

Sixteen minutes out they were climbing up that same wall. Maker led the way - as she had both hands and feet and no luggage. Kerry followed, the private strapped to his back. Rodriguez with a burned and wrapped hand and Gonzales with an oozing leg wound brought up the rear. Kerry nearly fell once, as an impact shook the entire structure.

Thirty-two minutes and they turned a corner into a Culler

stockpile. Crates and containers of every size sat next to what looked like data terminals. "Get whatever you can," Maker ordered Rodriguez. "You have three minutes." He immediately crouched under a console and pried off an access panel with his knife. Gonzales and Kerry kept watch while Maker set half of the ordnance they had with them. She pinged the location on a map and sent it on a wide band flagged for the 'legion'. She had no idea if the team leader she had heard over the comm would see it, but she didn't want any soldiers to walk into an inferno.

The regular impact of air strikes, not yet at the crater, but close, had begun.

Thirty-nine minutes out and Maker knew they would not reach safety. She peered around a corner in the tunnel - straight out onto the ridge of the crater. Cullers swarmed across the surface, manning laser cannons and shrieking. Chitinous bodies loped down other passages with frag and poison gas grenades ready for the Coalition. Maker tried to holster her gun so that she could get her rifle, but her hand slipped on the casing. She missed her belt and nearly dropped the weapon. Her hands were shaking, her head was pounding.

"Sergeant Maker," the wounded private called out softly through the proximity comm. "Thanks for not leaving me."

"Don't be stupid, Fuzz," Rodriguez said. Maker could not help a hysterical chuckle. Rodriguez was two months on duty, and in all seriousness calling another private a fuzz - a rookie.

"Yeah," said Gonzales, who was several years Maker's senior. "Sarge said everybody goes home. So stop yapping and pay attention. You're gonna tell this story for years." Maker could feel tears on her face, but she didn't think she was crying. She watched a Culler, taller and skinnier than the others, grip the controls for a laser cannon and swing it in a wide arc. The sound of his battle cry was like ice floes crashing together.

With my skull in the middle.

"You'll never have to pay for another drink," Rodriguez said cheerfully. Maker could hear him reloading his rifle.

"A real panty-dropper." Kerry's lack of inflection made them all laugh, even the private.

"Oh, ouch," he gasped. "Don't - that hurts."

"Okay," Maker said, glad to note her voice did not quaver. Her hands were still shaking. "Helmets on, weapons hot. I'll take a wide spray, you head-"

Loud, dangerously close large-caliber rounds beat into the ridge line. Cullers screamed and fell to the ground. Others were blown apart as they were caught in the fire. One alien braced his legs and threw himself with a shriek of rage straight into the air. Maker watched as his head snapped back, the force of impact from a heavy gun round stopping his flight and sending him plummeting. Her comm startled her.

"Zulu, Zulu, Zulu. This is Air Support One-Seven. Over."

It took a second of wild disbelief before her training kicked in. "Air Support One-Seven, this is Zulu. Over."

The bottom edge of the transport, side door open and a pair of legs hanging out around a gun mount, swung into view a few meters above what was left of the ridge. "Zulu, this is Air Support. We are holding at your position. Care for a ride? Over."

Maker was certain she was crying now. Her mouth tasted like copper and salt. She was fairly confident she recognized the voice. "Air Support. This is Zulu. Do you have room for five? One wounded. Over."

"Zulu, this is - ah, hell. Maker, get your ass in here. I'm tired of stayin' still while those lobsters are shooting at me. Over."

Maker laughed, feeling crazy and drunk on relief. She waved her team forward and brought up the rear. "On our way, Bretavic. Thanks for the lift."

CHAPTER 18: EVENING CONSTITUTIONAL

Lightfoot, noun. A person born in space, rather than on a planet or planetary satellite. So called because first generation space-ships and stations were set with gravity slightly lower than Earth standard.

Ex. John is a real lightfoot, he knows all the trade routes like the back of his hand.

Hour 1210
April 23, 2148

Ignition minus three hours thirty-eight minutes.

Malak barely contained a snarl. He had relied on the Coalition to do one thing - follow protocol. It was a simple task, but apparently beyond the capabilities of Captain Yamamoto of the *Ferox* class destroyer, the *Perry*. He hoped she was proud of her initiative, because it was most likely going to get her, her crew, and thousands of other soldiers killed. Giltine stood at his side in his ready room, and it was to her credit that she did not flinch at the low rumble of displeasure in his chest.

"How did they get around the Gravitron Apples?" She asked aloud.

"Patience," Parshav responded. There was a note of respect in his voice that, at another time, Malak might have echoed. As it was, he was too irritated that the rank-and-file of the Coalition had stumbled into his plan and made an enormous mess of it. "Yamamoto came to a halt here." Parshav highlighted coordinates on the wall display, just outside of VK10 sector, "and then sent a comm to her superior. The condensed version is that she requested permission to investigate some unusual readings and was given the go ahead, as long as she maintained her schedule. Yamamoto spent two weeks at sublight dodging the gravity wells I created. Her pilot must be a genius," he muttered, "or completely crazy."

"What about the other ship?" Giltine prodded.

"The *Pershing* received a distress call from Yamamoto. Almaut and I had a comm block in place. The signal shouldn't have gotten out to them, but for some reason the *Pershing* was scanning deeper frequencies than the SC normally does. Her captain is *definitely* crazy. *Pershing* changed coordinates during interstellar travel, and came out of ISG drive within 150,000 kilometers of the planet. One Culler ship was crushed in her disruption wave when she reentered sublight, but there were plenty of others waiting for her. Comms between the two SC ships show that they both took significant damage, but they were able to destroy the enemy."

"Is there a 'however' coming, Parshav?"

Malak was glad she had asked, he would not have been able to sound so calm if he had to question the soldier himself. After taking the trainees to base, Malak and Giltine had boarded a *Sica* class deep-attack vessel and headed back toward VK10. He had been preparing to fight Cullers and investigate their base, not save an army from slaughter. Malak did not often have his plans thwarted. He did not like it.

"Oh, a big 'however'." Parshav scrubbed a hand at his short hair. "*Pershing* deployed every battalion they had, including their rookies, to the surface. They lost about a quarter of the transports before they hit atmosphere. Neither ship is currently able to land, due to damage, and their ship-to-surface comms are still being repaired. Our comm block is still in place, so they can't call SC command for reinforcements. The battalions that survived entry have been pinned down by Culler forces here," he zoomed in on a map of the surface and highlighted an area along the southern edge of a massive crater, "for the last two weeks."

"So our comm block is responsible for the continued losses of SC troops, is that what you're saying, Parshav?"

"No," Parshav replied, "Two Captains with no concern for the lives of their soldiers – that's who's responsible. Idiots."

Parshav continued to describe the Culler defenses and situation with the Coalition forces, but Malak listened with only one ear. Most of his concentration was focused on the aerial images. He scrolled in on four dark openings inside the crater.

"Noticed those, did you?" Parshav smiled tightly at his Alpha and pulled up another, composite sensor scan of the crater. "This should look familiar too. It has a nearly identical chemical signature as on our training mission. The same high concentrations of zinc and lead in the rock - preventing deep thermal or radar scans. And it gets worse." Malak clenched his jaw and waited for news he would not enjoy hearing. "I've picked up some local chatter, several hours old at this point. It sounds like there is a really observant soldier down there who thinks the Cullers might be cutting tunnels under the crater."

Malak felt his adrenaline pick up slightly. It was not that he thought the Coalition forces were incapable of fighting the enemy. He had read reports and watched recordings of some respectable battle tactics and fighting techniques by humans. But the Coalition relied on superior numbers and technology for their victories. They were not prepared to fight such overwhelming odds. They definitely were not prepared for the Cullers to defend ground. The Legion was. There was also a high probability that if VK10 did have the technology he had been looking for - clues to what the Cullers were doing - the Coalition infantry would end up destroying it before it could be examined. Or worse, turning it over to the SIS.

Giltine swore.

"Oh, it doesn't end there." Parshav sounded disgusted. "That soldier with the good eye? Sent into the crater on a recon and destroy mission. Half a squadron was assigned to the job." Giltine's vocabulary became more creative. Malak wanted to crush something, preferably the idiot in charge on the surface. *Half a squadron.* Six weak-boned little humans infiltrating a secret Culler research station. *Suicide,* he thought darkly. If his own existence wasn't proof otherwise, he would have thought the Coalition leaders cared nothing for the lives of soldiers.

Malak opened a comm to the bridge. "Smierc, my ready room." As soon as she had joined them he gave orders. "Parshav, you have the ship. Giltine, Smierc, and I will each take a squad to the surface. We land here," he marked the location, "out of sensor range, and make for the north side of the crater on foot."

"The Coalition forces won't know we're even there," Giltine murmured, already drafting potential attack routes on her tablet.

Smierc stated the obvious, "The ground troops will be decimated without support. Even if we take out the Culler base, without reinforcements they won't make it off of the surface."

Giltine pointed out needlessly, "We're in a blackout."

Since before we first woke, Malak finished the thought. The responsibility of that designation weighed almost as heavily on him as that of his pack. He had the authority to terminate anyone, civilian or military, who discovered the Legion's existence, or anything to do with their objectives. He could order a wideband missile strike on the trenches, wiping out two thousand soldiers, and no one would ever know except Colonel Thomas.

As long as he gained actionable intel and killed every Culler on the planet, he would face no repercussions. If the Pershing had been able to request reinforcements, fewer humans would have died. Would still be dying.

Smierc seemed to read his thoughts, "The paperwork would be miserable."

It was true, and as good as any other reason he was willing to admit. "Parshav, loosen the block on their comms."

"They'll send out a distress signal," Giltine warned.

"I think the Alpha knows that," Smierc said with an eye roll.

"You want the Gravitron Apples disabled too?" Parshav asked.

"Hn," Malak pulled up a map showing nearby sectors. There were several Coalition ships that would be able to respond to the call. "Go ahead." He turned to leave. "Smierc, Giltine, transport bay in fifteen minutes." Alone in the corridor as he strode to his quarters to change, Malak allowed the scowl he had been repressing to surface. It was unlikely he would ever encounter Captain Yamamoto again, but if he did, he hoped he could see her face to face. He would have liked to scare some common sense into the woman. Her, and the idiot soldier investigating the crater too. *Curiosity and cats*, he thought with a frustrated growl.

***

Giltine landed with the same easy finesse she used for everything. Her voice came over the comm, clear and collected in the confines of his helmet. "We are solid. Engines spooling down."

"If you have enjoyed your flight on Giltine Transport, please fill out a comment card," Smierc said, causing a few chuckles to break out in the squads. Malak determined she had been spending too much time with Almaut.

"Silent running," Malak ordered flatly and his Legionaries immediately fell quiet. They had all read the mission brief compiled by Parshav. It was twilight on the surface. The time between day and night was exceptionally long, due to an odd rotational axis. The semi-darkness would only aid them in avoiding detection. From Cullers and humans. "Keep it fast. Execute the enemy on sight. Go."

The scents that came through his helmet filtration system were dulled, but he could still make out the musk of his pack. The dry, metallic odor of the ship. The doors opened and he was flooded with the wet, muddy smell of an unfamiliar planet. Vegetation, reedy and a bit spicy, nearly overpowered the faint traces of munitions on the air. The Coalition had been busy.

Malak left the transport at a quick jog, his squad behind him. A forest of grass lay between them and the crater. The close vegetation made good aerial coverage, but in some places he had to turn sideways in order to move forward. They still made acceptable time, reaching the wall of the ridge a few minutes ahead of schedule. According to the map, the crater was more than six kilometers across. The faint sound of heavy guns and the hot tang of laser cannons carried to him on a breeze. Coalition forces were fighting a losing battle, but they made an excellent distraction.

Not a single Culler patrol walked the ridge or the barren ring of dirt that lay between the grasses and the rock. One laser cannon, the muzzle hanging forlornly over the edge, had been abandoned. Either the humans were presenting more of a challenge to the Cullers than Malak would have expected, or the aliens had not defended their base as well as they should have. Malak hoped it was the former. Strong defenses meant something worth protecting. He wanted to see that something.

Malak pulled out a grappling kit and attached it to his sidearm. His shot sank into the rock just a meter over the edge. Others followed suit, and soon there were six ropes dangling from the top of the crater. Each of them could have scaled the surface without the assistance of climbing gear, but the ropes made the ascent faster. If necessary, they could also speed a descent. He reached as high as he could with one gloved hand and pulled himself up before getting another hand hold. He could not keep a weapon out as he did so. Soldiers at the bottom would stand guard until Malak and five others reached the top and secured the position. His biceps and shoulders were heated by the time he swung over the edge. He crouched, bringing his rifle into a ready position. "Clear," he said quietly.

"Clear," Smierc repeated as she completed her own scan of their surroundings.

Four others echoed the statement and Malak gave the signal for the rest of the team to ascend. The fine hairs on the tips of his ears tingled. There was some sound just out of his range, and it set him on edge not be able to identify it. A particularly poorly aimed cannon projectile soared over the far edge of the crater and crashed into the dusty bed. A cloud of pale dirt rose, obscuring Malak's view of the shafts. The distant battle could be heard, faintly, but not seen, except for that one shot. Instinct rose inside him, whispering, *something here, something here, pay attention.*

Giltine was the last to climb up, and she quickly organized a rear guard while Smierc lead a scouting team for the nearest entrance underground. Malak was hit with a sense of deja vu. It was eerily similar to the tunnels from eighteen years ago - right down to the grooves of melted slag on the walls. A desire for action swelled under his skin. Malak would not voice his feelings, but he knew they were close to answers. The stats for his team glowed on the edge of his display, adrenaline higher than it should be. They might have been eager for a fight. More likely Malak had not controlled himself well enough and they sensed his excitement. *Where the Alpha goes, the pack follows.* With each step, Malak took an even breath, willing his body to settle down. He flexed his muscles, releasing any tension that would not help to speed his response time. He slowed his breathing and heart rate. His team, unconsciously or not, followed his example until they were all within optimal parameters.

"Divergence, ahead," Smierc stated sharply. Malak brought his team to a halt and then he continued on alone, past Smierc's squadron, to where she crouched close to the ground. Her weapon was ready, her attention trained on the curve in the wall just ahead. He waited to speak until Giltine joined them.

"Assess," he ordered. After nearly two decades of missions together, the command wasn't really necessary, but Malak still gave it.

"Y-intersection, eight meters around the bend. Another twelve meters off of the main branch is a second Y. All three tunnels descend." Smierc traced a map in the loose dirt.

Giltine cocked her head to the side, and Malak knew what she was sensing, but waited for her to speak. "Cullers. Two on the left. At least four down the center. Dragging..." she trailed off.

Smierc finished, "It's human. Or it was."

Malak nodded shortly in agreement. The scent of human flesh, sweat, and blood was a stark contrast to the rotten-saccharine smell of the Cullers. He had never known them to collect trophies, but the body they were dragging was either dead, or had been so frightened and injured that it defecated. If he or she was still alive, it would be a kindness to end things. Malak pulled up his display, checking the countdown timer that estimated when Coalition reinforcements would arrive. The Legion needed to be off of the planet and preferably out of the system before then.

"Find those devices. Shut them down, if possible. Set detonations to block them in - we'll come back and dig them out after the Coalition has left. Kill the enemy on sight." He adjusted his display again, readying the instructions Almaut had given him regarding the device easily accessible in case he should need them. "I'll take center. Team Two, you have left. Team Three, you have right. Run silent. If you see any humans, stay low. Weapons hot." He started his timer. "Crater blows in I minus forty minutes. Legionnaires, keep your-"

"Team leader," a breathless voice interrupted him over the comm. Malak was so surprised he did not immediately react. "This is Zulu-actual." Malak held up a fist, signaling all of the soldiers behind him to remain silent. A woman was broadcasting on his team frequency, so they could all hear her. The soldier on the other end of the line, *how did she get comms through the rock*, punched in an identification code he did not recognize. "There are friendlies in the crater. I repeat, there is an SC unit in the crater, be advised. Over." *The curious cat survived*, Malak thought. He found the corners of his mouth trying to curl up into a smirk. It was rare to find a human so difficult for Cullers to kill. *Perhaps she is exceptionally skilled.*

"This is Zulu, I am sending you our coordinates." *Or incredibly lucky*, he realized, reviewing the map and comparing it to the aerial images. Zulu was directly under one of the shafts, right next to a device he needed. She had marked the other three shafts as well, clearly she knew, or had a good idea, what was there. It was his mission to retrieve the device - and to keep its existence a secret. She had most likely seen it, recorded it with her tech. If any of her team were still alive, they were witnesses as well. She continued speaking. Although her tone was calm, she rushed her words, implying anxiety. Understandable, given her position. "Do not, I repeat, do not fire upon the targets. There is unknown tech - extremely volatile."

That observation gave Malak pause. Although the one he had seen so long ago had emitted radiation, there had been nothing to indicate it shouldn't be destroyed. Almaut had not mentioned anything about the possibility either. However, the Legion's experience – only a few hurried minutes of observation – had been nearly two decades ago.

"Confirm receipt. Over." The command in her tone was obvious, but still laced with tension. Malak waited to hear if she would share any other pertinent information. "Team leader, do you copy. Over."

The scent of Cullers and dead human was moving closer. "Team leader," Zulu said again, more insistently, "This is Zulu. Do you copy. Ov-" Malak cut the transmission and re-keyed their comm channel so she could not break in again. The Cullers were on the move, he needed to be as well. That did not explain why he did not discard her authorization code or comms signature, but he did not have time to examine his reasons.

"Reset countdown," he said coolly. "I-minus sixty minutes. Go." Each team split up, and Malak lead his squadron down the center. If Thomas asked, he would state that Zulu's information warranted additional time to check over the devices before detonations were set. Privately, in a far corner of his mind that still held on to old lessons, he felt she deserved the extra minutes. Although Malak understood his conditioning, and actively chose to fight for the humans. Despite how he had been created and conscripted into their war, he still believed they should be protected. For the most part, humans were not unlike weak, frightened children. They had been wrong to think they could control the Legion, but they were not wrong to try to develop a weapon against their enemy.

Zulu had beaten long odds. She had lead an undermanned team deep into enemy territory and gathered valuable data about their resources. A soldier with that kind of skill and dedication, that fearlessness, deserved the chance to live.

As the tunnel flattened out, he began to feel a vibration in the floor. He discarded any thoughts of Zulu to concentrate on the obstacle ahead. Five Cullers were moving slowly towards him; one dragged a human body in its wake. He switched off the night vision provided by his helmet and relied on his own sight. The body was still wearing Coalition armor - although it had been shredded in places. Blood - thick, dark, and sluggish without a heart to pump it out - left a muddy trail in the dirt. The Cullers spoke to one another, and Malak was briefly frustrated by his reliance on the translator program built into his tech.

"Body is cold."
"It does not speak."
"Order same. Take it back. Get another."
"We have plenty."

Malak listened hard, holding back the signal to attack. He waited for more information.

"Fine. Not good enough to eat."

Useless program, he snarled internally, cursing whoever had designed it. Malak made a low-pitched sound in the back of his throat and his squad moved as one. Two legionnaires dropped to their knees, back-to-back guarding the tunnel. Another raced past the enemy, dragging his knife along the wall to throw out sparks. Two more soldiers attacked each of the first four Cullers, leaving the last one for Malak. He crossed the ten meters between them before the aliens realized what was happening. With a leap he stretched out one leg and flew over the dead body. His booted foot hit the last Culler high on the chest, knocking it to the ground and temporarily incapacitating its voice. He landed on his other foot, and continued his motion, swinging around with his blade drawn. The sharp edge caught the Culler just under the knees as it stumbled backward, and it fell to the side, fetching up against the wall. Malak was on it in an instant. One talon glanced off of his helmet, another snagged in the reinforced mesh of his suit, but did not puncture. The tip of his knife found the seam in the center of the chest carapace.

With quick, arching jab he sliced the nervous system. The Culler fell, and Malak turned to face his team.

One soldier was still pulling his weapon free from an alien corpse, but the others were all ready and at attention. Not a single enemy had managed to make a sound. *Good,* Malak chuffed into his comm. It was rare he gave in to the urge to speak in the primitive language that Bee had taught them all. A kill always brought the need to the surface. An easy relaxation came over the squad.

Pleased to have pleased. Feeling still the excitement of a mission, of prey ahead of them. Feeling pride that they followed their Alpha into battle. Malak faced back toward the direction the Cullers had been coming from, and gestured for the others to follow.

After another five minutes, Malak was irritated to note that they had not made adequate headway. It seemed that they had just finished dispatching one Culler patrol when another lone alien or small group would stumble upon them. It was perplexing as well as frustrating. The enemy did not seem to be seeking them out - were not aware of the presence of the Legion in their base until they crashed into suppressed guns, hard helmets, or quick fists. Malak flicked his knife to rid it of a stubborn layer of mucus and Culler blood. They needed to pick up the pace.

"Double time," he ordered quietly. "Kill on the move."

It would leave bodies behind them. Any enemy with eyes could have easily followed the trail right to Malak, but the pace did get him back on schedule. The Legion arrived at their destination to the sound of heavy guns growing louder. A small group of Cullers were surrounding one of the devices. It looked slightly different than he remembered, but Malak waited until his team had dealt with the paltry defenses before he took a closer look. Two of his people chased down a runner while he approached the device. The technician on his team stayed right beside him.

It was taller and sleeker than the earlier version, and no cooling pond was visible. Heat and radiation were seeping out, but in far greater quantities than what had been recorded before. Malak identified the access panel, in almost the same location, and pried it open. The technician had his tools out, but took one look at the gauges inside and halted.

"Exotic matter," he stated. "Maybe…" Malak waited while the soldier pulled a tablet out of his bag and synced it with his tools. Slowly and carefully he tested a few connections inside the panel. "Probably Souriau particles, can't say for certain without a sample, and I'm not qualified to take one."

"Hn." Malak tipped his head up to look over the device, conscious of the vibration that had grown stronger the closer they got to it. *Or as time moved forward,* he wondered.

"Even if I had the equipment, this is something that Almaut - or maybe one of the Falcons - should do. If I go poking around in there, I may start a reaction."

"And this?" Malak pointed to a rising meter.

The technician glanced at it as he took a few more readings. "It is definitely measuring the particles. Maybe charging them, somehow? Or filling up a space? I don't-"

An impact shook the crater. Malak held his ground, but a few of the soldiers stumbled. *Air support,* he thought. *The Coalition is here faster than expected.* "How much time?"

"At the current rate, I'd say 30-50 minutes." Malak leveled a glare at the technician. Although the male couldn't see his expression through their helmets, he understood perfectly. "I'd be more specific if I could, but the rate is fluctuating."

Malak had been given a brief overview on exotic matter as part of his physics lessons, but that had been years ago. From what he remembered, any amount of the rare particles could contain tremendous energy. If pressurized and then detonated, the blast radius would encompass the Coalition trenches. Maybe the entire hemisphere. Unless they were shut down. He could not leave the devices unattended. Whatever the meter was counting down, Malak wanted to stop it. Without Almaut and the Falcon scientists, he only knew one way to do that.

He summoned his two fastest soldiers. "Get to Smierc and Giltine. Don't waste time killing, just run." He outlined his message and then turned on the technician. "Get all the data you can, then take these three," he pointed out soldiers, "with you to the transport. Transmit everything to Parshav. We'll follow you out." He directed the remaining soldiers to set ordinance and timers around the device, then continued on alone, toward the southern edge of the crater. He estimated he was halfway up, and was twisting the head off of a Culler, when the airstrikes began. They were close, but not yet to the crater.

Malak kept running, nearly sprinting down the tunnel. He struck as quickly as he could, but the sheer numbers of Cullers he encountered were slowing him down. He resorted to incapacitating them whenever it was faster. It infuriated him to leave living enemies behind, but his schedule was too tight to allow the luxury of finishing every fight cleanly. The devices had to be destroyed before they could complete whatever task they were performing. Malak had the authority - the duty - to make certain it was done. No matter what the cost.

The Coalition had wasted more for less.

Around the last corner, dim light seeped into the tunnel. Two Cullers were silhouetted against the entrance, one holding a large gauge missile launcher. The sound of transport engines and rapid artillery fire was deafening. Malak drew his sidearm and fired without slowing down. He had not loaded any standard projectiles. Instead that magazine was filled with specialized armor-piercing rounds which only the Legion used. The tantalum rounds entered the armed Culler before either alien knew Malak was there. One pierced the back of his head, boring through the chitin and into the soft tissue. A second round slammed into the upper back, directly over the spine. Thicker plating there slowed down the projectile, but it still managed to hit the central nerve cluster. Malak's enemy collapsed into a pile of moist, gray flesh. The grenade launcher crunched down on the body as it fell.

His third shot went in through the side of the other Culler's head as the thing was turning to face him. The sensory organs just under its eyes were ripped apart, spraying out through the exit wound. Malak was on his opponent then, weapon first. He did not bother firing, but whipped the heavy barrel across large black eyes. The Culler shrieked, striking out blindly with his talons. Movements that would have been difficult for a human to follow seemed almost slow to Malak. He shackled one arm in his fist while the other talon to sweep across his ribs. The armor weave of his suit held, but the pressure caused him to grunt. Without allowing another opportunity for attack, Malak used his free hand to find the upper ridge of the chest plate. It had a raised edge where it met the skin of the jaw, and he worked his fingers underneath it. Then he pulled.

One booted foot braced on the ground, the other on the Culler's lower body, Malak gritted his teeth and ripped back as hard as he could. Shrieks, high-pitched and agonized, echoed down the tunnel. The Culler fell to the ground, exposing soft, vulnerable skin. Pink-gray mucus bubbling up from the massive wounds where the chitin had been attached and ripped out like a toenail from the root. Malak hefted the meter-long scale between his hands and brought it down hard where jaw met body. Abruptly, the screams stopped.

The air support vehicle outside was beginning to move away as Malak stepped out of the tunnel. He crouched, searching the battlefield below. More than a thousand glistening gray bodies were engaged in a fight to the death - with more pouring down from other positions along the ridge. Coalition forces had previously dug trenches to protect them from laser cannon fire. The trenches were rapidly becoming graves. They made excellent cover for long range guns, but as the Cullers closed the distance, they had the high ground and the human troops - already smaller and weaker, fought at a disadvantage. Wind was gaining strength, and it brought to him the smell of decomposing plant matter and hot, iron-sharp blood. One third of the distance from the furthest end of the trenches, a small bunker had been constructed of printed blocks. The crushed, dark rocks that had been used for raw materials allowed the structure to blend in with the surroundings.

Malak removed a comm unit from an outer compartment on his pack. It was a matter of seconds to sync it with his own tech. The air transport was flying high, dodging cannon fire as though the pilot had been drinking before he turned on the engines. A line of similar transports made a black haze in the distance. Malak estimated they were only a minute or two out. With line of sight on the bunker, which was the most likely location for headquarters, Malak used Zulu's authorization code.

"Hotel-Quebec, Hotel-Quebec, Hotel-Quebec," he repeated rapidly. "You are ordered to disengage the enemy and bug-out immediately. Repeat, bug-out. Over." He did not wait for a response, but contacted the incoming transports as well. He ordered half of them to descend as close as possible behind the trench and take on passengers, and the other half to provide air support. "This is a priority-one command. Do not engage. You are rescue and retreat. Over."

"This Hotel-Quebec-actual," a female voice brimming with authority and anger spoke. "That is not your authorization code. Over."

Malak ignored the question. "Hotel-Quebec. Disengage and re-treat. Immediately. Over." The transports were chattering over their comm line as well, and trying to contact headquarters. *Too much damn talk,* Malak snarled to himself. It was a perfect example of why the Coalition had needed to create the Legion. The humans couldn't follow simple orders.

"This is Hotel-" the woman in charge said at the same time as,

"This is Transport One. Who-"

"Pan-Pan," an emergency call sign came over all frequencies, bringing a halt to the arguments in Malak's ears. "This is Transport One-Seven. I have Zulu-actual onboard with - ah, hell," another curse followed as the pilot of the closet transport dodged a more accurate laser cannon. Malak watched him execute a barrel roll and narrowly avoid becoming a fast moving briquette.

"This is Zulu-actual."

Malak recognized that voice. He tracked the transport she was in with his eyes while on his display he painted a small group of Cullers a hundred meters away that had spotted him. She sounded far more confident than she had only minutes earlier. Malak purposefully did not focus on the countdown in his vision. Time was at a premium, but if the ground troop commander did not believe him, Zulu was the only thing standing between the humans and death. Anger welled up inside him along with frustration. He could not stop the detonation, not for an angry commander. Not for curious Zulu. Not for a thousand Coalition soldiers.

His purpose was *more.*

"Transmitting to you now, H-Q." Zulu must have taken her helmet off, because he could hear the wind - no doubt through the open door of the transport, the crackle of cannon fire, and the heavy thrum of the transport engines. "Recommend immediate bug-out and bombardment of the surface. Coordinates for missile launch are as follows." She read off and then repeated the exact locations of all four devices. Malak was grudgingly impressed. "Repeat, bug-out and immediate bombardment. Over."

"This is H-Q-" the absolute fury in the commanding officer's voice was tangible, "Zulu you are not authorized to-" Authorization codes and communication lines flashed on Malak's display. He focused on them instead of the gentle reminder of his clock. I *minus Fourteen minutes.* Malak's personal best time for five kilometers was just under ten minutes. The distance back to his transport was closer to seven kilometers. Over rough ground. With two descents and a climb, if he took the shortest route with the fewest enemies.

An encoded transmission overrode headquarters, "Pan-Pan. Calling all Coalition forces in VK10. This is General Batma." Malak allowed a small smile to creep over his face. Parshav sounded nothing like Batma, but it was a good bluff if the Coalition officers had not met the General. An authorization followed that matched Batma's. Enemies on the ridge were beginning to pay more attention to Malak. Parshav continued, "Ground Forces, you have twelve minutes to bug-out. *Perry,* you will begin aerial bombardment at that time." Another coded transmission, to authorize the commands to retreat and fire upon a planet, was sent directly to headquarters and the *Perry.* "Batma, out." Malak drew his weapon again, toggling it for a gravity net. Parshav had been smart to not allow any time for questions from the officers in charge. They were left with the decision to follow orders that had been verified by a soldier on the ground, or disobey.

Malak fired, taking down two Cullers that began to move toward him and knocking a third off balance. It struggled on the edge of the ridge for a moment, then artillery fire destroyed the ground under its feet, leaving it to fall to the rock below.

New communications lines lit his screen, although Malak did not have the equipment or training to follow more than two at once. What was said mattered little; activity behind the trenches assured him that the Coalition would do as they had been ordered. Zulu's transport touched down, and Malak could barely make out the small, armored figures that jumped out to help load injured into the ship.

He turned away, ignoring an unwarranted sense of satisfaction. Measuring around the crater edge, he was one hundred and twenty degrees from where his team had scaled the wall. *I-minus thirteen minutes* glowed on his display. Malak began to run.

He was fast enough, and the Cullers distracted by fire from approaching support craft, that he was not slowed at first. A few well-placed armor piercing rounds cleared his path. His lungs breathed in and out steadily. His legs pumped, the muscles heating and responding easily to his demands. His boots stirred up a fine cloud of dust in his wake. *One-two-one-two-aim-fire-kick.* A Culler body, bleeding but still thrashing fell into the crater. *One-two-one-two.* He continued to listen to the general comm line as he ran. Transport One-Seven was full and took off toward the *Pershing.* Headquarters organized a retreat, using cover fire from the transports and well-placed frag artillery to hold off the Culler advance. He did not hear Zulu again.

I minus ten minutes. Malak was nearing the end of the Culler defensive positions. One creature rushed him, and he turned to the side, gripping the slashing talon as it came down and using the Culler's momentum to swing it around in a circle. Malak pulled the alien in front of him, one razor sharp claw twisted between their bodies as a second enemy raked both of its talons across the space where Malak had been standing. Shrieks of pain, clicks, and screams overloaded his translator program so Malak muted it. He wedged one boot against the lower carapace of his captive and released his grip with a kick, throwing it into the other alien. The two tumbled to the ground, and Malak continued his run, firing an incendiary round into their heads almost as an afterthought.

One. He dug his left foot into the ground. *Two.* He planted his right, bending his knee. *One.* He sprang forward, arching over a laser cannon position. *Two.* He fired twice into the center of mass. *One.* His left foot touched down. *Two-one-two-one-two.* Only the sound of heavy guns, growing more distant, followed him as ran on.

I minus eight minutes. Headquarters was recalling the active troops. All the injured and support personnel had been taken back to the ships. Transport One-Seven was on its return flight.

Malak's motion came to an abrupt halt as two Cullers leaped over the side of the ridge from the inner crater. One swung a long, barbed spear that hummed with electricity. Malak had to drop to the ground to avoid being hit. He rolled, absorbing the impact, but the second enemy was waiting for him. It hissed and dug one talon into his armor - directly over his ribs. The tip did not pierce, but the heavy weight of the blow threw him off balance. The spear came around again towards his legs and Malak accepted the hit rather than be forced out of position. He had to grit his teeth to keep from biting his own tongue as electricity coursed through him. His display flickered, then began to flash with warnings for his health status.

Malak grabbed the barbed end that had snagged in the armor on his thigh and took another painful jolt. His grip forced the sharp points of metal bit into his right palm. He kicked out, catching the unarmed Culler in the side of the knee and snapping the joint. It fell. A moment was all Malak needed. With his left hand he brought up his side arm while he yanked the spear towards himself. One round at point blank range dropped the Culler and sent a vapor of cordite and burnt flesh to his nose. A talon from his living opponent pulled Malak's feet out from under him. He swung out with a fist. The blow hit the Culler on the shoulder, not even dazing it, but the distraction gave Malak time to aim. A frag round went through the soft tissue at its hip joint. The stuttering stop of movement and wail alerted the Alpha that the projectile had worked properly. He rolled to his feet. The second Culler was on its back, clawing at its chitin plates while molten copper, tungsten shavings, and sulfuric acid burst from the bullet and ripped through its organs.

I minus four minutes. Headquarters was ordering a last line to stand firm while the transports exchanged places. A lone Culler fled a tunnel - out into the slowly darkening twilight on the ridge. Malak shot on the run. As he passed he took off an arm at the shoulder joint with his knife.

I minus two minutes. The ropes were just ahead, still secured in place. Laser cannon fire ate through the ridge behind him. Malak did not look back, but his display alerted him to the approximate position the shot came from. *Finally realized I'm here.* He grinned in exaltation. There were few things that brought Malak true joy.

Alone on the ridge it was only him. The power of his own body. The quickness of his mind. Him against his enemy. He had no responsibility in that one moment, except to survive.

A growl of satisfaction, of challenge, of glory escaped him as a second blast carved a deep channel in the dirt in front of him. The hit was too accurate, too close, for him to escape. Instead he leaped over it. His trailing shin was so close to the energy pulse that his armor began to melt. Three more strides and Malak dropped to his hip, sliding across the surface of the ridge with his arm outstretched. His hand latched onto a rope and he was over the side just as another cannon fired. It was on target, if only a second too late.

Malak's rope snapped and he fell several meters before he could reach out and touch the rock wall. The friction of his glove against the sharp, glassy stone ripped apart the armor over his palm, but brought him closer to another rope. He seized it. The burn of synthetic fibers as he rapidly descended smelled like cooked meat. Two meters above the ground he let go and dropped into a rolling landing. Without stopping, he came up into a run, dodging through the grass forest.

I minus one minute. There was no more chatter he could pick up from headquarters. Malak burst into the narrow clearing around his *Sica* class ship. The doors were open and the engines spooled up. His breath was coming hard. "Take off," Malak ordered into his comm, just as he crossed the threshold. His cheeks hollowed as he gasped for air and his limbs shook with each step. His run was finished, but the mission was not complete. He nodded to soldiers he passed on his way to the bridge, but did not remove his helmet. Giltine and Parshav were waiting for him. Smierc was directing the helm. The planet was already far below them, and indicators on the nearest console signified they were entering the upper atmosphere.

"*Pershing* is fully loaded," Parshav noted without being asked.

"*Perry* has weapons charged," Giltine added.

As she spoke Parshav brought up the display, sensors showing two Coalition ships nearly on the other side of the planet. Even from a distance, the damage looked bad. Malak was sure it was worse.

Giltine continued, "Bombardment should-" A hot glow from the *Perry*'s forward guns was the only warning before twin streaks of fire broke through the atmosphere. Malak's ship entered space just as the surface of the planet shuddered, caving in. It happened only a split second before the *Perry*'s attack struck. The crater was obliterated, followed by most of the continent. Shock waves buffeted the ship.

"Deploy a satellite to gather information," Malak ordered. He spun back the way he had come. "Engage ISG."

"Something wrong with your helmet?" Giltine asked with one brow raised. Parshav set up the satellite and Smierc spoke over the comm, notifying the crew that interstellar travel would begin. "Clasp get stuck?"

"Hn." As the adrenaline wore off, his shin was began to burn where his armor had seared flesh. His muscles were quivering from the exertion of his run. His ribs throbbed, making every breath painful. His palms tingled with lacerations and rope burn. Malak kept his helmet on until he was alone in his quarters. He glanced in the small mirror over his sink as he finally took it off. The feral grin displayed all of his fangs. He chuckled, a deep and gravelly sound in the empty room.

It had turned out to be a good day.

CHAPTER 19: FEALTY

Burner. Noun. Slang. Citizen of the Sol Confederation who flees to avoid mandatory military service.
Ex. When the Home Guard caught the burner, he was sentenced to ten years of hard labor in a corporate mining colony.

Hour 0900
April 28, 2148

Ignition plus five days.

Maker barely suppressed the urge to fidget. Most soldiers managed to get through their mandatory two years without ever seeing a review panel. Most got through entire careers. It was her second time facing inquiry in less than two months. *Not a great track record,* she thought. She cracked the joints in her left wrist and hand nervously, then forced her palm to slide across her thigh. Maker pressed it there to keep herself still while she waited for the officers on the panel to enter.

It was not as bad as the last time. She was not alone. Kerry, Rodriguez, Gonzales, and Bretavic sat behind her. The rookie was still in the infirmary - drugged into a coma until his new vertebrae were done growing. Peters was conspicuously absent as well. Why the sniper wasn't in the hearing instead of Bretavic, she had no idea. *Seems to be the order of the day*, she griped to herself. She still wasn't entirely sure why the review panel had been called. As far as she knew, she hadn't broken any serious regulations. Everyone under her command had survived. *This time.* And while her breaking into the communications line to order a bug-out could be considered insubordination, that seemed like something that would be taken care of between her direct superior and Major Ben-Zvi. She could only assume that her mission had failed in some way - but if that was the case, it should have been Peters and not Bretavic in the room. She glanced at the sentry stationed by the doors, the crisp uniform of an MP in stark contrast to the haphazard look of her own group.

Bretavic, as usual, was just this side of out of uniform with his wrinkled jacket and fraying pant hems. Rodriguez would have looked the picture of the dapper soldier, if not for the over-sized burn glove on his hand, protecting his new skin. His hair might have been a bit too shiny and voluminous to be regulation, but he was a stark contrast to Gonzales. Every aspect of her appearance was staid and starched -except for the brace on her wounded leg and the IV pack of antifungals she carried around with her. A lot of Cullers carried diseases that might be worse than death. It was enough that most other soldiers gave her a wide berth.

A door opened at the far end of the room, and Maker could see the profile of an unfortunately familiar officer. Lt. Commander Soon was turned back toward someone else, talking, but even without his attention focused on her, Maker felt a surge of despair. Whatever she had done, the consequences were about to become much, much worse than she had imagined.

A stage whisper broke the tense silence. "Hey, Sarge."

Maker studiously avoided looking at Rodriguez.

He continued anyway, "Do you know the difference between a lieutenant commander and a private?" Maker closed her eyes and breathed quietly, hoping that whatever was about to be said wouldn't involve balls or recreational shower use.

"What?" she asked quickly, thinking maybe Rodriguez could get it over with before Soon heard him.

"The private *knows* he's stupid." There was an expectant beat, and Maker could feel Rodriguez's grin beside her without even looking.

"You're an idiot," she muttered quietly.

"That's what I'm saying!" His outburst drew a snorted chuckle from the sentry and a groan from Gonzales. Soon stepped into the room, his eyes narrowed with suspicion at them. "But obviously, the private is better looking," Rodriguez finished.

"Shut it," Maker hissed as they all stood at attention.

Soon was followed into the room by the Commander – Jones - she recognized from her first inquiry. The third figure made the blood drain from her face. *Captain Yardley.* It was one thing to be summoned to a performance review, without knowing what you had done wrong. It was entirely different for the Captain of the ship to oversee the hearing. She swallowed hard and did her best to look coolly professional. Maker had an uncomfortable suspicion that she failed.

"At ease," Yardley ordered. His silver buzz cut was bent over a tablet in his hand, reading glasses from another century perched on his nose. He found his seat, in the center of the panel of reviewers and looked up. "In consideration of your injury, you may be seated, Private Gonzales."

"Sir, I prefer to stand with my team, sir."

Maker did her best not to cringe. She knew it was a show of solidarity, but honestly she would have preferred to get the whole ordeal over with as quickly as possible without drawing any more attention than necessary. The last thing she wanted was a memorable inquiry. She already had enough officers that disliked her. Soon's perpetual sneer was difficult to ignore.

Yardley raised a brow, "As you will. This review board is con-

vened at oh-nine-oh-two-hours on April twenty-eighth, 2148."
The hearing room was equipped to record the proceedings for
the official record, and didn't require that date and time be
stated, but the Captain finished the formalities. "The actions of
Sergeant Clara Maker and Privates Daniel Rodriguez, Pilar Gonzales, John Kerry, and Petr Bretavic are under consideration.
" He noted the absent rookie would be reviewed after he recovered.

Yardley read their ID numbers off, then began, "While under
siege on planet VK10-RD48," it took Maker a second to recognize the designation of the hellhole she had spent two weeks
fighting on, "Sergeant Maker and Private Rodriguez showed initiative and disregard for their personal safety by planning, vol-
unteering for, and successfully executing, a maneuver which allowed two companies relief from pinning fire."

Wait, what? Maker actually felt her mouth fall open. Yardley had
sounded like he was complimenting them, but his expression
was stern.

"Furthermore," Yardley read from his tablet, "Sergeant Maker
planned and led an infiltration and destruction mission against
the enemy position, going above and beyond the call of duty
to ensure that her team survived against insurmountable odds,
weakening key enemy defenses, and retrieving data from en-
crypted enemy terminals."

Soon was glaring at Maker. She snapped her mouth closed. Her
thoughts were reeling. She had anticipated a slap on the wrist,
at best. She wasn't sure if praise from the Captain was better or
worse.

"Privates Rodriguez, Kerry, and Gonzalez showed courage
under fire and exemplary dedication to their duties, fighting
against overwhelming odds and undertaking tasks far above
their training and experience. Private Bretavic," there Yardley
paused and looked up. Something passed between the Captain

and the hulking man beside her, but other than the slight compression at the corners of Yardley's mouth, he gave no indication of what he was thinking. "Private Bretavic," he began again, "risked his personal safety to pilot a damaged transport ship to the surface, in advance of reinforcements, to provide an exit for the aforementioned team, without which they may not have successfully returned to base, and intelligence collected at great risk would have been lost."

Yardley scrolled through his tablet. "In light of these events, I am hereby submitting for consideration Privates Kerry, Rodriguez, Gonzalez, and Bretavic for Commendations for Meritorious Service during Combat. Sergeant Maker shall be considered for a Bronze Star." Maker felt like she must have taken a head injury. She wondered if the effects could be delayed. Soon was still scowling.

Soldiers," the Captain was speaking to them as he placed his hand on the tablet to sign the order. "Thank you for your service."

Bretavic shifted uneasily, blowing out a hard breath beside her. Rodriguez had puffed up his chest, but from the corner of her eye she could see his tight expression. Gonzales sat down with a thump.

"This inquiry has ended. Everyone dismissed." Yardley removed his glasses. Maker wanted to collapse in her chair, but oddly, the panel was not leaving. Yardley's voice took on a more dangerous tone. "Recording end, authorization Alpha, Foxtrot, two-niner-one-Alpha."

The Commander spoke next, "Sentry, lose the next twenty minutes."

"Yes, ma'am," the MP replied and left the room.

Confusion was rapidly growing into something resembling fear for Maker. Soon stood and walked to the nearest access terminal. He placed his hand on the wall pad and gave his voice authorization code, locking down the room. Maker's heart began to beat double time.

"Sir," Rodriguez began, but was cut off.

"Sit down, Private," Captain Yardley snapped. "All of you." Maker sat. Bretavic was stiff next to her, his arm pushing against her shoulder and supporting her frame. "You are in a serious situation here, and I truly hope you can grasp the importance of the next few minutes." His gaze focused on each of them in turn, and it made Maker feel small and unsure when it landed on her. "Classified information which is far above your paygrade came into your knowledge while you were in those tunnels, and while I would like to know what the hell you all thought you were doing, I have been informed that I don't have clearance to ask that."

Soon's scowl had turned into a sour little smirk, but it was completely overshadowed by Yardley's anger. "When the Sol Intelligence Service contacts me and demands records - I don't like it. When the Minister of Defense contacts me and orders compliance, I like that even less. Whatever garden stroll you took your team on, Maker, I suggest you forget it. Whatever you saw, whatever you heard, it might as well not have happened. Got it?"

"Our tech..." Rodriguez started, and then trailed off.

"Yes. Your tech." Yardley's jaw hardened. "Everything on this boat belongs to me, is under my command, and yet I have a dingy full of SIS on their way to rendezvous and collect your tech and scrub down my databases. Why is that, do you think?" Rodriguez opened his mouth. Only a sharp exhale came out as he was simultaneously kicked by Gonzales and Bretavic. He grunted, "It would seem to me to be a waste of time, given the number of individuals that now know about the comms transmissions. Who was that, exactly, that borrowed your authorization code, Sergeant?" His eyebrows were raised. "Well?"

Maker wasn't sure what to say.

"I, ah, sir, that individual did not identify himself to me, sir." Her palms were a little sweaty. She couldn't deny that she had thought about that gravelly voice, the Team Leader, since she returned to the *Pershing*. Most of those thoughts ended in telling him what a complete jackass he was for not responding to her communication. In light of what Yardley was saying about the SIS wanting to cover up the specifics, she was beginning to wonder if 'legionnaires' was a nickname for a special forces unit, or an intelligence gathering team. Either way, she was probably better off not knowing.

"Work on your answer, Maker. I doubt SIS will take it at face value." Yardley was still frowning, and for a moment Maker thought she saw pity in his eyes. "You will all debrief with SIS at the border station." He stood, tucking his tablet under his arm and sending one last glare toward each of them. "I suggest you spend what time you have left on your tours keeping your heads down and your noses clean. This meeting is over."

The captain stalked from the room, followed by a straight-backed Commander and a smirking Soon. The victorious smile he sent her way would have once chilled Maker, but she was too confused and had been too recently terrified to give it much attention. *The medals are a cover,* she thought blankly. It almost made her sick to think about. Pinning something to her chest that represented bravery and loyalty to the Coalition when all she had been was afraid and sick and terribly unlucky.

"Well," Rodriguez said, "now I'm really curious about that device we found."

"Shut it," Gonzalez snapped, struggling to her feet at the same time Bretavic ordered,

"Drop it, Fuzz."

"You drop it," Rodriguez fired back at the larger man. His voice was hot with anger and pent up frustration. "Debrief with the SIS? That could take weeks, if they don't like what we have to say. Those assholes - ! You pretend it never happened if you want, but I want to know what earned me this kind of sentence."

"It's not like you're going to prison, Fuzz," Gonzales tried to calm him down. "It'll probably be a cushy few days on some station inside the border. Free stale coffee and all the dried fruit supplements you never wanted."

"No, thank you," he replied tightly. It was the most honest emotion Maker had ever seen him voluntarily display. His wrist bracer chimed quietly with an incoming message, followed by each of the others'. Maker glanced down at hers as Rodriguez groaned. "Dammit, the new assignments have already been put through."

"I've been moved to munitions supply," Gonzales said woodenly. "I haven't done munitions since my rookie rotation."

"Third shift, cargo transport," Bretavic read off of his own screen. "Boring, but I've had worse. What'd you get, Sarge?"

"Second shift data core," she said, unable to suppress a wince.

"Isn't that Soon's detail?" Bretavic didn't wait for a response. "Shitty." *No wonder Soon was smiling, can't wait to have me under his command.*

"Yeah," Maker sighed. She still felt a little shaky. Just like Rodriguez, she wondered what the Culler device was for - why it was so classified. Unlike Rodriguez, she wasn't stupid enough to say so out loud. A little voice in the back of her mind also wondered what had happened to the Team Leader and his Legionaries. She shook her head, trying to get rid of thoughts that might end her somewhere worse than under Soon's thumb. *As if there was such a place*, she snarked to herself. Yardley was right. They all needed to forget they saw and heard anything that the SIS considered remotely interesting. She tried to change subjects. "Hey, no pity for me. I've only got three months left."

"Me too," Bretavic grunted, standing. "But I'll probably re-enlist. Nothing better to do."

"Nothing better than making greasy smears out of space lobsters?" Maker stood also, reorienting herself for the reality outside of the little room. Preparing herself to lie about what had happened inside the crater.

Preparing to convince herself that it didn't matter.

"Easy money," Bretavic replied.

Kerry, who had remained stoic throughout the ordeal, offered Gonzalez a hand and helped her to her feet. "It will make the rookie's story better, to have gotten a medal out of it." Everyone turned to stare at his placid, dark face. It took Maker a moment, but she finally remembered.

"That kid is going to be swimming in booze and uniform-chasing women," she laughed, grateful for the release of tension.

"And I'll be forever debriefing with the SIS," Rodriguez whined. "The best ladies will already be taken."

"Don't sweat it," Gonzales pinched his cheek, and they all began to file out of the room, "I'll save you a beer."

They were playing cards three days later when Rodriguez was called to report to his superior officer. Forty-eight hours out from their rendezvous with the SIS, and Bretavic had given in out of pity and let the Fzz into his game. Rodriguez was surprisingly good at cards, and unsurprisingly immodest about it.

"Ha," he crowed as he scooped up chips. "How did you not see that bluff, Sarge!"

"I was distracted by all the light bouncing off of your hair. Did you dump engine grease on it?" Maker folded her arms. She didn't really care that she had lost, she almost always lost, but teasing Rodriguez might put him off of his game enough that Kerry could win something back.

"Pomade," Rodriguez replied proudly, "it's made by collecting the placenta-" A message on his tech distracted him.

"Thank god," Gonzales muttered from her place at the next table.

Rodriguez frowned. "I have to report in, looks like our friends arrived early."

That the debriefing schedule, which listed Rodriguez first, had been moved up went unspoken. Their table grew quiet. Although most of the players at the Thursday games didn't know the specifics of why Maker's team and Bretavic were up for commendations, it seemed everyone on the *Pershing* was whispering about the unknown legion. *Comms travel fast,* Maker had thought the first time she overheard other soldiers whispering about it. It was true. Messages that went out on wide frequencies and resulted in a lightning paced bug-out and planetary bombardment tended to be repeated. Whether the gravelly voice Maker had heard on her line belonged to a special forces operative or an SIS spy, it didn't really matter. The rank and file had already chewed on the gossip and determined that there was a new, badass unit that Maker had met up with on a secret assignment. That neither she nor the other members of the team would talk about it only made the rumors worse. Rodriguez hurrying through the corridors just as a ship requested an unscheduled docking – in the Dark - would add fuel to the fire.

"Good luck, man," Bretavic said quietly.

"Try not to talk so much," Gonzalez advised.

"Keep a knife on you." Kerry's serious statement was met with surprised looks. He did not react as though he had said anything unusual. Rodriguez stood, and then waited expectantly by Maker's chair.

"What?" she finally asked.

"Aren't you going to say anything? Something encouraging and inspiring, maybe?" He waggled his eyebrows, "Or admit your undying love for me, Sarge?"

"Ew," Maker said flatly. The storage room erupted in laughter, breaking some of the tension. Maker stood too, and held out her hand for his. "Watch yourself, Rodriguez," she said quietly. "Anything they push you on, just tell them it was my orders, and they'll have to ask me."

He grinned lasciviously, his ultra white smile handsome against tanned skin, "See, you do care." Kerry and Bretavic stood too, and Gonzalez walked over, all to shake Rodriguez's hand. He whistled nonchalantly as he left for his debrief.

Everyone was surprised when Rodriguez returned an hour later, quietly letting the others know that the SIS unit had cleared the *Pershing* in a wide path to the server stations. After collecting the tech from the VK10 mission and scrubbing the servers, they left without debriefing anyone.

Maker did not feel relief.

***

Four months later.

"The recent skirmishes between Coalition forces and Culler detachments outside of the CSNS perimeter have been quoted by the Minister of Defense as being, 'the first of a new wave of aggression'.

"Sources close to President Sudarshan have indicated that she is committed to ensuring economic and civilian losses are minimized as the war continues. Approval ratings for the President remain strong after recent announcements of increased funding for a new fleet of deep space ships, with the intent to push the Cullers further from the Sol system. Whether the President has determined to run for a third term is still under intense speculation. Although the precedent has been for leaders of the Sol Confederation to step down after two six-year terms, the public has responded positively to the idea of Sudarshan continuing in office."

Maker took her beer as the bartender handed it to her and walked back to her booth. The screens placed around the small pub continued to drone on, reporting the news and showing highlights from the recent Sol Cup. It was only her second drink, and still early afternoon, but she hadn't eaten since she got on the train that morning. The alcohol was going to her head, but she nibbled on the pretzels at her table and stared out the window rather than order something. She had been discharged almost four weeks ago, her mandatory service complete, and had returned to the family farm with a mixture of relief and guilt.

"Hey, Dad," she said softly, stepping into the barn where he was putting away saddles. It smelled just like she had remembered. Dry and musky. Leather and horse sweat and the comforting notes of old wood, hay, and manure.

"Clara?" He looked up, startled, and she was a little surprised to see how much he looked the same. Bright blue eyes. Dark blonde hair that had faded to silver on top. His plaid shirt was rolled up at the sleeves and his denims and work gloves were dirty with leather polish. The man who had raised her by himself, who had attended cross country meets and spelling bees, who had taught her to ride, and mend fence, and grill steak. The man who had commiserated over quantum mechanics homework and spent hours setting up translation software so that she could learn Japanese - even though he didn't want her to.

"Daddy," she whispered. Tears welled in her eyes, and sud-

denly it came rushing back at her. She had seen people die. She had killed. She had been terrified. She was still terrified. Her bag fell to the ground, sending up a cloud of dust and crushed straw. And then he had his arms around her and they were sitting in the dirt. She was sobbing, and she thought he might have been crying too, but she couldn't tell through the snot and the tears and the painful way her heart was thumping. "I was so scared."

A waiter stopped by her table, shaking her out of the memory. "You need a refill, or something to eat? Or are you waiting for someone?" His smile was easy, his black hair carefully styled. It reminded her of Rodriguez. She wondered where he was. "Yeah - I'm waiting, I mean. But if you have a menu, I'll take a look." She didn't plan on ordering, wasn't sure her stomach was up to food, but it would buy her more time alone until Bretavic arrived. The news reporter on the screen behind the bar was speaking to another anchor.

"-indeed. The margin of five votes is significant. This will be a true indication of where the President draws the line in supporting the military. With such a small margin, she could maintain backing from either side of the issue. Vetoing this bill would allow First Tier Citizens to continue to inherit property and hold controlling shares in corporations. Although the bulk of the bill is dedicated to new reforms for punitive service and veterans' benefits, the property clause could have tremendous impact on re-enlistment numbers. Polls have shown that-" Someone changed the channel and a musical program came on. Maker turned back to the window.

That bill was why she had come to Seattle to meet with Bretavic. He had taken the Bering Rail line from Russia, and she wasn't sure if she wanted him to talk her into action, or talk her out of it. She stared at the enlistment office on the other side of a wide, cobbled courtyard. A few individuals were already lined up outside the door, waiting for their turn with the recruiter.

More than twenty years previous, Greg Maker had done his mandatory military service and then returned to Earth and his beloved farm. He had worked beside his great grandfather while he went to school and took courses in agriculture, veterinary science, and chemistry. He had traveled to institutions and research centers all over Sol-controlled space, pursuing his love of growing things and learning. It was how he had met the mother of his child. Lin Yamamoto had just reenlisted for her first tour and - despite their radically different views on the military, politics, genetics, and nearly everything else - they did have chemistry. Although all enlisted personnel were required to submit to a contraceptive implant, nothing was 100% effective. Greg had taken Lin to court to make certain she did not terminate the pregnancy. He had won then, the courts determined there was no physical or psychological detriment to the mother to continue the pregnancy, and Greg had gotten parental rights with no contest from Lin.

He had built a life for his daughter on Earth. Dedicated himself to raising Clara, crops, and animals. He made his home a center for education on historic food production methods and won grants to supplement his projects. He had done all of those things, and often stood on his soapbox about the genetic modification of humans in order to 'make them better'. He had not, however, re-enlisted. Greg was a First Tier Citizen, someone who had completed his mandatory service and never gone back to the military. The family farm was everything to him.Under the new law, when he died his property would revert to the government – unless it was deeded to a citizen with higher status.

Someone who had volunteered for service.

Maker let out a shaky breath. Second Tier Citizenship was not something she had ever desired. She had always assumed she would go home, perhaps pursue an education similar to her father's, and work on the farm. She certainly did not want to go back to the Coalition. The line in front of the enlistment center moved forward again. Ten years. That was the shortest period she would be eligible for, since she had no upper level education. A decade of her life, to preserve what her father had spent his life building. A decade to preserve two hundred fifty years of her family's legacy. She rubbed her shoulder absently. Kerry had not been helpful when she discussed it with him. He was absolutely loyal to her, and would support whatever decision she made. He had already re-enlisted - the same day they got back to Earth.

"What's the deal, Maker? You ask me all the way here and then don't even get me a drink?"

She glanced up and there was Bretavic standing by the table. His smile was large and crooked. His form looked smaller in civilian clothes. She stood too and offered him a smile and a handshake before waving over the waiter. "It's good to see you," she said, before they ordered. Bretavic got them each a beer and a plate of fried okra to share. It arrived quickly, and he ordered the most expensive, real meat entree on the menu and another beer while he salted the crispy vegetables and dipped them in mustard. "Seriously?" Maker wrinkled her nose.

Bretavic laughed. "I've been on leave for a few days, stocking up. By next week I'll be on military nutrition again. All printed meat and low-sodium reconstituted veggies. I need to enjoy this while I can."

"Make yourself sick, more likely," she retorted. He popped another piece into his mouth and smiled. He was halfway through his steak - all Maker could see when she looked at it was the outrageous price of beef - when she finally got around to it. "I'm thinking of re-joining."

He set down his knife and fork, wiped his mouth as he finished chewing, and leveled her with a serious stare. "You hated it."

"Yeah," she blew out a breath, and glanced out the window again. The line had grown shorter. Only one person was waiting, a thin man probably up for his mandatory service. *Man,* she thought, *more like kid.* He was on the short side and was fidgeting with anxiety or excitement. "Yeah, I did. Most of it," she admitted, turning back to Bretavic. "Have you seen the news?" He nodded, leaning back in his chair and folding his arms, the steak temporarily forgotten. "You know I grew up in the country..." She hesitated, wondering if maybe she was making a mistake talking to him about it. Bretavic was a career soldier. His family was huge, half of them lived permanently off-world, and none had owned property since before the last Russian tsar. *What will he know about it,* she thought, second-guessing herself. She then immediately felt bad.

"Your dad doesn't have Second Tier status, does he?"

"No," Maker confirmed quietly.

"You're thinking about enlisting to what, save the family farm?" His expression was unreadable, his posture stiff.

"Yeah."

"Don't." His flat response was so unexpected, Maker blinked. "There are already plenty of dumbasses who signed up just so they could get ahead."

Maker's cheeks burned with embarrassment and indignation. *That isn't what I-*

He interrupted her thoughts. "Idiots take a tour so that they can get a shiny bar on their shoulder or better pay. They want the SC to fork over the credits for school, or they want to meet a spouse. They sign up so they can run for political office or own a corporation. Those people are assholes - and I don't want to fight beside them."

"Who do you want to fight beside?" she asked. Her voice was

snide, but she couldn't seem to control it. She had thought Bretavic was her friend. Despite their age difference, he had acted like he respected her. Because of his experience, she had wanted his advice.

"Friends," he responded, quickly but without any anger. "Comrades. People who don't want to be killing or get killed any more than I do, but who still show up. Soldiers. That is who should be in the fight, Maker, soldiers. A real soldier is there, because he knows that without him the unit is weaker, his friends are more vulnerable. A soldier fights because he has something to protect, only a mercenary fights because he has something to gain."

Shame and fury washed through her like a tidal wave. Shame that she had fallen so low in Bretavic's estimation. Shame that she had only been thinking of herself and her family, not what the Coalition stood for - what it meant to so many others. Fury that Bretavic had forced her to see that part of herself. "Sorry," she mumbled.

"Don't apologize to me," Bretavic said gruffly, leaning forward again and cutting into his steak. "Thinking about it doesn't make you wrong. But if you do sign up, make sure it is for the right reasons." They both were quiet while he finished his meal.

"Why do you do it, really?" She spoke without thinking, and immediately regretted it as Bretavic winced. "No, never mind. You don't have to say anything."

Bretavic shook his head and took a deep breath. "During my two years, I was stationed on the border of Close Space Near Sol. SC was taking some pretty good hits at the time. The Cullers were losing big numbers, but they were wearing us down in places, testing the CSNS defenses." He took a sip of beer. "My Sergeant - he was a real prick - he pushed us further and further out from the main line. We were in a little short-range runner ship, and he saw a Culler detachment set down on an asteroid. We had no idea what they were doing, but Sarge wasn't going to let them get so much as a pinkie toe on anything in our space. We'd been going on forty-two hours without sleep, and you know there is only so much the stim packs can do for alertness." Bretavic was staring into his glass. The pale golden liquid swirled as he slowly turned the pint.

"He ordered us to do a free fall entrance to the asteroid and attack. There were only two of us that had ever been untethered in space outside of training. I remember one of the kids just about fainted at the idea. I called Sarge out, told him it was stupid. Prick punched me in the nose." Bretavic chuckled and looked up. "See," he pointed to his crooked smile, "didn't ever go in for correction. Broken nose messed up my face."

"What happened?"

"Sarge said I could stay on the ship, bleeding like a coward, or I could go down there and watch my team's back. Said he wouldn't report me either way - but I'd have to live with what happened." He took another drink of beer. "We all went down there. Sarge got killed. Most of the team got killed. But we got every last one of those slimy fuckers, and destroyed the supplies on the asteroid." He grinned, more feral than friendly. "They had munitions stockpiled. Enough to outfit a Culler fleet and take out ten or twenty destroyers. Could've blown a hole right through the perimeter. We stopped that." He threw back the rest of his drink. "Useugi was on that one with me."

Maker's gut churned, remembering blood floating out into space above VK10. "Useugi is dead."

"Gonzales isn't. Peters isn't. That kid with the broken back isn't. Even Rodriguez, who is just as likely to get shot with friendly fire for running his mouth, is still alive. They need good soldiers at their sides. The people here on Earth? The ones on Titan and Europa Station? At Gagarin and Aldrin colonies? At Gliese? They need good soldiers to keep them safe. If you're gonna re-enlist, do it for the right reasons, Maker. Be a soldier, or stay home." He didn't say it to be mean. He wasn't sneering, or questioning her bravery or loyalty. Bretavic called for the check while Maker sipped her beer, thinking.

He cursed, loudly and creatively, in Russian when it came. "Good thing I get a bonus for signing today. I'll need it just to pay. Two weeks' worth of credits for one steak. Highway robbery," he muttered, tapping his bracer against the waiter's tablet.

Maker smiled in apology and left a generous tip. "Come on, Bretavic," she stood and he followed her out of the bar. "Let's go get you that bonus check, then I'll thank you for coming out here with a real steak."

"A real steak?" he said, brows raised. He kept pace with her across the courtyard and up to the enlistment office. "What did I just pay for, printed protein?"

"Nah, that was inferior." She waved him off. "Before we have to report for duty, you'll come out to the farm and I'll get you some Nebraska beef. Trust me, there is a difference."

"*We* are going to report for duty?" He narrowed his eyes at her. "Are you still doing this for your dad?"

"Yes." She took a deep breath. "And for Rodriguez. He'll be scrubbing toilets for the next decade if there isn't anyone to make apologies for his stupidity. And for Kerry. He'll rush into enemy territory with just his bare hands if he's ordered to do it. He needs backup."

"Well, then," Bretavic leaned against the wall behind her, waiting his turn. "Welcome to the Coalition, Soldier."

CHAPTER 20: CHOICE

Wormhole. Noun. A connection between two positions that crosses both space and time, e.g. Einstein-Rosen Bridge, Ellis Wormhole. The first traversable wormhole was discovered by Andrae-Scott-Zurek in 2029. It was too small for human use, but numerous probes studied the phenomena and its destination in another galaxy before its practical collapse in 2036.
Ex. *Although the wormhole travel would be expedient, the probability of finding a stable instance, large enough for feasible use, and with both ends in practical locations, is infinitesimal.*

Hour 2230
May 14, 2148

Ignition plus twenty-one days.

"You don't seem pleased."

Malak controlled his expression while he watched the view screen. Colonel Thomas was leaning back in an office chair in the Sol System, a hundred light years away, crossing his arms over his dress uniform.

"Any feelings I might have are inconsequential." Malak's voice came out cool and even, but his jaw was beginning to cramp from being clenched tightly. Thomas was supposed to have met him at the base to debrief on the mission, as usual. A change in routine, particularly a last minute one, rarely brought good news, and Malak was vindicated as Thomas explained why he couldn't do the debrief in person.

"Cut the bullshit," the Colonel barked. His frown made the deep lines around his mouth more prominent. "You want to control your own destiny? Fine – but the Legion exists because administration says it does. You've got two choices, soldier," Malak could feel his spine straightening involuntarily at Thomas' authoritative voice. Any other Legionnaire might have lowered their eyes – but Malak was Alpha. He wasn't compelled to obey Thomas nor any other Coalition officer. It was a decision. "You can get with the program and maybe get a hand on the reins," Thomas continued, "or you can fight this and spend the rest of your unnatural life cleaning up someone else's mess."

In twenty years, Malak and Thomas had gained a relationship of mutual respect and honesty. At least, as honest as Malak ever was outside the pack, which meant that he didn't speak very often. Although they had never discussed the morality of the Legion's creation and quasi-employment, they shared an intense disgust for the manner in which the Sol Confederation was running the war. Over two decades, the SIS had become a more powerful voice whispering in the ears of Congressional Representatives, Senators, and at least half of the military establishment. Their agenda either included extending the fighting, which the manufacturing lobbyists no doubt supported, or they were the most inept military strategists since Colonel Custer. The amount of money to be made in a war, and the power derived from it, played a large part in that strategy. It ran against Malak's instincts not to seek out and utterly destroy his enemy as quickly as possible.

Thomas had always stated things more bluntly. "Like the feeling of an SIS burr up your ass, Malak? No? Then do something about it." He sat forward, leaning his elbows on his desk. The small window behind Thomas exposed a scenic view of one of Europa's more active cryogysers. Light reflected off of Jupiter and streamed through the water vapor and ice crystals to make faint rainbows. The beautiful image was a sharp contrast to the

Colonel's weathered face. "The SIS is currently the only game in town. This is an opportunity – if you can stop looking down your nose at it."

Malak repressed a sigh. He could not deny that there was some truth to what Thomas had said. The Legion was completely blacked out – which made bringing new support to their plans difficult. The SIS – although secretive – was an acknowledged organization. They had the upper hand when it came time to sway the Defense Minister, or Congress, toward a strategy. Malak hated the idea of exposing his people – even to a select, vetted, political echelon. He almost hated agreeing with Thomas more,

"I agree that a new fleet will greatly improve the Legion's efficacy." As the Alpha spoke, Thomas began to grin, and Malak nearly cracked a tooth trying not to frown. "However, I do not see the point of insignia."

That was perhaps the most surprising suggestion Thomas had passed down from Batma, and it was less of a suggestion and more of an order. Malak was not certain how he felt about it. Or what it meant for the future of the Legion. For his entire life, and long before that, the government had worked extremely hard to make certain there were no traces of Project Barghest or the Legion. That anonymity chafed at many of his people who disliked the idea of hiding from the humans they protected. Malak had no misconceptions, however. He was aware that while the shadows were a form of control over the Legion, they were also a layer of protection. If humanity was not aware of the Legion, they could not hate or fear them. A sudden disappearance of a blackout group would not be noticed by civilians, should the Coalition ever decide they no longer needed the Legion. It would also be more difficult to organize, if Malak put up a resistance. The biggest advantage the Coalition had over the Legion, if they ever became at odds, was size. But sheer numbers couldn't be brought against a covert group without alerting the public. Insignia would identify the Legion simply by their uni-

272

forms, eliminating the anonymity they had worked under for twenty years and making them a potential target for a billion prejudiced Coalition soldiers.

In a battle staged in the shadows, his people would win every time. He wasn't certain he was prepared to give up that advantage.

"Propaganda," Thomas stated simply, as if that one word brought sense to a complete reversal in policy. "There is no taking back your own actions, Malak. There are recordings-"

"Not for much longer," Malak interrupted.

"-witnesses," Thomas went on as though he hadn't heard, "soldiers who heard your voice on VK10. Who heard the name – Legion. Hell, once SIS gets a hold of the tech, we might even find an aerial image or two of you – running along that crater ridge like a one-man death squad."

"I did not state that in my report," Malak's forehead creased in a scowl. He had enjoyed his mission on VK10, at least the end of it. Having Thomas recount it muddied the experience.

"Of course not," Thomas sat back again, huffing. "Your reports are so brief they wouldn't make decent toilet paper. Smierc does not have that problem. And at least one Coalition pilot caught sight of you. Batma has blacked out comms for the *Pershing* and *Perry* until they reach CSNS and dock for secure data transfer, but the cat is out of the bag." The Colonel smiled, and it had the sharp edge of a hard lesson in it. "You haven't served on a cruiser or destroyer, so let me explain this to you. Five thousand humans stuck in a small space together don't have much to do but gossip and fuck. Science saved us from babies on warships with contraceptive implants, but they have yet to figure out a way to keep people from talking. Within a month of crew reassignments, every soldier in the Coalition is going to have heard some wildly exaggerated story about you and the Legion.

Batma is going to use that to our advantage – get ahead of it and start building more credibility and trust for what we are doing."

Malak could accept the decision. He still was not pleased. "Hn," he responded.

"I'll take that as a 'sir, yes, sir'," Thomas said dryly. He glanced down and tapped the tablet on his desk. The office lighting glinted on new strands of silver in his hair. Time had aged him far more than it had Malak. "I've already submitted the recommendations for promotions. You should be a Major by the end of the month. You're welcome. Forward your requests for the others as soon as possible so we can start the process. Although," he looked up and narrowed his eyes, "if you recommend anything higher than Warrant Officer for Almaut, I might deny it. His ego is large enough already." Malak nodded in acknowledgment. "Get some Falcons started on a work order for the new body armor and uniforms. I'll see you in a few weeks, after these emergency meetings are over."

"Agreed." Malak reached forward to shut down the link, but Thomas' voice stopped him.

"You did good work out there, Malak," he said quietly. "You saved thousands of lives."

He heard what Thomas didn't say: *good boy* and *thank you*. The former remained unspoken out of respect for Malak and his role as a soldier, not a research subject. The latter did not have to be said. It was his duty. His responsibility.

"Hn," he grunted, then turned off the comm.

The *Viper*, a *Sica* class deep-attack vessel, had docked at the base by the time his meeting with Thomas concluded. Most of the crew had already left to repair their gear, find a hot shower, or visit the infirmary. It had taken nearly three weeks to make the return trip from VK10 to the Legion base – more than twice as long as it normally would have. Unfortunately, the *Viper* had to take a circuitous route. First, dodging Coalition sensor sweeps and reinforcements. Then, to meet up with another ship and drop off Smierc with new orders. The *Viper* had ran into a few Culler short-range ships as well, resulting in some intel that would need to be examined by techs. And a few dozen dead enemy combatants. All those aboard the *Viper* were eager to stretch their legs and leave the small ship.

Malak grabbed his bag and helmet and strode through the empty corridors. With all of the delays, Smierc had returned before him. She had requested he meet with her in Almaut's office as soon as he arrived. Malak was still reviewing the *propaganda* and other changes Thomas had described as he stowed his gear and walked deeper into the base, towards the research center. Activity picked up as he neared the work area for the few humans that had security clearance to work with Keres Legion. The Falcons, as their squad was designated, were mostly scientists, engineers, and technicians. They were invaluable to Malak, whose people had been designed and educated to end life – not to explore the motives of their enemies. Although some, like Almaut, had taken to new information and tasks easily, most of the Legionnaires found it difficult to master skills so far outside their original programming.

The few soldiers he passed stood at attention and nodded sharply or tilted their heads at him. Humans were equally respectful in their own way; murmurs of 'sir' and 'Lieutenant' and salutes greeted him along with a smile or two. The corridors became more crowded the closer he came to Almaut's office, and the reason was obvious.

Every member of Keres Legion had excellent hearing. It was one of the priorities listed by the Erasmus Station research team when they first began experimenting with non-human DNA recombination. It surprised Malak though, that many of his own soldiers often seemed to forget about their enhanced senses. Perhaps they had spent too much time with human scientists.

They simply didn't expect anyone to be eavesdropping. Not that Malak intended to eavesdrop, but Smierc, Almaut, and one of the Falcons were speaking too loudly for it to be avoided.

"Has Malak seen this yet?" Through the closed office door Almaut sounded both serious and excited. It was a deadly combination for the highly intelligent and overly curious soldier.

"No," Smierc answered. "I ordered the engineers you sent to leave the data alone until we got back here."

Malak stared intently at the most senior Legionnaire lingering in the corridor. She took the hint quickly and ushered the other curious soldiers and scientists away from Almaut's closed door. The humans wouldn't have been able to hear anything, but Malak had no doubt that they would soon know the details of anything that had been gleaned by superior ears. The Legion wasn't designed to have much interest in fucking, as Thomas would say, but they were as proficient at gossiping as the humans.

"And you didn't have any issues getting on and off the *Pershing*?" Almaut asked.

"We're not exactly trained for covert ops, boss." Malak did not immediately place the voice, and so paused in the corridor and inhaled. A human male, one who smelled of standard issue detergent, excitement and the stale, pressurized atmosphere used in data storage rooms, was in Almaut's office. The Alpha mentally scrolled through the members of Falcon Company.

"Really, Lauraux?" Smierc sounded amused. "I would have never guessed."

"Sarcasm is the humor of a slow mind." Lauraux, a computer engineer, Malak remembered, did not sound offended.

"Your lack of appreciation wounds me deeply," Smierc laughed.

Almaut disregarded the exchange between the human and

Smierc. "Ignore her," Almaut ordered. "Tell me about the retrieval."

Malak hit the door control and stepped inside the office. Almaut and Smierc both nodded and tipped their jaws for a split second, exposing their necks. Lauraux straightened as though he had been hit with a tasing weapon, gave a half-hearted salute, and broke out in a sweat. Malak was used to the reaction. "Continue," he said quietly.

"Yes, well, uh," Lauraux cleared his throat and averted his eyes. *Prey,* Malak noted to himself. It was an instinctual reaction for the human, to avoid the attention of a more dangerous animal. "Ondrea piloted us to the *Pershing,* and their security officer accepted the codes Parshav gave them with no problem. There was a little bit of an argument, when Smierc told them to clear the deck between our docking bay and the data core, but they sorted it out. Just me and a tech went on board. The security crew seemed like maybe they share your feelings about the SIS, because they took one look at our false IDs didn't even speak to us."

Gradually, Lauraux's voice relaxed as he began to pull up files on his tablet and toss them onto the wall screen. "There was a technician waiting for us in the core, and he had all kinds of questions, but I ignored him just like Smierc said to. As soon as he opened up the ports, I kicked him out and we got to work. There was a lot more data there than we thought, and some stuff that had been recorded from orbit that might lead to questions about the Legion. We cleaned out the systems after we copied everything – even remoted into the suit tech that was still on board. The only information SIS is going to get is what the soldiers on the ground can remember."

"How much?" Malak directed his question at Lauraux, but Almaut answered.

"A lot – but no need for concern. We got this three days before

SIS was scheduled to arrive, and memory is a tricky thing. With that much space between the actual event and the debriefing, and with all of the talk among the crew, half of what they will recall won't be the truth, and most of of the truth won't sound believable. Hell, not sure I believe it. And I've seen the footage."

Lauraux pulled up a video file. The playback was only a few seconds, but it clearly showed an unusually large soldier, moving too quickly to be human, draw a knife and slice the arm off of a Culler. Malak briefly enjoyed the memory.

"This was taken from one of the transport ships, ah," Lauraux glanced at the file, "number seventeen." *Zulu's ship*, Malak thought. "It looks like there are a few more, from different angles, and some aerial still images. None that show the *Viper*, thankfully. Although there was some sensor data that we had to scrub before someone realized they had proof of another Coalition ship in the area."

"Your exit?" Malak asked.

"Clean," Smierc said, at the same time Lauraux rubbed the back of his neck. He was nervous enough that Malak could taste the salt of his sweat in the air, see it beading on his temple.

"There might have been a little confusion." The engineer glanced over at Almaut, who was rolling his eyes. "In order to get the security codes, we intercepted all of the communications from the SIS to the *Pershing*. Those soldiers that were inside the crater were supposed to be on lockdown until their debriefing, but the order was never received by Captain Yardley."

Malak did not see the problem, and Almaut filled him in. "Normally a captain would have isolated Zulu and her team, without the SIS involvement, until they were debriefed. But as you noted, Captain Yardley doesn't seem interested in doing things by the book. With the minor delay that SIS encountered-"

Smierc grinned at Almaut's words. "We diverted a subspace satellite station into normal space directly into the path of the SIS. They were lucky their ship didn't need a tow."

Almaut went on, "It looks like the ten-day window passed."

Malak raised his brows. The Coalition only certified intelligence gained from eye witnesses if it was recorded within ten days or the witness had been isolated to reduce memory contamination. Anything that Zulu's team could remember about the devices would be inadmissible in requests for intelligence funding or resource allocation.

"Good," Malak said. Lauraux visibly relaxed. Almaut grinned and Malak continued, "Show me what they saw."

"This is my favorite part," Almaut said with relish. He tapped away on his tablet and the wall screen separated into six sections, each labeled with a name and service number. "I had been wondering what they figured out that we didn't." The playback began, and Almaut muted the audio and began a commentary. "So, I already listened to them from when they left the Coalition HQ to this location. It was mostly routine checks and some chitchat. This one," Almaut highlighted the video labeled, *Rodriguez SC2148-E009-00425*, "is the mechanic. Not sure why he was selected for the mission. Apparently he is the second most junior soldier on Zulu's team."

"Is that a basebot?" Smierc asked. Malak felt as surprised as she sounded.

"Yeah," Almaut sped up the video.

Smierc whistled.

"That would take a bit of field rigging," Lauraux added with admiration, "and they're lucky that dinosaur of a robot didn't completely fall apart on them."

"Slow it down," Malak ordered.

"There is a few hours of this," Lauraux cautioned. Malak turned a hard gaze on the engineer. Lauraux smiled weakly.

"I should have brought popcorn," Almaut said, leaning against his desk and allowing Lauraux to sink into the office chair.

Smierc pulled a stool over from a work bench and Malak remained standing, watching intently. A bulky soldier, *Kerry SC2144-T001-00001*, led them into the tunnels. Malak assumed that was Zulu-actual, until the darkness closed around the group and Kerry removed his helmet. Even in the unnatural green lighting of SC night vision lenses, Kerry was clearly male. It was also obvious that he was not entirely human. Almaut and Smierc immediately began discussing it. Their interest in the GMH was understandable. Although it was popular for the non-regulated tubers, as the humans called them, to enter military service, it was strange to see one in any position of authority. And it was clear from the body language of the rest of the team that Kerry was respected.

The dark-skinned male was followed by a much shorter, slimmer soldier. Female, Malak guessed from the size. That one, *Maker SC2144-E056-00861*, looked sub-average – but then, Malak thought a lot of humans looked small. Her movements were clumsy and slow, especially in comparison to Kerry. The mechanic, Rodriguez, followed her. Almaut had stated he was a new recruit, but he carried himself well for it. His service weapon remained loose and ready in his hand, his visual display was clean, orderly, and constantly updated with location data. Another rookie was next, and his inexperience was obvious. Clumsier even that Maker, he stumbled often and his weapon wavered in and out of proper position. His display contained nothing but the location beacons of his team and his own health stats. Bringing up the rear was *Gonzales SC2146-M002-07845*. Gonzales also moved easily, a practiced sweep of sensor data on the display and routine visual checks to the rear confirmed the status of a more seasoned soldier.

Almaut and Smierc were still quietly debating the possible genetic makeup of Kerry, and Lauraux was studiously taking notes regarding the data feeds, when a Culler stepped around a corner and nearly ran into the point position. Kerry reacted nearly as quickly as Malak would have. His service weapon was already on repression rounds and in less than a second a projectile entered under the jaw of the Culler. The alien's surprise quickly morphed into anger and it charged. Kerry's quick action had silenced the enemy while giving the humans on his team time to prepare. Four shots hit the Culler in the upper chest - two from Gonzales' weapon - as Kerry slammed into its pelvis. The alien crumpled without a sound and Kerry stood, knife dripping with ichor, having cut the deep hip tendon to keep the Culler down while it bled out.

Malak was grudgingly impressed.

After that, Maker took point, which was a tactical error. Judging from his exposed head and body language, Kerry had exceptional hearing. He was also faster and stronger than Maker. Malak reminded himself to listen to the audio later to determine who had made such an asinine choice, and why.

It was not too much longer before they found the first device, and conversation in Almaut's office fell quiet. Malak easily recognized it as a duplicate of the one his own team had examined. More important were the scans that Rodriguez began to run. His visual display lit up with readings for radiation, geological composition, air quality, and too many other things for Malak to be able to concentrate on them and still take in the action of the other soldiers.

Almaut whistled, "That kid knows something is up."

"He's carrying non-standard equipment," Lauraux added. "Looks like a cannibalized x-ray and maybe some core sampling apparatus." The engineer's excitement was obvious. "Skip ahead to see his results."

"No," Malak ordered clenching his jaw. Maker's display focused in on a Culler, manipulating the control screen for the device. Its upper talons were withdrawn against its forearms, exposing the knobby finger-like appendages underneath. Maker dashed, head low, behind a pile of debris. Her health monitor flashed a heart rate that was higher than it should have been for such a short run. *Fear*, Malak thought, unsurprised. In the brief seconds before the Culler attacked, he caught a spike in Maker's stats. Her brain waves shot nearly off of the chart and appeared to increase in number. Her adrenaline escalated dramatically. Glutamate and dopamine levels rocketed while serotonin decreased radically. If Malak had not been watching her screen so closely, he would have missed it. Her stats suddenly returned to something close to normal for a combat situation, and then the Culler was on her.

The struggle was brief, and clearly displayed that either Maker was far worse at hand-to-hand combat than most soldiers or whatever had briefly changed her brain chemicals had incapacitated her. It was Kerry that took the alien down.

"He's good," Almaut noted.

"I'm better," Smierc replied.

No one refuted that, as the Zulu team began to examine the Culler device. "Slow it down," Malak ordered, but Almaut was already doing so. Rodriguez and Maker took readings, even climbing up on the struts to look inside. Rodriguez suddenly stepped away, and Maker moved to jump down.

"Stop," Lauraux whispered excitedly. Almaut did as requested. Maker's small form was frozen in mid-air. "Play it back, last thirty seconds, frame by frame." Almaut did so, and Malak thought he might know what had the engineer worked up.

"What is it?" Smierc asked.

"Pumping," Malak answered shortly. Almaut leaned forward, running the video through again to confirm it.

Lauraux nodded, "Yes, not just that but, look," he reached over Almaut and enlarged Rodriguez's screen. "See here? He confirmed what we were thinking. Souriau particles. It doesn't look like he has realized that yet, but in this frame you can see from the data..." As the video continued to play in slow motion, Lauraux brought up another window full of scientific equations and a diagram of an exotic matter particle. "The device is drilling down under the crust probably, maybe even deeper, and flooding the planet with Souriau particles. The quantity required – it's just massive!" Additional notes were quickly scrawled onto the screen. "I'll need a physicist – someone good, really good – but I think..." His voice faded away into mumbles. "Maybe, but why- only if..."

Almaut and Smierc were staring at the engineer, but Malak kept his eyes on the feed. Rodriguez and Maker were still talking, making small gestures toward the device. The man had removed his helmet. His dark hair was shiny and his lean face serious and worried. He was young. Younger looking than even the thirty-series, who had only recently reached maturity. Malak wondered, not for the first time, why the humans had taken so long to create his people. For nearly a century they had been fighting a costly war, sending their children – like Rodriguez – into battle. *To their deaths.* Malak also wondered if humans had far less attachment to their family than he did to his pack. He would never have sent a soldier as inexperienced as Rodriguez into the field with so few resources

As he watched he came to understand it was Maker who called the shots. She was Zulu-actual. She unclipped her helmet and pulled it off, using one gloved hand to push sweat-slick hair off of her forehead. A few long, black strands clung to her neck above her collar.

Suicide mission, Malak thought with disgust. Maker looked just as young as Rodriguez. Although her expression was calm, her pallor was startling and gave the impression that she might have been injured or ill. Malak had never seen such a pale person with such dark hair. Her eyes were bright blue, framed with black lashes, and she narrowed them and wrinkled her nose – no doubt at the smell of dead Culler. Given the opportunity, Malak would have liked to ask the officer in charge on the ground at VK10 what the hell they had been thinking. Two green soldiers, barely adults, with a scared boy, and only Gonzales and Kerry who looked like they knew what they were doing. It was a disgrace.

The boy was attacked, and they all watched as the small group fended off two Cullers. "Les enfer," Lauraux murmured, sounding sick.

"Sloppy," Smierc commented.

"It's like watching a PSA for new recruits," Almaut stated with a fascinated sort of disgust, "Kerry and Gonzales are the 'right way'. Maker and Rodriguez are going to be dead before the end of the scene." They hadn't died, obviously, since Malak knew they were quickly approaching the time of Zulu's transmission to him, but he almost questioned it. It was sheer luck that Maker wasn't mortally wounded in the struggle. And Rodriguez was the worst shot he had ever seen. The man was less than six feet from the Culler and still did not hit his intended target. After Maker managed to bring it down, Malak ordered Almaut to return the video to normal speed. The rookie was a good as dead with a broken back. Maker and Gonzales administered first aid, and then Maker began to search frequencies. Malak watched with interest, wondering how she had broken into his comms. The answer was startling and strangely unsurprising, given her actions as he had seen them so far. She shut down the thermal and kinetic armor monitoring functions of her suit and funneled the power to boost her signal. In addition to being dangerous, it broke several regulations for operating in enemy territory. Then she utilized a few simple but effective programs to break past Coalition secured lines. It was like sharpening a stick, and then inserting it between joints of an armored vehicle: low probability of success, and impossible to see coming.

Zulu team was on its way shortly thereafter, Maker in the lead and Kerry bringing the injured rookie. "Good for them," Smierc said in low, vicious voice. It was Coalition policy that bringing in bodies, or even mortally injured soldiers, was secondary to mission success. Malak had always ignored the edict. He refused to leave his people behind. His superiors had never questioned him; Legionnaires were too valuable to waste. He doubted many human soldiers would have risked their own lives, bucking Coalition warfare protocol, to save a man that was most likely going to die anyway.

Almaut sped through the rest of the video, only slowing when Zulu stumbled into the Culler data core and Rodriguez pulled information from one of the terminals. "We got that too," Almaut noted, glancing at his files. "It will need translation, but I'll get the Falcon techs on it immediately." When the playback finished, aboard the *Pershing* where Zulu team turned off their tech, Almaut stood and began pacing. "This is the ground breaking intel we have been needing, Malak. I can feel it."

"This data is going to require a team of physicists," Lauraux reminded them. "I can give you a list."

"Get whomever you need," Malak ordered.

"What about the clearances?" Almaut asked.

"It will be taken care of," Malak replied. He had the same feeling as Almaut, a tingling awareness in the pit of his stomach. They were close to something. The mystery that had been bothering him for twenty years, a key to what the Cullers were doing and how to stop them, was within his grasp. "Whatever you need," he said to Lauraux. "Tell Almaut and you'll get it." The engineer nodded and left, still talking to himself and making notes. "Get a secure copy to Kapziel, Giltine, and Skoll. Review and prepare to discuss at tomorrow's meeting."

"On it," Almaut said, immediately getting to work.

Malak stepped into the corridor, Smierc at his side. He mentally ran through the agenda for the conference with his betas. Almaut needed to update everyone on his attempt to undermine the SIS information blockade. Skoll was still knee deep in Culler corpses. If the enemy continued to send reinforcements he would be treading water before he was finished in his sector. Giltine had a new mission to brief them on and the results from the latest training exercise with the thirty series. Kapziel was on his way back from the other side of their arm of the Galaxy, and his intel was too sensitive to put on a subspace communication. Then there was the knowledge that the Cullers were filling a planet with exotic matter.

And, of course, the Legion's new role as a marketing tool for the Coalition. It would be a long meeting.

"If you have time, before you rest," Smierc began, "I still need your approval on those staff issues." Malak bit back a groan. He disliked dealing with personnel, and would have preferred to ignore them.

"I will get to it today," he answered instead. Smierc headed to the training section of the base, while Malak continued on toward his office. He had security clearances to request, personality disputes to settle, and leave to organize. He thought back to his bloody run across the crater on VK10 with something akin to longing before he quashed the feeling. His responsibilities came first.

***

Four months later.

Lauraux was fidgeting, the lead physicist next to him staring openly at Malak and his betas. Malak had ordered his people to remain seated. After working with the Falcons and then the newest scientists, he was too familiar with the human penchant for nerves when confronted with a large group of Legionnaires. Especially the officers. Malak refrained from glancing at the new bars on the cuffs of his gray uniform. The rank of Major did not feel any differently than Lieutenant had.

"We know what it is," Almaut announced from his place at the other end of the conference table, opposite Colonel Thomas. His satisfaction was palpable, and Malak could scent the rise in anticipation from the others. The mild smell of serotonin and adrenaline made his own heart rate increase. He breathed deeply and evenly, forcing his body to remain calm. *Theories are not knowledge until proven, and not useful until put into practice,* he reminded himself.

"We have a good idea," corrected Lauraux. He did not look excited at all. His expression was, at best, resigned. At worst, horrified.

"Well?" Kapziel asked impatiently. His arm, newly decorated with the bars of a Lieutenant, gestured for Lauraux to get on with it.

"Ah, Dr. Jawai can explain our hypothesis best," Lauraux said. Nerves made his hand shake as he reached for a glass of water.

Colonel Thomas, at Malak's left, nodded, "We are waiting, Doctor."

Jawai cleared his throat and tore his eyes away from Skoll's mangled right ear. Six months of fighting in the Dark had left Skoll with little but a hole in the side of his head and scar tissue that pulled his mouth into a perpetual smirk.

"Yes, well," Jawai cleared his throat again. "As you know, I was brought in to examine the possible purpose of this machine." He flicked his fingers across the surface of the table and a three dimensional representation of the Culler device from VK10 appeared above it. It turned slowly as Jawai spoke. "The design is not unlike many other alien technological advancements that have been reverse engineered since the Repulsion. When I began to examine the readings provided and the nature of the matter-"

"Get to the point," Kapziel growled. Malak issued a warning sound, low in his throat, and his beta settled back into his chair, frown firmly in place.

"Um, yes," Jawai stumbled, eyes shooting between Malak and Kapziel. "Yes, the point. Eh-em. Well." Sweat began to bead on his brow.

Malak suppressed the urge to let out a growl of his own. Dealing with humans was mildly irritating on the best day. Trying to convince one who had not had time to adjust to the reality of Keres Legion and who also held valuable information was maddening.

"Perhaps you could summarize, Dr. Jawai," Almaut suggested smoothly.

"Yes, I suppose I, that is-"

Skoll shifted in his seat, drawing Jawai's attention again, and once more his explanation ground to a halt. Malak determined the meeting was going nowhere.

"Lauraux," he said flatly. The engineer started, as he always did, but Jawai nearly jumped out of his chair at the sound of Malak's broken rumble. "Escort the doctor back to the lab." Lauraux looked relieved, and quickly obeyed. Jawai turned pale under his dark skin, and did not even remember to take his tablet with him when he left.

The door clicked softly behind them and Giltine muttered, "Good riddance."

"Almaut." Malak did not have to say anything else. A small part of his mind noted with relief how much easier communication was with his own people.

"It's a wormhole generator," Almaut said simply.

"Was that so fuckin' hard to say?" Kapziel threw up his hands, exasperated.

At the same time, Giltine asked, "What?"

Skoll questioned, "What for?"

Almaut reduced the image of the device and zoomed out, showing the general topography of VK10. "This is the planet, and the location of the drills, or pumps, that Zulu noted." Other tiny crosses appeared within the crater. He zoomed in again, cutting away the surface of the planet to show the side of a device and the geology below it. "You see here? Where we thought it might be some sort of extraction device? A drill for mining resources?" The drill began to move, driving down through the surface, under the planet's crust. "It was drilling, but, we are pretty sure, not to take anything out – but to put something in." The drill stopped moving, and a yellow substance began to flow from the device, down the narrow shaft, and then spread out into a thin, pervasive coating.

"Just under the lithosphere-"

"Skip the vocabulary lesson," Kapziel muttered. He slouched, arms crossed, form dwarfing the small chair. Almaut sighed.

"Are you trying to draw this out?" Giltine asked Almaut, for once agreeing with Kapziel.

"It's under the tectonic plates," Skoll said quietly, surprising Kapziel and Giltine into ceasing their complaints. He leaned forward, tracing the holographic image with his finger. "Does it cover the whole planet?"

"We think so, or at least it was supposed to," Almaut answered. "Based on the readings we have taken of the debris – which has been difficult. VK10-RD48 lost a lot of mass in the explosion and its orbit is becoming unstable. The particles are dissipating, but Jawai estimates there was enough to create a blanket about two micrometers thick."

"Is it a weapon?" Thomas asked, cutting to the heart of the matter.

"We don't know." Almaut zoomed out again, and played a re-enactment of the last minute of the battle on VK10 – up to the impact of the *Perry's* weapons. The image froze, showing the internal release of energy that occurred less than a second before the *Perry's* shot hit the surface. "The destructive force is unprecedented – but Jawai has argued that it would not be economical for the Coalition to use such a weapon, given the difficulty of obtaining Souriau particles in anywhere near the quantities necessary. Not to mention the deployment time, construction, logistics, et cetera."

"Dr. Jawai is still buying the story then?" Thomas asked.

"He hasn't questioned that this data is theoretical. Lauraeux told him it was retrieved from a Coalition research station that had a catastrophic accident, and he hasn't indicated that he has any concerns about the validity of our explanation."

"Good," Thomas said. His jaw was tight and his eyes hard. "The last thing we need right now is to clean up an information leak. If Jawai thought this could be an attack by the Cullers, we would have to permanently ensure his cooperation. As it is, he'll likely have to spend the rest of his career here."

Privately, Malak disagreed. He had no desire to start holding Coalition scientists against their will on his base, but he let the matter go. There were more important issues to discuss. "If it isn't a weapon?" All eyes turned on the Alpha, but he let the question stand alone.

"That's the crux of the matter," Almaut said. It was rare the blond male was completely serious, but his green eyes were focused and his shoulders tense as he spoke. "This is all guesswork. Really, really logical, founded-in-science guesswork – but there are no real answers. Not without getting data from another Culler device site for comparison." Discussions broke out along the table, and Malak leaned back in his chair to listen.

"If the Cullers are going to start blowing up planets, this is a lot bigger than Keres Legion can handle," Thomas said quietly.

Malak nodded, once. Not to agree, but to acknowledge that he had heard. Almaut was explaining that the composition of VK10 and other planets, like the one from their training mission so long ago, were similar. They naturally blocked comm signals and were relatively uninteresting – rocky, small planets not suitable for terraforming and far off from any trade routes or military positions. It made them ideal for covert experiments.

"I'm going to have to read in Batma – and probably the GA, Fleet Admiral, and the goddamn Defense Minister." Thomas scrubbed his face with one hand, something he only did under extreme stress and rarely in front of anyone other than Malak. "What the hell do they even think they'll accomplish with this? There is no way they can get to Earth, or any other inhabited planet, to set up something like this."

"They may not have to, sir," Almaut dropped his explanations to Giltine and quickly brought up a diagram of the VK10 system. "Aside from creating a fantastic trap for nearby Coalition ships that could get hit by debris, or an ambush site for ground troops, the bigger problem is gravity." He highlighted VK10-RB48 in red, then showed how its mass had changed since the explosion. "This simulation is accelerated a bit, but you can see how it begins to effect other planets in the system, even nearby systems. Given enough time." In less than a minute, the image showed the planet circling wildly outside of its orbit, destabilizing another planet, and sending six moons cascading off orbit. Two careened into the sun while the others were flung out into the edge of the system.

"That is a long-term strategy," Skoll said doubtfully. Malak had to agree with his sentiment. Cullers did not seem to have a broad plan other than eradicate humans as quickly as possible.

"How does it work?" Giltine asked.

"Wormholes are notoriously unstable. The few that have been observed were incredibly brief – on the scale of seconds – and end rather spectacularly. Jawai says that Einstein and Rosen theorized that an artificial wormhole could be created with exotic matter – and that it might be stable – but that any contact with normal matter would collapse it. In this case – a huge amount of Souriau particles creating a tiny fissure in time-space before almost instantly coming into contact with the normal matter of a planet. Boom." Almaut made an explosion with his hands.

"Expensive," Thomas noted.

"Especially when their usual weapons work so well to turn squishy little humans into space debris," Kapziel added. Discussions broke out again, and Almaut brought another set of diagrams up on the wall screen, adding notes. Malak kept his eyes on the slowly rotating VK10 system. Except for the remains of planet RB48, it rotated slowly and evenly. Although that one planet had left its orbit, the others settled into new, stable rotations around their star. IT took centuries, but the system found equilibrium.

"Kapziel is right."

Malak's statement drew five pairs of surprised eyes his way.

"Obviously," Kapziel stated after a beat. "About what?"

"Cullers are effective at killing humans," Malak began slowly.

Giltine interrupted, "Not so good at killing us."

Her statement was blatantly true, so he didn't acknowledge it. "They have one goal."

"Kill humans," Kapziel filled in.

"And one productive strategy for doing so," Malak continued as though he had not been interrupted. He fell silent, still staring at the map of VK10. The technicians were getting close on decrypting the data Zulu had taken from the Culler base, hopefully it would have more answers, but Malak could feel that tingling in his gut again. They were close to an answer, but they hadn't hit on it yet.

"Firepower?" Kapziel questioned.

"Numbers," said Giltine. "All the big Coalition defeats have been blamed on superior Culler forces. Technology being equal, if the Cullers have at least one of their own for every two or three humans, they win ground."

Thomas shook his head slowly. "Numbers," he stated thoughtfully. "In the beginning, before the Coalition was on its feet and humans were just getting our heads wrapped around all the tech our scientists were reverse engineering, this war was about superior numbers. We beat the Cullers out of the solar system, then out of Close Space Near Sol, all on sheer numbers." Thomas glanced over at Malak, then focused on Giltine. "Do you know how many soldiers died in the first decade after we figured out interstellar travel? One point five billion. Since then, we have barely kept up with population loss even with the fertility incentives the government offers. We turned their own plan on its ear."

"So up to now, the Coalition has been winning because they have more feet on the ground to go get killed. So what?" Kapziel crossed his arms in defiance, "That's what we're here for, right? To reduce loss of human life."

"You're missing the point," Almaut said. His eyes grew wide as realization dawned. Malak was still considering the possibilities, but he could tell that Almaut's impressive intellect had already jumped ahead to a conclusion. "Humans surprised the Cullers when they got the technology figured out to allow them to leave Sol. Before that, it would have been easy to overwhelm Earth. All they had to do was wait for the rest of their armada to arrive and then attack en mass. They would have had the numbers necessary for their method of rush-in-talons-waving-battle to overcome any defenses. Humanity jumped the gun. They went looking for the Cullers before they could grow their numbers sufficiently. Ever since then, the enemy has been trying to pick off any outposts, colonies, or ships it can outnumber. If they had enough troops they would hit Sol directly no matter what the loss would be." His mouth moved, but no sound came out.

"What is it?" Thomas demanded.

"A wormhole generator," Almaut said quietly. His breath came out in a long, uneven sigh.

Kapziel grunted. "You said that already."

Almaut was staring into the middle distance, his fingers tapping thoughtfully against his leg. "If they figured out how to do it, they could bring in thousands – millions, if it lasts long enough."

"What are you talking about?" Kapziel ground out.

"They'll wash over the Coalition forces in weeks," Skoll said. His hands fisted on the arms of his chair, nails digging into the plastic.

"Is that what it is for, then?" Thomas leaned forward again, demanding answers. "Did they really build it?"

"I'll need to have Jawai and the Falcons check it out, but it's possible." Almaut ran a hand through his short yellow hair, jotting down notes on his tablet with the other. "If it is..."

"If the enemy can create a stable wormhole," Giltine finished for him, "then they can bring as many soldiers as they want, from anywhere in the Orion arm, without the Coalition even noticing."

Almaut interrupted, "Forget Orion, think bigger. Galaxy. Universe."

Gilitine continued, "No more supply depots or repair spots. No more raiding Culler ships that are low on fuel and weapons."

Kapziel snarled, understanding the worst possible outcome, "It will be genocide."

"No," said Malak quietly. "Extinction."

The table fell silent, while they each considered the impact of that statement. The intelligence belonged to Keres Legion. Outside of their base, no one knew it existed. No one had any idea of what the Cullers might be capable of. All of Earth, the Sol System, an entire species was a breath away from finality and Malak held that information in his hand. He remembered what Thomas had said to another officer, so many years ago, on Erasmus Station.

Those aren't kids, they are killing machines. And if we are very, very lucky, they'll be somewhere deep, deep in Culler territory when they figure out what we have done to them."

"What's that? Made them soldiers?"

"Made them slaves."

There were few moments, in any life, where a clear choice was presented so perfectly. One action, it would only take a second to twist Thomas' head – snap it to the side like a dry branch, and then there would be nothing preventing Malak from keeping the information secret. From securing freedom for his pack and leaving humanity to their own fate.

Malak thought about his own people. Their purpose. Their creators. The reality that would exist if humanity was wiped out. Inexplicably, Zulu – *Maker,* he reminded himself – flashed through his thoughts. Her blue eyes too big in her pale face. Her hands shaking as she replaced her helmet after her team was attacked. Her promise to them: *Everyone goes home.* The Cullers would kill her. Rodriguez. Gonzales. The rookie with the broken back – if he was still alive. Kerry, the GMH who had the respect of his fellow soldiers. The pilot for transport one-seven who dodged enemy fire to save a mere half a squadron. The idiot Captain of the *Perry,* and the even crazier Captain of the *Pershing.* Thomas. Batma. Every researcher from Project Barghest. The Falcons. They would all die. Keres Legion could live, escape into the Dark and keep away from the Cullers and their hatred of humanity. But everyone else Malak had ever known would die.

Billions would die.

His responsibilities, to his pack and to the humans that had made them, had never been so at odds. *Choice.* The weight of it dragged on him, weighed him down like an albatross, so heavy he had to close his eyes against a terrible, horrible voice that whispered to him what sounded like truths. *Even if we could save them, they would not see us as people. Only experiments. Useful technology.*

"Guess we're hoping it's just a planet-bomb then?" Kapziel asked.

Skoll laughed, "Now there is something I never thought would be the better option." The tension eased – just enough that Malak could breathe again and open his eyes. Giltine was staring at him across the table. He had the feeling she knew where his thoughts had gone.

"We're going to stop an entire Culler armada." Giltine phrased it like a statement, but her green eyes posed a question. Whatever his response, she would follow it. Duty. To the pack. To the Legion. Malak smothered the voice that reminded him of all the suffering he and the others had gone through, in training, on missions. The deaths. At the knowing and unknowing cruelty of nearly every human they encountered. There was more to his life than that. More to his pack than the injustice in their lives.

"Yes," he said simply.

Keres Legion began to plan for a new kind of war.

Made in the USA
Lexington, KY
10 December 2019

58342788R00182